PENDULUM HEROES

JAMES BEAMON

Pendulum Heroes

Copyright © 2018 James Beamon
All rights reserved.

No parts of this publication may be reproduced, stored in a retrieval system, or transmitted in any form or by any means, electronic, mechanical, photocopying, recording, or otherwise, without the prior written permission of the copyright owner.

This is a work of fiction. Any similarity between the characters and situations within its pages and places or persons, living or dead, is unintentional and co-incidental.

Cover art by Micaela Dawn

Nadi Cat Press

Published by Nadi Cat Press 2018
Leesburg, VA United States
ISBN: 978-1-7323862-0-4

To Gina,

My muse, my measure, my magic for over twenty years.

I love you.

Quest Objectives

Chapter 1 1
   Heals for Hit Points

Chapter 2 13
   Progress Bar

Chapter 3 26
   Lunch at Runt's

Chapter 4 34
   Fort Law

Chapter 5 43
   Freedom Flight

Chapter 6 55
   Quest Proper

Chapter 7 69
   Tutorial

Chapter 8 80
   Trading Places

Chapter 9 90
   Maltepic Trails

Chapter 10 98
   A Proven Goodbye

Chapter 11 108
   Hollowers

Chapter 12 117
   Accomplished Accomplices

Chapter 13 129
   Clever Broad

Chapter 14 137
   Discovery Bonus

Chapter 15 151
   Taking the "!"

Chapter 16 164

Answers
Chapter 17...173
  Loose Ends Unraveled
Chapter 18...183
  Consequence
Chapter 19...193
  Risk Factor
Chapter 20...203
  Invite
Chapter 21...212
  Nasreddin
Chapter 22...226
  The Sprawl
Chapter 23...236
  Sons of Kaftar
Chapter 24...247
  Diversions
Chapter 25...257
  The Hollow Truth
Chapter 26...268
  In Mages Hands
Chapter 27...282
  Murderous Trip
Chapter 28...293
  Olukent
Chapter 29...303
  Family
Chapter 30...313
  Death Null
Epilogue...332

Chapter 1

Heals for Hit Points

Melvin Morrow experienced panic for the first time because of a forest. Alarm was Mr. Burney dropping pop quizzes on his desk as if algebra problems had cred in the streets while stress was finding Sophia Watkins standing behind him in the lunch line. Alarm, stress, they weren't even on the same plate as panic, which Melvin handled with virginal ineptitude. He felt near dizzy as his stomach rose and his heart dropped while his blood surged with roller coaster speed. His mouth, suddenly extra dry, tasted like salt.

The forest was his living room. That's to say, Melvin was just in his living room. Now there was no television, no coffee table, no game. There were no walls. It was all gone, replaced in a blink with trees that towered above him, a dense and impenetrable forest.

He had never seen trees loom but apparently that's what trees do when you allow them to congregate in groups of more than a dozen. Melvin wasn't that big into the outdoors, considering Dad would make him cut the grass every Saturday no matter how little it grew, but it wasn't like he was afraid of the outside. This, however, was two extra servings of outside. These pine and cedar trees stretched as far as the eye could see. Even with the sun shining brightly overhead, he couldn't see very far into the shadowy depths of the forest, but he was sure there were no stores on the other side, just trees and more trees.

Melvin looked down at himself, a "check to see if you're a ghost, are you still alive?" kind of moment, which is when he discovered he was both quite substantial and had women's breasts.

He couldn't entertain the illusion that he was a dude that had somehow grown extremely obese. The breasts were in a chain mail bikini top and outside of a leather strap across his chest, chain mail bikini bottoms that matched the top and calf-high brown leather boots, he wasn't wearing anything else. His skin was two shades darker than the russet potato color he had always known and there were very few places for fat to hide. Everything he saw looking down screamed woman. He, Melvin, was no longer a he. The steel bikini glinted in the sunlight. His chest heaved in sync with his panicked breathing, which only served to mortify him more.

"What the shit?!" a voice next to Melvin seemed to speak for him.

Melvin turned, immediately flooded with relief that someone else was here that could maybe help. The relief soured faster than it arrived. It wasn't a human standing next to Melvin but an aian, a being that didn't exist.

The sight stacked on top of the current things that were hard to parse, the equivalent a leprechaun riding a unicorn bareback through your living room. Only Melvin's living room was now a clearing in front of the world's biggest forest. The aian next to Melvin stood over a foot taller than Melvin with gray skin the color of charcoal ash and hair that was impossibly blue like sapphire. The aian, wearing a leather outfit that looked akin to tree bark, looked itself (himself?) over, as seemingly surprised that he existed as Melvin was.

The quiver of arrows and bow slung across his back sparked recognition in Melvin, mostly because Jason hadn't stopped showing him pictures of the bow and raving about its stats. This aian was Cephrin. It was his best friend Jason Streible's character in the game.

Melvin and the fictitious game being weren't the only ones there. Next to the aian, an old man with a thick gray robe and an even thicker, grayer beard stood, wild eyed and staring about. That was his friend Richard Bates' character, a mage Rich had named Razzleblad.

A roar erupted from the tree line. Melvin's head snapped like a rubber band towards the sound.

Melvin knew immediately the thing charging at them was a weagr. It was more mountain than man, as if Lou Ferrigno and Arnold Schwarzeneggar had made a baby and fed it nothing but protein shakes and gunpowder. Melvin had seen weagrs plenty of times in concept art and plastic miniatures, but none of that prepared him for a heavy jawed, nine foot tall, Cro-Magnon giant barreling at him. The weagr's roar seemed to crack the air like thunder, his brutish footsteps shook the ground and the axe he held raised to the heavens gleamed with wicked intent.

Before any of them could run, or put their hands up, or even scream back the weagr had closed the distance. He brought the axe down, deep into the aian's shoulder.

Aians always looked noble in the concept art, tall with angular features that stayed stoic as they struck battle poses. Not now, not here; gone was any sense of regal composure as this aian screamed in desperate agony while it stared at the axe in his shoulder. Blood showered from the wound all over the bearded face and gray robes of Richard Bates' character, the human mage Razzleblad.

Maybe it was the blood. Maybe Melvin had forgotten to breathe a long, long time ago. Maybe he had just plain reached his limit of mythical and impossible levels of crazy happening all at one time in a forest clearing that should've been his living room. Whatever it was, it caused his vision to tunnel, then darken as he stumbled on legs gone wobbly.

ଔଊ

"Melvin! Melvin!" Someone was calling his name, shaking him awake. Melvin looked down. He still had breasts. He looked up to the blood soaked Razzleblad.

"Rich?"

Razzleblad nodded. Melvin recognized Richard Bates' eyes behind the blood-streaked gray beard. Those eyes were afraid.

Melvin searched for reality: the sofa, a hint of living room carpet, the role playing game that make-believed everything he saw right now. What he found was short-grass plains on the outskirts of a vast forest, a weagr passed out and taking labored breaths, a bloodied axe, and an unconscious aian who was short an arm and spewing blood from the gaping wound at the shoulder.

If Rich was Razzleblad then the aian had to be Jason. Before Melvin could think to get up and check on his best friend, yet another impossible sight gave him pause. There was a megrym crouched over Jason. Megryms looked like gargoyles without wings. They were hairless and short, between four and five feet. This one wore brown linen pants and a matching vest that exposed sinewy muscles and purplish reptilian skin. It stopped whatever it was doing with Jason and looked up at Melvin and Rich with stern annoyance.

"You pussies get over here already."

Melvin found something familiar about the megrym. That look of annoyance came to him in an instant, across time and space and worlds. Melvin remembered begging his big brother to fill in as the fourth man for the game. His brother had chosen a megrym character and named it Ballztowallz.

"Mike?"

"Who else, jackass? Get over here!"

Melvin and Rich scrambled over.

"You, old white kid," Mike said pointing at Rich, "you supposed to know magic and shit, right? You need to conjure some fire and burn this shoulder wound closed."

"But—but—I don't know how."

"Figure it out, or this kid's dead."

Mike looked at his brother. "Melvin, you gotta kill that big motherfucker before he gets up and finishes what he started."

"What? Why me?"

"Who the hell else? Bloody Stump here or the pajama nerd that can maybe save his life? You're the one with the sword."

Melvin reached behind his back and found the hilt. Drawing it revealed his in-game favorite, the double-edged silver bastard. It was light in his hands but his nerves made the sword shake like it had a life of its own.

"You do it Mike." He extended the sword to the megrym.

"What? Negro, I'm four feet high—the sword's bigger than me. Plus I gotta stay with your loser friend here and see to it he makes this fire happen. Now ain't the time to be scary. Go over there and stab it already."

Melvin wanted to protest but Mike had already shifted his attention. He had picked up Jason's bow and brought it down across his knee with a crack. Rich shuffled around in his robes, produced a book and was racing through its pages.

"That a spellbook?" Mike asked as the bow broke with a crunch.

"I think so, but I can't read this language!"

"All the hours you put in this nonsense and you can't read it? You better try. He's spouting like a goddamn geyser." Mike started setting the broken bow fragments down close to Jason's bleeding shoulder

Melvin turned his attention to the weagr.

He was stirring.

Melvin advanced cautiously, holding the sword like a baseball bat. It shook more the closer he got.

The weagr was just a big man. Ugly for sure, his giant features misshapen and clothes rough and tattered, but still a man. The weagr laid there, his oversized brow furrowed in pain. Maybe Melvin could talk to him. Convince him to help them if he was made to understand they meant him no harm.

Melvin had played the game enough to know the bestiary and the character descriptions all said this was impossible.

The weagr's eyes blinked open.

Behind Melvin a boom exploded. His heart leapt with it.

Melvin screamed and ran toward the weagr. His screams were pure fear as he stabbed the weagr over and over. The weagr died with an expression of agony and helplessness in eyes that stayed locked on Melvin. And Melvin kept stabbing until his arms gave out and he panted for air. His breasts heaved in their steel bikini.

"You gonna stop now?" his brother asked, "or are you just taking a break?"

Melvin turned. Rich was sweating buckets. Behind Rich a small, sooty fire crackled. Jason was still out, his wound well burned. Mike shook his head.

"You see, Mel? That's why black folks don't play these games."

಼಼

This morning he was Melvin Morrow, a sixteen-year-old math hating drum major in the eleventh grade. Just another half-black kid in an average suburban home.

Now he was Zhufira, warrior woman. Full lips, frizzy black tresses, bearing a sword that had more material in it than her current fashion choices.

His big brother was a little megrym. His friend who wouldn't be the same age as him until December was an old man. And his best friend was an aian who had lost the battle for limb and was now fighting for life.

None of them knew why they were there. Or how.

They could worry about why or how later. Melvin asked the question that was pertinent now. "How do we get back?"

"Click your heels, Dorothy," Mike said. "How the hell do you think we get back?"

Mike held his hands up to show Melvin the expansive countryside. Neither the forest line in front of him nor the endless grass behind offered answers.

A lesser question, the question of where, had an answer. They seemed to be on the edge of Kazawood; the place was distinctive with its giant cedar and pine trees. This is where they had started the game.

There was also an answer to why the weagr was down when Melvin woke up. Rich explained it to him.

"Like the bestiary described them, weagrs are primitive minds driven by blood or lust. When you fainted you landed with your very attractive ass in the air, an invitation so strong the weagr's gears switched momentarily. When it hesitated Mike used his club and bashed the weagr's balls until it passed out from pain. Then Mike told me to wake you up while he checked on Jason. You were only out for like thirty seconds."

Other questions were weights. Were there more weagrs out there? Would Jason live?

"I dunno. He lost a lot of blood while what's-his-name was pulling his head out of his ass to make fire," Mike said.

"It's Rich," Rich retorted. "You try deciphering this book next time we have a crisis."

"If I had the kind of hard on you have for this shit I would've had it down cold, believe that."

"This isn't helping," Melvin said. He turned to Rich. "You're a mage. I know mages aren't clerics, but you can cast spells. Can you cast a heal on him?"

Rich considered. "There's no reason why I couldn't. A cleric's heal would definitely be a better grade, but basic spells are accessible to all casters. Let me look through the book."

Mike snorted. "Welp, guess I'd better start digging his grave."

Rich snapped the book shut. "How about you start shutting up?"

Mike fingered his club idly. "How about I get to cracking your skull like a ripe melon?"

Rich glared at him.

"I see you cutting your eye at me, boy. Any time you want to try something, my four foot ass is right here."

Melvin stepped between them. "C'mon, Rich. Jason needs you."

Rich took a last look at Mike and walked off leafing through pages.

"That's right, keep it moving," Mike said.

Melvin looked at his diminutive big brother. "What the hell, Mike?"

"What you mean 'what the hell'? Do you fucking see me?"

"I see you. Look at me. And Rich. And Jason who's got one arm. You're not the only one who's jacked up. So stop taking it out on us."

"Are you serious? Fool, I didn't even wanna play this stupid game. I let you talk me into it and here I am stuck looking like a chupacabra. Stuck in some shit none of us know how to get out of, and you telling me not to take it out on y'all. Who do I take it out on, then?"

"We didn't put you in the middle of this. We're stuck too trying to figure all this out."

That only made Mike madder. "Y'all are supposed to be experts," he said, waving his hands at everyone. "This is supposed to be y'all's shit. Not only don't none of you know shit, but here I am saving all y'all's asses. I didn't come back from a war zone just for you to send me to another one. Or are you saying it's all right that I'm spending my first week of R&R bashing balls open in a dream world of magic?"

Mike pointed his gnarled purple finger at Melvin. "You know what, don't say shit else to me."

He didn't. For a moment there were only the gentle sounds of birds chirping, squirrels rustling in the boughs of the cedars, the sound of Rich turning pages. Behind him, shrub grass plains stretched to forever. In front, the widest evergreen trees he'd ever seen seemed a dark and forbidding wall.

The dead weagr was a giant mass of torn, bloody meat. Melvin's carnage had spared his head though. His eyes seemed to follow Melvin whenever he looked at the corpse no matter where he stood. He went over to Rich as he stood over Jason's broken body. Jason's shallow breathing punctuated the silence between the turn of pages.

"Any luck?"

Rich shook his head. "Not much. I'm really just

guessing at what these words say. You rarely see this stuff in the game outside of decoration. And never with translations."

"How'd you conjure the fire then?"

"I used a quote I remember from the Conquest storyline that had both the words and the meaning."

Rich said the words. They were gibberish to Melvin, but they had a nice flow to them. Rich translated.

"Fire from figment, wind from wish, water from word, your soul at risk."

Rich ruffled through some more pages. "It was a warning to apprentice casters in the story. Now it's kind of my Rosetta Stone to deciphering this book. None of those words exactly say 'heal' though. So I have to proceed carefully."

"I don't think we have time for careful."

"Yes, you're right, Melvin," Rich said, looking up from the book, his countenance angry. "Rushing and arbitrarily picking are much better options. I guess I should just pick a spell that doesn't have any of the words I do know, which is like ninety-five percent of the book, and hope I don't turn Jason here into a block of ice or summon a tree out of his pancreas. I'm ashamed I didn't think of it."

Melvin's anger flashed, but he exhaled it down. He was half a second away from beating Rich's face in with his sword pommel and doing the same thing to Mike. But that wouldn't help matters. His best friend was dying and they were all still in danger.

"Look, I'm not telling you to rush it," Melvin said. "I'm saying that we may have to just carry him away from this forest and hope he makes it. We can't afford to run into more weagrs or whatever else is in there."

Rich's robe started fluttering erratically. He looked down. Jason was tugging at his robe with his one good hand, his gray aian face pale and clammy looking.

Rich and Melvin knelt down. Jason grabbed Rich close and mumbled something before passing out again.

Rich looked up at Melvin.

"I think he just told me the spell for heal."

"You sure?"

"No. But Jason does know more about this game than all of us put together. If anyone would know it, it'd be him."

Rich's look was solemn. "What do you think, Mel?"

Melvin shrugged. "It's about our only option."

They stood up.

Rich cracked his knuckles, shook his wrists, and held his hands over Jason's body.

He cleared his throat.

"I wouldn't stand so close if I was you, bruh," Mike called from a few yards away. "He's fixing to turn you into a peanut butter and jelly sandwich."

Rich glared at Mike. He looked back at Melvin and motioned for him to back away.

Closing his eyes, Rich said the words Jason gave him. Jason's body glowed in a soft white light.

Jason's face contorted into a grimace. He reached for his shoulder and winced when his fingers touched the burnt nub.

"What the fuck happened to hit points?!"

Everyone was silent. None of them knew what to say to a person who just lost his arm to an axe-wielding weagr.

Jason shambled to his feet, using his one good arm to wave off their attempts to help him up. He looked around frantically. He went searching by the weagr until he found his severed arm. Holding the arm up to his burnt shoulder in a crude facsimile of how it should be, Jason looked at Rich.

"Cast the heal again."

"Jason, I, uh, don't see this working."

"It'll work. Just do it already."

Rich cast the spell. The white glow spread from Jason through his body and into the severed arm. He smiled and stopped holding the arm up to his shoulder.

Melvin stared in disbelief at the arm.

Then the arm fell and rolled down to the weagr's foot.

Jason roared his frustration and started kicking the meaty mass of the dead weagr.

"Hey! Hey!" Mike yelled at Jason, who stopped kicking.

"You healthy enough to kick, you healthy enough to walk… let's bounce."

Mike pointed to the woods towering over them.

"Unless you wanna wait for more ridiculous shit to pop out of the woods over there. Cry later. Walk now."

Chapter 2

Progress Bar

Melvin was managing the simple task of one foot in front of the other until it devolved into a question quest. Rich was the first one to go. He turned around to face Kazawood, which was still an impressive line of trees even now that they were more than a mile out, and shook his head as if he was Lot's wife longing to return to Gomorrah.

"What if the way home is back there, where we started?" he asked. "I mean, we kinda just left without looking, without even trying to look. We should be back there, turning over stones or something. We shouldn't be out here."

A jolt of happiness surged through Melvin, who felt vindicated that it wasn't just him. "You too? I was thinking, 'what if there's some kind of stargate or something in a partially covered hole, a tree hollow, a secret cave, you know, something."

Mike shook his head. "Stop tripping. You think a stargate is something you won't recognize if you see it? How they running it? Y'all see some power lines out this bitch?"

He tried to get them walking again, but Rich stayed rooted. "Ok, so not a stargate," Rich said, "but they have mages here and portals. Same difference. Something that could be just waiting for us to find. We need to go check."

Mike grimaced. "No, we don't. We didn't walk out of a cave or a tree hollow, so what kind of sense does it make walking into one to get back?"

"Maybe we can't remember it," Melvin suggested.

"Maybe we blanked out for a moment. There's no way to be sure. We should go back and look." Rich nodded in agreement.

Mike grit his pointy megrym teeth. "Y'all wanna know what's in the woods… danger. And we already found it once. It's. Why. We. Left! Y'all catch a lil bit of fresh air and now everybody wanna be Tomb Raider? We need to get some distance from this place."

Melvin was ready to argue the point more, hell he was ready to bolt back to Kazawood, until he heard an unexpected voice.

"Mike's right," Jason said.

Thanks to Rich's healing spell, Jason seemed a lot better since his brush with death. His skin was a much richer shade of gray and looked a lot less clammy. If not for the bloody, torn sleeve that rustled in the wind, Melvin would've forgotten he had just lost an arm.

"Weagrs are tribal. There's never just one. So yes, getting some distance is a good thing."

Jason turned his gaze to Rich. Melvin found it a strange sight, as aian irises moved constantly, an autonomic function that gave their eyes the appearance of dancing perpetually.

"And Rich is right. There's magic here, with mages and portals. And if there's a portal to be had or one to be seen near those woods, we're probably gonna need a mage to help with that."

He knelt down and began to scrawl in the dirt. He made a row of triangles.

"Here's Kazawood. If the terrain is anything like the game maps, if we travel due south we'll reach the town of Tirys," he said scratching out a crude X below the row of triangles. "We reach the town, we may find a mage, someone with some magical background that can help us."

He stood up. "The question is, where's south?"

Mike squinted at the sky and panned his head all around. "Well, if this place is anything like back home, we should already be going south," he said. Melvin assumed his brother's confident answer came from some training the Army had provided. He wasn't going to question it.

Jason performed a one shoulder shrug. "Guess we'll find out." He turned to continue the trek, exposing the severed arm on his back. Before leaving Kazawood, Jason had the guys tie it around him using the dead weagr's belt. The hand flopped up and down as he walked in a crude hello wave. It bounced in rhythm with the quiver of arrows on his right shoulder.

Melvin fell in step on Jason's left, a decision that immediately weirded him out as the severed hand seemed to be reaching for him from his peripheral vision. Rich had already taken a place on the quiver side of Jason and Mike brought up the rear. Funny enough, taking the lead would've been even weirder, so Melvin chose to ignore the reaching hand and focused on the landscape. The grasses and shrubs of the steppes were getting sparse as the land turned rockier.

They walked in silence. The plan was simple enough. It felt solid. Magic was the only thing that made reasonable sense as to how they got here. The town of Tirys may have a mage or someone conversant in magic, someone who could maybe help them.

Melvin tried to stay positive. Just because all this was incredibly new and extremely bizarre for him didn't mean that someone in Tirys hadn't seen this kind of thing before and knew what to do. Even if this was strange to the townspeople, maybe between everyone putting their heads together they could arrive at a plausible way to get back.

Above all else, he did not try to think of the alternative. His life was pretty mundane back in the suburbs, but that didn't mean he wanted to be stuck here. He hadn't even fully gotten into manhood yet. He'd never get the chance to if he was stuck living the rest of his life as a woman.

They crested the top of a hill and were greeted by more hills. A road would have been a blessing, an indication they were heading somewhere civilized. Instead, the occasional spattering of small, hearty brush among the rocks seemed to whisper the opposite as they rustled. The party crested these hills and was greeted with more of the same. And again. And again.

"Let's rest a minute," Rich said. He was sweatier than everyone else, and wheezed between exhales.

They all sat in a circle. A gentle breeze stirred and began to dry the sweat from them. Silence was thick.

"Wish one of us had thought to imagine our character with a water skin," Melvin said to no one in particular as he wiped sweat from his brow.

"Maybe I can conjure water," Rich said. "Do you know the spell for that, Jason?"

Jason looked at Rich for a moment, his irises dancing unnaturally. "I know the spell," Jason said, "but what makes you think I can't cast it for us?"

"Cause I'm a human mage and you're an aian archer. I know aians have their own magic but you—"

"You," Jason cut him off. "You are Richard Bates looking like a made up mage named Razzleblad. I'm a tall, gray dude with one arm. Point is, underneath the stage make-up we're the same people. If you can cast spells, I can cast spells. I might as well cast it—it's not like I'll be doing much arching. How many one-armed archers you ever heard of?"

"Well, that was that one dude who was an Olympian," Melvin answered. "Had one arm and one leg and used his teeth to fire. Pretty badass."

"One dude," Jason said.

"I'm pretty sure there were a couple of lady amputees that are archers, too," Melvin said.

"Whatever!" Jason cried. "I'm not them!"

"Hey, you wanna cast spells, "Rich said. "Knock yourself out."

Jason held out his hand, closed his eyes and spoke flowing gibberish. He opened his eyes and nothing. He said the words again with care. Still nothing.

Rich held out his hands and repeated the words. Blue light emanated from his chest, to his shoulders, down his arms and into his hands. Water filled his hands, which he cupped together. He took a sip.

"It's cold!"

"It's bullshit," Jason said. "It doesn't make any sense."

"Yeah, and the rest of this makes perfect sense." Mike said.

"Just because he made a caster shouldn't mean squat. He's still the same dude—he can't even read the spellbook!"

"You a hater," Mike said. "No one made you choose that weak ass character."

"I'm not a hater. Being an aian archer's cool, but you want to know what's even cooler? Not being stuck here!" Jason shouted, answering his own question. "Look at us. A warrior woman in a steel bikini," he said, causing Melvin to look down at his well endowed chest. "An old mage complete with robes and long gray beard," Jason said, pointing to Rich, whose robes and beard were stained red with his blood.

"We're walking goddamn clichés."

Mike grunted "I dunno about them, I ain't much into this fantasy crap. But I know you ain't no cliché. Only one of us in this circle has ever heard of a one armed archer, boss."

Jason's brow furrowed at Mike's jab. His obvious madness prompted an idea Melvin recalled.

"Maybe this is *folie à deux*," Melvin said.

"Hell's that?" Mike asked.

"Shared psychosis," Melvin explained. "I learned about it on Wikipedia. It literally means madness shared by two."

"Seriously dude?" Jason asked with a sneer. "Wikipedia? You know why it's not called *folie à*… uh, four? Because four people hallucinating all this is impossible. You'd more likely to win the lottery while being struck by lightning while dating a supermodel who's reading the winning numbers from the passenger seat of the Chevy Nova you're delivering pizzas in."

A distant roar killed Melvin's response before he uttered it. The sound was unmistakably angry. It came from the direction of Kazawood, which was now only visible as a long line of treetops on the northern horizon.

"Weagrs maybe found their dead kinfolk," Mike said. "We gotta move."

They ran, down this hill and up the next one. They kept running and the hills kept passing with no town in sight. Jason turned around, his eyes dancing as he looked.

"Weagrs," he said.

They were just blots on the horizon to the others. Jason said he could see them well enough. He reported fourteen of them, coming their way and making huge strides.

They kept running. Up and down more hills and there still was no town to be seen. Now all of them could see the weagrs getting bigger behind them.

Jason saw something to the west.

"It looks like a house. I'm sure it's a house."

"We head there then," Mike said. "If it ain't the start of the town then at least that's more in number against these weagrs. Our odds are bad."

They set course toward the house. The weagrs changed their direction too. No question they were in pursuit.

Melvin's lungs burned. All of them were moving as fast as they could. The house was getting closer. But so were the weagrs. He could hear their yells growing louder.

The house was a simple rectangular structure made of what looked like bricks of dried mud with a wooden door and window shutters. Smoke puffed lazily out of a hole in the roof. It stood alone on a hill with a few trees behind it. There was no village to speak of. Melvin hoped whoever lived there would help. He couldn't imagine someone reacting positively when strangers show up with fourteen angry weagrs in pursuit.

They sprinted the gap to the house. As they got within a couple of feet of the door, it opened and a giant head popped out.

It was a weagr.

"What are you all doing here?" he asked.

Wait. Weagrs don't talk.

"Weagrs… chasing… us…" Melvin explained between gasps of air.

The talking weagr looked past them. "I see." He came out of the house and Melvin saw, although he was big, he was much smaller than the weagr from Kazawood. Maybe he was just a massive man after all.

"Bad odds," the big man said. "I don't too much care for weagrs."

"Will you help us?" Melvin asked.

The weagrs were advancing up the hill towards the front of the house.

"Let me see what the trouble is," the man went forward and started yelling at the weagrs. A real broken, guttural sound, Melvin realized he was speaking to the weagrs in their language.

The weagrs walked up to the big man, who was small by comparison and started speaking back to him. They pointed at Melvin and his party and started beating their chests and yelling.

"I didn't know weagrs talked," Rich said.

"It's never mentioned in the companion texts," said Jason. "But I guess it makes sense. Tribes gotta communicate some kind of way."

The harsh dialogue continued between the weagrs and the big man for some time. It seemed like a very tense conversation. Melvin wondered if all weagr conversations were like this.

"I wonder what they're saying," he said.

"I can guess," Mike said. "They wanna end us."

The big man nodded at the weagrs, said something akin to clearing his throat and came over to the party.

"You killed one of their own," he said.

"It was self-defense," Melvin told him.

"He hacked off my arm," Jason said.

"Don't matter," the big man said. "Their law demands blood."

He stayed silent for a moment, looking at them all. Weighing them maybe. He continued.

"Their law allows for a custom called *akhta*. One-on-one blood for resolution of group grievance. About best anyone could have managed for you."

"What are you saying?" Melvin asked.

"One of yours against one of theirs. To the death or worse."

"Oh shit…" Melvin considered the likelihood of any of them surviving against a well prepared weagr.

"Their other requirement for *akhta* is to settle debt with blade bearer. Sword kills weagr. Sword swallows debt."

"Me?"

"Wait," Rich said. "You said to the death or worse. What's worse than to the death?"

"Bondage." Big man answered, looking at Melvin. "I know what that is if you don't. That happens and you'll wish yourself dead a million times over before you finally find it."

Melvin looked at the lead weagr. He was looking at him, gliding his thick fingers up and down his club and licking his lips. Melvin looked down at his bouncy breasts and curvy hips.

He shook his head as if it would negate the fact that this was happening. He spoke in a near whisper. "Please… there has to be some other way."

"Afraid you have little option," the big man said, his face grim. "You're lucky they've conceded to *akhta* at all. Easy for them to capture you and kill others. Me too for good measure."

Melvin looked at the ground. His heart felt like it had sank into his stomach. He wished he was back home and he had never heard of this game and that he had never stabbed that stupid weagr and that he wasn't a woman that these sick fuckers wanted to have their way with.

"This is bullshit, dude," Mike told Big Man. "You tell them I was the one that dropped their partner. And tell them I'll drop any one of their big asses if they step to me."

"You don't understand. *Akhta* not with you."

"Naw, bruh, you don't understand. They get *akhta* with me. I damn sure ain't gonna watch them make my brother into their bitch."

"Look. Either your…" Big Man cut his eye at Melvin as he spoke, "…brother… agrees and fights alone or disagrees and there's no one left to dig graves. Decide. Weagrs not keen on dialogue."

Melvin looked at the big man "I'll *akhta*."

The big man nodded as if he already knew. "Prepare yourself." He returned to the head weagr.

The weagrs cheered and hoo-ha'ed at the big man's news.

"Mel…"

The lead weagr smiled a big grin on his big face. He looked back at his weagr buddies and began to pump his waist in demonstration of what he was planning to do.

"Mel…"

Melvin barely heard Rich calling him. He was too busy looking at the massive man he would have to kill or… else. "Huh?"

"Mel, it's important. You can beat this weagr. Focus. Put yourself into your game persona. Just like I can cast spells because I'm Razzleblad and Jason can see further than any of us cause he's aian. Be Zhufira."

The big man motioned for the others to clear away from Melvin. They all backed away and Melvin took a hard swallow, feeling more alone than he'd ever felt in life. Then the big man walked north of the weagr and Melvin until the three formed an equilateral triangle. He extended his arms out and pointed at the two of them. Then he brought his hands together to meet and yelled "*Akhta!*"

The weagr charged. Melvin didn't even have time to

draw his sword. The weagr's open hand came up swift and caught Melvin on the cheek.

The smack sounded like thunder and felt like a truck. Melvin screamed and tumbled to the ground. He scrambled to get up, holding his stinging face. The weagr smiled and advanced slowly. The other weagrs yowled with glee.

He's already making me his bitch, Melvin thought as he backed away. He reached for his sword and brought it up with a shaky hand. The sword trembled like it was still recovering from the weagr's smack.

Can't let it win. I am Zhufira.

Melvin charged. The weagr sidestepped easily and smacked Melvin's ass with authority. The force of it lifted him in the air and sent him crashing back down to the ground. The weagr yowls sounded out again.

He was bruised and cut from the hard landing. He got up and set his jaw.

I am Zhufira. Zhufira. Zhufira.

The weagr rushed in and gripped Melvin's face in his oversized hand. He picked Melvin up off the ground and let his legs dangle before tossing him like a half empty sack. He tumbled and skidded across the grass.

It was a miracle Melvin was still holding the sword. Fear and despair washed over him like tidal waves as he fought to get up and steady himself.

The weagr took a moment to stroll over to the other weagrs and laugh with them about the fight. He made more pumping gestures with his waist and they all got to yowling.

Humiliation consumed Melvin. His body stung and his face throbbed where the weagr had smacked him. He tasted his own blood on the corner of his mouth. From somewhere deep within, his frustration boiled.

The weagr saw him standing and charged.

Melvin would be damned before he spent the rest of his life beaten and raped as a weagr toy. His frustration boiled over into red hot rage.

He charged to meet the weagr.

A cry rushed from his throat as if dying to be released. "*Ildasleen!*"

The weagr threw a hard punch. Melvin side-stepped and his sword met the fist at the wrist, loping the hand off. It was effortless, and he spun with momentum and kept the sword moving. Moving and cutting and piercing in strikes so precise and quick the sword seemed a natural extension of his arm. He put no thought into it other than his anger; the sword translated it into pain.

When he stopped, the blade was red and the weagr staggered two steps before crashing down. Melvin faced the crowd. The weagrs looked stupefied. His friends and brother had their jaws hanging open. The big man had a smug grin on his face.

Rich ended the silence.

"Beautiful…"

As if that broke the spell, Jason and Mike cheered and rushed over to him.

The big man started yelling at the weagrs, who trudged past and collected their dead comrade.

Rich was still stuck where he stood, shaking his head. "Beautiful…"

"Good fight," the big man told him. "Would have hated tracking the weagrs down later to put an arrow through you. Never sits right, killing a helpless woman, megrym brother that you are and all."

"Uh, thanks," Melvin said.

"Right thing to do. Believe me, I know. Name is Runt. Runt Half-weagr. Come in and I'll see what I have to offer the lot of you."

Chapter 3

Lunch at Runt's

Runt was a broad man of about six foot three who kept his hair prickly short and his face clean. The furnishings in his home were simple: a bed, a chair, a table. It was not made to accommodate guests, but he accommodated them anyway, offering the chair to Melvin while the others found space on the floor or bed. Rich made use of a bucket to wash Jason's blood out of his face and beard.

Runt prepared a stew in a small cauldron suspended over a hearth. Set in the middle of the room, the hearth was little more than a raised platform of bricks where a bed of embers quietly glowed. Melvin recounted their story as Runt made trips back and forth from table to cauldron.

"Magic of a powerful kind." Runt said while stirring and adding spices to the pot. "Likely leads to the Hierophane."

"What's the Hierophane?" Melvin asked.

"You should know," Jason answered. "We ran a campaign around it once. It's the body of human arcane leadership, located in Ardenspar."

Runt nodded. Melvin tried to think back to the Ardenspar campaign and saw only fragments. Ardenspar, Seat Esotera, people in robes, an illustration of a marbled promenade… that was about it.

Everything he remembered about this world was just bits and pieces. Before now, it was all disposable information, just a way to play with the few friends he had. He wished he had paid more attention to the scenarios and settings instead of being so impatient to jump ahead to the action.

Runt left the ladle in the pot and got settled on the floor with his back to the wall. "You all have time before this is ready. Should probably use it for rest."

As if on cue, a light snore came out of Mike's mouth. He was sprawled across the bed and drooling a little. The run had been the hardest on him and his little legs.

"How far away is Tirys?" Jason asked.

"Little over a day, due south. Not much in Tirys for you. Few mages, if any. None I'm sure powerful enough to help."

"I need healing, for my arm." Jason said.

Runt looked at Jason with steady eyes. "Jason Cephrin, your arm is dead. No healing to be done for it."

"How would you know? You're not a healer."

"Seen enough battles. Arm is gone. Should bury it before rot brings creatures."

Jason's face reddened. "You underestimate the power of magic. It can do anything. All I need is a good healer."

Runt said nothing. He just leaned back against the wall and closed his eyes.

"What he's saying kind of makes sense though, Jason," Rich said, dabbing his beard with his robe sleeve to dry it more. "Heals are used to augment the regenerative qualities of living tissue."

Jason's oscillating eyes looked Rich up and down. "Now you're an expert? Are you sitting here trying to scientifically analyze magic?"

"Just because it's fantastical doesn't mean there aren't rules and mechanics to it."

"I've played the game enough to know any rule can be bent. It's just a matter of figuring out the angles."

Rich shrugged. "I just don't see how you can bend the rules on healing living tissue."

Jason shook his head and sighed. "Can't read spell one and you're already so quick to discard twenty-first century knowledge. Let me explain for all the slow mages out there." Then he spoke with deliberate care. "From a medical perspective, the ability to save appendages directly correlates to how much time has passed since said appendage was severed. Why? Because the appendage still has living tissue. It's just been cut off from the life source. Rejoin it to the life source and it's back to life again. But you're right. So stupid of me to think magic trumps needle and thread."

Rich was clearly getting mad. He didn't say anything else, though. Melvin knew why. Jason was understandably bent out of shape; he had been hacked out of shape. He just wanted to save his arm.

It was quiet in the house for a few moments. Jason spoke to Rich.

"I need to put it on ice. Let me see your spellbook. I can teach you some spells while we go through it."

They began to go over the book. Rich held the pages and Jason told him what things meant and what the spell was likely used for.

Mike was asleep. Jason was teaching Rich. That left Melvin, Runt and a simmering pot.

"Are you asleep, Mr. Half-weagr?"

He kept his eyes closed when he replied. "Only relaxing. Have to stir the pot every now and again."

"I just wanted to say thanks again for helping us out like this."

He nodded.

"So… uh… what's your story? Why are you out here in the middle of nowhere?"

"You should likely rest now, Miss Melvin."

"Kind of hard to. So much has happened. Besides, I've never met a half-weagr before."

"Hmmm. Likely never meet another. I never met one."

"Why are you guys so rare?"

"Human males don't take a liking to weagr women. Big. Hairy. Smelly. Aggressive. And human women almost always die birthing half-weagr babies."

Melvin was about to ask what kind of woman took a liking to a weagr male. Then he thought about what the weagrs had wanted to do to him and he thought better of asking. He knew how Runt had come to be.

"Guess, uh, your mother was lucky enough to survive it."

Runt opened his eyes, stirred the stew. He looked into the pot as he spoke. "Depends on how you see it. I was lucky. She didn't think herself that until years later."

"What happened years later?"

"I stopped being selfish. About her. About her life. Ended it for her."

Melvin sat in mute shock. He looked over to Rich and Jason, who were staring open-mouthed at Runt, the spell book all but forgotten. Jason was the first to recover.

"Uh… as I was saying… we could go for the ice spell but I'm thinking the sleep spell would be even better."

"I don't see how casting sleep on the arm would do any good," Rich said, eager to get back to something less awkward.

"It'll act like stasis. It'll put the living cells to sleep. It'll also put any microorganisms to sleep. Since the cells don't have a complex mind to fight off the sleep spell, it'll stay in stasis until its reattached. And it'll be much easier to carry around than a cold block of ice."

Rich mulled it over. "That doesn't sound half bad."

"Half bad? It's perfect! Plus you won't have to keep refreezing it when it starts to thaw. Let's do it."

He reached behind his back and grabbed the arm by the hand, pulling it up and out like a club. He placed it on the ground and looked at Rich with expectation.

Rich stood over the arm. "*Yorgun hal*," he intoned. The arm glowed yellow.

Jason pushed Rich. "Dude, it wasn't *hal*. It was *bolge*. You changed the sleep from affecting a specific area to saying sleep and something I don't even recognize."

"No worries, I'll just cast the right one."

"Don't be a nub. You know what happens when you start layering spells. Not on my arm."

"Look, dude, I'm sure it's fine." Rich went to pick the arm up, but the moment he touched it he fell out on the floor, snoring soundly.

Jason and Melvin looked at each other then back to the arm and then back to each other.

"You touch it," Jason said.

"No way. It's your arm."

"Nice going, Rich," Jason said to the sleeping mage. "How is anyone going to carry an arm that induces sleep?"

"Maybe it won't for you," Melvin answered for Rich. "It is your arm, after all."

Jason thought about it for a moment. "Guess I have to try. Runt recommended a nap anyway. Here goes."

He touched it with a finger and nothing happened. He grabbed it by the hand, lifted it, waved it around a little. It did not move at the joints. Either rigor mortis or the sleep spell had made it very rigid.

Jason smiled. "Back in business."

"Have about two hours before stew's ready," Runt said.

"After we eat, we'll clear out of here."

"Wait," Melvin said. "You're coming with us?"

"A ways," was all Runt said as he settled back against the wall. Melvin settled against the back of his chair as well. He closed his eyes to rest, allowing himself to focus on the sounds of stew simmering, fire crackling and hushed chatter between Jason and Runt. Occasionally a diminutive snore from Mike punctuated the air. The smell of the stew wafted to Melvin's nostrils, a scent that hinted at exotic spices and game meat.

A person emerged out of the darkness. It was the weagr, the same one Melvin had killed at the forest. His body was mutilated, his eyes locked onto Melvin, a mixture of shock and accusation on his face.

"Aaah!" Melvin yelled himself awake. Jason and Mike looked at him as he nearly jumped out of his seat.

"Welcome back to the nightmare," Mike said.

"How long was I sleep?"

"How the hell should I know? All I know is the stew's gonna be ready in about half an hour. That's why I'm up. Smells kinda like gumbo."

"I can put you back to sleep if you want," Jason said, waving his stiff, severed arm. "This thing rocks!" he pointed it at Rich, who was still snoring on the floor.

"Shouldn't we pick him up off the floor?" Melvin asked.

"Sheeet," Mike swore. "I ain't giving up my seat for him. He'll be alright. He getting better rest than you got."

Melvin conceded Mike's point with a nod. He noticed Runt, sitting on the floor, tightening the straps of a leather backpack. He remembered the big man had volunteered to come with them.

"Thank you for coming with us, Mr. Half-weagr. That's

extremely hospitable of you." It would be nice to have a guide through the area to get to the mages and, hopefully, a way home.

Runt grunted. "The magic that brought you here is too strong. Concerns us all. Besides, no longer safe here for some time. Weagrs will come back."

Melvin's heart raced with panic. "What? Why? I settled the *akhta*."

"Yes. *Akhta* settled. Not coming for grievance. Coming because they want to."

"If they don't want to settle the score, what do they want?"

"You."

"Oh."

"There is a reason why no one lives within a day's march of a weagr village," Runt said, checking the compartments of the backpack as if what he was talking about was routine. "Weagrs take what they want. They will always want more women. No *akhta* can change that."

"Well, shouldn't we leave, like right now?"

"Road unpredictable. Can never trust when another meal will come on it. We eat first."

Melvin got to pacing, "But, oh my god, this stew is taking forever. Weagrs could be right outside the door by the time it's finished stewing."

"You won *akhta*. Victory rules keeps them from harming you for another eight hours."

Melvin only paced faster. "Rules? What rules? What if they don't follow the rules? I'll be getting dragged back to weagrland by my hair, and all because of stew. This is bad."

Runt stood up. His massive frame gave Melvin pause. Runt's look was serious, his tone was calm.

"Weagrs take what they want. But they have some few rules. Simple rules. They will follow them."

"But how…" Melvin started to ask how he could be sure. But he was looking at a half-weagr. Runt knew. Melvin shut up.

Melvin sat back down. Mike was hefting his club, getting a feel for its weight and balance. Jason was looking outside, at a beautiful day and a horizon full of danger. Rich was still snoring; in about twenty minutes he'd be waking up to stew. Then everyone would be out of the door and making time against a very big menace.

Chapter 4

Fort Law

It was one thing to walk a couple of blocks to the store or walk around your high school between periods. This was walking for hours on end. All their feet were well tenderized by the end of the third hour. Except for Runt, who had tried to make the pace brisk but gave up after leaving them as indistinguishable dots on at least three occasions.

The sun was setting, turning the sky afire with purples and oranges. The countryside, still quite rocky, was now a touch greener with the occasional copse of trees and batches of colorful wildflowers on fields that stretched as far as the eye could see. Melvin had never seen so much nature all at one time and he so desperately wanted to see something else. Something that looked like civilization because that meant he could stop walking.

Mike voiced their concerns. "Yo, can we punch the timecard? My dogs are barking."

Runt looked at them all and stopped. "Briefly. You all take your boots off."

"I can't believe you understood him," Jason said.

Runt grunted. "Don't have to. Mike Ballztowallz like most megryms. Overly wordy. Understood he wanted rest. You all want rest."

They all sat down save Runt and pried their boots off with earnest. A concert of groans and ahs went up into the air as they began massaging.

"We make poor time," Runt said. He stood with his

back to the group, facing the mountain range on the horizon that was glowing gold from the light of the fading day. The sunlight glinted off of the unconventional weapon that ran the length of the big man's back, a stout staff with axe blades facing in opposite directions on either end, like a deadly letter "Z".

"Thanks for bearing with us," Melvin said. "Walking's a lost art for guys like us. And thanks for the stew earlier. It was really good."

"No thanks needed, Miss Melvin Zhufira."

Mike snickered. "Miss Melvin."

Melvin felt his face grow hot. "Uh, yeah, Runt, about that. You can just call me Melvin. I'm not really Zhufira and I'm definitely no miss."

"But you are. You are Miss Melvin Zhufira."

"I don't think you understood our story fully. I'm Melvin Morrow. I'm a sixteen-year-old guy. I'm just stuck in a woman's body right now."

"Understood story. Zhufira fights. Melvin walks. You are both. Miss Melvin Zhufira."

"Speaking of fighting," Mike said, "you still have a big ass hand print around your thigh from when that weagr spanked that ass. I noticed your nasty ass friends looking at it when we was walking."

Shock hit Rich's face like a lightning strike. "No I wasn't!"

"You was looking at my brother's tight, brown-sugary ass, you old pervert. I saw you."

Rich's face turned red behind the beard. "Um. What? No—no—that's crazy." He shook his head.

Jason shrugged. "I was looking. Sorry Mel, but right about now your brown-sugary bottom is the most scenic vista out here."

"We should leave," Runt said.

They set out once again. The sun had all but vanished behind the mountain range. An army of stars twinkled into existence. Runt stopped, little more than a giant silhouette against the growing darkness.

"Mike Ballztowallz, walk with me. I need your eyes. We go to the mountains, the base of the mountain with the horse head shape."

Melvin looked at his brother and noticed his eyes shining like a wolf's. That's right; megrym vision was better suited to night. Melvin wondered what it was like for Mike to see the world right now.

"I don't remember Tirys being in the mountains," Jason said, looking down at his feet as he talked. Melvin imagined his eyes were pretty useless in low light.

"Not going to Tirys," Runt said. "Tirys is for tomorrow, in daylight."

"I don't see why we need to deviate," Jason said. "Going to the mountains puts us farther from Tirys than we would be if we just headed straight for it."

Runt explained without breaking his stride as he walked beside Mike. "We would not make Tirys at our pace. Exhaustion would claim you all. Easy for weagrs to find us as we slept out here in the open. A grim end."

Melvin shivered. It had been so calm and peaceful on the plains that the threat of weagrs seemed distant and surreal until now. The prospect of them finding their camp out here in the middle of the night destroyed any thought about sore feet.

"What's in the mountains?" Rich asked.

Runt explained as they made their way. A fort lay there, abandoned for ages. It was one of many forts that dotted the landscape and in disrepair since the days of the Nigev Endeavor. Jason had heard of that; when mankind had attempted a manifest destiny of sorts leading to fierce warfare with aians and nasrans. Men named the forts after idealistic principles that ran contrary to their sense of entitled conquest: Fort Noble and Justice and Vigil. They were headed to Fort Law.

    Jason was telling stories of history's hard lessons, of famous battles and heroes in the Endeavor when Mike called for the group to stop. Melvin could see the oppressive pitch of mountain outlines against the starlit sky all around him.

    "Prolly best to go single file through here," Mike said.

    "What's here?" Melvin asked.

    "Graveyard."

    They all fell in step behind the megrym. He snaked a course through the graves that felt erratic to Melvin's feet. Despite the low light, Melvin was able to spot a few grave markers. Some were innocuous rounded stone but others were crossed swords or spear heads affixed in granite. This was definitely not a safe place to wander through aimlessly.

    "That's not all," Mike said. "There's holes all over the place, like some giant badger went crazy."

    "Hmmm," Jason said, "I don't recall reading anything in the bestiary about an animal that would do that. Seems a lot of trouble to get corpse meat."

    "Few troubles in easy meal," Runt said.

    The graveyard was massive and by the time Mike led them through it, the team was within a stone throw of the mountains. Within a mile they found a mountain pass, host to an old and broken trail overgrown with weeds. As the trail led them around a bend, Fort Law came into view.

    Even abandoned and age worn, the fort was awe

inducing. The gates alone had to be the height of a three-story house and made of dense wood as thick as a bank vault. Sharp iron spikes bigger than Mike protruded from the wood, a clear and imposing message that no one was welcome here. One gate hung ajar and beyond it blue flame flickered in sconces, casting an eerie glow on the stone steps leading to the entrance of the fort.

"Netherfire," Rich said breathlessly, his eyes never leaving the blue flamed sconces as they approached the gates. "Stuff'll burn for a thousand years."

The netherfire illuminated the face of Fort Law. Shadows danced across foreboding features. Melvin imagined an era long gone when behind the slit windows men fired arrows or from the balcony they poured boiling tar onto the entryway. His gaze flitted, along with the flickering blue light, across the expanse of the entryway, carved to resemble the monstrous maw of a hungry beast.

A sound in the not-too-distant darkness behind them broke Melvin's reverie. A yell. Followed by another.

"Weagrs," Runt said. "Going through graveyard the hard way. Will be upon us soon. Help close the gate."

They all strained as they tried to coax dense wood well settled after being ajar for countless years. It fought the change, issuing its own massive groans as it gave up inches. Melvin could hear the weagrs getting louder, closer and sounding angry as they were no doubt dealing with the many holes and sharp markers of the graveyard. The butterflies in his gut made him nauseated and the gate's slow progress only made them flutter faster.

When the gate finally shut it sounded like a loud knock on hollow walls. Runt looked around and retrieved what must have been the doorjamb, a giant four by four beam.

The beam was worm eaten in some places, heavily splintered in others. It would not hold long against banging weagrs.

"We got another problem," Mike said, his eyes shining as he looked across the courtyard.

Melvin followed his brother's eyes and saw another pair of eyes shining back at them from the darkness. The eyes approached until the netherfire revealed an animal that looked like a hyena. Instead of the short, spotted fur of a hyena, this creature had a mane of long brown hair erupting from its neck and down its back. It seemed to regard them all with curiosity.

"Strandwolf," Runt said. "Will kill for its meat when necessary or in large groups. Mostly scavengers."

Scavenger or not, Melvin didn't like the looks of it. There was a nasty and intelligent gleam in those shiny eyes. The strandwolf rose up until it looked like a man on two legs leaning forward, its front paws hanging down in front of it. Then it started to laugh, revealing wicked teeth. "*Ke ke ke ke...*"

The gate behind them jumped with a sudden thud. Another thud followed, as jarring as the first. The doorjamb splintered a little more.

"*Ke ke ke kiyiya... yeya!*" the strandwolf's laugh got louder, bouncing off the mountain walls of the courtyard. It ended its taunting laugh with an ear piercing howl.

Eyes started appearing in the darkness. A sea of them, too many to count, all of them shining with nasty intelligence. From various places amongst the eyes, a low laugh came. "*Ke ke ke ke...*"

Boom! The gate shuddered from another attack.

"Inside the fort!" Runt yelled.

They raced to the door. The strandwolves broke into a run to cover the courtyard grounds and beat them to the entrance. The door grew closer quickly but so did the shifting tide of furry bodies all around them. The closest strandwolf, the one that had roused its family, lunged at Jason, its jaws open.

It yelped as an axe blade landed on the side of its face. Runt had pulled his Z-weapon and was bearing it in both hands as he ran. He did not break a stride as he struck the strandwolf. Neither did the remaining pack.

Four strandwolves covered the courtyard grounds before the group could make the entrance. Runt's Z-weapon went up, cutting one in mid-lunge. Then the other end came down, swiping another. Mike's club crushed the hind quarters of the strandwolf trying to hamstring Rich. The last strandwolf lunged at Jason, who undoubtedly looked like easy prey, one-armed and weaponless.

Its teeth sank into Jason's arm. It was the severed arm tied to his back. The strandwolf bit down and a moment later crashed to the ground, deep in sleep.

Jason was the last one inside the fort. Runt closed the doors while Mike slid an iron bar across them. Outside, they could hear the scratching and howling and braying of the strandwolves.

They all backed away from the entrance cautiously, as if any sudden movement would cause the door to break down and allow an army of strandwolves to descend upon them. The netherfire sconces were sparse inside. Their blue light illuminated errant patches of pitch blackness, making the desire to tread carefully that much more pressing.

Melvin could make out the entrances to a few cave-like passages that disappeared into darkness. Four netherfire sconces in the center of the room illuminated a large portion of the antechamber. They retreated to this well lit square, watching the door the whole time.

"What do we do now?" Melvin asked.

"You can start by getting your sword out, jackass," Mike said.

Melvin drew his sword. The sight of it shaking made him feel even more unnerved than when it was sheathed. He brought the sword tip to rest against the stone floor to keep it steady.

Jason reached behind him and grabbed his severed arm by its hand. He hoisted it like a club. It was a strange sight, with the rigid joints keeping it up and shoulder socket meat exposed at the top.

"Not sure how this unfolds," Runt said looking at the door. "Door could hold, proof against strandwolves and weagrs. Door could fall to either or both."

He went quiet. Melvin hoped he was thinking of battle strategies or alternate plans. Melvin couldn't get his own mind to think beyond what he was seeing and hearing. He was seeing a door surrounded by darkness. He was hearing scratching and braying outside the door, the occasional shuffle and scurry of rats inside the fort.

Runt spoke at last. "Depending on weagr numbers, strandwolves may retreat. We want somewhere dark for weagrs, to ambush and confuse."

The sound of Runt's voice calmed Melvin. They had no definite plan yet, but the sound of him working through their precarious situation without fear in his voice strengthened Melvin's resolve.

"But there are many strandwolves. More than I thought possible in a land scarce of meat like this. Possible they will take down all weagrs, forget about us entirely. Possible too they defeat weagrs and still come for us. Must fight them in light."

It sounded like they would have to wager on who was going to win outside: the rock or the hard place. Inside, Melvin heard more rats shuffling, closer this time. Normally rodents move away from strangers and danger. He thought about the state of decay this ancient fort was in.

"Are there any other ways into this fort?" he asked Runt.

Runt shook his head. "Carved into mountain. One way in, one way out. Highly defensible."

Melvin was about to explain about the rats and what he thought he was hearing, but the rats announced themselves with a loud shuffle of movement directly behind them. They all turned to face the noise.

Blue netherfire shed flickering light on some of their questions. Now they knew how the strandwolf population had grown so dense. What was moving toward them was no errant rat.

They were corpses. Some in full and rusted battle raiment, some in tattered rags, but all of them were walking corpses. The men long dead and buried in the fields outside the gates had returned from the grave to occupy Fort Law.

Chapter 5

Freedom Flight

Melvin, Rich and Jason screamed. All their voices were so high it was impossible to tell which shriek came from the woman's body.

"Hell naw," Mike cried in disbelief as the ever-increasing number of corpses shuffled their way. "What the fuck is next, vampire dragons? A kung-fu killer werewolf priest? What the hell did you fools get me into?"

Vacant-eyed and slack-jawed, the undead warriors dragged their spears and swords along the floor as they stumbled and shuffled. They stopped in unison, and all the ones that still had mouths spoke as one.

"Free... me."

Runt twisted his Z-weapon in the middle. The shaft separated; now the big man wielded an axe in each hand. The undead warriors took another step, unfazed by Runt's gleaming twin blades.

Melvin heard a splintering crash behind him. He snapped his head around to see the fort's entrance door imploding, taking the iron bar and hinges with it. With a loud yell, the first weagr came through the entryway, charging toward the closest thing in sight. That was Melvin.

Melvin was close to reaching his shock tolerance level again. All he could do was look up with his mouth open as the weagr's massive axe came down.

A violent shove forced Melvin forward. As he collided into Rich and Jason, he looked back to see Mike had pushed him out of harm's way. But now Mike was in the weagr's path.

The weagr was too busy looking at his target escape to notice the tiny megrym. Mike got tangled up into the weagr's legs, getting knocked back and forth between them as the weagr stumbled. The weagr crashed head first into the corpse warriors while Mike was sent tumbling across the room. Runt rushed over to Mike's aid.

On his hands and knees, the raging weagr took wild swings with his axe back and forth through the undead throng like he was cutting jungle brush with a machete. Many swarmed him, stabbing with their weapons. Many others stumbled past him as if he was not even there.

The undead began splintering off into a "Y". The left branch headed toward Mike and Runt, the right toward Jason, Rich and Melvin. And the stem of the "Y" was stabbing the weagr, who had already dropped his axe as he succumbed, in wet, bubbling wails, to the onslaught.

More weagrs were piling into the entryway, making a "Y" of their own as they pursued the split party. Melvin knew getting across the room to rejoin Mike and Runt was suicide at this point. Mike pointed behind Melvin, to a tunnel made visible by a nearby netherfire sconce.

"Run!" Mike cried. With that, he and Runt fell back into a passage on the opposite side of the room, corpses and weagrs either in tow behind them or fighting each other.

Melvin, Rich and Jason turned and fled into the tunnel. The netherfire light that illuminated the tunnel entrance quickly disappeared and they found themselves running into inky blackness, their hands out in front of them. Despite the near perfect darkness, they did not slow. When their hands hit coarse cave wall, they groped around frantically until their hands met empty air and their blind dash continued. After a few awkward turns, they saw a faint blue light at the end of the tunnel.

The tunnel opened up to a vast chamber. The solitary pole sconce in the center of the room showed it used to be a mess hall. Rows of wooden tables and benches disappeared into the surrounding darkness, the light too faint to show where they ended. Empty cups and bowls lay scattered across the tabletops, the chaotic place settings of a ghost garrison.

"What do we do? What do we do?" Rich asked, wheezing to get his breath back.

"I don't see another tunnel," Melvin said. "There could be one on any of these walls, or nothing at all."

"We need more light," Jason said.

Melvin looked at the pole sconce and came up with an idea. He whacked at the pole with his sword, his strikes hurried and imprecise. When he had whittled enough away, he pulled at the pole until it broke away into his hands.

"Nethertorch," he dubbed it, raising it up. "Let's find a way out of here," he said, proceeding down the row of tables.

It did not take long to reach a wall. This one offered no adjoining passageways. As they moved along it, Melvin heard yells and footstep as their pursuers made their way toward the mess hall.

"Hurry!" Jason cried.

They ran along the wall until they found the corner and ran the length of this new wall. They came to another corner. Still no new tunnels.

Commotion in the room stole their attention. Yells, grunts and the clatter of plates and cups crashing punctuated the air. Something was in there with them, hidden in darkness. Melvin's good idea for a nethertorch also meant they were now huddled around the room's only light, a beacon in the corner that advertised their presence.

"Run!" Melvin cried, taking off in the direction of the newest wall in hopes of finding a break in it. Wood splintered. Dishes crashed. The sounds of the room being wrecked got louder and closer.

A break in the wall came into view just a few feet ahead. A weagr stumbled into view at the same time. It crashed into the table closest to them before hitting the ground. A dozen strandwolves covered him. A couple more advanced on the boys.

"Into the tunnel!" Melvin said. He waved the nethertorch at the strandwolves, forcing them to back away as his friends made the passage. The two strandwolves turned their attention back to the downed weagr and the easier meal he offered.

They ran. The tunnel sloped downwards and began to curve. The walls became narrower, the roof lower. Melvin could no longer see what was up ahead beyond Rich and Jason. He kept glancing back, sure a strandwolf was about to leap onto his back despite the only sound being their footsteps on stone.

Jason and Rich stopped abruptly, causing Melvin to nearly collide with Rich. He noticed the tunnel had opened up a bit more. They were at a "+" intersection. No going back meant left, right, or forward.

"What if these tunnels start criss-crossing and intersecting?" Rich asked. "We could wind up back here, all turned around with strandwolves waiting for us."

"Let's keep going straight," Melvin said, casting a glance backwards. He didn't want to spend any time down here standing still.

"No, no," Jason said. "We have to go left."

"Why do we have to go left?" Melvin asked, looking

into the dark passage as if a way to tell its potential merit was going to jump out at him.

"Dungeon rules," Jason said. "Any serious dungeoncrawler knows you always go left."

Melvin couldn't believe what he was hearing. "We got three different flavors of the Apocalypse chasing us and you want to treat it like we're in it for experience points? This is crazy; do you see any 1-ups? There's no save file to load if things go bad. We're going straight." He took a step down the middle.

"No, no, no," Jason said, shaking his head and waving his arm club like a truce flag. "Most mazes are built in what's called a 'simply-connected' design. To keep from getting lost or going down the same tunnels over and over, you keep your left hand on the left wall and follow it around. Do that and you never go down the same tunnel twice."

"Why can't we do the same thing with the right?" Rich asked.

"Talk about this later!" Melvin cried, taking off down the left passage with Jason and Rich scrambling behind. The tunnel opened up into a barracks room. The wooden frames had caved in on most of the bunk beds, spilling mattress and support slats onto the bottom bunk. Dust lay thick and undisturbed on footlockers. Netherfire in wall recesses told them this room was a dead end.

They turned around and saw three pairs of eyes shining in the darkness. Strandwolves, and this time there was no escape route.

Melvin brought his trembling sword up as he backed up into the barracks. Beside him, Jason raised his arm club, a look of menace etched into his gray aian face. Behind them, Rich looked around the room frantically as if something useful lay hidden in the dilapidated wood.

The strandwolves lunged. A massive hairy body dominated Melvin's field of vision as it jumped at his face.

He flinched, stabbing wildly at air while his eyes stayed squinted shut. He felt his sword hit something, followed by a yelp.

He opened his eyes and saw his blade stained with blood tinted blue under the netherfire light. One of the strandwolves was down, blood steadily seeping from a wound in its chest. Beside that one, another strandwolf lay asleep. Jason must have hit it with his arm club.

Jason was yelling. The third strandwolf was on his good arm, its maw full of sleeve and the forearm underneath. Apparently, Jason's swing had knocked out the one but had left his arm exposed. Now the strandwolf was shaking its head violently, pulling an already off balance Jason down.

Rich kicked the strandwolf in the face. It yelped and released Jason's arm as it backed away snarling. Melvin readied his sword, but he noticed the strandwolf was looking beyond them, snarling at something low to the ground.

He turned and saw the strandwolf he had stabbed in the chest was back on its feet. Its eyes were vacant. The beast was clearly dead... and freshly risen.

"What the...!"

Melvin didn't get to finish the expression, as the living strandwolf exploded past them and launched itself at the undead beast. The two went at each other, snapping and growling in the barracks. Rich pushed Melvin out of the room and grabbed Jason by the arm. Together, they fled back to the intersection.

When Melvin looked at the three identical passages, a surge of panic rose and died a moment later. The "always go left" trick meant the way to the mess hall was on their right. Their only options were left or straight. He was able to keep it all clear in his head, despite his heart racing and the fear rising.

"Left," he said and began proceeding. He stopped short because Rich had followed him but Jason had stayed in the intersection. Jason was shaking his head, staring into the tunnel that led back to the barracks.

"Might as well give up," Jason said to the empty tunnel. "Nothing stays dead here."

"Jason…"

"It all comes back. It all comes after us."

"Jason… c'mon man…"

Melvin took a step toward his friend. Hands emerged from the darkness of the tunnel behind Jason, several hands, their fingers caked with dirt or missing nails in places.

"Jason!"

Jason looked back and screamed as the hands grabbed him and pulled him into the darkness. Melvin ran forward to see the briefest glimpse of his friend getting pulled into a sea of corpse warriors. The undead shuffled toward Melvin and Rich.

"Free… me."

Melvin raised his sword. Rich grabbed Melvin's arm and shook it.

"Mel! There's too many. We gotta run!"

Melvin shook his head, looking for his friend in the mass of bodies growing closer.

"Mel!"

Rich was right. Melvin yelled out, a mixture of anger, despair and frustration before turning to run with Rich down the tunnel.

C3&O

Jason was in the midst of festering rot. Slimy, putrefied

hands pushed and pulled him. Every second he expected all their mouths to start biting into him. But their hands just kept pushing, pulling, herding him where they wanted.

He was ushered through a grand chamber. The netherfire light revealed four weagrs in the center of it, fighting against an undead army of weagrs, men and strandwolves. One of the undead weagrs put his axe through a living one's forehead. His eyes went vacant around the axe handle before pulling it out and turning on the remaining three weagrs.

Jason was pushed out of the chamber, down tunnels and through halls until he could no longer tell where he was. When the undead finally stopped pushing, he was in a small room with a high ceiling. Dead men lined the walls and blocked the way back.

A creature occupied the center of the room. It was black, as if its skin was made from total darkness. A white aura of sorts surrounded it, allowing Jason to see the humanoid contours of its legs and head. Jason saw it was kneeling down and looking back at him with white, pupil-less eyes.

The creature opened its mouth and only white light escaped. However, the corpses in the room spoke words in sync with the creature.

"Free... me."

Jason saw no bars, chains, nothing holding the creature down. He looked above the kneeling creature. A glowing, red crystal floated at eye level.

He had seen this before, in the *Secret Blades* expansion. A Majora witchlock. Resembling a twelve sided die, it created an invisible magic prison. The creature was helpless beneath it.

As helpless as the ruler of an undead army; some of the dead pushed Jason forward while others spoke their master's wishes. "Free... me."

Jason had never seen this creature, not in any bestiary or expansion or even in the background of any artwork. And he knew if it was under a witchlock, it was for a good reason. They were difficult to make and too rare to waste on even dangerous criminals.

"Uh..." was all he could say as they pushed him ever closer to it. He was pretty sure the creature wasn't going to take no for an answer. "Can't you, I don't know... free yourself?" he indicated the legion of the dead around him.

One of the undead stepped out from the ranks lining the wall. It reached a hand out to the Majora witchlock. When its fingers touched, the red light swelled within the crystal and melted the fingers. The red light continued to travel along the corpse's body, incinerating as it went, even burning up the ancient armor it wore. In seconds there was nothing left but ash.

"You want me to touch that?!"

The all white eyes of the darkness creature stared at Jason. The corpses spoke around them.

"You... give... to me. I... give... to you."

Jason felt pain shoot through his shoulder blades. Hot, excruciating, unbearable; he screamed as the pain consumed him.

◌◌◌

Mike bashed another corpse in the head, sending it tumbling to the chamber below. He knew it was a useless win. A fall like that would seriously injure or kill most folks. This enemy was just going to get up and shuffle his ass back up here.

Him and Runt were on a stone bridge spanning a huge chamber. Runt was on the other end of the bridge, dual axes flying, while Mike was on this end, doing his level best to crack skulls. They were both giving ground slowly as the dead kept coming.

Mike had no illusions about what was going to happen. He had seen four weagrs in the chamber below go from alive and angry to Night of the Living Dead. Eventually, this crowd was going to push him and Runt back to back. After that, even if he decided to jump to his death, he knew he wouldn't stay dead for long.

He bashed another one, sending it over the side. "There's your freedom!" he told it. "Give me a chance, I'll free every one of you bitches," he said as the grasping hands forced him another step back. Between strikes he thought of Melvin, hoping his dumb ass had made it out alive.

◊

Melvin and Rich were fresh out of left turns. An undead pack of strandwolves followed them. The strandwolves had lost their sense of urgency after rising from the dead, and were just plodding after the two. Behind the strandwolves, dead men shuffled in their own slow pursuit. If they had leashes, it would look like zombies taking their dogs for a walk.

Melvin had run out of steam two tunnels back. Now the two of them just kept backing away from the encroaching corpses, occasionally looking behind them to see what lay ahead.

"This doesn't look good," Rich said.

They were slowly approaching a chamber. It was hard to make out very much in it. But Melvin saw the undead lining the walls, waiting for them.

"Do something!" Rich cried to Melvin. "We can't walk into that!"

"What the hell do you want me to do?"

"Turn on Zhufira mode and cut us out of here!"

"Zhufira mode? What, like I'm a lightbulb with a

sword?! You're supposed to be Razzleblad, superbad super mage. Razzle already!"

Melvin turned to see the chamber had grown much closer in the time they spent arguing. The undead still lined the chamber, making no move toward them.

They were almost at the entrance to the chamber when Melvin noticed the person in the center. It was an aian standing over something black and reaching out to something with a red glow. A severed arm protruded from his back.

"Jason!" Melvin called out as Jason took the red thing in his hand and crumbled it. A shock wave boomed through the fort, knocking Jason down and shaking the walls and ceiling with earthquake force.

Melvin and Rich rushed over to Jason. He looked up at Melvin. "It—it—made me," was all he said. Jason reached out to Melvin, an act that made Melvin jerk back in horrified shock.

Shiny white bone protruded from the cauterized wound of Jason's severed shoulder. He had an arm of bone, and he had reached out to Melvin with skeleton fingers. Jason pointed the skeleton hand at the black shape.

It was a man of total darkness. Melvin could only see how giant he was because of the white outline around him. He was twice the size of Runt as he stood up and stretched. Four pitch black wings unfurled behind him. Then he lowered himself to one knee, as if he was going to charge at them.

The winged man exploded upward, fast as a bullet, breaking through ceilings of solid stone. He was gone in the night after a moment, leaving massive holes in his wake.

All the undead men lining the walls fell where they stood, once again lifeless.

Fort Law began to shake much worse than before. Stones started falling from the roof. In the middle of the room, a circle of blue and white light swirled into existence and grew bigger.

"Is this making the fort shake?" Melvin asked, looking at the growing circle of light.

"No, that's a portal," Jason said. "Between the Majora witchlock breaking and that creature making its own exit, this place is coming down around us." As he finished talking more stones, bigger stones, started falling.

The quaking got worse as more of the roof fell away. Even if Melvin knew the fastest way to get back to the entrance of Fort Law, there was no guarantee they wouldn't get buried under tons of rock first.

He knew about portals. They were magic gateways that could lead anywhere. The few times he had used one in the game he had met a quick and cheap death.

Also a quick and cheap death was getting crushed by roof rocks. He looked at Rich and Jason. He said nothing; he didn't have to. They nodded.

As they plunged into the swirling portal, Melvin looked up through the massive hole left by the creature. He caught the briefest glimpse of Mike looking down from a bridge many stories up. Giant rocks fell on the bridge, as Fort Law collapsed in on itself.

Chapter 6

Quest Proper

Melvin saw nothing but blue and white light for long, tense moments. When the light finally died, he wasn't quite sure if their situation had improved.

They were in a grand circular library. The polished marble floors, the smell of oiled leather and the soft glow of paper lanterns were all things that made him want to exhale a much needed sigh of relief. But he couldn't. A man and woman, their faces twisted in rage, kept his breath bated. In their bare hands they held blazing fire raised as if to throw at them.

The woman yelled at them. "What have you done?! Explain this malice or burn!"

"Whoa! Whoa! No malice here," Melvin said as he waved his hands. Then he realized he was waving a sword at two people who had fire aimed at his head. He dropped the sword on the floor with a jarring clang.

"We didn't mean it," Jason said. "But the undead were chasing us. And the weagrs and the strandwolves. And the black thing made me. And the fort was falling on our heads. And we're not even supposed to be here. We're from the suburbs!"

The man and woman looked at each other. The woman nodded and the two of them closed their hands, smothering the fire. She stood with poise, wearing what seemed to be a soft green nightgown. Asian features and skin the color of honey gave an exotic look to the expression of concern on her face.

"Wait, I know you," Rich said pointing. "You're the Hierophant Majora."

"I am," she said. "And one of you broke my lock. I need to know why."

They explained in sloppy, broken fragments the events that led them there. One would tell the story and then someone else would interject with details or corrections and pick the story back up. Hierophant Majora and the man with her said nothing the whole time. When Melvin, Rich and Jason finally reached the present, the lady spoke.

"It is late, and you three have been through much. My questions, and yours I'm sure, will keep until morning." She looked at the man. "Druze, please show them quarters."

"Wait," Melvin said. "What about my brother?"

Majora looked at him. "Who can say? Just as you hope for his safety, put faith in those hopes. That is all you can do at the moment, my dear."

She left them with Druze, a dark featured man with black robes. He took them out of the library and onto a breezeway. Wide marble columns ascended into an arched ceiling and both sides of the breezeway revealed a majestic garden, with colorful flowers, lush plants, and sculpted fountains that sprayed water. It all twinkled in the light of paper lanterns.

"The Hierophane," Rich said as he looked around in wonder.

The breezeway ended at a tower. The interior of the tower made Melvin feel like he was inside a giant bottle. He stood in the atrium courtyard looking all around at doors and windows ascending up to open sky.

It was a clean, elegant design. Perhaps that was due in

some part to the fact there were no stairs. Doors, no matter how high up, opened up to empty air.

Druze led them on the path until they stood on a section covered with charcoal colored gravel. He knelt down and traced out a pattern into the gravel. Once he was done, the strange character he had drawn glowed orange and the square of gravel they were standing on rose into the air.

It coasted up gently several floors, stopping in front of a door. When Druze opened the door, the light came on and he put his hand out for them to go inside.

Rich and Jason went in but Druze put his arm up to block Melvin. "These are not your quarters."

Before Melvin could understand the what's and why's, Druze was drawing in the gravel again. The square rose up a few more floors, leaving Rich and Jason with an open door and quizzical looks on their faces.

Melvin understood when he walked into the room Druze opened. Sheer gossamer curtains surrounded a bed layered with furry throw blankets. The wall, the bed, the curtains—it was all a soft shade of pink. He whirled on Druze, anger etched into his pretty features.

"I'm not a girl!"

Druze's reply was written in gravel, leaving Melvin with an open door.

Melvin shut the door, but not without a dizzying look down first. He knew the height was intentional. Hierophant Majora wanted answers from them; there would be no leaving until she had them.

Right about now, Melvin didn't care if he was stuck in a pretty pink prison. It was the safest place he'd been since reality shifted. He looked through his quarters.

He found a rectangular tub of cut stone. His day had

consisted of hours of traveling, dueling with weagrs, and running from the undead in a decrepit fortress. The grime of it all felt like glue stuck to him.

He saw two pictographs on the tile wall at the head of the tub, one of a raincloud and the other a row of waves. He touched the raincloud and water sprayed out from tiny holes cut into the ceiling directly above the tub.

He peeled off the steel bikini and let the hot water work its own kind of magic. Worries dissipated into the steam. Troubles swirled down the drain.

He was beyond exhausted. Once the water stopped raining down, he was barely cognizant of toweling off, finding some night clothes, and getting under the fuzzy throw blankets of his bed. Soon as his head hit the pillow it was like a knockout punch.

A loud, powerful knock woke him up. Melvin opened up crusty eyes to a bleary world. Daylight was streaming through the windows.

"I will come back to collect you in thirty minutes," a man's voice said through the door. Must be Druze, Melvin assumed.

Melvin got up, his legs stiff and sore. He looked out the window and his breath caught in his throat.

A giant river wove a course from the top of the horizon to almost the base of the tower before bending around, its water sparkling blue and violet. Dense tropical foliage lined the banks of the river. Melvin's eyes followed a flock of majestic white birds as they flew over a lush copse of palm trees. The birds flew in a triangular formation, a living arrow that pointed to fog shrouded mountains barely visible in the distance.

Melvin stretched, eyes closed as he enjoyed the feeling

of release that came with extending the muscles. As he opened his eyes, he caught the reflection of himself in the room's full length mirror. He was on his tip-toes, arms raised, body only modestly covered in a pink nightie.

"God, I'm ridiculously hot," he said as he eyed the gracious curves of his legs, breasts and butt. "Why can't I meet you in real life?"

The thought brought him back to Majora. If anyone could help them get back to their world, it was her. Melvin had only seen a fraction of the Hierophane and he was already astounded by its magic and grandeur. The Hierophant Majora had probably already devised a way home for him and his friends and brother.

The thought of Mike made his stomach lurch as he put on his steel bikini. Mike was tough; he came back from some pretty hairy scrapes in Afghanistan, after all. And he had Runt with him, who was thoroughly badass with those Z-blades.

But the last time Melvin had seen Mike an ancient fortress was crumbling down around him. How far away was Fort Law from the Hierophane? Surely the mages could conjure up another portal close to the fort and search for Mike and Runt.

This was the issue foremost in his mind as Druze came back for him. The expressionless man had Rich and Jason with him. Druze just opened the door this time instead of knocking, giving Melvin's friends a chance to see inside the room.

"So this is why you couldn't bunk with us?" Jason said with a wry curve of his lip. "Too many peas under the mattresses in our man cave?"

"Shut up." Melvin got on the gravel platform and looked straight ahead.

"Mmmm… you smell good too," Jason said, sniffing

close to Melvin. "What kind of soap they give you in the Princess Suite? Is that—lilacs and lavender?"

"I hope you stab yourself with a finger bone the next time you pick your nose."

"Pretty cool huh?" Jason held up the bone arm, curling and uncurling the fingers. It was completely mobile despite being devoid of sinew and muscle. The thing was simultaneously compelling and disturbing to watch. Jason seemed at home with it though.

Once the platform reached the ground, they followed Druze as he led them through the Hierophane. Many people bustled about now, making the place feel like a city unto itself. Women wore muslin dresses and men wore long flax tunics with a severe "V" cut that exposed most of their chests and stomach. A belt separated the top and bottom halves of the tunic, which stopped at the men's knees. It all seemed very Egyptian to Melvin.

Few people wore robes like Rich. Druze in all black and a handful of random others were the exception. Of course, no one had on a steel bikini or aian-style tree bark leather. As they walked by, people everywhere stopped and stared. Melvin didn't know if they were looking at Rich's robes, Jason's bone arm, or his own barely covered ass. He felt his face turn warm.

Druze took them to a villa. Lavishly furnished with high, domed ceilings and marble columns, it was a place that made Melvin's nice room shabby in comparison. Druze led them out to a veranda, where Majora was sitting at a table and looking out at the gardens of the Hierophane while birds chirped good morning.

She was wearing regal white and purple robes as opposed to the green nightgown they first met her in. When she saw them, she smiled warmly.

"Please, sit down. Breakfast is due."

They all took seats around the table, except for Druze. He sat on the sofa behind Majora and looked stoically at the party in front of him. No sooner had they sat down than servants start bustling about, bringing out plates.

Sweetfish patties, flat cakes of shredded fish cooked with green onions, was the main course. Mushroom slices and generous chunks of tomato, both cooked and steaming, were heaped along the sides. They were served a hot, spiced tea and a green fruit juice that was just a touch tart. Maybe it was the hunger talking as he dug in, but Melvin couldn't remember the last time he had had a meal this good.

Famished as he was, Melvin was still able to ask about his brother between bites of sweetfish patty. "After we eat, can you make another portal back to Fort Law so I can find my brother?"

"I'm afraid portals do not work as simply as you assume," Majora said as she nursed her spiced tea. "A mage, no matter how powerful, cannot just open a gate to anywhere they want to be. Portals are a form of recall magic. A mage would have to go to the location in question and craft the portal spell for his or her return later. If it is or ever was possible to get to an unprepared location via portal, that magic is lost to us now."

"Then I have to get there the fastest way possible. I need to find him."

Majora shook her head. "We must discourse, plan and prepare. No good will come of rushing into the unknown. 'Cook your food before you eat it,' as they say."

"Wait a minute," Rich said, "if a mage needs to be present to set a portal, how'd the one we took get there in the first place?"

Majora looked at him and smiled. "Rich is it? I like that name. Rich as in sweet, like a butter-orange cake. The portal was there because I placed it there myself, in the event the dark creature you encountered tried to escape. I had been using that portal every fifty years to go back to Fort Law, where I would renew the witchlock and refresh the portal. It was a flawless system for three hundred twenty odd years until last night."

Rich's jaw dropped. "Do mages live that long?"

Fine wrinkles gathered at the corners of Majora's mouth as she smiled, and her eyes displayed the faintest touch of crow's feet. For a woman over three hundred years old, she didn't look a day past forty. "No," she said simply.

"Your inadvertent reprieve to the creature leaves it free to endanger this world," she continued. "It is not exactly fitting to send you all home while we're left to deal with this obscene mess."

"What exactly was that thing?" Jason asked. His bone hand came up from the table as in emphasis.

"What you've seen is more than most know," Majora said. "But it is a terrible sight, is it not? This being, able to control the nameless and countless dead. The puppetmaster to an unkillable army, an army that too easily converts the living into more of their ranks. Such a thing cannot be allowed to pervert the balance of nature. And I need you all to stop it."

"Us?!" Melvin, Rich and Jason spoke as one.

"Who else? From what I see, you three make the ideal combination to contain this threat," she said as she took a sip of spiced tea. From behind the cup, her gaze went between the three of them. Melvin wondered if she was smiling as she sipped.

"You got us all wrong, lady," Melvin said. "You're

looking at a fumble-handed swordswoman guy, a mage that can't cast his way out of a wet paper bag, and an archer who's never fired a shot. We're not the badasses you're looking for."

"My dear, you are more badass than you think," Majora said, rising from the table. "And I know this because I fully understand what you are and how you came to be here."

The three looked at each other then back at Majora. She was stepping off of the veranda and into the garden. She turned to them. "If you all are done with breakfast, I'd be happy to show you," she said.

She took them across the gardens and into a grand building. Their boots clicked on polished tiles that rippled like water as they tread on them. Marble statues and curious devices decorated the hallways. Melvin had to fight the urge to touch stuff every time something new came within reach.

"It is no big secret how you got here," Majora said. "Magic from the Hierophane pulled you into this world and into these bodies. The only real surprise is your level of awareness and attachment."

"What do you mean?" Jason asked.

"Jason, right? Not as cute as Rich," she said, smiling at Rich. "Well, Jason, magic pulls your consciousness from your world into these constructed bodies for a limited duration. Normally, your consciousness is never fully entrenched and aware of this world because you interact with it through an interface device."

"The game…"

"Exactly. What you call the game is the interface device that our magic uses to bring your consciousness here."

"I've never heard of this kind of magic," Jason mused.

"Well, prepare to look upon what you've never heard of," Majora said. She waved her hand across the granite wall and tiny fragments of stone scurried out in either direction, leaving a giant passageway that they stepped through.

"I present the cause of your current predicament, the Rift Pendulum," Majora said, extending her hand toward the giant device in the center of the room.

For its namesake, it did look like a pendulum, an unconventional kind called a Foucault pendulum, something Melvin knew solely because of his Wikipedia habit. The pendulum was a giant, golden bob suspended from a wire affixed to the ceiling. The bob itself consisted of a sphere with a cone extending from the bottom of the sphere to terminate into a needle fine point. The golden sphere of the bob contained light that swirled like a constant storm. The ceiling where the wire hung looked as if it was a night sky made of liquid metal with stars and nebulas changing colors as the pendulum swung. The floor under the swinging bob looked like an ancient map, the highly stylized ones Melvin always saw in pirate and adventure movies. The air shimmered in the space between the pendulum's swinging arc as if it was tearing a hole in the air itself.

"The Rift Pendulum is the apex of nasran hexation, megrym clockworks, and human ingenuity. It performs a thousand functions, to include powering the magical tools and devices throughout the Hierophane. One of those functions was bringing you here."

"I don't understand," Melvin said. "Why bring anyone here at all?"

"You and yours are the major force preserving law and order here," Majora said. "You all have the strength, skill, power, and most importantly, the desire to do things others don't. Few would sanely volunteer to walk into weagr-infested woods looking for trouble, or track down cut-throat bandits, or tangle with a demented mage. Not only do you all do that, you eagerly want to."

"We've played this so much, acting like it was real, and the whole time it was," Rich said, looking at the pendulum swing.

"I'm afraid it's not that simple," Majora said smiling at Rich. "Every time you play your game doesn't necessarily predicate your presence here. Pendulum hero visits can be directed by mages, but they are largely automated based on perceived threats as calculated by the Pendulum. It appears your goals of culling a weagr threat in Kazawood matched one of the Pendulum's calculations that the weagr population had grown dangerously high there. Only when your goals align with the ours does the Pendulum pull you here."

"So if this is routine business, what's the difference now?" Jason asked. "What changed that made us so we're aware of our circumstances and stuck here?"

"That is difficult to assess, Jason," Majora said. "There are many variables at work. As you can see, a myriad of moving parts. But I assure you it was merely a hiccup, something easily remedied once your quest is complete."

"You make it sound like a trip to the mall but it's all deadly and dangerous and a bit much for a bunch of kids from the burbs, so I'd just like to find my brother and go home," Melvin said.

"I agree," said Majora, "It is dangerous. But a bit much, no. Your bodies are created, every fiber pure magic. They are perfect. The amazing things possible to you when you feel it's just a game are still possible. The problem is your minds."

"That's a big problem," Melvin said. "Our minds aren't right. We don't want to do it. So why us and not some new guys you pull out of the pendulum?"

Majora looked at the pendulum as she spoke. "Pendulum heroes achieve much, but they are only good for limited engagements. Though, I do wish you had their eager, accepting nature. Only you can change that. More to the point, you all are already pendulum heroes, and much better suited to the task at hand."

There was nothing in Majora's proposal about finding Mike or sending them home. The thought of going out there in a crazy fantasy world to contain an evil menace did not set well with Melvin. They had barely survived a day out there.

"We're not pendulum heroes," Melvin said. "We're kids. We know only fractions about this world and the possible dangers. The super skills you're trying to sell us on are buried to the point of being completely unreliable. You're better off sending out a group of mages to deal with this. We're useless."

Majora turned and faced Melvin, her jaw tight. "How many robed mages did you see this morning? The mages of the Hierophane are already dispersed throughout the world, dealing with problems you three didn't actively create. There aren't even enough robes left here to properly instruct the acolytes. You are pendulum heroes, but you stand before me and have the gall to call yourselves useless?"

Majora walked over to Jason and snatched a finger off his bone hand. The bones came off in a crunchy snap while Jason yelled out more from shock than pain. "*Suchanaa*," she intoned and a bowl of water appeared in her hand. She dropped the finger in and showed them.

"What keeps his arm together is the magic cast from the source. His arm will always seek to come back together first and then find its way back to the source second," Majora moved the finger opposite of where it pointed and it slowly moved itself back to its starting position. She tossed the bowl to Jason, who fumble-juggled it while she went over to Rich.

"Rich wears gray robes. His command of magic is overwhelming in its magnificence; only a handful ever live to reach gray. He is nothing short of living splendor. We need this kind of power to contain the monster."

Melvin tried to protest. "But…"

"No." The way Majora said it; the way her eyes sparked with cold anger, Melvin knew to shut the hell up.

"Your enlarged sense of self-entitlement does not grant pardon here. This is the consequence of your actions, unintended or otherwise. You released it. This is your weight to bear. But you are also ideal candidates for this task, with Jason able to track it and Rich able to contain it. And if you want the Rift Pendulum to return you to your rightful place you *will* contain it."

Melvin cast his gaze down. He knew she was right. "My brother," he said. "I need to find him."

"You mentioned last night you were all headed here before you got separated. It is my hope he is still inclined to journey to the Hierophane. Ultimately, I feel it best if we let him come to us rather than turning over a thousand stones looking for him.

"But I understand the strength of family ties. And you are not directly necessary to find and stop the creature. If you choose to go in search of your brother, I will not stop you. But please realize you possess more martial skill than Jason and Rich combined. Your absence will surely be felt."

Melvin looked at his friends. Rich was nodding at him, eyes clear behind the gray beard. Jason had reattached his finger and was flexing it in amazement. Melvin had a decision to make.

"You do not need to rush your decision," Majora said.

"I need to keep you here for a day before sending you out to task."

"Why?" Rich asked.

"Sweet Rich," she said smiling, "in that time I will have taught you a few necessary spells. And it will be time enough to see if you can survive the cost of magic to your soul."

Chapter 7

Tutorial

Rich said "*baana gaelin ateshi*,", his voice confident. The small flame from a candle streamed from the wick into his hand, growing to the size of a small fireball.

"Excellent, Rich," Majora said with a smile. The two of them were in the circular library where they had met last night. "You sound much more sure. You have picked up bending fairly well."

"Thanks," Rich said, smiling through his beard. Sweat had made his hair damp and his robes slightly sticky.

"I see you are tired. Let us recess from practice and discuss magic philosophy while your body recovers." Majora sat on a divan and patted the other cushion for Rich to sit next to her.

"Sounds good." Rich had been practicing the art of magic bending for two hours now. Using magic made him tired in a way he couldn't quite describe. The closest he could place it was a combination of muscle failure, like doing pushups until you can't do another one, and the mental fatigue of taking a two hundred question exam and having forty questions left.

"Let's see if you were paying attention to me speak or if you were just eager to play with your newfound power," Majora said as Rich took a seat on the divan. "Describe the levels of magic."

"Well, bending is when you take something that already exists and bend it to suit your purpose. Altering is changing the properties of materials, like oil into vinegar or lead into gold. Creating is making something out of nothing. And destroying is unmaking something."

"Excellent," Majora said, reaching over to a coffee table. She poured two cups of strong black tea. "Which levels should you try to utilize most?"

"Bending first, then altering."

"And why is that?"

"I don't know…" Rich paused to think. "I guess because it's faster."

Somewhat," Majora said. She smiled at him like he was an adorable kitten mewing. "Depending on the spell and what you're trying to bend or alter, they can be very fast spells to weave in terms of speech and necessary focus. This is important in the heat of battle, where an arrow flying at you leaves very little time to speak and very little ability to concentrate. But that's not all."

Rich rubbed the back of his head, drawing blanks. "I can't think of anything else you might have said. I think maybe I was too busy worrying about getting roasted by the fire."

He shrugged and went to take a sip of tea. Majora's smile evaporated. So did Rich's tea, as she pointed to his cup and said, "*chaybuhar haalinay.*"

"No tea for bad students," she said.

Rich frowned, feeling thirstier now that he was without. He looked at the teapot. "*Chayfin jonum gael,*" he said and a stream of tea came from the spout of the teapot to fill his empty cup. He smiled a wicked grin at Majora before he took his first sip.

She nodded. "Well-earned, sweet Rich. As you can see, a clever mage is able to improvise on the fly. The term 'powerful battlemage' is a misnomer, as an effective battlemage chiefly uses bending and altering but largely abandons the more powerful acts of creating and destroying in the course of a fight."

Majora set her cup down. She moved a bit closer to Rich and put her hands over his as they held his cup. The warmth of her fingers and the softness of her skin made it feel like they radiated more heat than the tea in his cup. Rich became very aware he had never been this close to a girl, let alone a woman this attractive. He dry-swallowed. Her fingers gently wove between his, pulling the cup from his grasp, where she set it beside hers on the table.

"We still haven't addressed the other reason mages rely more on bending and altering," she said, her tone level. "The cost."

Now he remembered. The higher order of spell, the greater the cost. It was hard to focus on intangibles like cost when you have fire burning in your hands and your robes are flammable.

"Doesn't seem that big a deal," Rich said. "I cast a few spells yesterday and with all the bending today, all I am is sweaty and in need of a quick nap. The whole 'cost to your soul' thing seems a bit over-exaggerated."

"You wouldn't see a cost your first day here. That's about as long as any pendulum hero can possibly stay, but they all leave this world before magic exacts its cost. You are not so fortunate… your cost is coming."

"Coming?"

"We teach beginners here that magic is a tapping into the Onesource, the unifying essence of life, the Celestial All. The different races do this differently, but humans take directly from the Onesource. It is the most straightforward, flexible, and reliable way to use magic. But in turn, the Onesource collects payment from your soul."

One side of Rich's mouth curved up in a grin. "How am I supposed to pay the Onesource… soulbucks?"

Majora shook her head, that look of finding a helpless kitten on her face. "Oh, Rich, your innocence is one of the things I find endearing about you. I hope you will be able to smile about it tomorrow. But in the meanwhile, you have rested enough. Come," she finished, putting a hand on his knee and rising.

"What? More bending?"

"No. Now, we alter."

☙❦

Melvin watched as Jason's arrow hit the target with a dull thunk. It was a bit off center, but still a bullseye. All the shots Jason had landed after the first errant few had been bullseyes.

"Man, this isn't fair at all," Melvin said. "How come you can tap into your inner Robin Hood so easy? Today's your first time ever firing a bow… and one of your arms doesn't even have any meat on it!"

Melvin was taking a break from his own practice with a scarecrow Druze had found along with Jason's target. They had passed a few hours practicing their skills in the courtyard. Occasionally, Hierophane residents would gather in small groups along the walkways to look at them and talk in hushed murmurs.

Melvin looked up to the window where the library was. Every now and then, he'd see a flash of light and knew Rich was in there working magic with Majora.

"And it looks like there's nothing stopping Rich from using magic," he said. He looked at his sword and the scarecrow he had been taking clumsy swipes at for the past few hours with zero improvement. Then he looked at Jason.

"How come I still suck?"

"I like to think it's not that you suck so much as I'm beyond awesome," Jason said, squinting one eye as he looked down the draw of another notched arrow. His bony fingers loosed and this time the arrow split one he had shot earlier… bullseye.

Melvin let out a small growl and whacked his scarecrow. It took his serious blows like he was joking as it rocked back and forth from the swings. Druze had enchanted its wooden support stake to bend like rubber. The harder Melvin swung the more the scarecrow rocked, making his attempts to connect awkward and uncoordinated.

Jason scored another bullseye. "Nah, I think I know what it is," he said, shouldering the bow.

He walked over to Melvin. "You remember when I first tried to shoot this bow, I was craptastic. You had to stand directly behind me just to make sure I didn't put one in your ass."

Melvin nodded. "Yeah."

"I thought about when you fought that weagr in *akhta*. So I looked at the target and started thinking about my character, Cephrin, Fane archer of Nasreddin. I recalled all the best campaigns I ran, the ones where I shot my way through legions of trash mobs and took down big nasties I had no business going up against. Those were the times I was most in character, when the game almost disappeared. So when I'm looking at the target and I'm thinking about this stuff, it's like Jason disappears and Cephrin's the one hitting the target. That make sense to you?"

Melvin shrugged. "Sounds simple enough. If I just get into character, then I can unlock an untapped reservoir of asswhip."

"Yep," Jason said. He nodded toward the scarecrow. "Give it a shot."

Melvin held his sword up at the scarecrow. "I am Zhufira, warrior lady. Ample of breast, round of butt…"

"You're not taking this serious, Mel."

"That's the thing, dude. I've never taken this serious."

It was the truth. Melvin had only started playing six months ago because Jason had become so fascinated with it. He figured it better to join in rather than lose his best friend altogether. That's when he had met Rich, who was fun to hang out with too, and a whole community of avid gamers. Melvin enjoyed the game while he was playing, but once it was done, he didn't give it any more thought.

"This is your character, Mel," Jason said. "And you're her now… at least for awhile. What do you remember from your character stats?"

"Um…" He envisioned the decorative stat sheets and the page with the bio, but he couldn't remember a word of it. What's the point of memorizing it when it's already written down?

"Seriously?" Jason looked at Melvin as if he had just wandered in drunk off the street. "Zhufira of the Khermer Tribe. The Khermer live far to the south, one of several tribes that populate the high plains of the Transvaal. Fierce warrior tradition—women, old people, hell, even cripples graduate with honors from the School of Rumble. Make great mercenaries… any of this ringing any bells?"

All Melvin remembered is wanting a female character so at least he'd have something pretty to look at while he was playing. He regretted how that worked out.

Jason nodded his head toward the scarecrow. "Just

think about who Zhufira is and try."

Melvin raised his sword and locked his gaze on the scarecrow. He was Zhufira, warrioress of Khermer, lady of the plains. He charged.

It only took one hard whack to send the scarecrow into a wild pitch. Melvin couldn't keep up with its unpredictable path, striking haphazardly until the scarecrow's return arc brought it crashing directly into him. He yelped as he took a face full of scarecrow and got knocked on his butt.

Melvin sat on the grass, looking up at the scarecrow. It took an arrow to the face, which sent it rocking back. Another arrow hit the face on its way up from its return swing. Melvin looked back at Jason, who was smiling at him.

"I think I just saved you from the wicked scarecrow menace."

"Once I figure this thing out when we're on the road, I'm going to whip your ass," Melvin said, making an effort to stand.

Jason held out his bone hand to help him up. "So, you decided to come with me and Rich?"

Melvin took the skeleton grip. "Yeah, it's probably better for everyone this way." Until he learned how to use his latent sword skills, going off alone was probably suicidal. At least with Jason and Rich developing some sort of expertise, there was a degree of safety in their company. Mike had already proven he was capable of handling himself out here. Plus he had Runt with him… provided they had made it out of Fort Law in one piece.

"It is wonderful to hear that," said a voice behind them. They turned to see Hierophant Majora walking through the courtyard toward them. Rich walked beside her, drenched in sweat, looking exhausted.

"I guess 'anti-perspirant' wasn't one of the spells that made today's lesson plan," Jason said.

⋘⋙

In the dark of night, Rich found himself alone in one of the Hierophane's courtyards. The subdued glow of paper lanterns left shadows to fall along the paths. Nothing stirred.

"How'd I get here?" he wondered aloud. Faint echoes of his question bounced around the dark, empty spaces.

The last thing he remembered was dinner. The food was good, something weird, reminiscent of chicken but not. Everyone was having a good time, except for Druze… he was perpetually like the Grim Reaper.

"You already know how you got here," a voice said from the shadows. "The Rift Pendulum wanted you here. Or were you talking about something trivial like the courtyard?"

The voice sounded familiar. "Where are you?" Rich asked it. He looked up and around at the stillness surrounding him.

Movement caught his eye. A figure in black trousers and shirt emerged from the shadows. Rich gasped.

He was looking at himself, the spitting image of a teenage Richard Bates.

The Richard Bates clone smiled. "Why, I'm everywhere you are. Everywhere you go, Razzleblad."

Rich stared as the boy circled him, his lips trembling behind his gray beard. "H… how?"

The boy continued circling around Rich. Clone Richard Bates closed his eyes as he walked, smiling, inhaling deeply as if he was enjoying the smells of a backyard barbecue.

"You're my newest plaything, Razzleblad," he said as he looked the mage up and down. "And gray robes!"

Rich blinked and the boy was gone. Then he felt an icy grip, strong as steel, grab him from behind. Rich looked down to see hands holding his chest, the fingers clutching at his robes as if they were trying to get at his heart. A voice, his own voice, whispered in his ear.

"You're afraid. I can feel your heart beating, blasting its way out of your chest. If you don't calm yourself, you'll die here. You won't be the first mage I've killed like this."

Rich was frozen, unable to move or struggle. He closed his eyes, telling his heart to slow. It didn't listen. He felt one of the hands move upwards, the fingers scurrying up like a spider. The fingers were on his neck and chin.

He opened his eyes and saw it really was a spider. Black and bigger than a fist, with a swollen white tail section that flared out with black spikes. It hissed.

"Yaeergh!" he batted it off and kept batting. He remembered when he was a little kid, the neighborhood bully had terrorized him with a spider like that. It was called a spined micrathena... only this one was twenty times bigger.

He felt the same scurry up his back.

Rich pulled at his robe, craning his neck to see what was back there and shake it off. There was nothing on his back. But the young Richard Bates was behind him, a wicked gleam in his eyes.

"Oh, Razzleblad, you're much too old to be afraid of a little spider. And you wield too much power. Do you have any idea what you can do as a gray robe? Let me show you."

Around Rich, the Hierophane started to crumble and fall. It melted in places. He looked and saw its grand towers collapsing, the gardens burning to cinders.

He was in the middle of a sea of burning ruins. The screams of the tortured and dying pierced his ears from all around. His nostrils were full of the pungent bite of sulfur, the acrid smell of burning flesh. Richard Bates held his arms out like this was a gift.

"Make no mistake, Razzleblad. Before you and I are through, I will make this happen. Or more specifically, you'll make it happen, gray robe. The only question is: will you be sane when you do it, or stark raving mad?"

"Stop this!" Rich yelled at his younger self. The sound carried him into the waking world, where he struggled against a hand holding him in his chair. It was Druze.

He was at the dinner table. It was well into the night, the room dimly lit by paper lanterns. His unfinished meal was on the table in front of him. Majora sat next to him, her face creased with worry.

"My sweet Rich," she said in a hush. "Can you still smile about the price we pay for magic?"

"What was that?"

"It is past and future, dreams and nightmares, truth and lies, all seamlessly woven into a horror you must endure."

Rich was quiet, still reeling from the experience. He wanted to call it a dream but it had all felt so real and vivid he halfway believed he was dreaming right now. Druze pulled his hand away and went over to stand behind Majora. She smiled at Rich.

"But you survived it," she said. "And you are lucid. I think you will be able to handle the burden. Unlike today, I expect you will not have to cast magic as often during the course of your travels."

"Is it always… like that?"

"The severity and duration are dependent upon how much you draw from the Onesource. But it is always very real and very haunting."

Rich closed his eyes and exhaled, trying to get the smell of sulfur and scorched skin out of his nostrils. Majora leaned over, offering him a glass of water. He gulped it down, spilling water down his beard as he drank.

"Would you like to eat?" she asked. "I can warm your food for you."

He shook his head. "Where is everyone?"

"Several hours have passed since supper. Your friends are in bed. When you fell asleep at the table and could not be roused, I knew the cost had come upon you. Druze and I stayed with you, to see you through it. You must be exhausted; the cost looks like sleep but it does nothing to restore fatigue."

Rich nodded. He felt like someone who had gotten shaken awake every thirty minutes for the last four days, a tiredness that was a weight in his muscles and a cloud in his brain.

Majora nodded at Druze. She smiled at Rich. "Rest well, Rich."

Druze led him to the living quarters and up to his room. Jason was in bed, snoring loudly. Rich, tired beyond what he had ever known, collapsed onto his bed.

Tired as he was, it took a long while to find sleep.

Chapter 8

Trading Places

Mike woke up in the strangest place ever, stranger than waking up in a fantasy world as a megrym. He was in bed with Runt. The big man took up most of the bed, but Mike was in it all right, nestled in the crook of Runt's arm.

He didn't care what world he was in; there were some things Mike Morrow wasn't down for. He bolted up in an attempt to get out of bed but ended up falling to the floor as his head pounded in agony.

It felt like his brain was swimming. Least he wasn't in bed with another dude anymore. As he lay on the floor trying to get his bearings, memories of the recent past started filtering in through the grog.

He was cracking undead heads over and over and over again in a battle he was sure he couldn't win. Then this flying, pitch-black movie monster thing flew past, punching a hole in the ceiling on the way out. One of its wings cut through the stone bridge he was on. Then the corpses dropped dead and stayed dead. The whole place started falling apart.

Melvin. Him and his stupid friends had jumped into some disco light whirlpool. Meanwhile, him and Runt had to book it out of Fort Law. Last thing he remembered was looking up as a baseball-sized rock was coming down.

Mike sucked in his breath as the pain stung where he touched the throbbing spot on his head. He looked around at a room of brown wood floors and mud bricks walls. The rock to the head must have knocked him out, which meant Runt had carried him here. The room only had a window, a chest of drawers, and a big man on a small bed. Where was here?

He got up from the floor wobbly, feeling like he had a hangover without the benefit of a kickass night prior. He managed to steer himself over to the window. What he saw was better than an old fortress and rotting corpses, but it wasn't exactly inspiring either.

It was a small dusty town. Most of the buildings were single story and uniformly square, flat-roofed and built of brown brick and wood. A lot of the roofs were hosts to clotheslines and dudes who lounged and played board games. The street below buzzed with activity, where Mike saw various shops selling stuff he recognized, like meat and jewelry, and other stuff he didn't.

"What is this, hood B.C.?"

"This, Mike Ballztowallz, is Tirys." Runt stayed motionless on the bed, talking without opening his eyes.

"Ain't a whole lot to it," Mike said.

"Never was. Most likely will never be. It is trade land. People come to make deals, good and bad. That is all it has ever been."

"You think that light show my brother hopped into brought him here?"

"Doubtful," was all Runt said. He looked like he had fallen back into sleep, but hell, the whole time he had talked it looked like he was asleep. He was still recovering from a long night. And the peaceful look on his face was almost inviting enough to coax Mike back to bed. Almost… Mike opted to stay awake and feel like roadkill.

"What now?" Mike asked.

"Hierophane still. Best place for answers. Soon, I'll work on getting transport for us. You should clean up and eat.

Meal's paid for."

That was good advice. A bath and some food would probably do wonders to clear the cobwebs. He followed some more advice, this time from his inner voice, and grabbed his club on the way out.

Outside the room, nothing in the hallway or on the other wooden doors looked promising. He headed downstairs and discovered a big open room full of tables and chairs and a bar.

"Bathroom," Mike said to the wiry dude behind the bar.

"Town baths are around the corner on the right," the barman said like it was scripted, pointing to the open doorway.

Mike made his way through the throng. Different people and races pushed carts and hawked wares and moved about. Almost everybody was taller than him. A sign with a rough picture of steam and water let him know to turn the corner. At the end of the street was a big domed building with the same sign out front… had to be the bath house.

Two guys preoccupied with talking blocked the walkway in front of the bath house. They both looked aian like that kid Jason, all gray with the eyes that couldn't keep still, but these two had animal traits. One had antennas sticking out of his head and the other had a lion mane and cat ears. Despite their differences these two held common ground in they were both in Mike's way.

"Yo, could you move?"

"Go away, we're talking, twee," said Antennas. His hands and forearms were armored like an ant's exoskeleton.

Mike had never been called 'twee' before. It wasn't a name he dug.

"Problem is this here's a walkway. That looks like the

talkway," Mike said, pointed to a bunch of small rocks that lay on the side of the path. "You best to get on that if you wanna conversate."

Antennas looked down at Mike, a sneer on his lips. "You had best use that same talkway to go around or you may find your brains on this path you're so fond of, twee."

"Word? So that's what you do when somebody calls you out for being wrong? Go all fire ant on people… or am I just the lil' dude you think you can punk in front of the bath house?"

Antennas looked at lion-cat guy, maybe for backup or maybe because this was strange new territory for him. Mike kept at him.

"Why you looking at your friend? He knows you wrong, too. Everybody knows you don't hang out in the middle of a walkway when people are trying to walk on it. Bet them antennas can get you free cable so I know they can tell you something that simple."

"You mock me?!"

"You movin' or what?"

Before Fire Ant could respond, Lion-cat put a hand on his shoulder.

"Avus, think of our contract work today. How would we explain any unnecessary violence to the local peacekeepers? Or to Taldin? Don't ruin our payday. Let it be."

They exchanged looks until Avus nodded in agreement. Then Avus looked at Mike with daggers in his eyes. "Fortune favors the small in large doses," he said as he turned to go.

Mike shrugged. "Yo, it's whatever."

His immediate vicinity free of dumbasses, Mike headed into the bath house. There were different chambers with swirling hot water pools and steam rooms and even a courtyard in the middle where folks just hung out. It was definitely nicer than he expected or was used to. Coming from Afghanistan and the conditions on some of the forward operating bases, he would have been cool with two bottles of water and a bar of soap.

He had no trouble enjoying the bath or finding his way back, where Runt was at a table eating. Mike pulled up a seat next to him, feeling a lot more refreshed. He had his appetite back and didn't hesitate when Runt nudged the plate in his direction.

"Caravan leaving today," Runt said as Mike ate things he didn't completely recognize. "Headed to Maltep to trade with nasran hexers, then onto Hierophane. Our best option."

Mike smiled between mouthfuls. "Bet."

It took longer than Mike thought possible to find the caravan. Asking about Ruki Provos or his caravan either got them indifferent shrugs or guys trying to sell them something sworn to be at the lowest price ever. And not buying their junk meant not getting any info. Tracking, backtracking and asking around in a sea of people who feigned deafness made for a grueling search.

They finally found the caravan on the outskirts of town. The caravan consisted of four wagon cars attached in line to a small steam engine contraption with tread wheels like a tank. Folks were moving about checking the engine or loading the wagons.

One man sat in a chair underneath a four-post canopy shade, calling out instructions. His linen shirt and pants were white, which meant he didn't do any dirty work. Mike and Runt made their way over to him.

"Ruki Provos?" Mike asked. "We wanna ride this caravan."

He didn't bother to look Mike's way as he watched people haul crates. "Sorry, caravan's full."

"We can pay." Runt said.

"It's still full."

Runt got into Ruki's direct line of sight to the caravan. "Telling us our money's no good offends us."

Ruki rose from his chair. Now his gaze lingered on the big man and occasionally drifted down to Mike when he spoke. "You got me all wrong, friends. Don't take my distraction with the caravan or my rejection as offense. Honestly, I would love to take along two paying passengers. It would no doubt please uncle that I exceeded expected profit when I finally return to my homeland. But there's no room unless I remove some of the shipment. These goods have been prearranged. Spoken for. I refuse to sully the name of the Provos Trading Company by not honoring established contracts."

"So you telling us there ain't a single passenger on this ride?" Mike asked.

"Just me and the security detail."

"Then make us security."

Ruki shook his head. "I already hired a five-man team of locals. Not only will they provide security, but they're going to guide me through the dry flats to Maltep—and all at dirt cheap prices. I like the size and stature of your friend here," Ruki said, looking Runt up and down, "I mean, I stood up and I'm still intimidated. But I just don't have the room to accommodate more."

"Is there a problem, boss?" a voice asked behind Mike.

"Not at all, Taldin," Ruki said. Mike turned to look, bothered by the familiarity of hearing that name before.

If Taldin was the guy in the lead, then he was backed by four more, all of them aian. Four of them sported the ant antennas and armor, and a fifth one in the back had a lion's mane and cat ears. Now the name clicked. Directly behind Taldin, the sneer Mike remembered from in front of the bath house returned to the guy's face.

"Friends," Ruki Provos said, "this is my team of local security. As you can see, they're a mean looking outfit. So procuring your services would be a little redundant at this point."

Mike whirled to face Ruki. "You can't be serious?!"

Ruki looked confused, like he had missed out on the punch line of a joke. "Why… wouldn't I be?"

"These guys are a comedy act, not security. 'Giant Pussy and the Picnic Raiders'. You'd get more security from wishful thinking than these clowns."

Ruki laughed hard, then his face straightened. "As entertaining as you are, insulting my security detail won't get you hired. It'll likely get you into trouble more than anything else."

Mike's megrym ears twitched. Behind him he heard the voice he recognized as Avus saying, "Allow me, Taldin. I owe this twee."

Mike put up a closed fist and looked at Runt. This signal meant "freeze" in Army close range engagement. He hoped Runt would get it. Mike kept talking to Ruki, seemingly oblivious that he was pissing off the aians behind him.

"Look, I got five good reasons why you shouldn't hire these dudes."

Being so close to the ground, Mike didn't just hear footsteps behind him; he could almost feel and taste them too.

"One…" Mike began as the footsteps were nearly upon him.

He whirled, bringing his club around at the sound of

that last footfall. It smashed into the side of Avus' knee with a sickening crunch. The leg bent inward and Avus collapsed with a roar of pain.

The remaining four aians unsheathed their swords. Runt disassembled his Z-blades into twin axes.

"No, no, no!" Ruki Provos got into the middle of the standoff. "I do not have the time to go rooting around for another security detail because the lot of you are violently disagreeable."

"I cannot allow this insult to stand," Taldin said, his teeth clenched and sword pointed.

"What insult?" Mike asked. "Last time I checked, I put down a grown ass man… and a security professional. Am I wrong? Is Avus really your daughter? You mad cause she'll never dance at her wedding the way you always dreamt about?"

"Insolent twee!" Taldin roared.

"No!" Ruki yelled. "He's right. Avus approached the megrym with hostile intent and he defended himself. There is no insult to hold. Any more violence and I will summon the peacekeepers. Stow your weapons."

Grudgingly, the aians complied. Mike and Runt followed suit. The cat guy helped Avus to his feet. Avus had to hop on one foot, as the leg Mike clubbed was bent at an awkward angle.

Ruki looked at Mike. "I'm afraid all you've done is shorten my security staff by one. I'm still not going to hire you."

"Don't you want to hear my other four reasons why you shouldn't hire these dudes?"

"You actually have reasons? I thought your other four reasons were just euphemisms for clubbing my remaining guards out of commission."

"I mean, I guess that woulda worked, even if it's kinda played out. Naw, I got real reasons. One, as you saw, is that they're short one. Two, judging by how easy it was for me to drop him, it's obvious they're not pros."

"Damned twee!" Avus roared. "You're a cowardly wretch, sneaking an attack before I was ready."

"Three," Mike said pointing at Avus while he spoke. "If you stay ready then you don't have to get ready. Four," he turned his gaze back to Ruki. "This is the most important. These guys are all local. They're all boys, tight with each other. And you're out-of-town Rich Guy. What's to keep them from leading you away from town, killing you and taking all your money and all your product?

"You know what keeps that from happening? Reason number five: a diversified security detail," Mike finished pointing to himself and Runt.

Ruki looked down at Mike then at Runt, then at the aians, chewing on his lip. Long moments of silence stretched. Finally he turned to Taldin.

"One more comes off of your team. The new guys come with us."

"That was not our deal," Taldin said.

"No, our deal was for five guys in working order. You cannot provide this. So I'm augmenting the deal. Meanwhile, I will pay you for four men even though you're only providing three. You two," he said to Mike and Runt, "I won't pay anything. But neither will I charge you for passage. We all come out ahead. Deal?"

Mike and Runt agreed. Taldin spent a long time looking back and forth between his guys. None of them spoke the whole time, which was weird... like they were all playing poker and trying to figure out who was bluffing. Finally, Taldin looked at cat guy, the only one of his folks who he hadn't been making eyes at, who was still holding Avus up.

"See he gets care. We'll have a share for you when we return."

"Then it's all settled," Ruki said. "And just in time, seeing how the caravan is loaded and ready to leave." He put out his hand to Mike. "Welcome to the temporary unpaid employ of the Provos Trading Company. Since I can't call you 'friends' any longer, seeing our affiliation is a business matter now, what are your names?"

Chapter 9

Maltepic Trails

Ruki Provos' caravan moved at a decent clip. Mike figured the awkward steam tank was treading ground at about thirty miles an hour. He also made the mental conversion to approximately forty-eight kilometers an hour. Army training put to good use. He looked out the window at the same dusty, sparse plains that hadn't changed much in the hour they'd been riding. What else was he going to do?

Ruki and the security detail all shared the first wagon of the caravan. It was linked directly to the engine; Ruki, wearing goggles, sat up front steering the contraption. Mike was in the back with an ant dude, the one who wore a loud ass red shirt instead of the drab brown of the other ants. Runt took up a side all by himself. Directly opposite of Runt sat Taldin and his remaining henchman, whose mouth hung open because of an overbite.

The wagon was really just a covered canopy with benches inside, more open windows than walls. Mike hated looking outside the wagon, cause everything was so damn bright in the daytime, but when he did look, he saw nothing but desert shrubs in any direction.

Occasionally, Taldin would lean toward Ruki and tell him directions. He must've been going off of rock formations cause wasn't no street signs out here. The ant dudes would look at each other often enough, but they'd never speak. Mike was never one for small talk and Runt seemed to be the same way, which suited Mike fine. But there was something he was curious about.

"Yo, Runt."

"Yo." The big man acknowledged him with a quick glance and a raised eyebrow, but mostly he looked straight ahead at Taldin and Overbite.

"I'm curious. How'd you know what this meant?" Mike asked, holding up his closed fist again, the close range engagement signal for "freeze".

"I didn't. What does it mean?"

"It means to stop. So how'd you know to chill?"

"You looked at me and made a sign. Took it to mean you were aware of what was developing behind you and had a plan. Otherwise, why make a sign?"

"Well, what if I had wanted you to do the opposite and bust him up?"

"Protecting your back was the standard action, Mike Ballztowallz. There would have been no point to look at me and make a sign."

Mike had to admit, the logic made sense. He settled back on his bench, squinting out to look out over the dry flats as the little tank that could chugged along. As far as he could see, nothing moved out there. The whine and *ga-gunk ga-gunk* of the engine filled his ears and the warm, dry air lashed his face.

Taldin and his ant goons remained quiet, sharing eye time with each other. And kept sharing, eyes looking back and forth between the three.

"Yo, Runt, why these dudes keep staring?" Mike could have asked Taldin directly, but he had no respect for the clown. Besides, the ant bastard had called him a twee. Fuck Taldin.

Runt didn't take his eyes off of the two in front of him. "They look to indicate who they are speaking to and to acknowledge who is speaking to them. Same as us."

"But they not talking."

"They all follow the aian god, Yol. Yol gives his followers ant qualities. Armor. Strength. Hive mind."

They were all talking inside each other's heads. By the look of their eye trades, they had been talking a lot.

It's paranoia if a scheme's going off in your mind... when others are having whole conversations in their minds around you, well, that's when someone's plotting on you.

Mike looked at Taldin. Taldin was looking at Mr. Loud Ass Red Shirt beside Mike. None of these ants had bothered to chime in while him and Runt were talking about them. They had nothing but idle time on this ride, plenty of opportunity to butt in and explain or correct them, or even to just tell the two of them to mind their own business.

Maybe the time wasn't idle. Maybe they were busy talking about something... something so important that they didn't even hear the conversation Mike and Runt were having outside of it.

At this rate of speed, an hour's ride provided a solid distance away from Tirys. Nothing out here but thirsty shrubs.

Mike looked at Red Shirt. Not his eyes; despite what they talk about in movies, eyes don't tell you squat. Mike watched his hands. His right was creeping, ever so slowly, almost as if by the accidental jostling of the wagon, toward his dagger.

"Ambush!" Mike yelled. That was the trigger to an explosion of action.

Taldin and Overbite pulled out their swords and jumped from their bench. Runt sprang to meet them, elbowing the henchman and fighting to deflect Taldin's sword. Mike grabbed Red Shirt's hand as he freed the dagger from its sheath.

Red Shirt leveraged his weight to pin Mike down on the bench. Both of Mike's hands were holding the dagger arm, trying to keep the knife from stabbing him in the face.

"What the hell is this madness?!" yelled Ruki's voice over the whine of the steam engine.

Out of the corner of his eye, Mike saw Runt punching Taldin. But Overbite had recovered and was approaching Runt's back with his sword.

Mike kicked out with his little legs. They scored Overbite's hand, knocking the sword out of his grip.

That's all the help he could give Runt. Red Shirt's dagger was edging closer to his face. The bastard was strong.

Instead of pushing the hand away, Mike pulled it hard toward him, moving his head as far to the right as possible. The dagger found empty wood, and Mike turned his head to bite the ant's wrist.

Megrym teeth are sharp. Mike clamped down, driving them through the ant exoskeleton. He felt the shell splinter and crack, tasted the metallic salt of aian's blood, and heard Red Shirt's roar of pain.

Red Shirt's grip weakened, Mike pushed the aian off and grabbed his club. He saw Runt trying to manage Taldin, who still held a sword, while Overbite had his arms wrapped around Runt's neck and was squeezing.

Mike leapt off the back bench and brought the club down onto Overbite's head. That got him off of Runt's neck and put him face down on the floor of the wagon.

"Duck," Runt said. Mike hit the deck on top of the laid out henchman as Runt tossed Taldin towards the back of the wagon. Taldin collided with Red Shirt who was trying to work his knife out of the wood. Mike saw Red Shirt fall out the open window and heard him scream as the wheels of the trailing caravan car rose over the sudden bump of him.

Ruki was slowing the caravan down. Taldin pulled his former henchman's knife out of the wood and whirled to face Mike and Runt. He held his ground, pointing the knife back and forth between the two of them. The engine came to a grinding halt.

"You can either walk off or get your corpse tossed off," Mike said. "Make the call, Taldin, you slowing us down."

Taldin was smarter than Mike thought. After a moment, he tossed the knife out the window.

They let him collect his unconscious henchman. It'd be a stroke of good luck if Overbite would ever contribute anything useful to the hive mind again.

Taldin glared at Mike as he stood out in the dry flats. He carried his limp henchman with an arm draped over his shoulder.

"I'll get you for this."

"What you need to get is a move on," Mike said. "It's a long walk back to town with you dragging that bag of vegetables."

Mike waved goodbye to Taldin, cheesing a smile the whole time as Ruki cranked the engine back to life. The caravan shot a cloud of dust over Taldin and continued on its way.

Ruki yelled over the drone of the engine. "This direction should take us all the way to Maltep. If not, we'll be in a bit of a bind trying to figure out where we are on the maps I brought."

Mike nodded; wasn't much to say to that.

Ruki continued to yell despite the fact that Mike was standing right next to him. "How'd you know Taldin was setting me up to rob me?"

"Game recognize game."

"I seriously want to know. If I wanted nonsense gibbered back to me I would have just asked the engine."

Mike sighed. "I grew up in a place like Tirys. Looked different but the vibe's the same. We was thugs on a come up, every one of us. Point being, I knew what Taldin was about cause if I was Taldin I woulda done the same thing."

That seemed to settle the matter for Ruki. He nodded, adjusted his goggles and returned his attention to driving. Mike took up the seat across from Runt.

Runt looked at Mike. "You grew up in a different place than the land of suburbs your brother spoke of."

"Much different."

By the time dad's business allowed them to move to the burbs, Mike was halfway a man and definitely all knucklehead. He'd probably be locked up right now if it wasn't for the army. But his upbringing came in handy out here. The last thing he thought he'd need was survival skills when he agreed to play Melvin's stupid game.

No one talked for long moments, letting the engine's whine fill the silent spaces. Runt had his head down and eyes closed. Mike squinted out at the desert, seeing the dust dance on swirls of wind.

"Hey!" Ruki craned his neck and yelled back to them.

"Yo," Mike answered.

"I'm still not paying you guys."

It took about another hour and a half to reach Maltep. At first Mike thought it was just some kind of supply stop at an oasis. There wasn't but six buildings or so, all of them made out of mud brick and resembling giant beehives. They were sandwiched between a small lake and a few hills that were almost big enough to be mountains.

As Ruki took the caravan around the lake to the buildings, Mike wondered what was worth the trip. That's when he saw bunches upon bunches of people emerge, but not from the crummy buildings.

Holes dotted the hills. It looked like most of the town of Maltep lived in homes they had dug into the hillside. Now that the caravan was fixing to pull up, the townsfolk were coming out in droves. All of them wore similar tanned leather pants and long-sleeved shirts. They weren't human, aian or megrym.

"What are these guys?" Mike asked, looking at folks who looked back with eyes spaced far apart on their heads like deer.

"Nasran," Runt answered.

Big ones walked and little ones ran toward the caravan on legs that bent forward at the knees, like a stork. Their hands only had four fingers, but each finger was long and slender, ending almost at a point that was icicle sharp. They had fluffy little tails that poked out of the back of their pants where holes were cut.

"They don't eat megryms, do they?"

Mike was about to find out. Ruki brought the caravan to a stop and stepped out of the wagon. He was greeted by swarming nasran kids. The kids cheered and shouted and held out their long-fingered hands.

Ruki seemed to enjoy the attention, patting kids and smiling as he cut a path through to get to the second wagon. Rummaging under the burlap tarp over the wagon, he finally pulled out a big glass container that held red licorice. The kids cheered even louder as Ruki started handing them candy.

Ruki paused long enough to pull his goggles up to rest

on his head. Trail dust made for a dirty face with two clean circular spots around his eyes.

"Uncle warned me about this kind of thing," he said, beaming a smile.

By this time the older nasran had made their way to the caravan. They waved the kids off to play and enjoy their candy.

The one leading the adults, an old dude if gray hair was any indication of age with them, offered his hand to Ruki. "You are well received in Maltep, Provos Trading Company."

"You're just saying that because I have wagons full of stuff for you," Ruki said. "But I'll take it," he finished with a smile, taking the hand and shaking.

The nasrans fell to unloading the wagons while Ruki and the elder talked. Every now and then Ruki called out to the handlers to be careful with one box or another. Mike sighed; this looked like it was going to take awhile.

He felt Runt's hand on his shoulder. He looked up at the giant.

"We are here and idle. And no town is without a bar."

Mike could get with that. He was halfway scared Ruki was going to pull off and leave them stuck in Maltep, but he figured nobody was crazy enough to ditch free employees.

"Let's make it happen."

Chapter 10

A Proven Goodbye

Rew Majora studied Rich throughout breakfast. He seemed pensive, managing an occasional smile while his friends talked and laughed. His appetite was scarcely there.

"The day ripens," Rew said, setting down her spiced tea. "Soon, you three will depart on a noble undertaking. Druze and I have done our best to prepare you for the road ahead. Are you ready to begin?"

Her words killed the mirth that was vibrant between the girl and aian a moment ago. The three friends nodded their heads slowly.

"Excellent." She pointed two fingers at Jason and Melvin. "Druze will outfit you two for the journey." Then she looked at Rich.

"I need to see you in the library."

The friends looked at each other and Rew could almost see the conversation behind their eyes.

What'd you do? Jason and Melvin's eyes asked.

I don't know; I'm just as dumbstruck as you are, Rich's eyes answered.

The youthful honesty of it made her smile.

"We're not going to go over more spells, are we?" Rich asked when they were in the library. The sunlight streaming through the open windows washed out the gray of his robes.

"Only if you feel the need to," Rew said. "But that's not why I asked you here." She stepped toward him. "I want to know what's wrong."

Rich shrugged. "I don't know. Nothing's wrong."

"You would rather keep it to yourself?" she asked. Her fingers found his chin and lifted it so his eyes met her gaze. "Do you think I would not understand?"

"I...," he began then fell silent. "Why do you trust us with something so important?" he asked.

"You, your friends, you all have good hearts. And the power you wield…"

"That's just it, the power!" Rich said, cutting her off. "I mean, what if I go nuts? How much worse off would your world be with a crazy gray robe running around lighting up the people you care about and burning down the places you live?"

He went over to the window, where he looked out over the Hierophane like there was an answer to his turmoil among the towers and gardens. "I don't want to destroy a world you're trying to get me to save."

She came over to him. "Then don't," she said, grabbing his hand. "You alone have ultimate say over what you do and how you wield your magic."

She led him over to a bookcase. Her finger ran across book spines until she found the *Birleshik Arcana*. She took it out and handed it to him.

"Keep this with you, in your library pocket. It is the unified theory of magic. I think it will help you understand the nature of your power and help ease your fears about the cost."

"How did you know I was worried about the cost?" Rich asked taking the book.

"It is a burden you must endure alone, but is also one I share with you," she said with a smile. "The first time scares us all."

Rich nodded. Then he looked at her, confusion etched

across handsome features and boyish eyes. "What's a library pocket?"

He was so adorable it was charming. "It's sewn into mage robes," she said. "It helps distribute the weight of books, allowing mages to carry a handful without feeling lopsided."

"Oh, that's what that's called," he said. She watched him fumble a bit with his robes before getting the book into his library pocket. Still, he was more confident of his movements and his spells than many acolytes who had trained and studied a full year. She wished she could have met him under different circumstances; he would have made a wonderful student.

"Now, are you ready for the task ahead?" she asked.

"As ready as I can be, I think."

"Then, Grand Razzleblad, present to me your spellbook." She held out her hands.

He produced it after a quick rummage through his library pocket. She flipped through the thick tome until she got near the end where the pages were blank.

She spoke a creation spell, her focus locked on the empty page. Her hand glowed white as she held it over the blank space. Ancient words scrawled themselves onto the page, flowing from the bottom up.

When she was done she presented the open book to Rich. "This is a replica of Mage-Scholar Kaftar Friese's spellbook, page one hundred seventy-three. The spell you'll need is the third one."

"I can read it, but I don't know what it means," he said, staring at the stylized calligraphy.

"The language is very ancient. Not even I know what it means. But, as far as we know, only this spell of Kaftar Friese's design can contain the creature, as evidenced by the last mage who captured it."

"I thought you captured it last time," Rich said, his attention half given to reading the new page in his book.

"I'm afraid that was a bit before my time. I just kept it contained through the use of the witchlock which bears my name."

She gently closed the book he was preoccupied with and studied him. "You can do this, Rich," she said. "Are you ready?"

Rich nodded.

When the two of them returned to the courtyard, Melvin and Jason were watching Druze demonstrate the finer points of controlling a hava-chaise. Essentially a platform that hovered a foot above the ground, the hava-chaise moved depending on foot placement and the manipulation of two levers that extended from the platform to waist height. Druze stopped the hava-chaise and dismounted when he saw Rew and Rich.

"Jason, Melvin, teach Rich," he said.

Through excited chatter, Jason and Melvin explained how to control the hava-chaise. They talked in terms she could scarcely decipher like aviation layout, control scheme and played stations. But Rich had no trouble following along, and soon enough all three of them could control their individual hava-chaises fairly well. They laughed as they raced around the courtyard.

A thunderclap from Druze got their attention. They brought their hava-chaises to a halt in front of the mages. As they dismounted, the platforms settled gingerly down onto the ground.

Rew looked at the three of them. Jason and Melvin already wore the packs she and Druze had prepared. It was standard traveler's gear: bedroll, jerked meat, waterskin, and other odds and ends. She held out the third pack to Rich.

Rew knew Druze had given Jason and Melvin items specifically meant for them as well. She looked at Jason, the one who seemed the most knowledgeable of the world. "Are you able to read the map we gave you?"

"Yep," he replied, a smile creeping up the corner of his mouth. He pulled the map from his pocket with that disturbing bone hand. "I've spent hours staring at maps like this, pre-staging my game time. Yours isn't the most detailed and stylized, but I can work with it."

Meanwhile, Rich rummaged through his pack, exploring the contents. Rew turned her attention to Melvin. The girl was looking down at her boots.

"My dear, you should wear the hooded cloak Druze gave you."

"Why? I thought that was for inclement weather." She looked up at a clear blue sky.

"I know your attire is derived from the customs of the Khermer, but still, look at you. Your attire is barely there. The cloak protects against bad weather as well as your bad sense of decorum."

The girl glared at Rew. Rew looked back nonplussed by whatever thoughts the girl entertained. When you're trying to move efficiently from place to place without harassment, it just made sense to not parade around like you're the head priestess of your own fertility cult.

Having either swallowed what she was going to say or acquiescing to sound advice, Melvin put on the blue cloak. A red-jeweled clasp at the neck held it in place, allowing the material to cover a body that only exposed itself in brief flashes of movement. Much better now.

Druze spoke before Rew could. "It's time," he said as he looked at Rich. "Create a water bowl so Jason can determine your direction."

Rich took a step back as if Druze was asking the impossible of him. He stood there for a moment without reply or motion, then he took off his pack and started going through it.

"I got an idea," Rich said, "much faster and easier than making a bowl." He dug out the waterskin, set the pack down and then he did the most ridiculous thing imaginable. He filled his hands with the water.

He carried his cupped hands over to Jason. "Ok, drop a finger in."

Druze smacked his cupped hands. Water sprayed into Rich's face.

"It is just as I thought," Druze said, his eyes full of anger. "The cost rides this boy."

"Druze, it will be fine," Rew said. "Rich will…"

She stopped talking as Druze's look fell on her. She had not seen that hard glare in a century. There would be no placating or reasoning with him on this. His baleful stare went back to Rich.

"Look at you, a child scared to go out in sunlight because you'll cast a shadow. How can you cast the containment spell when it is time to?"

Rich looked at him with defiant eyes. "I won't fail to cast."

"You fail to cast now!" Druze yelled. He spoke esoteric words in a heated flurry. Then he pushed out with open palms and tornado-strength winds erupted from his hands. The winds knocked Rich back and down, causing him to tumble in a roll across the courtyard.

"Your endeavor is not child's play," Druze said to Rich, who was on his stomach spitting out grass. "You leave here to face unknown dangers in unknown places and you hesitate to cast even basic spells."

Rich looked at Rew.

"Don't you dare look to her for aid!" Druze altered and bent his sleeve. The black fabric stretched the distance to where Rich lay and whacked him across the face, knocking him on his back.

"She has no say on this," Druze said as his spells expired, causing the sleeve to shrink to its original form around his arm. "Now cast the spell or we dance."

Rich licked his lip, tasting the blood on it. He stared at Druze. Rew could see the anger behind his eyes.

He got up on one knee and threw a handful of dirt. "*Guuch kir*!" he yelled and the dirt hardened and sharpened in midair.

Druze spoke and the blackness of his robe expanded, swallowing most of the projectiles. A few errant pieces whizzed past Jason and Melvin, ricocheting off the marble columns behind them.

"Shouldn't we stop this?" Melvin asked Rew.

"No."

Druze advanced on Rich. "Do you think altering dirt is going to save you from marauders or walking corpses? We need a gray robe for this task, not a boy at a costume ball."

He spoke a succession of spells so quickly he made it look easy. The sky darkened with clouds and a tornado wrapped itself around Rich, hauling him up into the sky. Druze looked up at the swirling winds, controlling them with hands that he spun around in circles.

Somewhere up there in that swirling vortex, Rich was

spinning around. He may have shown a lot of promise, but the time Rew had spent with him was nowhere near enough to prepare him for a mage duel. Her eyes frantically searched the twisting winds for a hint of his robes.

Then he appeared. Not only appeared, Rich emerged from the tornado riding a giant icicle. Druze leapt out of the way as the icicle crashed into where he stood a moment ago. On top of the ice, Rich looked at the black robe with fury in his eyes.

Druze killed his wind spell. Then he bowed his head to Rich.

"Mage of gray, do you still hesitate to summon a water bowl?" Druze asked him.

Rich glared at him. He did not respond to Druze, but jumped down from his perch of ice.

"*Suchanaa*," he intoned, thrusting the newly created bowl to Jason.

"Badass," Jason said, looking at Rich as if he was a total stranger.

Rew shared that feeling. Nothing she had shown him could account for that level of spellcraft. There was more built into his gray robes than he could possibly know.

"That was truly remarkable," she told him.

"Yeah," he said, "well, you can thank your trigger happy bodyguard for that."

"What ever makes you think Druze is my bodyguard?"

Confusion replaced the anger etched on Rich's face. "Well… um…" he began, not knowing what to say to her question.

"Is it that you thought the Hierophant needs protection… or that my body should be guarded?"

Rew watched Rich's cheeks redden as he stammered

through speech. It had been such a long time since she had felt this kind of nervous energy from a man. Everyone saw her as Hierophant Majora, Voice of Seat Esotera, someone to either fear or revere. Rich saw none of that and so much more. Rew couldn't help herself.

Jason saved Rich from further embarrassment. "Dude, it's pointing northwest," he announced, looking at the finger in bowl.

"Then go northwest," Druze said. He looked at them like a father who knows his children are procrastinating.

Jason reattached his finger and tossed the bowl, which disintegrated into air. Melvin, finally decent in the cloak, threw on her pack. The three of them made their way over to their hava-chaises. Druze presented Rich with a ring.

"Wear this. It will reduce the cost somewhat."

Rich nodded and took the ring. "Thanks." He put it on right there.

"And thank you, Majora," Rich said "for helping me with my casting and everything."

The way he looked and talked to her made her smile. She approached Rich. "Call me Rew." Then she leaned and whispered into his ear.

"You really are sweet, Rich. If you ever want to talk and you feel I'm worth the cost, remember this…" she told him, in slow, hushed whispers how to create a scry and how to attune to her. She hoped he would remember and, better yet, use it.

When she stepped back Rich's friends were giving him eye language again.

What's going on with you and her? Jason and Melvin's eyes asked.

Rich's eyes only flickered briefly to his friends. Then he cleared his throat, started his hava-chaise and turned it northwest.

Rew watched them depart into the unknown. She felt Druze come to stand beside her.

"What was that you gave him?" she asked. Nothing mitigates the cost.

"Insurance," Druze said. "I do not like this task in their hands, Rew. Our very lives at are stake."

"I know," Rew replied. Druze was sounding every bit like the father he was to her. "That's why I wanted to take care of this myself."

"Your role is here, daughter, to guide the Hierophane. It is not to meander around the world in search of monsters. And it is not to develop crushes on children."

Rew looked at him with steel in her eyes. "I am over three hundred and fifty years old, father. What man isn't a child to that?"

"Do not be fooled by the length of his beard. He is baby fresh."

"And he has risen to a challenge men twice his age would cower from."

"Hmmph." He walked off, his purpose and destination unknown to her. Even now, after centuries, his ways were sometimes utter mysteries.

Rew stayed in the courtyard, watching the three silhouettes grow smaller in the distance.

Chapter 11

Hollowers

Mike was impressed with the beer. They kept it cold. And it was good, even though it smelled like breakfast cereal.

One of the beehive buildings near the lake served as the bar in Maltep. The high domed ceiling made the barroom feel big, which Mike could appreciate after being stuck in that little wagon for hours. Only a few of the nasrans were in there with him and Runt; everyone else was outside checking out the caravan. The ones that had stayed didn't seem happy about out-of-towners.

They probably weren't happy about anything. Mike wouldn't be if he lived here. Seemed like the only thing to do in this town was get drunk on part of his complete breakfast. Speaking of, he sipped his cereal beer. Hopefully by the time they finished drinking, Ruki would be ready to push off.

Ruki's appearance in the bar settled that mystery. An old nasran was with him, probably the same dude he had been talking to during the wagon unload. They came over to Mike and Runt's table.

"Ah, my team's already procured a table for us to finalize our transaction. Excellent," Ruki said as he and the nasran filled in the empty chairs. He motioned to the bartender for more beers.

"Damn, you not done yet?" Mike asked.

Ruki took the question with a smile, his road-dusted face and clean circles around his eyes making him look like a reverse raccoon. "We've hit a bit of a business snag, Mike.

Nothing a little discussion over drinks can't fix."

The nasran shook his head. "I'm afraid there is naught you can say to sway us on this matter."

Ruki's smile brightened as he leaned toward the nasran. "Hear me out, Gazi. The original agreement the town officials made with Provos Trading was for six crates of nasran craftworks and three crates of hexes. You can't just substitute three more craftwork crates for the hexes like the only factor here is box arithmetic."

Gazi didn't respond to the smile. "We understand craftwork and hex are not the same; we make them both. The extra craftwork crates are compensation for the hexes that we will not provide."

The beers had made their way to the table, but neither Gazi nor Ruki seemed to notice. Mike noticed; the waitress had brought him and Runt another one. It was the only perk to being stuck in the middle of their haggling.

Ruki dropped the smile. "Let me get this straight. Barring all other factors, you have enough hexes here in Maltep to easily fill one crate with offensive hexes, another with defensive hexes, and a third with utility hexes, yes?"

"Yes."

"But you won't?"

"No, we won't."

"Let me tell you something, Gazi," Ruki said, pointing a finger at the stone-faced nasran. "I didn't make this trip to Maltep to feed kids licorice and to pick up some extra blankets and pottery. The only reason I'm taking craftwork in the first place is because I have a perpetual grudge against empty space in the caravan. I came for the hexes. You can give me what we agreed upon, so why are we even discussing it?"

Gazi didn't answer right away. He looked at Ruki, his

slender fingers massaging the wide open space between his eyes like he was trying to work just the right words into his head. At last he spoke.

"Hollower attacks come almost daily now, threatening nasran settlements from here all the way to the Burai Plateau. Hexes are our best defense; we cannot trade them away, reserve or otherwise. Times have changed since we first made our arrangement."

"You want to know what else is changing?" Ruki asked, his face screwed in angry disbelief. "My reputation is changing, Gazi. And you're the one who's changing it. You think I can show up at the Hierophane with none of their order and go 'Times are hard for the nasran'? You think they'll say 'Can't wait to put in another order with those Provos Traders'? Or 'That Ruki Provos has my confidence; I wager he would follow a demented mage through a megrym's asshole if it meant delivering what he promises'? You think they'll be saying that when I deliver nothing but excuses?!"

Mike guessed he was the only one who thought that was funny. Runt was in his frosty new glass like everyone else at the table was speaking in a foreign language. Gazi's stone face didn't twitch.

"My concern lies in protecting nasran lands, not kept promises to factory mages," Gazi said.

"Well, kept promises are my concern. Ruki Provos delivers what he promises. Protect this dirt pile after you settle your debts."

Ruki's words broke Gazi's poker face. His anger was obvious. "Maltep is a sacred site," he said in a low growl.

"Then treat it as sacred!" Ruki cried. "Or is this the holy site of broken deals? Maltep stands as sacred as the dust between my toes if it comes between honest agreements."

Mike didn't know if Ruki's words persuaded or angered Gazi; they all became victims of bad timing. A little nasran kid ran into the beehive bar, his eyes wide with panic.

"Hollowers!" he cried.

All the nasrans in the room jumped out of their seats. Ruki looked in confusion as they all ran out of the bar. Mike and Runt went back to their beers. After watching the nasrans pour out of the bar, Ruki's head jerked back to his security detail.

"My caravan!"

The three ran the short distance to the edge of town where the caravan sat. Coming around the lake and heading toward Maltep were four guys. It was hard for Mike to see with all the sun glare, but one was a man in armor, two were aians, and the last was a man in white that hurt Mike's eyes the most to look at.

Why were they almost at the town? The nasran should have seen them coming from the dry flats miles out. Mike wondered how worried could the folks of Maltep be about attacks if they didn't even keep a decent watch.

Swarms of nasrans armed with hatchets, daggers and glaives ran out to meet them. Those nasrans were fast runners on their backward knees, and they looked like serious business. Near the caravan, Gazi stood waving his hands, yelling for the armed nasrans to stop.

"Wait for the Hexenarii," he cried. "We'll need their expertise!"

The nasran warrior in the lead turned to face Gazi but kept his pace. "We've no time to wait for expertise! The Hollowers will make Maltep if we don't stop them now."

Mike couldn't understand what the fuss was about; the nasran fighters outnumbered those Hollower dudes five to one.

The Hollowers seemed unconcerned about the approaching swarm. One of the aians dived into the lake. Moth wings unfurled behind the other aian and he took to the air. The guy in white just stood there while armored man unsheathed his sword and continued his stroll forward.

"Doesn't seem that dangerous," Ruki said as he shielded his eyes with his hand and peered out at the Hollowers. His words echoed Mike's thoughts.

The moth aian fired his bow from where he hovered while reaching for another arrow. One of the rushing nasrans dropped. Moth fired again and grabbed another arrow as a second nasran dropped. Then a third fell as Moth reached for another arrow in the quiver between his fluttering wings.

The armored man dropped three just as fast without breaking his stroll. The first nasran ran past him, disemboweled. The second and third dropped from single strikes faster than Mike's eyes could track.

Armored man dashed into the fourth, cutting a violent "X" that produced a cloud of red mist.

The nasran closest to the armored man took a step back. He caught an arrow to the neck, death by moth archer.

Now all the nasrans were backing up. But their backs were to the lake. Some of the nasran were already at the water's edge.

Three tentacles shot out from the lake and wrapped themselves around the faces of the nasrans closest to the water. They pulled the nasrans into the lake without ceremony. A pool of red started spreading in the lake.

The aian emerged from the lake, floating on his back. One hand held a short spear. His other three limbs had morphed into long squid tentacles. He threw his spear into the back of a nasran on shore. Then his three tentacles shot out;

one retrieved the spear and the other two grabbed more nasrans to drag into the water.

There wasn't but six nasrans left. Five now that the flying moth dropped one. Four after armored man cut another one into confetti. Those four bolted back towards town.

"The living gods…" Ruki muttered.

These guys were like the special forces of special forces. In less than a minute they had completely encircled a combat force five times their size and reduced them down to equal number. That was some serious long division.

The nasran reinforcements had arrived. A dozen archers had assembled on one of the hills overlooking the lake. More warriors were coming down to where Mike, Runt and Ruki stood at the front of the caravan. The seven warriors in the front were the strangest Mike had seen yet.

They didn't have any weapons, at least none he could see. Each of them went shirtless, instead wearing a black cape with a hood. The exposed skin of their arms, chest and abs was covered in black tribal tattoos. They each sported a belt with bunches of little wooden figures attached to it.

Every belt had to have hundreds of those wooden figures, all of them carved into various shapes, their edges dipped in silver. Mike swore no two looked alike.

Meanwhile, the archers on the hill let fly a volley of arrows. They all came down on the armored man.

Most of the arrows glanced off the armor. But one arrow lodged in his neck. He did not drop. There was no blood. Armored man kept walking as if nothing had happened.

"What the fuuhh…" Mike's words trailed off, his mind still trying to work out what his eyes had just seen.

The Hollower in white, motionless this whole time, raised his hands in the air. The sun pulsed like a light bulb getting extra current. Mike had to shield his eyes with his hands as he saw a bolt of light come down from the sun and crash into the Maltep hill. The nasran archers screamed as the explosion blasted them off the hill or into ashes.

Rock bits rained down on the town below.

The tattooed, caped nasran in the lead turned to address the traditional warriors behind him.

"These are Hollowers, not timid deer! Tell your remaining archers to scatter, not congregate. Focus their fire on the flyer. If they see his arrow point in their direction, they must take cover; he will not miss."

He pointed to the nasrans with hatchets and glaives. "You all need to circle back, behind the town and around to get to the Sun Cleric. Form two attack circles around him, hatchets in front, kneeling down for waist high attacks. Glaives stand behind the hatchetmen, stabbing his upper body. Do not let lack of blood be the measure of your success—keep stabbing. And be quick, as the Sun Cleric will surely bring a sunpulse down on his own head just to kill all of you around him.

The hatchet and glaivemen left without a word.

"Hexenarii," he said, looking at the caped nasrans around him. "We focus on the knight."

The Hexenarii proceeded slow and cautious, fanning out like they were trying to corner a rabid animal. The armored man continued his stroll toward them, devoid of expression to this change in adversary.

When they got close to enough to spit, the armor man rushed the Hexenarii in front of him.

That Hexenarii pulled one of the wooden figures from his belt and yelled "Pyre!" He burst into flames.

The two Hexenarii on either side of him pulled wood

from their belts too. One yelled "Stone" and the other yelled "Life". They tossed their wooden figures at the Hexenarii covered in flame.

He turned to stone just as the armored man was upon him in mid-strike. His sword bounced off harmlessly. The nasran made of burning stone moved, apparently alive and well underneath the flaming rock. He embraced the armored man, bringing him deep into the fire.

Another trio of Hexenarii did the same sequence with the wood pulled from their belts. The new burning stone man moved behind the armored man and hugged. The armored man was trapped between two burning stone walls.

The remaining five Hexenarii pulled wood pieces and yelled "Heat". They threw the wood, which stuck on the trapped man's armor. Within seconds, the armor turned molten red.

The arrow that had protruded from armored man's neck had burned away awhile ago. If he had any reaction to being broiled alive in his armor, he didn't show it… not even through sweat. He just struggled wordlessly to get free of the stone arms hugging him tight.

The sun stole Mike's attention. It pulsed. He looked and saw the Sun Cleric surrounded by nasrans going to town with hatchets and glaives.

The light pulse never came down. The Sun Cleric dissolved, as if he had been made of nothing but crinkled parchment paper.

Mike looked back to the armored man to see him dissolve as well. In a matter of seconds, the stone men were only holding themselves.

The moth guy had four arrows stuck in him. He kept in a state of fluttery, sporadic movement to avoid arrows that came from random directions. His arrow was constantly drawn and ready but stayed unreleased as he was forced to switch targets when the nasran archers dropped out of sight.

The two burning stone men were back to normal. All seven Hexenarii dove into the lake.

Moth aian fluttered around for several minutes. The archers who ducked behind cover whenever his arrow tip pointed their way left him nothing to fire at. Likewise, the archers couldn't get a bead on him, with him moving like a moth dancing around a light bulb.

The Hexenarii emerged from the lake. They pulled a wood piece from their belts and uniformly yelled "Web." The wood became what looked like spider webbing, which they threw into the air at moth aian.

All the lines missed him except one. That brought the moth's attention to the Hexenarii below. He released his long held arrow at the nasran that snagged him with the web.

It was too fast to counter. The arrow embedded itself deep into the Hexenarii, who crumpled.

The moth's pause allowed the remaining six Hexenarii to catch him in their webs. The six lines kept the moth from reaching his quiver or flapping away. They pulled the moth down, where waiting glaive and hatchetmen descended on him and stabbed it into nothingness.

Ruki Provos turned to Mike and Runt. He pointed behind his back to the where the last Hollower had been, his eyes wide. "You don't see this kind of shit sitting behind a counter in Suusteren!"

Chapter 12

Accomplished Accomplices

If nothing else, Mike learned that nasran women were passionate mourners. None of that quiet grief for them. They wailed like air raid sirens as they threw dirt on their faces and held their freshly fallen loved ones. For any one dead warrior, there were several women clutching the body and several men trying to console them.

"We should prolly go," Mike said to Ruki. Them being there seemed a little too invasive for his taste.

"I'm not letting these shriekers run me off," Ruki said, crinkling his nose as if an odor offended him. "These women believe they have to wail their sorrow to keep the spirits from coming back angry. Until I get what's mine, you'd better get used to the sounds of bereavement."

He looked around at the various groups of nasrans holding or hauling off their dead. "Where's Gazi?" he asked.

Mike panned through the crowd with his sorry excuse for daytime vision. There were too many nasrans and he was still at a point of racial unfamiliarity where they all sort of looked alike. Despite this, one nasran woman held his attention.

Her hair was black, streaked with gray. She sat on the ground, her hand resting on the body of a fallen archer. She didn't wail and her face wasn't covered with tear-streaked dirt. There was no crowd around her or the body she silently mourned for. Instead of looking down at the body, she looked dead straight at them, a cold intensity burning in her eyes like this was all their fault.

Mike's search ended there. His eyes stayed locked on hers and hers on him as the moments stretched. Her grief was beyond platitudes or reconciliation. Mike had seen this look from Afghan women more times than he cared to remember. Her eyes forced him to remember those women as his mind cycled through mortar rounds and bomb blasts and the wake of villages after the Taliban swept through.

Gazi found them and broke the woman's hold on Mike. He put a hand on Ruki's shoulder, his jaw tight as he spoke to the merchant.

"Now you see firsthand what we deal with. It is something guests we welcome should not have to witness. Come."

He led them back to the beehive bar. The place was both full and quiet as the many nasrans nursed their beers in silence, either drinking to remember or drinking to forget. Gazi spoke to two guys at a table, who grabbed their beers and went to join others standing at the bar. Soon the four of them sat with a glass of their own.

"What are these Hollowers?" Ruki asked.

"They are hollow people. There is nothing inside them to reason with or bleed out. They seek the blood of others. This is as much as anyone can tell you about Hollowers."

"But why do they attack?"

"Who can say? They do not talk to state their purpose. Stories of them have existed since before I was a child, talk of unkillable demons who turned whole villages to cinder. Attacks and sightings used to be so rare that Hollowers were myth, tales to frighten children. This goes back to what we spoke of earlier; they are the reason we cannot give you our hexes."

"That's your plan then?" Ruki asked. "Keep all the

hexes and die a slow death of attrition?"

Gazi looked at him with sadness in his eyes. "Do you have a better plan?"

"Hollowers are too impossible to be physical. That means they're magical. The Hierophane can help. They are my next stop on this caravan and the hexes I can deliver with a promise of more to come from Maltep would do wonders to procuring mages to root out the cause of your Hollower menace."

Gazi shook his head. "Many here believe the factory mages are the source of the Hollowers. These attacks only became more frequent when the nasran clans stopped supplying the Hierophane with hexes for their infernal devices."

Mike had heard enough. At this rate they'd be here all day getting a history lesson for a world he wasn't supposed to be in. He moved his beer out of the way and leaned over to point at Gazi.

"You know that don't make sense, right?"

"What do you mean, little one?"

"You said yourself these attacks been happening since way back when. If y'all were hooking the Hierophane up with product all that time, it sounds like you shoulda had a Hollower-free childhood. Seems like the mages are just an excuse for y'all to renege on a deal."

Gazi's eyes turned cold. "Excuse or no, there will be no hexes on your caravan."

He stood to leave. Ruki grabbed his arm.

"If you don't mind, I'd like to stay here until morning. I'd hate to be out in the dry flats at night with the threat of Hollowers lurking in the dark."

Gazi bowed his head. "It is the least we can do, friend

Provos."

Once Gazi was out of earshot, Ruki turned to his security detail. "I don't think he'll be calling me friend after what I do tonight."

Mike raised an eyebrow. "And what's that?"

A crooked grin crept up on tradesman's lips. "Ruki Provos delivers what he promises."

Mike leaned in and whispered. "You're gonna heist them."

"I just want my three crates. We got three guys. This should be easy. So why not?"

"Because there's nothing in it for me and Runt," Mike said.

"Because they will kill us if they discover theft," Runt said.

"Guys! What do you mean?" Ruki asked as if he was offended by their legitimate observations. "Of course you're getting something; you're getting the ride you wanted. You think I'm going to the Hierophane with nothing to deliver?

"And you," he said pointing to Runt. "You're already guilty by association. They catch me with a crate full of contraband and they won't hesitate to lop your head off for good measure."

"We can just snitch you out," Mike said.

"Or I can kill you right now," Runt said flatly. He was looking more at Ruki's pointing finger than his face.

Ruki seemed to realize that pointing and making veiled death threats to a half-weagr wasn't the smartest play in the book. He retracted his finger and smoothed out his shirt.

"Was I coming off as hostile? This isn't hostility, guys. It's passion. We can do this. Besides, I'm the only one who can drive the caravan. So whether it's you or the nasran who kill me the result is the same; you two are stuck walking through the dry flats with few supplies and only a vague idea of where you're going."

Mike had to hand it to him, Ruki was a hustler. The whole point of riding the caravan was to get to the Hierophane as fast as possible. Besides, Mike had more of a problem with snitching than he did with stealing.

He looked at Runt. "What do you think?"

Runt nodded. "Rather ride than walk. And like him, I would take what I'm owed."

Ruki's grin turned into a salesman's smile. "Excellent, men! You'll see, it'll be as easy as getting a wheel downhill."

He began to sketch out a plan, which basically amounted to a smash and grab. Mike had a few issues with it, as it didn't account for any lookouts or Ruki staying back to keep the engine running. He was fixing to bring this up when they were interrupted by a nasran woman taking a seat in the empty chair.

"You will fail," she said, her tone flat and matter-of-fact. Mike recognized her face and gray-streaked hair. She was the lone mourner.

"My dear, whatever do you mean?" Ruki asked, his brow furrowing up in confusion. "I'm just having a business discussion with my security team. If you don't mind, I have to ask you to find another table so we can get back to that."

She did not budge. "You do not fool me, Provos Trader. I can see it in your eyes. I see it shimmer all around you. You will pursue what's yours like a dog on a scent. And you will die like a dog unless you take my help."

"I'm not entirely sure of what you're talking about. And even if I did, I don't see you being of any help."

She leaned in. "Do you know where we keep our hex

stores?"

"Um…"

"Were you planning to just wander through the sacred mounds of Maltep opening doors and looking in as if that wouldn't attract notice?"

"Err…" Ruki leaned back and looked at Runt and Mike like he had forgotten how to form words. Asking her to elaborate or help would be an early admission of guilt. Telling her to go away would leave them paddling in waters she clearly pointed out were way over their heads. Mike stepped in, asking a question that did neither.

"Why you want to help us?"

She looked at Mike long enough to only speak one word. "Passage." Then she turned her attention back to Ruki. "On your caravan. There is nothing left for me here."

Ruki shook his head. "A ride doesn't seem like reason enough to go to the lengths you're going."

"It is a better reason than any reason to stay. Staying just makes more graves, and I am not content with that."

"But how—" Ruki started.

"She's in," Mike said, cutting him off.

"This doesn't seem prudent to me, Mike."

"Seems to me that having an insider will keep us from tripping over ourselves in a place none of us knows squat about. Also seems to me that this isn't a set-up… what's the point of working so hard to get us to do something we were gonna do anyway? If you want prudent, then get over getting screwed out of your hexes and let's head out."

Ruki nodded. "Prudence is overrated."

The woman called herself Savashbahar. Her plan was simple, clean, better.

"This goes off like I think it will and you'll have

yourself a ride," Ruki said with a smile. "Where do you want to go anyway?"

Savashbahar's response was flat. "Right now, to a place where no one asks questions." She left as suddenly as she came.

The three strangers to Maltep passed the time amongst themselves while the village tried to recover from a day of tragedy. Nasran men mourned by drinking in silence for a long while. Every now and again, one would stand on their table or the bar and regale the whole room with their favorite story about one of the fallen, tales of mischief and escapades. At the end of the story, everyone would raise a glass and cheer the dead's name. It went on like this well into the night.

Wordlessly, Ruki rose from his seat. Mike and Runt followed him out of the bar. The night air felt like walking into a refrigerator; Mike hadn't realized how stuffy the bar had gotten.

Without the sun's heinous glare, Maltep looked like an entirely different place. The lake shimmered like it was full of silver sequins; the roads and lakeshore buildings had a subdued orange glow under the brown of the mud. Mike looked up at the sacred mounds, where they were fixing to tempt fate. Countless torches burned, hints of pale green light with angry red, dotting the many holes carved into the hills.

Ruki Provos continued to walk toward the lake where his caravan waited. Mike and Runt broke off and walked around the back of the tavern. They found Savashbahar there, facing the sacred mounds as she sat in the dirt. Her backward knees let her legs fold up into the air, where she rested her arms across the soles of her boots.

She rose without a sound and proceeded to the furthest mound. *It would be that one*, Mike thought. Images of him struggling to carry a big ass box of hexes from the mound to the caravan flitted across his mind.

He understood why the nasrans considered the mounds sacred when they got inside an opening. It wasn't so much a cavern as it was a meticulously carved hall, perfectly round from floor to ceiling, as if a giant earthworm had tunneled it out. The ceiling was decorated with colorful, tiny tiles stuck together to form a pathway of designs. These were not just a bunch of raggedy caves.

Savashbahar led them through twists and turns without pausing. Within a few minutes their path opened out into a huge expanse shaped like a sphere. A town bigger than the Maltep outside filled the bowl of the sphere, full of small beehive buildings and avenues. Mike marveled at a miniature green sun suspended high in the air, bathing the entire town in chlorophyll colored neon. The roof of the cave was covered in glittering tiles that his eyes got lost in.

Savashbahar grabbed onto Runt's meaty arm and sobbed into it. "Lead," she whispered after a sobbing spell. "I'll guide."

They sob-walked their way through the busy streets of the cave village. Runt and Savashbahar drew only token attention, as the sound of chicks wailing their lungs out could be heard from several buildings and out on the streets. Savashbahar's sobs were tame in comparison.

"Up ahead. Guarded," she whispered and took her sobbing up a notch. Sure enough, Mike saw the guard standing in front of a building the size of a small warehouse, his glaive held out.

When Savashbahar had sobbed her way past the guard, she stopped and faced him. "Why, you're a hex guard. Do you know, my dear Dushunmek wanted to become Hexenarii?"

The guard turned his head to look at her, the disdain apparent in his voice. "I don't care. His death gives you no quarter among us, witch. Now move along."

The guard's head turn was all the angle Mike needed. He clonked the guard with his club, just hard enough to force an early bedtime.

They pulled the guard into the building. Green-tinged torches lined the walls, revealing a room packed with boxes. There had to be more hex crates than people in Maltep.

Mike shook his head. "You stingy packrats," he said to no one in particular.

Savashbahar picked out three crates. Then she went over to an open crate, rooted around and pulled out a handful of hexes.

"Be fast but cautious. Stay in the alleyways. Unescorted foreigners alone in Maltep are cause for suspicion, even more so when carrying whole crates of hexes."

Her words made Mike rethink the plan she had devised.

"It'd be easier and less suspicious if you helped us with these boxes," he said. "We got here easy enough. I don't think we need whatever distraction you're planning."

"Sus," she said in way so quick and sharp that the word could only mean "hush". "I am no one to explain to others how you have these boxes. They need their attention on other things. I will meet with you before you realize." She mumbled something that Mike couldn't quite hear then smacked him on the back. "Be manly."

Those last words stung. "Word? You attack a dude's manhood over a box?" Mike grumbled but went to the nearest crate. He lifted it easily enough but carrying it was awkward because of its relative size. "No wonder that cat I knocked out called you a witch."

Savashbahar's lip curled up into a grin. "Remember, alleyways, back to the tunnel." She was out the door, gone to cause a commotion somewhere else.

Runt had no problem holding a crate under each arm. He led the way, Mike's visibility reduced because of the hulking container he had to crane his neck to see past.

They made good time, darting from alley to alley. The cave sat in near-daylight conditions because of the green mini sun, but most of the streets were narrow enough that Mike and Runt only had a couple of seconds at most of street exposure. When they got to a large avenue, Runt cast a quick peek around the corner, then set a crate down and raised a closed fist—the freeze symbol.

"Six nasran men, two women approach. Will pass this alley in twelve paces."

Twelve paces, not enough time to run back they way they came. Any one of the eight pairs of eyes would likely see them if they stayed. Running out across the wide avenue was a suicide on stealth.

"Hide!" Mike hissed, setting his crate against the wall and ducking behind it.

Runt looked at the two boxes he had carried like they were puzzle pieces. Even if he stacked them and hid, his linebacker girth would leave half his body visible. Finally, he set the boxes side-by-side and lay down behind them in the fetal position.

For the first time today, Mike was glad the nasran ladies were loud and active grievers. He heard the group come and go without any difficulty.

Runt checked for clear coasts again. He shook his head. "Two more approach. Twenty-five paces."

"Dude, I say we crack these fools over the head. We

gotta do something. I ain't hiding behind this box all night."

They wouldn't have to. The green light from the mini sun started to flicker. Mike looked up and saw clouds forming inside the cave, obscuring the glittering tiles on the ceiling.

Then the rain came. Heavy rain. Mike could hear the sun sizzle and pop, trying to fight the water. But the sun didn't have enough juice to match this level of storm and after a few moments it turned gray like a used piece of charcoal.

Darkness fell. Mike's vision came alive in that darkness. Being megrym had some perks.

"I'll lead," he said.

They ran through rain-slicked alleys and side streets, Mike craning his neck to see ahead of him. The rain slowed to a drizzle, making it easier for Mike to navigate obstacles. What wasn't easy was remembering which streets they needed to take to get out. A map would've been nice, or…

Think of the devil. Savashbahar burst out at a "T" intersection in the alley, her hair wet and clinging to her face. Mike almost dropped his box in surprise.

"How'd you find us?"

"Satisfy your curiosity after your safety. Not before. Keep straight; I will guide your course."

Mike was starting to hate how she talked to him. But she had a point. He took off, her in step right behind. She called out the streets, the lefts and rights. Her distraction had caused many nasrans to come out of their homes and into the bigger avenues, but very few torches were among them. Apparently, they were not used to their sun losing light. Mike navigated in the near pitch and dodged light sources with ease.

They passed a last side street and entered a clearing, where Mike saw the opening to the cave dead ahead. He had to admit, the old lady's plan had gone off picture perfect.

A ball of orange flame hit the wall next to the tunnel, blasting the darkness with light that made Mike's eyes shriek in pain. Fiery rocks rained down around them, making them stop in their tracks.

"Feral witch, stop your blasphemies, now!"

They turned to face the voice.

Three Hexenarii stood at the ready a few paces behind them, looking pissed.

Chapter 13

Clever Broad

The three Hexenarii approached with caution, each holding green torches in one hand and a hex in the other like a loaded gun. Mike recognized the one in the lead; he had given the other Hexenarii and fighting men their battle orders when the Hollowers had attacked. Now he was seething as he spoke to Savashbahar.

"You would extinguish the sacred fire? And for what, to aid foreigners in our destruction?"

"I have seen what you hold as sacred and what you hold as *yasak*," Savashbahar said. "Neither holds a place in my heart, Demirtash."

"Have you gazed upon your own death, witch?" Demirtash asked. "Tell me, I'd like to know if you die by my hand or by Eclipse, looking down at the city you betrayed while the whole host of Maltep watches you burn."

Savashbahar pulled out a dagger, slow and steady. She raised it in the air with the same deliberate care. Mike knew any fast moves and these guys would bake her on the spot. He didn't get what she could possibly do with that little knife that would do them any good. He stood a better chance of defending himself with the crate he was carrying.

She turned the blade on herself.

"I would rather die by my own hand than yours, lawseeker."

Demirtash paused in his approach, causing the ones in tow to follow suit. Behind the sickly green tinge of the torchlight, his lip curled up into a sneer.

Savashbahar plunged the knife down, toward her own gut.

Before it found a home in her flesh, she pulled the knife to the right, cutting a wicked gash through her robes. With her free hand she grabbed the cut garment and pulled a handful of fabric free.

"Burst!" she yelled and flung the swath of fabric toward the Hexenarii. Mike saw a silver dipped piece of wood, stuck on the fabric, glow red before disintegrating. The fabric shredded itself and flew out like daggers toward the Hexenarii, forcing them to shield their faces from the impromptu shrapnel.

The clever broad had slipped a hex past them.

Now she had a hex in both hands. "Barrier," she named the left one. "Raise," she named the right. She smacked them both together and then she brought her hands down to smack the ground. The hexes dissolved and the ground shot up to make a wall a foot thick in front of her.

Her wall came just in time. No sooner was it up than the wall shook with the force of three explosions. Mike could tell by the sharp orange light and flaming rock chunks that the Hexenarii had thrown their hexes as fireballs.

Savashbahar turned and looked at Mike and Runt.

"Hold onto those crates and run, you idiots!"

She didn't have to tell Mike twice. He didn't even pause when he saw her cut across her own wrist with the knife. The relative safety of the tunnel was a few scant paces uphill, and that's all he cared about.

"Flood," he heard Savashbahar say behind him as they all ran toward the tunnel. "Oil."

As he made the tunnel, Mike ventured a look behind him. Runt and Savashbahar were close behind. Savashbahar brought up the rear, running backwards and facing the direction of the Hexenarii. She was holding her wrist, which was gushing blood. It streamed out like a river, black in color and running a course down the side of the hill.

It was impossible to get that much blood from a wrist. Hell, Mike didn't remember Melvin's friend shooting that much blood when the weagr lopped his arm off.

Down below, the Hexenarii had made it around the rock wall and were in pursuit, hexes at the ready. When their boots encountered Savashbahar's coursing blood, they all lost their traction and began to stumble and slide.

Demirtash yelled "Fire." He went down on one knee and dropped his hex into the river of blood. Flame sprang up, blazing a trail toward Savashbahar's wrist.

Savashbahar was in the tunnel entryway now. She swung her bleeding wrist over her head, causing black blood to splatter the walls and ceiling inside the tunnel. Then she held out her wrist toward the encroaching flame and brought a hex up.

"Burst!"

Blood shot out of her wrist as a projectile stream. It collided with the approaching fire and was like a grenade going off. The mountain shook with smoke, fire and a wave of dust. The force of the explosion knocked Savashbahar off her feet. Mike hit the deck.

When the smoke cleared, the tunnel was blocked by a cave-in at the entrance. Savashbahar lay on the ground, reaching for the dagger in front of her with shaking hands. Her wrist still spewed blood.

Mike rushed over to her. She looked at him.

"Burn it," she said. Her trembling fingers held up a hex. "Heat," she said, then placed the glowing hex on the blade of her dagger.

Wisps of smoke emanated off the dagger. Mike grabbed the hilt and pressed the hot flat of the blade into Savashbahar's open wrist. Her clenched teeth did little to suppress her growl of pain.

"Crazy broad," Mike said as he took the blade away from the freshly cauterized wound. "You can't lose that much blood as fast as you did. What the hell were you thinking?"

She raised an eyebrow at him like that answered the question. Weakly, she turned her head to Runt.

"Can you carry?"

"Leave the crates," Mike said.

"You will not," Savashbahar said with a barely-there shake of the head. "I bled for those. They are ours."

Runt hoisted her onto his back. "Hold and brace," he told her. She gripped his shirt and leaned her head against his massive neck, as if to take a nap. With his free hands, Runt picked up his crates.

They were off. Mike ran full steam with his little legs, hauling ass with his crate. Runt had little difficulty keeping up, despite the extra weight of two crates and a semi-conscious nasran lady. It seemed to take forever, much longer than it did going in, to make the exit.

Finally, they emerged out of the tunnel and into the cool night air. A brief glimpse of the lake was visible in the distance. If Ruki still had the engine running, they'd make it out of this after all.

"Transgressors! Profane!"

Six Hexenarii, led by a soot-covered Demirtash, charged out of another tunnel and were running down the side of the hill in pursuit. Great, they had doubled up.

The lake was growing closer but it still looked so far

away.

Mike turned his head to check distance from the hex tossers. They had gained a bit of ground. Mike wondered what the range was on those fireballs.

Eyes back on the lake, he saw salvation heading their way. Ruki's train was closing the gap.

Mike put as much sprint as he could in his legs. If he ever got out of this and got his body back, the first thing he was going to do was take a jog and enjoy his long stride.

A fireball exploded behind them to the right, close enough to feel the wicked heat of it.

The engine of Ruki's caravan rolled past. Mike had no time to pussyfoot the awkward logistics of entering a moving vehicle while you're moving in a different direction. He jumped, crate first.

The crate landed on the floor of the open train car and slid, scuffing Mike up along the way. He should have let go when he landed in the car, but his adrenaline had kept his fingers locked on the wood like it was some sort of cubed safety net.

He turned on his back, looked out of the moving car and saw Runt tossing a crate at him. Mike rolled out of the way and dodged again as the other crate and then finally Runt landed in the caravan, still bearing Savashbahar on his back.

The Hexenarii were still coming down the mountain in chase. The only difference was now the train was en route toward them. Two of the Hexenarii's hands lit up with flame.

Ruki took a hard left. It almost threw Mike out of the car. Two fireballs exploded where the train would have been if not for the turn. Mike looked up to see the train headed straight for the beehive bar.

Ruki, in the driver's seat, didn't turn the wheel. He

cranked a lever all the way down, then turned his head and ducked down. The train leapt with even more power.

Crap. Mike followed Ruki's example.

All he heard was the splinter and crack of wood giving way. The train groaned and shook but it kept on going through the wall. Mike looked out and saw flabbergasted nasrans, sitting at their tables and holding onto their beers, staring mutely at the train as it plowed through their watering hole.

Gazi was one of the gaping bar patrons.

"Ruki Provos gets what he's promised!" Ruki shouted at him with a smile.

They broke through the other wall and found themselves free of Maltep. The endless expanse of the Dry Flats stretched out in front of them. Behind them, the town was growing smaller and smaller by the second.

Now that they had escaped, Savashbahar released her grip on Runt. Her legs touched the floor and they gave out like they were made of paper. Mike rushed over to her.

"You aight?" he asked as he helped her to lie back against the wall. She nodded.

"You know you crazy, right? Of all the possible ways to hex your way outta there, you pick the most suicidal."

She shook her head. "This just shows how little you know about hex magic," she said. "Four things have to align: the intent of the user, the design of the hex, the word spoken and the materials on hand. Blood wasn't my first choice. It was my only choice."

"I dunno. Couldn't you have said 'escape' or something?"

She gave him a weak laugh. "You cannot just speak a word hoping your intent is clear. Each hex is designed to pay the cost for a certain kind of magic. Speaking 'escape' to any random hex with no materials to guide it would just as soon find me instantly buried under a mountain of rock or a thousand spans in the air in freefall. My way was safest."

"Doesn't look it."

"Looks deceive, Mike Ballztowallz," Runt said. "Her grip is strong. Her strength will return."

They were all quiet for a moment. The train's engine whined as it chugged along the lonely stretch of barren turf. Well outside the reach of the train's spotlight, Mike could see desert animals looking up in puzzlement of this noisy intruder. Another question came to him.

"Hey, lady, could you teach me hex magic?"

"No."

"Damn, that's cold. You could've at least looked at my job app before turning me down."

"It takes years to learn. Reading hexes is a nuanced skill. Not only do you have to read the basic form of it, whether it's for aggression, defense or utility, but you have to understand the tone of it. Did the crafter carve sharp lines for fire or smooth curves for water? Once you've mastered that, you have to master yourself. If your intent strays when you speak, if you think of home or a hot meal or any errant thought when you name your hex, it will bend the hex. Many aspiring Hexenarii die learning the ways. It is not for everyone."

Before she said that, Mike figured anybody with a tongue could be Hexenarii. Between the self-bloodletting and her explanation of how hard it was to work the hexes, he had grown a lot of respect for her.

"Aight. One more question; how come you ain't a Hexenarii yourself?"

Her eyes turned sad. "It is *yasak*. Forbidden. Because I

am a woman. So I left Maltep when I was young, learned the ways among a clan who were more open and accepting. I am Hexenarii among them, but will never be to my people." She looked at him, tired resignation on her face. "How much more appetite does your curiosity have before it's satisfied?"

That reminded him of a question he had earlier. "One more and I'm done. How'd you find us after you made that distraction?" She had just come out of nowhere, like she knew where they were the whole time.

A grin crept up on her lips. She pointed at Mike, then patted her own back.

Mike reached around his shoulder to pull a stuck piece of wood off his back. The hex glowed green.

A tracker. He thought about when she had patted him on the back and told him to be manly.

"Clever broad," Mike said with a smile.

Chapter 14

Discovery Bonus

Melvin, Rich and Jason formed a semi-circle around the body. An arrow from Jason's bow protruded from the corpse. This was one unlucky rabbit.

"What do we do now?" Rich asked. He looked around like an answer was lurking in the grassy plains around them. But there was no answer, or much else other than grass and occasional shrubs, for miles around in any direction.

"We clean it and cook it," Jason said with a shrug, smirking with satisfaction at his kill.

"How the hell do we do that?" Melvin asked. Jason may have been celebrating his martial proficiency, but Melvin wasn't.

They didn't even need to make a meal of poor Mr. Rabbit. The Hierophant Majora had seen to it they had plenty of field rations in their packs. But as they had cruised along in the hava-chaises, the rabbit had shot out from some undergrowth and made himself a tempting target to a guy who had recently learned he was a crack shot.

None of them had experience with meat that wasn't prepackaged. Before the fatal arrow, Jason's statements of "I need the practice," and "we need to preserve our rations anyway… we don't know how long we'll be out on the road," had sounded great, but didn't go a long way for Melvin now that he was standing in a semi-circle looking down at a dead rabbit after the hunt.

If Jason had any qualms about Step Two, he didn't show it. "Well, we take a knife and skin it," he said. "And gut it." Apparently, a person could learn a lot watching cable TV.

"But we don't have a knife," Melvin said.

Rich and Jason stopped looking at the rabbit and turned their gaze on Melvin. His brow furrowed as he thought through his last statement for any evidence of nonsense. No, it made sense, so why were they looking at him like he held a solution?

Because he was a warrioress with a double-edged bastard sword on his back.

"No!" he cried. "Not me. It's not even a knife."

"It's a big knife," Jason said.

"Big," Rich mumbled in agreement with a nod of his head.

"C'mon, guys! How am I supposed to skin something this small with a sword this big?"

"Slowly?" Jason asked.

"Carefully?" Rich asked with a shrug.

They both patted Melvin on the back and walked back to the hava-chaises, leaving him alone with the tiny carcass. For long moments Melvin wrestled with indecision. He wanted to leave it. But the least he could do was eat it… otherwise the bunny took an arrow for nothing.

What would Mike do? He probably wouldn't have a qualm about skinning a rabbit. The thought of his missing brother sent fear pangs through Melvin, and he had a mind to forget everything, jump on his hava-chaise and head back to the Hierophane. Maybe Mike had made it there and was waiting for him.

But how would his friends fare out here without him? Hell, they didn't even have a knife between them to skin a rabbit. Mike wouldn't leave friends in need. He also wouldn't stall on creating carnage. Melvin looked down at the rabbit and pulled out his sword with a sigh.

After a minute or two at the task, Melvin knew with certainty he would have nightmares about it. Pulling blood-stained fur, cutting into muscle, it was unadulterated gruesome with every sloppy slash of his sword. He didn't think a little rabbit could possibly hold so much blood. It stained his hands, smeared his boots and legs, streaked his face as he wiped away the mounting sweat.

"Finished," Melvin said at last. He held up his hard-earned bundle, a little mass of bloody meat. Small tufts of fur still clung wetly to the creature.

"Dude," Jason said, "it looks like an aborted fetus."

"Yeah, Mel, that looks worse than the weagr you chopped up," Rich said.

"Well, next time you bastards can do it. Then I won't be the one looking like a crime scene."

"Wouldn't dream of it," Jason said. "I couldn't pull off that look. Nothing says dangerous like a woman who shows she's not afraid to get dirty, and right now Mel you are a dirty, dirty girl."

Jason looked at him straight-faced, like it was a statement of fact. Melvin cut his eyes at Rich and swore he could see Rich's smile under that bushy gray beard.

"We gonna cook this thing or what?" Melvin asked. Some battles just weren't worth fighting.

Melvin and Jason both had to cajole Rich, who wanted

to gather dry sticks instead of casting a fire. The obvious argument of where to find dry sticks in the middle of a grassy field held little sway until they coupled it with the observation that everyone should contribute to the meal. It took even more prodding before Rich would create a bowl of water for Melvin to wash the blood off his hands, legs and face.

After their resident mage made fire and water, grumbling the whole time between casts, Melvin took to washing up while Jason manned the grill. He overcame the lack of sticks by impaling the rabbit with an arrow, kebab style, and holding the shaft low to the flame with his bone hand. The bones might be disturbing to look at, but they didn't suffer from muscle fatigue and were impervious to fire. Lucky him.

Thirty minutes worth of slow turning over the fire, lunch rabbit was ready. It was the hardest meal Melvin ever had to work for. And it was still teaching him things.

It taught him rabbit was indeed tasty and delicious. It also taught him one rabbit did not stretch very far between three guys, or two guys and a warrior woman.

"Anyone else think all this wasn't worth it?" Jason asked.

Both Melvin and Rich's hands shot up.

"Yeah," Jason said with a nod. "But it'll be better next time. You two'll be more efficient. Me? I was awesome."

Jason pulled his index finger bone off at the knuckle and dropped it into the blood-tinted water bowl. He pointed West with the nub digit.

They headed out, hava-chaises sounding like little tornados as they lifted off. They made good time through the grasslands. Melvin cast wary gazes at any undergrowth, hoping no more rabbits decided to make a dash.

"I've never seen so much grass without houses," Rich said. "This would suck to mow."

"Yeah," Melvin said. "Back home somebody would've turned all this into civilization… condos or a subdivision. Something."

"I like it better as grass," Jason said. "Just grass."

They rode on in silence for a bit, looking at the endless sea of green. Jason spoke again.

"I gotta be honest, the more time I spend here the more I don't want to leave."

"Dude, you're tripping," Melvin said.

"Not really, I thought about it," Jason replied. "Here, there's all sorts of stuff to do. Adventuring, slaying monsters and other baddies. No school. Quests. Wide open, exotic locations. Back home, I'm just another kid from the burbs, being bland and working toward college, motivated by the prospect that I can maybe get an average job so I can continue being bland."

"Yeah, but here you're also gray skinned and your eyes won't stop jumping around," Rich said. "And you have a skeleton arm."

"I still have my original arm," Jason said, pointing behind him to the severed appendage strapped to his back. His hand flopped up and down, perpetually waving as he cruised in the hava-chaise.

"Besides," he continued, "small price to pay. Now I'm a badass with a bow. And according to Cephrin's stat sheet, I'm only thirty-two years old. Aians live to be like a hundred and fifty, so I've cut out all the awkward puberty years, skipped the prom, and woke up in the prime of my life with a pretty wicked muscle-to-fat ratio. It could be worse."

"Like being older than Abe Lincoln?" asked Rich.

"Like being stuck in a woman's body?" asked Melvin.

"We can't all be enviable characters," Jason said. "Well, I guess we can, since, technically, we made them ourselves. You guys need to learn how to enjoy the wish fulfillment."

What?

Melvin couldn't believe what he was hearing. "Hello? I never wished to live my life as a warrior woman."

Jason smirked, never taking his dancing eyes off the fields in front of them. "Part of you did, otherwise you wouldn't have made the character. Zhufira's an extension of you."

"You can wipe that smile off of your fake, created character's face," Melvin said, his anger rising. "Just because you took psychology as an elective doesn't mean you're qualified to psycho-analyze me. I made Zhufira cause she's hot. That's it."

"If we had been playing something called 'The Rap Game', would you have created a rapper with tight gear and an even tighter ride or a video vixen who's shaking her ass as the guys pour bubbly over her?"

"What?!"

"I'm just saying. Video vixens are hot."

"That's not the same thing!"

"If being hot is the only prerequisite for your character creation process, then, yes… it is."

Melvin didn't even know what to say to that. What could he say? He knew it was different, but he didn't know why.

"Whatever," he finally managed. "You can stay here and fall in love with yourself all you want. Me? When we finally get to go home, you'll see how fast I get away from here and Zhufira, extension of me or not."

"You don't see it yet," Jason said.

"Psssh! There's nothing to see."

"No," Jason said, pointing. "Up ahead."

It took another two miles before Melvin could make out what Jason was talking about. Little smudges popped out of the horizon, breaking the monotony of grass and brush. The smudges grew until Melvin could make out individual homes and buildings.

"Wait," Melvin said, "we're not going there, are we?"

"Of course we're going there," Jason replied. "Dude, it's a town."

The town was growing ever bigger. All the houses were simple brick and wood, reminding Melvin of Runt's house. And Runt's house reminded him of running from weagrs and hungry strandwolves and the shuffling undead army and angry mages out of portals and rabbits that needed skinning.

"Do you know what town that is?" Melvin asked.

"Nope," Jason said. "This place never made a map I ever saw."

Unknown towns meant unknown dangers. "Can't we go around?"

Jason stopped his hava-chaise, causing the other two to shoot ahead before circling and stopping. He had a look of disbelief on his face and he paused before speaking as if trying to find the right words to express.

"When'd you turn into such a girl? And I don't mean badass bikini warrior girl, I mean a girl."

Melvin scowled. "The sooner we cage that creature the sooner we go home. I just don't want any unnecessary stops."

Jason spread his arms. "Look around, man. We're in fantasy land on a quest to save the world… this is the stuff of movies! Every stop is necessary. How often do they just go from point A to point B and then roll credits in the movies? Never, that's when."

"This," Melvin began, pointing into his palm, "is real, not a fantasy. Or a game. Or a movie. Our lives are at risk. Unnecessary stops increase that risk. When are you gonna realize that and stop playing around like you're trying to level up?"

"I thought I was talking to my boy Melvin, but obviously you're my grandmother. I'm sorry Nana, are you and Gramps here afraid the townsfolk eat travelers?"

"Hey," Rich said, "I never said I didn't want to go into town. And if you keep speaking to your Nana like that old Gramps is gonna bend you over his knee."

Jason smirked at Melvin. "Looks like you're outvoted, sugarplum."

"Are both of you crazy?" Melvin asked, the exasperation in his voice making him sound like a hysterical woman even in his own ears. "We're in pursuit of a monster here. We can't afford to waste time sight-seeing."

"Meh," Jason said. "We've made good time since leaving the Hierophane. Looks like we've got about two hours left of daylight." He shielded his eyes to look at the low-hanging afternoon sun.

"When the sun goes down we're going to have to stop anyway. I don't know about you, but when we stop, I don't want to be in a field surrounded by hungry nocturnal critters. I want to be in an inn, with a mug of beer in my right hand and a key to a room in my left."

Rich's eyes got wide. "Dude! Beer! The only perk to being this old. Let's go already."

Rich started up his hava-chaise. Jason followed suit and together they took off toward the town. Melvin swore as he put his hava-chaise in pursuit.

Jason and Rich talked about the different beers they remembered in the game as they approached the outskirts of town. With names like "Dead Bard Ale" and "Strangled Puppy Stout", the ones that sounded the least appetizing managed to get them the most excited. Melvin was quiet, looking at the modest homes and simple, straight streets.

It looked like a quiet, sleepy town. Melvin felt it was a universal truth that nothing ever happened in towns like this. He began to relax a little but then he realized there was no one out and about. Where were all the townspeople?

He found the answer to his question when they got to the town's center, easily identified by the wide avenue that cut through the town. There, at the inn Jason and Rich were making a beeline towards, was the sound of cheering voices, music, and laughter.

When the three of them entered, the music died. It looked like the whole town was there, and now many of the faces were staring at them. Everyone was gathered around one table, where two men sat drinking while a third stood, his foot on a chair and a large sword on his back. Apparently, the man standing was in the middle of telling a story and since his back was turned to the door, he kept telling it despite the abrupt lack of attention.

"You gentle folk should have seen it," he said. He talked like he loved the sound of his own voice. "It was the size of two bears dancing, teeth as long as miners picks…"

One of the guys drinking nudged the standing man and nodded toward the door. The standing man shut up and turned. Now all eyes were on Rich, Jason and Melvin.

Jason took the lead, weaving through the crowd with Rich and Melvin following closely behind. "Excuse us", "Pardon us", "Nice day", he spoke to the nonresponsive onlookers as he worked his way to the bar.

"Do you have a tap?" Jason asked the bartender. "Cause I'd like to know what beers you've got on it."

The whole bar erupted in cheers.

"Guess they don't see much in the way of new business," Rich whispered to Jason.

A balding man with a big pot belly and even bigger smile made his way over to Rich and grabbed him firmly by the shoulders.

"By the Onesource, we thought the Hierophane wasn't taking our request seriously. We don't hear anything for months and now, out of sheer mist, they send us a gray robe." He turned to face the crowd. "A gray robe, everyone!"

The bar erupted in another round of cheers. "Pints for the gray robe and his friends!" someone shouted.

Melvin found himself getting handshakes, smiles, cheers, and "thank you's" from a dozen random faces all around him. Rich and Jason were getting similar star treatment, especially Rich, with women pressing the back of his hand up to their foreheads. Beers flew down the bar and were thrust in their hands.

Rich and Jason looked at Melvin then at each other. They both shrugged in unison like it was choreographed, raised their glasses and drank.

Another round of cheers broke out, this time with Rich and Jason joining in at the tail end after taking huge gulps of beer.

"Now wait a minute!"

The cry came from the center of the room, loud enough to make the crowd's raucous cheers seem like mice squeaks. It silenced the whole room with its bass. The townsfolk cleared a path as a man came striding through the throng to stand in front of Rich. It was the same guy who had been telling the story earlier, the one with the sword on his back.

"He's no gray robe," he shouted to the crowd. He looked Rich up and down, a sneer curling his thin lips. "He's a charlatan, a flam-man. He's here to drink and dine on your backs, not do a job!"

"Um…" Rich started. "I was gonna pay for the drinks."

The man kept talking to the crowd as if he hadn't heard Rich. "Tell me, good people, why the Hierophane would slight you for months on end and then send a robe leagues beyond your needs? A Magelord in your charming but small village is like sending an army for a bread thief!"

Jason set his beer down and looked at the man like he was passing out unwanted flyers. "Dude, relax. He's a gray robe."

That didn't help.

The man twisted his finger up to the sky as if Jason's

words proved his point. "As if I needed any more proof," he said, "answer me this: what gray robe has need of an armed escort?"

Murmurs and nods rippled through the crowd. The man was winning them over. Before he had started talking, Melvin didn't know the crowd was something to be won, or what they got for winning. This guy could have them for all he cared.

Done talking to the crowd, the man eyeballed Rich. "Stop playing with these good people's emotions, hope spinner, before I get angry. Just enjoy their fare at their modest, honest prices. Tell your stories for tips perhaps." He leaned over toward Melvin, his eyes still fixed on Rich like he was a cancer.

"I'm sure you and your friends would be welcome here without pretense," he said. "You all look like you have your uses."

Melvin felt pressure; not just pressure, more of a weird tickle, like a jab of heat on the edge of his skin. He looked down. The man's dirt covered hand had found one of his breasts and he was giving it generous, greedy squeezes.

The sight of a guy's hand, this dirty, meaty, chip-nailed hand--groping and questing and gripping him--set Melvin to a boiling rage. He didn't think. There was nothing to think about as the anger took over.

Melvin smashed his beer glass into the man's face. He took the offending hand and in two quick flashes broke the thumb and two fingers. As the man jerked his head back to howl, Melvin gripped his head with both hands and slammed the back of it into the bar.

It only took a second to drop him.

The two guys that had sat with him sprang into action. The closest one lunged at Melvin, his knife seeking that same breast.

Melvin brought a knee up to the hand, connecting with a crunch at the wrist. He didn't stop with the knee, Melvin pulled the knife from the man's weakened grip, spun it and stabbed it into the man's thigh. As the man opened his mouth to howl in pain, Melvin stuck a foot in his chest and kicked the air out of his lungs while sending him flying across the room.

That took another two seconds.

Melvin whirled to face the third attacker. That guy never made it. Jason's severed arm smacked him across the face and the man fell out, skidding to a stop in front of Melvin's feet, snoring loudly.

Melvin was still a torrent of red hot anger. He whirled around, glaring at everyone.

"Anyone else think they can squeeze some fun out of me?!" he shouted.

The same bald, pot-bellied man from earlier held his hands up. "Now, now, miss," he said, "no one here means any disrespect. Those men you bested aren't of this town."

Cooling off now, Melvin turned to Jason and Rich. Jason was smiling like he just remembered it was his birthday. Rich was staring at him like Melvin was a unicorn in the zoo.

The bald guy spoke again. "Trespin was only speaking the obvious. Gray robes don't need escorts. But even if our friend here isn't what he appears to be, I believe this warrior maiden has enough skill alone to handle our problem, let alone the three of you."

The man rested his hands on his pot-belly. It was a

practiced gesture that gave him a look of authority when he spoke.

"And it looks like you three are going to have to, handle our problem that is. You've just decommissioned our commissioned bounty hunters."

Chapter 15

Taking the "!"

When Rich had made Razzleblad, he didn't realize being a gray robe was all that special. He had just liked the default spells, the bonus to his intelligence stat, plus the color scheme wasn't bad. Now it was a matter of respect he didn't understand or feel he deserved.

He sat with his friends and the bald fat guy, named Nestor Grade, at the only available table in the bar. Melvin and Jason had recently made it available by pummeling trained, hardcore bounty hunters. Nestor served as the town mayor and resident blacksmith; now he served as the face of the town to the extremely welcome gray robe and friends.

"Well, it's obvious by your lack of familiarity the Hierophane didn't send you here on purpose," Nestor Grade said. "But we'll take happy accidents the same—Ha ha ha!"

His laugh was a deep, throaty bellow, like Santa Claus. The genuine mirth behind it made Rich want to laugh with him. He would've but a feeling of dread tightened his throat as he waited for Nestor to explain what was going on.

"As you all can see, we're in the middle of nowhere out here," Nestor said. He raised an eyebrow and talked in a conspiratorial tone. "You have no idea what kind of strange happenings befall ordinary folk in the middle of nowhere."

Screaming from outside hit Rich's ears. He looked toward the open door and saw a giant wheelbarrow rolling past. The townspeople had piled the three bounty thugs into the barrow and were rolling it through town. Nestor said it was a tradition for undesirables they ran out of town. The screaming came from the only conscious thug, who still had a knife in his thigh and was getting pelted by villagers with all manner of refuse.

"Strange stuff like what?" Jason asked, taking the time to lower the mug. He was finishing his second round of "New Morrow Bitters".

It was a good beer, something Rich wouldn't have known in his real body, because the few beers he had tried all tasted like dog piss. Apparently, Razzleblad had developed a taste for beer. Now at least he could enjoy the path to getting drunk as well as just being drunk.

"Well, I'm sure it's nothing for you, sir," Nestor said, looking at Jason's bone arm clutching the near empty mug. "I'm sure you've seen all manner of the weird and exotic in your travels. But things find us out here. Things we could do without."

Rich and Melvin leaned in to listen to Nestor. Jason looked back at the barkeep and pointed a skeletal finger at his empty mug.

"This past year alone a gang of bandits took over the town, convinced we all collectively knew the secret of a local gold mine. Only thing is, we're in the middle of grass plains; there is no gold mine.

"Then a pack of strandwolves got a peculiar taste for town sentries. It would make sense if they tried to eat everybody, but no, they just went after the town sentries. The only way we could make them stop was to disband the nightly patrols. That caused all manner of nighttime foolery.

"We reached the last straw when our town became the

battleground for two rival resurrection cults. I mean, we don't want our town to carry that kind of reputation. Tell your friends, this is not the place to come to kill off your rivals and then try to bring them back. I'm just glad none of their resurrection rituals worked... otherwise it could have gone on forever."

"Sounds like a fun place to level up," Jason said, taking a drink from a foamy new mug.

"Erm..." Nestor Grade chewed his lip in thought, trying to work out Jason's meaning. "Yes, well, we're good, level-headed folks. So, finally fed up, six months ago we procured the services of a megrym tinker. He made Sentry Triptoe."

Rich remembered the game definition of tinkers. They were a megrym-only, playable class that built cool gadgets out of wood and metal, cogs and steam. He had been curious about the class but had never made a character. Thinking about Melvin's brother, he was glad he hadn't. Life was trying enough as a geezer.

"So what's the problem?" Rich asked.

"Sentry Triptoe," Nestor replied.

This particular tinker had made a mechanical sentry guaranteeing it would perpetually patrol the streets of the town at night, guarding against crazies. The problem was Sentry Triptoe worked too well. No one could go out at night without fear of a beatdown from Triptoe, or worse. A few of the braver men in town got fast-tracked to the cemetery by going up against it. Now the residents lived under Triptoe's harsh curfew, unwilling hostages to their own town guard.

"Don't you worry, Nestor," Jason said with a big smile and glazed eyes. "We'll take care of your Triptoe problem."

"What?" Rich and Melvin uniformly cried. Their

question was drowned out by Nestor Grade's raucous laughter.

"Ha ha ha! Excellent!"

"What are you *doing*?" Melvin asked in a harsh whisper.

Jason kept talking to Nestor as if Melvin hadn't said anything. "Gone by dawn, Nestor, you'll see. Last thing we're afraid of is a dumb bucket named Triptoe. What kind of stupid name is that anyway?"

Nestor's smile evaporated, his face red and serious. "It's the name of the town."

Jason started laughing like Nestor had just dropped a punchline.

Melvin smiled at Nestor. "Excuse me, Mr. Grade, can my colleagues and I have a minute to talk among ourselves?"

"Sure, miss," he said, casting a couple of glances back at Jason before finally focusing on Melvin. "I'll leave you lot to plan a strategy. You've got about an hour before Sentry Triptoe arrives."

Melvin kept his pretty-faced smile while Nestor got up to leave. As soon as his back turned, Melvin gave Jason a wicked elbow.

"Hey!" he cried, sloshing beer onto the table.

"Hey, yourself! How the hell are you going to volunteer us to take on a killer robot?"

"Dude," Jason said with shrug. "Don't worry. We got this."

"What do you mean, don't worry? The whole town's afraid of it, it's already put bodies in the ground, and you say don't worry about it?!" Melvin snatched Jason's beer as he was in mid sip.

"Dude, you really need to lighten up," Jason said.

This time Rich agreed with Melvin. At first he thought Melvin just worried all the time, preoccupied with getting home as soon as possible. Rich figured worry was a by-product of being stuck in a body that was differently gendered but very, very easy on the eyes. But if they had just listened to Melvin an hour ago, they wouldn't be in this mess.

They should've gone around this town.

"I'm doing us a favor," Jason continued. "We need to get our feet wet."

"No," Melvin said. "We don't."

Jason turned indignant. Rich caught that look all the time from Jason when he had to explain things about the game he felt Rich should know. Jason started his words with a deep sigh.

"So what's your plan… talk nice to the death creature's undead army and hope they'll let you through? Ask the creature to stay still so Rich can chant over it and pray Rich doesn't mumble or misspeak a spell of insane magnitude?"

"We need *battlefield* experience. What's crazy is trying to take on death monster in this state. You're unreliable." Jason pointed at Melvin and then pointed to Rich without taking his eyes off Melvin. "He's unreliable. Just hoping your inner ass-kicker's going to manifest itself when you want it is plain stupid. Where was she in Fort Law? Where was she when I got this?" he asked, holding up his bone arm.

Melvin's eyes softened. "Jason… this robot… it could kill us."

"If it does, we would've never finished this quest to begin with. The only difference is that at least here they'll be people to bury us. Better that than shuffling around with the rest of death creature's zombie party."

Even though Jason wasn't talking directly to him, Rich felt the same way he always felt whenever Jason finished doing his long talks that started with a deep sigh. Stupid. Either Jason was a master tactician or incredibly convincing.

"So what do we do now?" Rich asked.

Jason shrugged. "We wait. Then we kill it."

Rich looked out toward the door. Behind the wood buildings on the main avenue, the sky was starting to purple. Inside, the bar's crowd had thinned out considerably. The sun was setting.

In the space of what felt like mere minutes, the sky went from orange to red to purple to black. Night couldn't have come this quick. Rich jumped out of his seat and looked to his friends.

They weren't there. He was alone in the bar.

"You're alone with a monster, Razzleblad," a familiar voice said.

In the darkness of the doorway emerged a boy with a black suit, dark eyes and twisted smile.

It was Richard Bates.

Rich's breath caught in his throat. The cost must have come while he was waiting for the sun to set.

He closed his eyes tight. It didn't matter if he felt creepy fingers, oozing slime or heard hissing in his ears. He wasn't going to open his eyes. The cost could swirl and swarm all around him; if he didn't look it wouldn't matter, right?

Rich didn't feel anything creepy. He felt a punch to the face. Hard and jarring, the force of it knocked him to the ground and made his eyes water.

Richard Bates stood over him. Even though it was a face Rich had grown used to in the mirror, the look of rage etched in it was so intense it made Rich's heart leap in fear.

"Is that what you thought, Razzleblad? That you could cast and not pay?!"

Richard Bates punched his face and kept punching. Each blow was a lancing, biting jolt of pain. Dream or hallucination, it didn't matter. The only difference from real punches was the point where his nerves should've gone numb to the pain never came. The last blow stung as fresh and raw as the first. And still Richard Bates kept punching.

When he stopped, his knuckles dripped blood. His other hand gripped a handful of the gray robe. He spoke in a shout, spittle flying as he loomed over Rich.

"I am the cost, mage! And you will pay me. If you try otherwise, I'll make it so you *wished* you paid."

This was too much. Rich tried to say he only made a little water, a little fire, but he talked through swollen lips with loose and knocked in teeth. It was all mumbles.

"A little water? Is that what you call that glacier you made at the Hierophane?"

Rich recalled his fight with Druze. He didn't even know how he had made that thing, he just remembered being stuck in the tornado and being more afraid than he had ever been. The words just came from nowhere. It shouldn't count. He shook his head, tried to bargain.

Richard Bates turned him around and hauled him up by the waist. A hand jerked Rich's head back by the hair.

"I know what you do, what you owe," Richard Bates

whispered. "And I swear, before I'm done tonight, you will know. I. Must. Be. Paid."

Rich felt himself careening, pulled along by his back and head towards the wall. He didn't have the strength to fight as the wall grew closer. All he could do was close his eyes as the impact came with a hard crunch and dull thud.

He felt himself getting pulled out of the wall. Rich opened his eyes and saw a red outline in the wall, a ghostly specter of his face dripping blood. Then he felt himself getting pushed again. And the wall grew closer.

Rich woke in the dark, screaming his head off. He flew out of the chair and scrambled across the floor, trying to get away from the invisible, screaming the whole while. A hand clamped over his mouth, which he tried to claw and scrape at, his chest taking great heaves as his panic began to overwhelm him.

His eyes adjusted to the dark and he saw the person clamping his mouth shut was Melvin. The look on Melvin's face was serious. He was holding a slender finger up to his lips, silently calling for Rich to shut up. Rich obeyed.

Jason was peeking out of the bar's open doorway, staring out into darkness.

"We thought you were going to do that trance sleep thing all night," Melvin whispered. "Triptoe's already made one pass and will probably be headed this way soon, especially with you screaming like that. You ok?"

Rich wasn't. He wanted to tell Melvin he was scared and confused. That he felt helpless and trapped. But he didn't say any of that. He nodded.

Melvin helped him up and they joined Jason by the door. Jason's dancing pupils scanned the darkness, his gray brow furrowed with strain.

"My eyes suck at night," he said.

Rich looked out at the dimly lit streets. The occasional lantern illuminated the avenue, but most of the town stayed draped in pitch. Somewhere out there, Sentry Triptoe patrolled.

"Plan's simple," Jason said. "When I see him I'll step out and distract him with some arrows. He's all metal and wood, so I won't be of much use. But while he's focused on me, Melvin will charge from the rear."

Jason looked at Rich. "While Melvin is lopping off body parts, you cook up some fire to toss at him."

The pain and helplessness of the last cost was fresh in his mind. He never wanted to cast another spell again. Ever. He shook his head.

"No… I can't…"

"Agro time!" Jason said and darted out the door.

Rich looked down the street. A figure stood under the light of a solitary lantern. The thing looked like a combination of training dummy, scarecrow and tank. Its chest was all turning gears and chains in a wood casing, its face wood with blinking lights for eyes. It stood with its pipe-like arms extended, like it had been caught in the middle of picking up an oversized box.

"I've been doing criminal acts in this town for hours," Jason hollered at it. "And now I've finally found the toilet!"

He loosed an arrow. In keeping with his newfound marksmanship, the arrow hit Triptoe in its left eye, shattering it.

Triptoe's right eye stopped blinking and went dark. It

stood under the light, inert.

Jason looked back at his friends and shrugged.

"Man, was he trumped up for nothing," he said.

Triptoe's remaining eyelight came back on. It wasn't blinking, but glowing a steady, angry red.

It dashed toward Jason with its pipe legs at breakneck speed. As it raced toward him, it pulled a giant double-headed axe from its back.

"Oh, crap!" Jason said as he saw the speed of the robot bearing down on him.

He had wanted Triptoe's hostile attention, or agro as they called it in the game. Now that he had it, it turned Jason into a wreck. He tried to fire again and the shot went wild. He backed up and tried again and he almost shot himself. Finally, he ditched trying to shoot and just ran.

"Melvin!" he shouted.

Rich looked at Melvin. He wasn't in Zhufira mode. Zhufira was graceful with her weapon, amazing, beautiful. Melvin couldn't keep the sword still, he was shaking so bad.

Nevertheless, when the dashing robot was almost at the bar, Melvin ran out. He swung his sword at a pipe leg and connected, cleaving the foot off above the ankle.

Triptoe fell forward on its hands. The moment its hands hit the dirt, they dug in for traction, supporting a body now parallel to the ground. Its body swiveled on its hands, whirling like a powered turnstile. Triptoe's extended pipe leg whirled around, smashing into the back of Melvin's knees and knocking him on his butt.

Triptoe's pipe leg came around again with crushing force. This time Melvin's head lay directly in its path.

"Duck!" Rich yelled.

Melvin flattened out just as the pipe leg rushed past.

Triptoe stopped whirling. It dug its knee into the ground and raised up in a crouch. Now it kneeled in front of Melvin, who was flat on his back.

It raised up its huge axe.

Thwip! An arrow lodged itself into the doorway next to Rich, far off its mark. Jason was still shaken up, his aim worthless.

The axe came down.

Melvin rolled away and the axe stuck into the packed dirt of the street. But Triptoe was inhumanly fast and strong. The axe came back up like the robot was pulling a knife out of warm butter. Triptoe's free hand shot out and grabbed Melvin's leg. There would be no rolling away this time.

Rich ran out into the street and grabbed Triptoe's axe-wielding arm. Rich was no match for Triptoe's strength. All he did was slow the descent of the axe. It came down, steady and sharp, to cleave Melvin apart.

Melvin brought his sword up to meet the axe. Their combined strength slowed the axe to a crawl, but did not stop it. Now the only difference would be that Melvin would be killed by his own sword as the axe forced it down.

"Rich! Cast!" Melvin yelled between clenched teeth. All his strength was tied into keeping his own sword at bay.

There had to be another way. It was just gears, spare parts. He didn't have to cast, he just had to think.

Rich started kicking Triptoe's arm, the one that held Melvin in place. The arm didn't budge. Melvin looked up at him with desperation.

"Cast!"

The sword was almost at Melvin's exposed belly. Rich kicked again. And again.

His third kick dislodged Triptoe's grip. Melvin rolled away. The axe bit into dirt.

This time Triptoe left the axe where it was. The sentry grabbed Rich by the hair, just as Richard Bates had done.

Rich fought against it, but Triptoe pulled. It was going to bring Rich's face down onto the axe.

Rich's heart threatened to beat its way out of his chest. The axe was like the wall Richard Bates had slammed him into. It was coming. He was helpless against it. Fear overcame him, like it had when Druze had trapped him inside a raging tornado.

The words came. He didn't know what he spoke, but the words came naturally. They sounded foreign and familiar all at the same time. And they kept coming.

Rich's hands erupted with energy. Red light burst forth like a lava flow. He grabbed Triptoe's axe and it melted into sludge at his touch. He dug his hands into Triptoe's gearbox chest and pulled. The robot separated like freshly torn bread.

Rich's final words were a shout, his voice reverberating with authority and power. The red light consumed his vision in a violent explosion. When the light finally faded to the dark of night, the only thing left of Triptoe was a couple of pipes that were slowly eating themselves into cinder.

No one spoke in the space of several moments after Triptoe's demise. Finally, Jason broke the silence with a shout.

"Badass!"

Jason and Melvin shook Rich with enthusiasm. They

patted him on the back and spoke with excitement about how crazy awesome he was.

Rich was numb. He was too busy worrying about how the hell he had done that and how much it would cost.

Chapter 16

Answers

The town of Triptoe celebrated their liberation from Sentry Triptoe with wild abandon. Streets that were once bathed in darkness sparkled and flickered in the light of torches, lanterns, sconces, and bonfires. People danced in the streets, their doors open, and the light from their homes flooded out to join the bright displays up and down the avenues.

Rich sat in the bar with Melvin and Jason. Now it was full of life, with people singing and cheering and drinking and dropping rounds off at their liberators' table. Each of the guys nursed at least three full glasses apiece.

The good mood of the townsfolk didn't rub off on Jason. He sat grumbling, looking down into his near empty mug. After he drained the glass, he looked up to address his friends.

"We were garbage out there."

Melvin was leaning back in his chair, his long legs crossed as he held his mug. He shrugged casually. "At least we did it."

Rich didn't say anything. The last thing he cared about at the moment was letting Jason down.

"It's okay if you guys are garbage," Jason said. "I mean, I expect that from you two. But me? As soon as that dumb robot came at me, I imploded. I was a total nub out there."

Melvin smiled and drank. Apparently, he was enjoying Jason's self-directed hatred.

Rich was too busy thinking about the magic he never

wanted to use again. He couldn't imagine what kind of cost that last spell would incur. Plus these guys didn't understand; later on they'd ask him to start a campfire or create a drink of water or magically make their dreams pleasant. Their whining only added to his cost. The only spell he wanted to cast was the one to cage the death creature so he could get out of this body.

Out of nowhere, a smile crept up on Jason's face.

"I think I got it."

The only response he received was Melvin's raised eyebrow.

"We all have a character-mode trigger," Jason continued. "It's something we have to trip to before the skills of our characters emerge."

"Huh?" Melvin asked.

"Yeah," Jason said. He leaned closer and talked excitedly. "I thought at first it was just a matter of concentrating, but it's not. After I was out of danger, I concentrated, I focused, and still couldn't hit the side of a barn, let alone Triptoe. The problem was I couldn't trip my trigger to put me back in Cephrin mode."

"And what's your trigger?" Melvin asked.

"I have to be calm. Cool and relaxed. That's my trigger. Anything else and I'm just Jason in a gray body."

"I tried being calm," Melvin said. "Back at the Hierophane with the practice dummy, remember? That didn't work out so well."

"That's the thing," Jason said. "Your trigger is completely different. I've seen you go Zhufira mode twice now. Once in the akhta with the weagr and again in this bar when that dude groped your goodies. How were you feeling those times?"

Melvin nodded, his pretty features scrunched in anger. "I was mad," he said.

"Anger's your Zhufira mode trigger," Jason said, pointing at Melvin as if that validated everything he said.

"Of all the triggers to have…" Melvin stated flatly, blowing hair out of his face with a heavy sigh.

Rich could understand. He hadn't known Melvin very long, but Rich knew Melvin to be extremely level-headed. A person would have to step over the line and then step out another mile before Melvin got angry.

Melvin and Jason were both looking at him. "So what's your trigger?" Jason asked.

Rich thought about being stuck in Druze's tornado, the wind ripping at him and tossing him about. He thought of Triptoe's iron grip at his hair, pulling him relentlessly toward the axe. And how his heart had felt ready to rupture, the waves of panic striking him like lightning bolts.

"I dunno," Rich lied.

"You need to figure it out," Jason said. "You unlock those gray robes, and the rest of this trip will be on easy mode."

Rich dry-swallowed and nodded. He looked down into his beer glass to keep from meeting the eyes of his friends.

Jason's theory made sense. Until they found another way to access the potential of their characters, they needed those triggers. Jason would be able to tap into Cephrin virtually all the time. Zhufira would be much harder to call on for Melvin, who largely stayed afraid, level-headed, or worried.

And Rich? He wanted nothing to do with Razzleblad. He was mortified to use him. But now that he knew his trigger, the thought of turning into Razzleblad would linger in his mind and only heighten his fear the next time he was afraid. His mortal fear of turning into Razzleblad could likely cause him to turn into Razzleblad.

Talk about a repeating cycle of irony.

Rich told the guys he was tired, drained from the spell he cast on Triptoe. It was only part of the truth. He got up, made his way upstairs through a throng of people dancing, cheering and thanking him profusely.

Alone in his room, Rich looked at the bare walls like they held an answer to his problems. If not an answer, a way to escape. The dull throb of the party filtered in through the closed door. That was all.

It was tough going through this alone. He knew he couldn't talk to the guys about it. Without having ever experienced the cost, they would just chalk it up to a bad dream or something imaginary. Rich needed to talk to someone who understood how different and terrifying the cost could be.

He remembered Majora's last words to him. She told him she was there for him if he ever wanted to talk.

She had given him the words for a scry spell. Casting it was worth it. He already owed plenty for the spell he had woven to obliterate Triptoe so this little bit wouldn't even register next time Richard Bates came to torture him.

He created a bowl of water and set it on the nightstand beside the bed. Then he spoke the spell she had told him. He never doubted the words; she had burned them into his memory by whispering them into his ear.

Rich looked at the bowl of water for what felt like forever. He finally began to question whether he had said the spell correctly.

"Why did you bring the bowl of water?" a soft, feminine voice asked behind him.

Rich turned and saw Majora. She was right beside him, wearing the same green nightgown she wore the night he first saw her. Her lips curved up and eyes turned down in an expression that couldn't help but make Rich feel welcomed.

"I thought I needed it," Rich said, looking back at the bowl. "I figured your face would appear in it or something."

Her face scrunched up in confusion. "What made you think that?"

"I dunno," he said with a shrug. "I thought that's what mages do when they scry."

Majora giggled. "A scry is a meeting of two minds," she said, putting her two index fingers together. "We share our environment."

Rich looked past Majora and saw the Hierophane, the same library where she had taught him magic fundamentals. The bookshelves were just as he remembered, even the empty space where Majora had taken out the *Birleshik Arcana*. The tea set on the table glittered in the subdued light of paper lanterns. The windows were open and the soft glow of the garden lights revealed trees that swayed in a gentle breeze.

Majora herself sat on a divan. Between her and Rich a yellow line stretched across the divan, the floors, walls and ceiling. Past that line, Rich sat on his ratty inn bed. He looked behind his back and saw his nightstand with the water bowl and the featureless wooden wall of his room a mere two feet away.

"Talk about not putting up my fair share," Rich said as he looked up at his squat ceiling.

"You don't need to offer any more than what you are now," Majora said. "I'm glad you decided to scry with me," she said with a smile. "The last time I saw you, you seemed so shaken by the cost."

Rich scratched his head. "I still am. I tried to shut my eyes to it… you know, avoid it."

The pity in her eyes was unmistakable. "I wish I had had more time with you, Rich," she said. "There are a lot of things we teach beginners, years worth of instruction that I had to condense into a single day. I'm sorry you went through that.

"You're not alone," she said. "Even though we teach the cost is unavoidable, inevitably a young practitioner becomes full of themselves, headstrong with their own growing power."

She looked up at the ceiling, her eyes dancing as she reminisced. "I remember when I was a young girl; I was mastering spells graded two years above my class. My teachers said they had rarely seen the like of it, but I, I had never seen so steep a cost before. I tried to close my eyes to it, despite the warnings I had learned. I thought to myself, the price for avoiding the cost couldn't be any worse the horrible alternative of bearing it."

She fixed Rich with another look of sympathy. "It's a hard lesson few ever repeat."

Her words about the steep cost for advanced spells reminded him of Sentry Triptoe.

"How'd you handle the cost—you know, for the highly advanced spells?"

"Well, I approached it with the mindset that higher learning demanded greater sacrifice. And like anything, if you're willing to sacrifice then the mind and body can endure all sorts of strain. When I needed a break, I would go back to practicing my bending and altering, spells where the cost was little more than a few bad images. That's what you should do. And when you're ready, challenge yourself to loftier goals."

"But why cast at all?" Rich asked. "You don't pay for what you don't use. I don't see why anyone uses magic."

"You don't? Wonderful things happen because of magic. Look around you. You are sharing your world with me right now, and I with you. From what you told me, your friend Jason is alive because you healed him. What is the cost to wonders like that?"

Rich nodded. What she said made sense. He hadn't liked his first cost one bit, but it was definitely better than trying to avoid it. And he had done great things in the short time he had wielded magic. Surely it was worth the price he silently paid. And the more he paid it the easier it would get.

"Thank you, Hierophant Majora."

She smiled. "I asked you to call me something else, yes?"

"Yes, Rew." Rich smiled with her. Then he looked back at the empty wood walls two feet behind him compared to the spacious finery of the Hierophane library. "I'm sorry about the world I'm sharing with you right now. This is pretty crappy."

"Where are you anyway?"

"Some little town you've probably never heard of.

Triptoe."

"Oh, Blessed Onesource!" she said with a shake of her head. "I know where you are."

"You've heard of it?"

"That town has more problems than empire capitals. It's as if the place is the focal point for all the world's absurdities. The residents may hate their mechanical sentry, but believe me, it was the best thing to ever happen to them."

"Um…" Rich said, "Not anymore."

"What happened?"

"I kinda disintegrated the sentry with a spell of ridiculous power."

"Oh no… that sentry was the only thing keeping the legion of crazy things at bay," Rew said, her mouth making a moue. She gave Rich a look of feigned malice. "If that town gets taken over by sentient mole people or some other nonsensical menace, I'm holding you responsible."

"That's not fair at all, Rew. If I beat Sentry Triptoe then I know he wouldn't have been any match for the mole people."

They both laughed a good while. As Rich looked at Rew, he realized all his feelings of despair and isolation had melted away. Her words and company had given him strength and resolve. He no longer feared the cost so much. After all, Rew had been casting powerful magic for centuries.

They finally stopped laughing and the silence grew from seconds into moments. "I see you were about to go to bed," Rich said, looking at Rew in her dainty nightgown. "I guess I should go. Or cut the feed. Kill the scry? How do you break the connection anyway?"

"You just have to want it bad enough, to leave that is.

But you don't have to. It doesn't look like it right now, but we're both in a state of sleep."

"You sure I'm not putting you out? I don't want to be blamed for bags under your eyes and mole people."

Rew smiled. "Let the scry itself be your proof. It can only hold if both parties want to be here. So as long as we want each other's company, the scry will persist until the deeper levels of sleep extinguish it."

She winked at him. "But that still won't excuse you if something ludicrous happens to that town."

He held his hands up. "I didn't know the robot I was blasting into fine powder was your unwitting henchman. How can I make it up to you?"

She leaned closer and rested her chin on her hand. "Tell me about the world you come from. You know a good deal about my world, but I'm afraid I'm completely ignorant about yours."

Rich shook his head. "Oh no, that wouldn't make us even. See, I know a little bit about this world," he said pointing down to his simple bed. "But I don't know anything about *your* world. If this is gonna be even, I tell you about my world and you tell me more about your childhood."

He liked the way her eyes danced when she spoke of her childhood, like she was a world away. There was something magical about it.

"If you wish," she said with a smile. "But you owe me, so you first."

So Rich began, talking of the modern conveniences now gone that he had taken for granted. He and Rew shared their worlds as they shared their minds, talking back and forth until the time sleep would come to finally claim the scry. Maybe it was just Rich's imagination, but it felt like that moment never came.

Chapter 17

Loose Ends Unraveled

Druze Wozencraft hoped the barbarian girl's megrym brother was quietly resting beneath a mountain of fortress stone. But centuries in the world had taught him never to rely on hope. So he wasn't shocked when a megrym showed up with a caravan trader—few things ever shocked him—but he was annoyed.

He didn't abandon all hope right away. Perhaps this megrym wasn't the brother of the barbarian girl. After all, his basic order was for the workers to directly report any strange megrym presence. By definition, "strange" encompassed that whole race of slimy lizards.

Druze walked with the shipping steward who had reported the megrym. The morning air was brisk as they walked through the gardens to the exchange yard. In a week or two the leaves would start changing and another autumn would have its turn in the world.

Despite the fact that the sun was just beginning its climb, the Hierophane was bustling with activity down at the exchange yards. The mages traded with all flavors of nations and groups. Not only that, the Hierophane moderated transactions and guaranteed security of goods, so many traders came there to trade with one another. The shipping steward led Druze through various crowds: high-cheeked Hillanders haggling with Agoni nomads, aian bakers unloading confections preserved from the ovens of Nasreddin, nasran *Denizbashi* showcasing delicate carpets made from the rare kelp of the Azure Coast.

On a small patch of grass on the outskirts of the exchange enclave, one trader had parked his contraption engine. The megrym was there, completing the ensemble of a thoroughly motley band of rabble.

"Hey! You the one running this theme park?" the megrym asked Druze as he approached.

"Theme park?" Druze asked. The steward had been right to report this megrym; he was strange even by megrym standards.

"Yeah, rides, guys in costume," the megrym said, pointing to a mage apprentice who was traversing the courtyard on a floating tile. "You should add concessions and charge for this, but whatever. I'm looking for a warrior chick. Steel drawers, big ass sword on her back. Seen her?"

Druze let out a sigh. So much for optimistic thinking.

"I have," Druze said. "Mike, is it? I was told you may come here. You and—" Druze went up to the small fellow with a face that looked like he routinely washed in road dirt except for the clean circles around his eyes. "—a man named Runt, I believe."

"Yo," said a different man, one as big as a weagr.

"You would think otherwise, right?" said the dusty faced man, offering a friendly smile and hand. "I'm Ruki Provos of the Provos Trading Company. I'm just a businessman with a pleasantly settled contract."

Druze took neither the hand nor returned the smile. These people were all irksome and confusing. If the big one was named Runt the tight-lipped nasran woman must be named Straight Legs.

The shipping steward whispered in his ear that Provos

had delivered three crates of Maltep hexes. That got an eyebrow raise from Druze; none of the other merchants had been able to trade with the tight-fisted bastards for months now.

At least something good came out of this caravan. Druze turned his attention back to the thing that wasn't.

"Follow me," he told Mike.

"Word," the megrym said with a nod. He turned to Provos and stuck out his little purple hand.

"Aight, Ruki. Preciate the ride. Stay up, playboy."

The tradesman grabbed the megrym's hand and shook it vigorously. "You all have been the best investment ever. I'm going to remain in Ardenspar for another day, restocking the caravan and all. Once you finish your reunion, come and celebrate our good fortunes with me. I'm lodging at the *Exquisite Promise*."

"Bet."

Druze turned and began the walk through the trade exchange. But he heard more than just the megrym in tow. He turned and saw Runt on one side of the megrym and the nasran woman on the other. He looked down at the megrym.

"What?" the megrym asked with a shrug. "Following you."

It was bad enough playing host to a bunch of pendulum rejects. Now he had to extend the courtesy to their hangers-on as well. But Druze nodded, kept walking, and kept his tongue still.

The moment the fake gray robe completed his mission couldn't come soon enough.

He led them out of the exchange yard, through the

gardens to the dormitories. They could stay in the same rooms as the last guests. High up and out of the way, cooling their heels until the others were done.

The megrym must have grown restless passing by the various enclaves and buildings to get to the dormitories. Druze heard him stop.

"Ok, so where's Melvin?"

Druze turned his head to speak as he continued walking. "First, I am going to show you to your rooms."

"I don't want a room. I wanna see my brother."

Why, thought Druze. *Why do these people make everything so complicated*? He turned to face the megrym. He was going to have to explain what happened to his brother, in tedious detail, until Mike nodded his little purple head and got on the walkway so Druze could float him up to his room and forget about him.

Something was missing. Not something. Someone.

"Where's the nasran woman?" Druze asked.

"Took off for the pisser," Mike said. "So where's my brother?"

Druze found it hard to understand more than two words at a time from Mike, but he got that the nasran had left to relieve herself. She'd likely pee all over the floor rather than figure out how to use the fixtures. Yet another reason why he just wanted to get this brood in their rooms and contained.

"Your brother is on a vital quest on behalf of the Hierophane. He will return soon enough. Meanwhile, I'm sure you and your friends are tired from your journey here. I will show you to your rooms where you can relax and recuperate."

Mike looked at Druze, his face scrunching up in

disbelief. "Vital quest? What vital quest?"

"You were at Fort Law. The creature your brother and his companions freed cannot be allowed to roam unchecked. So they have gone to contain it."

"Contain it? You mean the big black monster that crashes through solid stone walls like he's a stripper popping out of a cake? Big as four Runts, with wings, lives underneath the zombie apocalypse and has no problem getting along with the neighbors? You sent my little brother to go heads up against that?"

"I assure you, your brother and his friends are well-suited to the task."

The little lizard looked up at Runt. "You believe this dude?" he asked the oversized man. "He's assuring me of something my own eyes can't."

The megrym turned his attention back to Druze. "I'm also well-suited to a task, the task of finding my brother. Where is he now?"

Druze shook his head. "I'm sure you will understand when everything is explained fully. For now, know that pursuit would be impossible. I cannot allow it."

"Man, you may be able to get kids on board with that, but I don't follow the orders of a dude in a snuggie. Where is he?"

Mike was starting to become the loose end Druze had wanted to prevent. The last thing he needed was some half-informed, half-crazed megrym running around trying to stop the others from completing their mission.

He had lost some of his proficiency in interacting with people over the centuries. It was always easier to incinerate them or wait a few decades or so until they died.

The thought of incinerating Mike popped up, as warm a thought as his charred body would be, but the repercussions were something Druze wanted to avoid at all costs. His daughter had grown unduly fond of the fake gray robe and she would be livid. Her good-intentioned, guilt-filled heart would drive her to tell the fake robe and he would tell the barbarian girl and maybe they'd all quit the quest. So, no, he couldn't incinerate Mike, at least not here. He changed his tack.

"You are right, megrym. I cannot tell you what you can do. So allow me to offer help. I will escort you to your rooms, where you can wash up and refresh yourselves. While you two are doing that, I will prepare some maps and some packs filled with rations and travel supplies. Is this agreeable?"

Mike looked up at Runt and they exchanged brief nods. "Word," Mike said to Druze.

Druze led them the rest of the way to the dormitories. Soon enough they'd be lifted up on a tile and locked away in the tower. And when he found the nasran woman, Druze would incinerate her just for associating with this annoying megrym.

Inside the dormitory tower, Mike looked up at the doors and the few people that floated to them on tiles. "Sweet," he said. He smiled as he looked at Druze, little razor teeth peeking out behind thin lips. "We get to ride on the tiles up to our room?"

"Of course," Druze said. "Right this way."

Mike approached Druze but stopped suddenly. He stared at something beyond Druze in the courtyard gardens. He walked up to a flower carefully.

"Oh my god, they got Gahniytues! How'd you get

these?"

"I think that's a daisy."

"Did you say a damn daisy? Man, I know the difference. Those are daisies," he said, pointing to a bunch of identical flowers. "This is a Gahniytu. Don't you see the difference in the petal and stem?"

Mike looked at Runt. "I thought you said these dudes were smart."

Frustrated, Druze went over to the stupid flower to see what this insufferable toad was talking about. He leaned closely to look at the flower and compared it to the other white and yellow flowers.

"It looks the same as the daisies," Druze said looking at one and then the others.

Behind him, Druze heard Mike's voice. "Good night to you."

He felt a thud at the back of his head, and everything went dark.

ଔଞ

Savashbahar ventured a peek around the corner. At the opposite end of the hallway, two factory mages were engaged in conversation. Soon their path would lead them elsewhere. Then she could see where the stairs going down led.

It might be enough for her people to blame the Hierophane for the Hollowers and just sit idle on their accusations, drinking and crying over needless deaths. It was not for her.

The coast was clear. She darted down the hallway and into the safety offered by the darkness of the stairwell. She took a few cautious steps down into the pitch-blackness.

These stairs had no torches. Good. When humans had things to hide, secrets that lived among their bright and shining towers, they buried them. What she sought would be deep in the dark.

She felt the walls and stairs turning like a corkscrew as she descended. The stairs emptied out into a passageway, and she could see torches flickering at either end. The torchlight illuminated damp, moss covered walls.

One end of the passageway opened into another passage, this one clean, free of dust and well lit with torches hanging in neat intervals. She turned around and went back the other way. The other end was in disrepair, the moss thick on the walls, and lit with only the briefest touches of torchlight.

This was her path. She crept along, keeping silent and straining to hear anything outside the occasional crackle of the torches. Getting discovered down here would be hard to explain.

The passageway turned, but offered very little in ways of options. When she got to her first intersection, there was a young, brown-robed mage at a table hosting a pile of thick books. He was leafing through one of them.

Savashbahar saw the glow of the mage's soul about him, a shimmering that never lied like mouths did. His shimmer told her he was innocent and unburdened. A good person. Behind him were stairs.

She watched from the shadows awhile. A brown-robed woman came, a warm shimmer about her and a sour look on her face. She and the one at the table talked, discussing the tragic circumstances that got them both stuck down here.

They were students serving some sort of punishment. Now it all made sense to Savashbahar. What better way to guard something without showing you're guarding it than by forcing the unwitting to stand watch in the guise of something else? These students didn't know they were supposed to guard the stairs. But they would read their books in penance and be present to stop intruders like Savashbahar all the same.

Savashbahar looked down, at the dozen hexes that hung from her belt. She grabbed a utility hex, one that bent and flowed like wind.

"Serpent," she named it in a whisper. She bent down and the snake wriggled from her hand and turned the corner. The girl screamed and the boy jumped out of his chair in surprise.

It was a utility hex; the snake would not bite. But it would serve its purpose and distract. The girl tossed books at it while the boy chased it around the corner, shooing it. While their backs were turned, Savashbahar made the stairs and descended.

These stairs were another dark corkscrew. As she descended, a slow steady drone grew in volume, like she was falling into the maw of a machine.

There were two rooms at the bottom of these stairs, both lit by the blue demon light humans called netherfire. One room had nothing. The other held shelves laden with golden bricks, silver coins, and gemstones.

No one guards in secret the things they should guard openly. She went back to the empty room. Walking slowly, she pushed along the walls.

Her hands fell through at one point. There was a passage way, disguised by factory mage illusion. She stepped through the illusion into the entryway of a dungeon laboratory.

Two rows of netherfire burned in floor channels

running the length of the room, bathing everything in their unnatural blue light. The walls were host to dangling chains and strange apparatus. Shelves and tables held devices, books, even hexes.

Despite only having eleven hexes, she wasn't tempted to pick up the extra hexes that littered the various tables. Who knew what the factory mages did with them, bending them, perverting their purpose.

A clinking of glass got her attention. A mage was engrossed in work at one of the tables. He wore purple robes, the mark of the nightmare bringers. He looked up from his task and their eyes locked.

His shimmer stabbed out in angry, piercing bursts like lightning. What she saw in those sporadic lightning strikes of shimmer told her he was as twisted as the robes he wore.

But it was what his shimmer told her when it wasn't lashing out that made her blood boil. For when there was no lightning there was nothing at all. An unholy void of soul. He was her proof.

He was a Hollower.

Chapter 18

Consequence

Savashbahar pulled an attack hex, its wood lashing out in all directions. "Reap," she named it and hurled it at the Hollower.

The hex transformed into spinning scythe blades and expanded beyond the length of the room. The deadly fan carved out gashes into the walls but did not slow. It careened toward the mage at dizzying speeds.

The Hollower hit the floor right as the blades shot past and buried themselves deep into the back wall. A shower of dust and stone fragments shot out from the force of impact.

The Hollower pushed up into a defensive crouch. "*Ateshim gael!*" he shouted and the netherfire from the channels in the floor leapt up and came to his hands. He launched his netherfire volleys at Savashbahar.

She pulled a defense hex, its wood carved in ripples. "Gust," she named it, put it up to her lips and blew. Wind erupted from her palm, churning a narrow passage through the netherfire.

The blue flame licked on either side of her, its heat nauseating, but it passed by without touching her.

"Well, aren't you a resourceful little hex witch," the Hollower said with a smirk.

"So, you demons can speak," Savashbahar spat. "Tell me, Hollower, what magic brings you here?"

"I should ask you the same thing," he said, running his fingers through his short hair, so blonde it was nearly white.

"This place isn't exactly easy to find."

His presence alone proved the factory mages were in league with the Hollowers. The sporadic bursts of darkness stabbing out from his otherwise lifeless shimmer proved he was more than just the average Hollower. This one could speak. He could tell her where they come from.

Savashbahar would pry the secret from his mouth. Then she would end them all.

"The restless spirit of my fallen son brought me here, to you," she said. "He requires your life. And I, I need answers. Tell me why."

"Why, huh? You're not gonna like the truth, which is why I'm gonna tell you," the Hollower said as he circled Savashbahar. "We do it because it's fun. Killing your boy… fun for us… *korkma zinjeerlair*!"

His last words summoned chains from the folds of his robe, demonic, talon-clawed chains that pulsed with a dark purple glow. The chains shot out and wrapped themselves around her, the claws digging into her skin. They dragged her towards the Hollower.

Savashbahar's anger melted into fear. This was the strength of the purple robes. They were fearmongers, using the emotion as weapons against their foes.

She fought down her fear, grabbed a utility hex and named it "weagr". As it dissolved, she felt her muscles bounding with strength. She grabbed handfuls of the glowing chains, and pulled with all her newfound might.

She launched the Hollower at a wall. He spoke a rush of words, and as he hit the wall, he disappeared into his robe as it became a jumble of purple stormclouds.

The Hollower emerged from the clouds, holding a chain. A massive, purplish-black demon beast dog was at the end of the chain, slavering and pulling the chain taut as it strained against its master to get at Savashbahar.

The Hollower let go of the chain. The dog leapt at her, too fast to dodge.

Waves of dread and panic hit Savashbahar, so intense they drove her into hysteria. She screamed and screamed, shutting her eyes to keep from seeing the dog tearing at her flesh. She felt herself hit the ground where she scrambled backwards until she hit the wall, trying to get away as best she could from the threat.

She knew the dog wasn't real, that it had passed over her as harmlessly as smoke. But the terror it had driven into her made these facts seem surreal, myths it had devoured as easily as it could her bones.

"Stupid girl," she heard the Hollower say. "Someone should have told you not to bring sticks to a firefight."

The Hollower was real, she told herself. He was going to kill her if she didn't open her eyes and fight back. Dushunmek's death would go unavenged. The thought of that didn't dispel the overwhelming, impossible terror. But it got her to open her eyes.

The Hollower was tossing two chains, one wrapped around each arm, into the netherfire channels. A sickly blue and purple flame spread onto the chains.

Savashbahar looked down at her hex belt. Two attack, three defense, and three utility hexes were all she had.

She couldn't bring down this fiend; it took a whole team of Hexenarii to defeat a Hollower.

It was impossible to separate her true feelings from the fear the Hollower had induced. What she felt didn't care whether it was manufactured or not. Her heart beat so hard she could hear it in her ears. She didn't want to fight, she wanted to run as fast as she could and never look back.

The whole of the Hollower's chains now danced in flame. The fire cast deep shadows over his face, giving a frightening hue to his sinister grin.

Her trembling fingers closed over an attack hex. If she couldn't kill all the Hollowers, she could still kill this one with a single word. Even if that same word killed her as well.

The Hollower whipped a fiery chain at her.

For Dushunmek.

"Boom!" she yelled, naming the hex as she threw it at him.

The explosion ripped out of the hex. The room disappeared in a flash of brilliance. Fiery waves of pain washed over her.

Silence. Savashbahar still felt. Pain was there, steadily decreasing. She wasn't dead.

She raised her head. The laboratory was wrecked, bathed in dust and soot. The explosion had collapsed the roof in heaps of rubble, turned the tables and shelves into splintered firewood, and set books alight.

Why wasn't she dead? The explosion had blasted her through a wall, into what appeared to be an old fireplace. Her clothes were tattered and smoking, but she was whole.

Only a weagr was thick-skinned enough to possibly survive a blast like that.

Weagr. She had forgotten in her fear. Weagr was what

she had named her utility hex earlier.

Inside the ruined laboratory another boom sounded, smaller this time. A chain bathed in purplish blue flame erupted from a pile of rubble.

Savashbahar's dread came back strong. One attack hex left. Dying here would not avenge her son. She looked up at the rounded hollow of chimney.

She pulled another utility hex. "Geyser," she named it, wiping sweat from her brow on it before tossing it on the ground. The saltwater spray shot up, carrying her with it through the chimney tunnel. When she reached the geyser's apex, she grabbed the walls and began to climb.

Soon the darkness claimed everything. She couldn't even see the geyser below. She kept climbing. Then she heard a clinking below, the sound of metal digging into stone.

Below her, the purplish light of the fiery chains illuminated the gloom. They were digging into the stones. The Hollower followed the chains, pulled up by the snakelike tethers. His face was a torrent of rage.

He was gaining fast. She looked up at the neverending darkness. She looked at the stones in front of her.

She hoped she still had weagr strength.

Savashbahar punched the chimney stones with all her might. They fell away, and sunlight streamed through the small hole they left.

"You think you get to leave, after this?!" The Hollower shouted. He was making huge leaps with the chains pulling him up.

Savashbahar punched out more stones. It was barely big enough, but those chains were frighteningly close. It would have to do.

One attack hex left. She pulled it, named it the same as the last attack hex, and dropped it as she fell out of the hole into daylight.

She landed on her back on the grass as the explosion went off. The tower she fell out of groaned. Smoke billowed out of the hole and began to fill the sky. With a sudden crash, half of the building dropped a floor, making the whole tower look staggered.

"What the hell have you been up to?"

She looked to the side. It was Mike. He was holding the legs of the black-robed mage, the one whose shimmer was so thick and convoluted it looked like a stormy sea. Runt held the mage's arms.

She raised an eyebrow as she spoke to Mike. "What the hell have you been up to?"

Mike looked up at Runt. "So much for the discreet exit," he said.

They tossed the mage into a clump of bushes. The three of them hurried in the opposite direction of the people who were approaching, amassing into an ever thickening crowd around the broken tower.

⋘⋙

Druze's head pounded. More than the injury made by the club, the insult was an unforgiving lash. The insult fueled his rage.

His daughter didn't help matters. She stormed about his den, fury etched in her features.

"So all you can tell me is someone or multiple someones infiltrated the bottom levels of the Aphelion Tower and set off an explosion," she said, her voice climbing as she spoke. "This person or people then ascended through a forgotten, walled off exhaust chimney and set off another explosion, turning the tower into a misshapen, unusable monstrosity. But you have no idea who or why or how many or what's next."

"I told you, Rew, I was unconscious."

She glared at him. "How easy is it to incapacitate a mage with five hundred years of acumen?"

He returned her glare, his blood running cold. "I will not be scolded by you, daughter."

"Yes, you will!" she said, standing her ground. "You relinquished control of the Hierophane to me, remember? And for three hundred years it's been me, guiding it, doing the administration, being the face of Seat Esotera while you do whatever it is you do in the shadows. So when it comes to matters of the Hierophane my say is absolute, not yours. And when my head of security lets someone destroy one of the original five esoteric towers in bold, broad daylight, I will scold him."

She looked out the window, at the tower that now looked like a broken shoulder. "Do you understand me, Druze?"

There were few times in the last three hundred years he regretted giving up control of the Hierophane. He enjoyed moving about in the world without the recognition or restrictions as Hierophant. This time, with his own daughter talking down to him, was one of those times when he did not relish his lack of authority.

"You are Hierophant," he told her. "And you are right."

She turned to face him, her manner cold and business-like. "What steps have you taken since the attack?"

"It looks like hex magic was involved. I have sealed off Ardenspar. We're coordinating with the local peacekeepers who are sweeping the city, looking for Hexenarii."

"Keep me abreast of any development. I want answers," she said and stormed out of his quarters.

Druze ran his fingers through his black hair. His gaze drifted to the ruined tower, one of the few that had stood since the beginning of the Hierophane.

For five hundred years the Hierophane had served as a beacon for humanity. It was the bulwark against aian aggression, nasran barbarism and megrym imperialism. Before today, it had seemed impregnable and unassailable. Now that the beacon was tarnished, what message did that send to those who sought to marginalize humanity?

The purple-robed man whose presence Druze had masked stepped out from unnatural shadows along the wall. He looked at Druze, his lips curled up into a wicked grin.

"You know, your daughter... when she's mad she is smoking hot."

"Nevermind my daughter. You should concern yourself with your own future when it comes to smoking hot." Druze opened his palm and called netherfire into existence, a spell that took experienced destruction mages an hour or longer to craft.

"You let this happen, Samedi," Druze said looking at the tower. He balled his hand into a fist, extinguishing the netherfire with his lack of will to maintain it.

"How was I supposed to know some part-time Hexenarii hag was roaming the dungeons looking for a brawl?" Samedi asked. He leaned against the window and looked out at the tower. "I gotta admit, though, she was pretty resourceful."

"I want her pretty dead," Druze said as he looked at the purple-robed mage. "Her, the megrym, the big man, all of them dead."

Samedi's smile broadened. "Why don't you just tell your daughter who it was? Instead of sweeping the city looking for any nasran who looks Hexenarii, the peacekeepers can target a megrym, nasran lady and a big man. You'll probably have their heads before dinnertime."

"I know why you smile," Druze said. "You see my tactics and know I'm hiding something from Majora, something I figured you wouldn't notice. You make one fact glaringly apparent. It seems my centuries of life have made me arrogant in my own intelligence and dismissive of the faculties of others."

Druze's eyes drifted to the staggered tower. "I swallowed the megrym's bait, a ruse for fools. We all make mistakes, apparently even after half a millennium. The megrym's mistake was injuring my pride. He must die. And no one will come between that, not even Majora."

"Yeah, she wouldn't kill him for a bump on the head," Samedi said. "She kinda has that good girl aesthetic."

Rew's sense of truth, justice and fairness were the biggest reasons the Hierophane was regarded as a beacon of hope. She was known for making hard choices, some which had been disadvantageous to the Hierophane, for the sake of fairness and equity. This was the reason he had ceded control in the first place.

"Well, that's where you and I come in, Samedi. To do the things in the dark that Majora and the Hierophane can't or won't do in the light."

"Always more fun with the lights off," Samedi said.

"The *Exquisite Promise*," Druze said. "You'll likely find

our new friends there, with a trader named Ruki Provos. Kill him too, for bringing them to our doorstep."

Samedi nodded and retreated into the shadows. He never complained about tasks that allowed him bloodletting.

Meanwhile, Druze looked at the broken tower. He would make some good come of the desecration. Everyone already talked about the Hierophane's lack of master robes and their dwindling influence. Seat Esotera was an overextended, crumbling relic, lacking manpower to do much outside their own demesne.

That would change. When sacred Maltep lay in ruins and the Hierophane had possession of their hex stores, no one would question the might of human mages.

Chapter 19

Risk Factor

Mike was grateful the city of Ardenspar was so big. Carved into several districts, separated in two by a river, it would take time to find any needle in this massive haystack. This alone gave them time to plan.

"You guys are the worst investment ever," Ruki Provos said scowling.

He looked out the window at the mayhem loosed on Ardenspar. The distinctive chrome armor and white cloaks of peacekeepers were everywhere—running through the streets, riding the skyrails, storming businesses and buildings, grabbing cloaked individuals and checking their faces.

"Dude, not our fault," Mike said, sharing the view out the window. "You can't lock me up while you send my brother off to die. Not having it."

"Fine, but did you have to blow up the Hierophane?" Ruki asked. He looked at Savashbahar, who now blended in perfectly with the wall thanks to her hex magic. Two different squads of peacekeepers had already stormed the *Exquisite Promise* looking for Hexenarii.

"Yes," was her simple reply. Considering what she saw down there, Mike didn't blame her. But her time to hide as a chameleon was limited; she had already burned two hexes concealing herself from peacekeepers. Unless she had some that weren't on the belt, she only had two hexes left.

They had to get out of the city.

Ardenspar reminded Mike of old school London.

Cobbled streets, tall stone and brick buildings, lots of steam boiling out of grates, gutters and vents. Only things missing was Oliver Twist and Jack the Ripper.

It wasn't all Sherlock Holmesy. Giant iron bars crisscrossed the skies of Ardenspar, joined at massive cylindrical towers. Passenger cars shot out from these towers and traveled sideways along the giant bars. It was the equivalent of a skyrail, which was impressive considering it ran on steam and gears.

Ruki Provos grimaced. "Well, I'm not the type to inform on others. But I am a businessman, and harboring fugitives isn't my business. You guys need to think of a way to get out of Ardenspar before I'm seen with you."

"We got it, Ruki," Mike said. "We just needed a place to lay low for a minute."

"Well, that minute is getting stretched rather thin," Ruki said, looking down onto the street. "We've got another round of peacekeepers heading inside, this time with a terrormancer."

The blended blur of Savashbahar moved quickly. "We must flee," she said, panic in her voice.

"Why?" Mike asked. "You still got some hexes, right? Just hide. They'll come and go like the others."

"No, this is different," she said. "He is the Hollower."

Crap. If the same Hollower from the Hierophane basement specifically came to the *Exquisite Promise*, then that meant the black robe Mike clubbed told him where to find Ruki Provos. It also meant the Hollower knew who to look for rather than any random nasran.

Ruki opened his room door. "Flee to the roof; I'll try to stall them."

Mike looked at him. "Dude, you need to come with us.

They're coming for you too."

Ruki dismissed Mike with a hand. "Nonsense. I wasn't even with you guys. Once they see I'm not harboring you, I'll be fine." He pointed up. "Now get going, quick."

Mike, Runt and a well-disguised Savashbahar ran up five flights of stairs and emerged on a flat roof overlooking the city. The sun lay at the horizon, changing the sky into shades of oranges and reds as dusk came to Ardenspar. Soon nightfall would arrive, making it easier to move around undetected in the city.

Sooner than that, though, peacekeepers would burst out onto the roof. Runt blocked the door with rain barrels. Mike ran around the perimeter of the roof, looking down.

They were twenty stories up, the tallest building in the neighborhood. The second tallest was right next to the *Exquisite Promise* but only ten stories high. Jumping ten stories with nothing to break the fall but four barrels was a hard, hard crunch.

Bambambam! Hard, violent pounding hit the door, shaking the barrels. A frantic, muffled voice came from behind it.

"It's Ruki! Open the door, open the door, open the door!"

Runt pulled the door open a crack, Ruki quickly squeezing through the thin crevice like he was covered in butter. He looked like he had seen his own ghost.

"Those bastards tried to kill me!"

Runt closed the door as peacekeepers arrived. Mike and Ruki wedged the water-laden barrels back into place as the door started jumping from the peacekeepers. Their pounding was even more violent and insistent than Ruki's had been.

"They may get another try at it," Runt said. "Few

options this high up."

"Gather to me," Savashbahar said. She was waving a half rotted plank of wood, which seemed to be dancing in the air because she was still invisible.

"Follow the wood," she said. "Aim for the water."

In front of him, Mike saw the plank go dancing off the roof, plunging toward a roof ten stories below and a hard, hard crunch.

Behind him, the barricaded door exploded into toothpicks, shooting the barrels in random directions. A squad of six peacekeepers shot out from the darkness, followed by a mage in purple robes.

Mike turned back around. Savashbahar's track record for escaping without a scratch wasn't exactly stellar. She'd probably risk two shattered ankles for a shot at crawling away from capture.

He saw the wood ten stories below, waving. Next to the dancing plank, a geyser was shooting out from the rooftop like a Christmas miracle.

Mike didn't have to turn to feel the peacekeepers bearing down on them.

Aim for the wood.

He dived toward the geyser. Time seemed to crawl, giving him plenty of opportunity to feel his heart beat in his throat and think about the circumstances that led him to the point in his life that he was freefalling above a fairytale city in a little purple body.

His little purple body had little short legs with very short jumping power. He almost fell completely shy of the geyser. But his head came into contact and the rushing torrent of water slowed his fall by blasting his face. He landed on his back, safe and stinging.

As he lay sputtering next to the geyser, Ruki hit the stream on his butt and bounced out onto the roof. Runt came last, belly flopping onto the water. His mass plus gravity was a bit more than the geyser could keep buoyant and he landed with a dull thud as water sprayed in all directions at everyone already on the roof. But it cushioned his fall, and he rolled off the shooting water unharmed.

On the roof of the *Exquisite Promise*, the peacekeepers looked down at them as if they were unsure how to proceed. The purple robe didn't seem to have that problem; he turned and said something to one of the peacekeepers.

The peacekeeper jumped.

Runt pushed a nearby rain barrel into the geyser stream. Unable to lift the full barrel's mass, the water stream sprayed everywhere but up.

The peacekeeper's scream was cut off abruptly as his face hit the barrel. The impact put the peacekeeper out of the chase. But it also broke the barrel and now the stream was back to blasting upwards.

Everyone lent Runt a hand carrying the remaining three barrels. With the three of them over the geyser, the water flowing out looked like it was a harmless leak from the barrels, no shooting spray. Now there was no way the peacekeepers could follow.

The purple robe pointed to four of the peacekeepers. They backed up. A chain shot out from the mage's sleeve and wrapped around the fifth peacekeeper. The mage hoisted him up into the air.

"Time to go!" Mike yelled.

As they beat a path toward the roof exit, Mike heard the telltale crash behind them. Another peacekeeper was out of commission, but now there would be four extremely motivated peacekeepers with a cleared landing pad in hot pursuit.

The stairs down ended abruptly on the sixth floor. Apparently, these people built with total disregard for fire safety. Runt, in the lead, burst through a door at the base of the stairs and the gang kept going.

People screamed and darted into rooms as the half-weagr barreled down hallways. The halls opened out into what looked like a factory. A giant steam-powered device occupied two floors. It looked like its only job was to press ink onto sheets of paper.

"Great," Ruki said as he ran. "We busted into the *Ardent Parse.* Nothing keeps a lower profile than running through a news agency with peacekeepers in pursuit."

"Just keep running," Mike said. "Better to make headlines than the obituaries."

Runt continued charging through the factory, plowing down anyone not fast enough to get out of his way. Ruki, bringing up the rear, kept knocking over anything within reaching distance as he passed. Amidst a symphony of screams, protests and an ever-present whine of press engine, they found the remaining stairs down.

The stairs led them to an alleyway. It was great to be on the ground again.

"Wait," Savashbahar said. She was still invisible, so it looked like the wooden door they had come out of closed by itself.

"Bulwark," she said and placed a hex on the door. The door turned from brown to gray and expanded in width until it was several times thicker. Now, instead of a door, it was an immovable stone block.

Ruki Provos looked at the general area of where she

should have been. "Why didn't you just do that when we were on the roof?!" he asked, pointing to the sky in exasperation.

"What suicidal trait drives you people to ask questions in the most dangerous places?" she asked in return.

Ruki gritted his teeth. "Right. Let's get out of here so I can keep living to hate you. Follow me."

Ruki took them through a mazeway of back alleys and side streets. Night darkened the city, and gas street lamps cut through the gloom and rising steam. All around them, the sounds of heavy footfalls on cobblestone reminded them that peacekeeper patrols could be around any blind corner.

After an hour of navigating alleys, peeking around corners and ducking from the roving eyes aboard the skyrail, they emerged onto a wide avenue. A bit on the beat-up side, the buildings on the street were nevertheless lit up with orange, yellow and red lights. Music and laughter emanated from any given building and the occasional drunk wandered down the street.

"This is your solution?" Savashbahar asked, a scowl visible on her face now that her hex had worn off. "You take us to flesh dens?"

Mike looked at a building laced in red lights before his own light bulb went off. This was the red light district.

"Worse places than this to make a last stand," Runt said with a smirk.

"This is our ticket out, guys," Ruki said. "Before my uncle let me handle some of the business, I had to prove myself. That meant an aspiring businessman had to make a few risky deals. I'm taking you all to the king of risky deals."

Ruki led them all into a three story, orange-lit building named *Fracas Catawampus*. The orange lights continued inside, subdued to create a soft glow. Scantily clad human and aian girls danced or ran playfully from eager male pursuers. Smoke curled from censers to fill the air with a scent of musk and sandalwood. The only furniture was pillows, large and small, thrown about or gathered together to support the weight of couples making out on top of them. In some places there were more people than a couple.

Moving with purpose, Ruki waded through the smoke, prone bodies, and giggling women into another room full of gaming tables. He made his way to the back table, to a card game between two aians, a human and a megrym smoking a cigar.

"Any room at this table for a real player?" Ruki asked.

The megrym, more greenish and less purple than Mike, scrunched his face up and talked around the cigar. "Unless you've learned a new talent of shitting out real players, I don't see where you're going to get one. But you're in luck, Provos. Who needs real players when we can fleece a greedy son of a bitch like you?"

Ruki held his hands up defensively. "I'm stung, Grandlevoss. Do you kiss your mother with that mouth?"

Grandlevoss took a pull on his cigar. "No. I kiss your mother with this mouth."

Ruki nodded. "Yeah, I'd rather kiss my mother too than that ancient lizard you call a mother. I imagine it's like kissing a ball sack. But we don't need me to imagine when you can tell us from experience, right?"

Grandlevoss slammed his cards on the table and got up, looking livid. He walked over to Ruki. Then out of nowhere both Grandlevoss and Ruki started cheesing big grins.

"Ay!" they said in unison and grabbed on another firmly at the forearm.

They talked about old times and caught up to new ones,

asking a million questions about one thing or another, correcting each other on the false rumors they'd heard about the other. One rumor wasn't too far from true.

"I heard you joined some rebellion and hatched a plot to blow up the Hierophane," Grandlevoss said, half laughing about it.

Ruki laughed half-heartedly with him. In the quiet space after, Ruki spoke with a serious look in his eye. "I sort of need your help, Grand."

Grandlevoss nodded. "Let's go to my office." Then the megrym shouted. "Hey, Delightful, come and finish my hand!"

From the front, an aian woman with kitty ears and a silk top that was virtually see-thru bounced over to the table. If nothing else, the competition was bound to be distracted.

Grandlevoss took them down some stairs. Mike was expecting a basement, but the stairs opened out into a cavernous underground chamber. Dozens of tank-trains like Ruki's were lined around a station house. Six tunnels were cut into the walls, leading out to who knows where underneath the city.

Ruki moved with familiarity down the gangplank toward the station house as he spoke. "It's probably best if you don't know the details, Grand, but I really need to get a caravan out of town the discreet way."

"So," Grandlevoss said. "You need passage on one of my mules. Passage for three doesn't come cheap, you know."

"I know," Ruki said. "Wait. There are four of us." He looked around. Their most visible member had disappeared.

"I never saw but three of you guys," Grandlevoss said and shrugged.

That's when Runt entered from the back room. He

trudged down the stairs, adjusting his belt.

"Where the hell were you?" Ruki asked.

"I'm half-weagr," Runt said, his eyebrow raised. "Easy puzzle to piece."

"Well, if we can't afford the cost per ticket, I know who's walking," Ruki said.

"No worries," Grandlevoss said, "I wouldn't dream of charging my good friend Ruki Provos hard currency for this trip."

"Really?" Ruki asked. "Well, that's splendid! That's incredibly generous of you."

Ruki stopped and looked at the megrym. "On second thought, I'd rather pay the hard currency."

Grandlevoss lit a cigar. "Anyone would rather pay. Unfortunately, you don't have enough money in those short pockets to warrant me getting involved in your little tiff with the mages."

The megrym blew smoke out, thick wafts that floated up into Ruki's face, making him cough and sputter.

"What you have that warrants my involvement is your reputation, Provos," Grandlevoss said. "You're known for making deliveries at whatever cost. And I have something that needs delivering."

Grandlevoss took another pull of his cigar, the smoke coming out of his nose and mouth like he was a little mini dragon as he spoke.

"There may be a little risk."

Chapter 20

Invite

Melvin was coming to hate the travel part of this quest. Everything was too far from everything else. They had been traveling on these hava-chaises for hours after leaving Triptoe. So far they had passed grass and a stream and some more grass. There was also a pond where Melvin spent ten minutes convincing Jason not to shoot a deer because he wasn't about to clean it. And after that, yet more grass.

Maybe the scenic countryside vistas would be more welcome if he had the city to go back to. He missed the suburbs, the concrete, street lamps with powerlines that fed lookalike houses with electricity. That was home.

Maybe he was just irritable because of last night. Before Rich melt-blasted Sentry Triptoe, the robot had worked Melvin over pretty decent. Then the townspeople had come out in droves and their relentless partying and plying him with liquor made for a slow morning start and a cloudy head. Hell, even his breasts were sore and heavy-feeling, probably from the rough night's rest on that crappy bed.

So now, he just wanted to be there already, wherever there was. What he got was more grass—lush, green and promising to never end on the horizon. It was making his mood dark.

Rich seemed to have had a better night. He barely focused on the view; his eyes had been stuck for hours in his book. That thing was denser than the thick clumps of grass they routinely passed.

A brief visual of Rich crashing his hava-chaise while he was in the middle of turning a page made Melvin smile. He would skid and tumble across the grasses, yelping and cursing all the while.

"Hey guys, check this out," Rich said, engrossed in his book. "It says here that Kaftar Friese was the first Hierophant. He believed in a principle called ritual equivalence. His theory was a mage could pay for the cost of casting spells physically and mentally before or during, not just after a spell."

"So?" Melvin asked sourly. The last thing he cared about was Rich's dumb book.

"So, I have to cast a spell designed by Kaftar Friese on the death creature to trap him," Rich said, not bothering to look up from his book. "Not only am I casting a spell made by the first Hierophant, but he was working on a whole different way to use magic, like a sort of mystical pay-as-you-go system."

Crash already, Melvin thought.

Rich didn't crash. The three of them continued on without incident for another hour. They encountered a stream and Jason called for lunch.

Melvin let out a sigh of relief as he sat on the grass and took off his boots. Butt was sore, legs were sore, breasts were sore… all he wanted was to go back to bed.

"You know, I'm sure wild animals come to this stream to drink," Jason said. "If we just wait a little while, something'll get thirsty and I can shoot us some fresh meat for lunch."

"No! That's OK!" Melvin cried. Rich was shaking his head emphatically. "Look at our packs," Melvin said, "we should really eat some of this food before it gets old."

The packs were full to bulging. The people of Triptoe

had bestowed them with all they could carry. Fresh bread from the baker, sweets from the confectioner, dried meat from the butcher who also happened to be the mortician.

Melvin's pack was especially overstuffed. The town's women had shown a fondness for him that bordered on mascot adoption. Before his backpack screamed at the seams and forced them to stop, the ladies of Triptoe had stuffed it with a make-up kit, countless silver and gold hoop earrings, bangle bracelets, a necklace of amber-colored stones, and three sundresses. Even though he was essentially wearing a steel bikini, the thought of wielding a double edged bastard sword in a sundress was comical to Melvin.

They rummaged through their packs, pulling out the Triptoe bread and meat, Hierophane cheese and apples. The stream gurgled its water past their picnic to destinations beyond. A gentle breeze stirred, rippling the grass to tickle Melvin's toes. This was a much-needed break.

Jason fished an ornate bowl out of his pack, one of his rewards for saving the town. He leaned over the stream and dipped the bowl in. After taking a drink, he pulled off his pinky bone and dropped it into the bowl.

"I knew it," he said, pointing toward where they had been traveling. "I'm starting to feel the direction," he said with a smile. "In my bones."

"Good," Melvin said, "That means we're getting close, or at least closer. I can't wait to get this done and get back. I have never wanted a freshly toasted Pop Tart so much in my life."

"Meh," Jason said, his mouth half full of bread, "The way I see it, the burbs can wait."

"Easy for you to say," Melvin said, cupping a sore breast. "You're not differently gendered."

"I'm differently species'ed," Jason said with a shrug. "But really, gender or race doesn't have anything to do with what I'm saying. It's just logic."

"How is waiting to get back to our real bodies and lives any form of logic?"

"Once we've captured the death creature, we'll have an open invitation to return home," Jason said. "The Hierophane's been standing for five hundred years, so it's not going away any time soon."

Jason kept going, snacking on meat and cheese between sentences. "Whether this new world of ours is in an alternate universe or a billion light years away or whatever, since time wasn't a factor in our instantaneous arrival here it's indicative we're operating outside our known understanding of time. That means we stand a fifty-fifty chance of returning home at the exact moment of our departure. Granted, if we take our passes back to Earth when we're old and gray here, there's a chance we'll be just as old when we get back. But there's an equally good chance we'll return exactly when we left. If that's the case, we're throwing away an extra lifetime for nothing. And even if that's not the case and we're a week away from the mortuary, at least we had fun over here."

"Wow," Melvin said, raising an eyebrow at his best friend. "Looks like you've thought this through."

"Hells yeah," he said. "Besides, I'm kind of in a different state than I started out in."

He held up his bone arm and looked at it. "Who knows how this will translate through the pendulum. I know I don't like the possibilities."

"Maybe after he finishes that book Rich will be able to cast a real fix for your arm," Melvin said. He looked at Rich, who had been quiet the whole meal.

He saw the reason. Rich was lying down next to a half-eaten piece of bread, asleep.

Melvin started to nudge him with a toe, but he saw Rich twitch. He was in the middle of a mage-trance. Melvin hoped this time he wouldn't wake up screaming his head off.

Jason nodded toward Rich. "He's got it the best of all of us," he said. "I mean, you saw the way he melted Triptoe. He's got insane amounts of power, and the only drawback is a bad dream every now and again."

Melvin looked up at the sky. The clouds were wispy thin, as if they had been lightly dabbed against the blue background with a paintbrush. "Guess our break's gonna run a bit longer than we thought," he said.

With his stuffed pack acting as a pillow, Melvin lay down to take a nap while Rich tranced it out. Lying on his back was measurably more comfortable for his sore body. The sound of the stream and the sight of lazy clouds drifting added to the tranquility.

Then his stomach started cramping.

"Oh come on!" Melvin muttered. What the hell was that dried meat they got from Triptoe, strandwolf jerky? His stomach never cramped to a warm maple and brown sugar toaster pastry.

He sat up, annoyed by his body's refusal to find comfort. Jason was also sitting up, his dancing eyes squinting as he looked at something invisible in the distance.

"I think company's coming," he said.

A bolt of panic shot through Melvin. "What do you see?" he asked. Whatever it was, Melvin had already banked on it not being good.

"Aians, it looks like," Jason muttered. "Hard to make out how many."

"We should try getting Rich up so we can get out of here," Melvin said.

"C'mon, you know there's no waking him up," Jason said. "Six… seven… looks like eight of them. I'm sure they see us."

Melvin looked at the horizon. Whatever Jason saw was just a shimmering smudge to Melvin.

"I say we prop Rich up on one of our hava-chaises and cut out of here," Melvin said.

"And run? We'd look guilty of something," Jason said nonchalantly, his eyes still on the growing smudge in the distance. "Yep, definitely eight."

"Doesn't matter if we look guilty if they don't catch us," Melvin said. "I can carry Rich. You grab his pack."

"No," Jason said, shaking his head. "These hava-chaises are light craft, built to support one passenger. Your combined weight will slow it to a crawl."

Jason took his eyes off of the smudges to focus on Melvin. "They're riding destriers."

Melvin remembered destriers from a campaign they had run called "Siege of Andalus". The hardest part was getting through the aian cavalry. They rode the destriers, massive warhorses, big like leftovers from the Jurassic period when everything was supersized.

Melvin could see them himself now. Eight distinct riders, moving at a gallop, and clearly heading straight toward them.

Jason was right. Even with the each of them on their own hava-chaise, it was likely the destriers could still chase them down. In this open country, there was nowhere to run for miles.

"What if they're bandits?" Melvin asked.

"Why do you think I'm acting so calm?" Jason asked. "You'd better think of something to get mad about."

Melvin couldn't think of anything but his own fear. The riders were two football fields away. He could see they were all armed, some with sword pommels protruding from their backs, others with bow and quiver. His hand trembled as he reached behind his back for his sword.

"Don't draw," Jason said smoothly. "We'll run the risk of turning neutral intent into hostile. We're gonna have to let them make the first move."

They were now one football field away. They all wore the same black leather with swaths of red fabric. Jason looked at the approaching riders as he talked.

"If they're bandits, then maybe emptying our wallets will satisfy them."

Jason gave Melvin a friendly smile and looked his body up and down with his dancing eyes. "If they want something else, then that's when we may have to get messy."

Melvin dry-swallowed.

The eight aians were upon them. The riders fanned out to form a circle around them. The massive bulk of the destriers blotted out the view of anything beyond. Now there was no option for escape.

"Ho, brother," one of the riders said, looking at Jason. "What business brings you to the High Veldt?"

"I should've known this was the High Veldt," Jason said, looking around like he could see through the horses. "Me and my companions are just passing through, brother."

The rider looked at Melvin and a tranced out Rich. "You keep strange company."

"These are strange times, are they not?" Jason asked. He kept a smile on his face and his manner calm.

"Indeed," the rider said. He raised an eyebrow at the hava-chaises. "On what orders of the Hierophane do you come here?"

"Just passing through to lands beyond," Jason replied.

"I ask because the Hierophane doesn't have much say here or in lands beyond," the rider said.

The rider paused and looked Jason over. "Where are your marks?"

Jason looked himself over. "What marks?"

The rider brushed his own neck, indicating the gray skin that looked like scales. He stuck out his tongue and it was forked.

"The Marks of Passing," the rider said. "You have none."

Melvin looked at the riders. All of them carried animal features of one kind or another. Two had bug antennae, three had feathers along their necks, and the remaining riders had gills.

One of the feathered riders shook his head in disbelief. "Impossible," he said.

"Not impossible," the scaly rider told him. "We may not have believed it, brethren, but the teachings were always clear on this. Here is the proof. We live in the last days of Onus."

The scaly rider dismounted and approached Jason. "What is your name, markless traveler?"

"I am Cephrin," Jason said. "Uh, sorry about having no marks."

The scaly aian held up a hand to dismiss Jason's words. His hands were as scaly as his neck. "No apologies needed, Cephrin. I am Mors, Knight-Marshall, Armsguard of the High Fane."

Mors looked at the riders with bug antennae. "Sapr,

Restan, send word to the Fane."

Mors dropped on one knee in front of Jason, who looked down and around as if trying to get a clue as to what was happening.

"Allow me the honor of escorting you to Nasreddin," Mors said, his head bowed.

"I'd love to see Nasreddin," Jason said, "but I'm afraid I have business elsewhere."

Mors looked up at Jason. His tone was deferential, his eyes deadly serious. "You're the one of prophecy. I'm afraid this isn't a request."

Chapter 21

Nasreddin

Paying the cost was bad enough. Paying and then waking up to eight new friends was definitely worse. Rich's new friends weren't used to seeing him jolt up with a blood-curdling scream after the cost. So he had to introduce himself at the point of their drawn weapons.

Now everyone was cool. Everyone was en route to Nasreddin.

"Why are we going to Nasreddin anyway?" Rich asked, looking at the horses surrounding their hava-chaises. "That on the way?"

"Not exactly," Jason said. He led their triangle-shaped hava-chaise formation. Surrounding them at a distance of roughly ten yards on every side, the mounted aians formed a diamond. They traveled upstream from where they'd made camp.

"Then why are we going?" Rich asked. Having freshly paid the cost, Rich was thinking more like Melvin than ever before. The sooner they could cage the death creature, the sooner he could get these robes and the cost off his back.

He could still smell them, burning. Richard Bates had pumped him full of fear until the mage Razzleblad took over. Rich had no control of his own hands as Razzleblad used them to incinerate whole towns, men, women and children. While Rich screamed on the inside, Razzleblad laughed, a madman enchanted by a symphony of bodies crackling under fire and voices wailing.

Jason's mouth curved up into a wry smile. "We're going

cause they like me."

Rich looked at Melvin for a better answer. His face was a sullen, dark cloud. Apparently, he wasn't a fan of this detour either.

"It seems the markless wonder here is the one of prophecy," Melvin said.

"Marks? What marks?" Rich asked.

"That's the same thing I asked," Jason said. "I had to dig into what I remembered about aian folklore for the answer. When an aian kid comes of age, one of the eleven aian gods will welcome the new adult into their house. That means giving them new animalistic abilities and the distinctive markings of that house. Look around for examples."

Rich took a quiet survey of the surrounding formation. Scales and feathers and antennae and gills, it was a regular box of animal crackers on horseback.

"So why don't you have any marks?" Rich asked.

"Cause they messed with my stats," Jason said. "Sure, I would have gained some new talents, but choosing any one house would have reduced the primary stats that go into being an archer. Since choosing a house was always optional, I just never did."

"Never did," Melvin echoed. "Only his folklore never told him an aian without the marks is their equivalent of the Immaculate Conception."

"The folklore might have mentioned it," Jason said with a shrug. "But after awhile, all that backstory just gets in the way of gameplay."

Rich could almost hear Melvin's teeth grinding in frustration. He could relate. Who knew how long the aians would want to keep them in Nasreddin because Jason fit the description of their prophecy?

Melvin didn't say another word. Rich didn't feel much like talking either. They followed the horses, which were following an ever widening stream back to Nasreddin. Jason filled the silent gaps between horse clomps with the aian history he knew.

Aians used to use magic the same way as humans. But spell casting made them undisciplined and feral. It drove them mad. Out of the chaos, twelve heroes rose up and communed with the Onesource, cutting off access to it for aiankind. Now the twelve acted as intermediaries to the Onesource, gods who invited the rest of their people into their houses to share the benefits of intercession.

"Wait," Rich said. "I thought you said one of the eleven houses gives you their mark. But you just said there are twelve gods. Where's the twelfth house?"

"Dude, I don't know," Jason said. "The folklore I remember just says aian kids get adopted by one of the eleven when they come of age. Only eleven marks are playable. Maybe the twelfth mark makes you ridiculously overpowered so it wasn't an option. I know the stats of the other eleven all suck in some way when it comes to my pedigree."

"What if all this goes south on us?" Melvin asked.

"We are heading south, or at least south-west," Jason said. "Totally the wrong direction."

"No, I mean what if they get mad when they find out you're a game construct," Melvin said. "Instead of their chosen one, you're a fluke, made to look this way based on Hierophane magic and the whim of a kid trying to max out his stats."

"We tell them from the start it's a simple misunderstanding," Jason said. How mad could they possibly get?"

"Remember that wheelbarrow those mercenaries got dumped in at Triptoe?" Melvin asked. "Those guys just messed with the townspeople's money. You're messing with the belief system of an entire race."

Jason looked at the galloping riders in front and beside them.

"Shit," Jason said. "They're going to kill us."

"C'mon," Rich said, "we're on a noble quest on behalf of the Hierophane. How can they get mad about that, given the circumstances?"

"Dude, you were asleep for that part," Jason said. "Aians aren't particularly fond of the Hierophane right now. The game notes always talk about how tension between The Temple of Houses and Seat Esotera has been rising lately. How do you think the Temple's going to react to finding a Hierophane-crafted Chosen One on aian turf?"

"Shit, they're going to kill us," Rich said.

"We gotta think of something," Melvin said. "We can't tell them the truth."

A forest was coming into view. Beyond that, the peaks of a tiny mountain range loomed over the trees.

"We better think of it quick," Jason said. "We're getting close to Nasreddin."

"Ok, how about we go soap opera on them?" Rich asked. "You know, we all fake amnesia. We just say we woke up in Fort Law. That's where Jason got his arm cleaved by a weagr, we found the death monster, yada yada yada."

"Amnesia would keep us from having to explain awkward past questions," Jason said. "Like my childhood as an aian, or how our extremely diverse party came to be."

"Think they'll go for that?" Melvin asked.

"It's better than trying to invent a whole life story on the spot," Jason said. "Besides, I got my bone arm—that alone proves there's something crazy out there."

"And it gives us a reason for chasing the death creature besides getting back home," Rich added. "We say it's because the creature's our only real lead to getting back our lost memories. We can throw in some stuff about having a feeling that killing it will restore the natural balance or fulfill our destiny. It's gotta work."

"That is good, Rich," Jason said with a smile. "I almost feel sorry for us."

Rich nodded, glad to have Jason's approval on one of his ideas. Finalization of their alibi couldn't have come at a better time. They crested a hill and the city of Nasreddin bloomed into full view.

The city looked ancient, weathered, timeless. The stone walls surrounding it were densely covered in ivy. The stream they had been following had widened into a river that coursed through one of the three openings in the wall.

Their aian escort steered them to another gateway, the biggest of the three. As they neared the gateway, a crowd of people came into view. Every aian in the throng was standing at the gate, looking at them and waiting.

"Enclave formation," the scale-covered rider said in a quick military bark. The riders fell into a tight circle around Jason, Rich and Melvin. Rich was glad they had finished discussing their strategy, because now the horsemen were too close for conversation.

"Uh, Mors, is it normally this crowded?" Jason asked the scaly aian.

"No," Mors said. He looked at the two riders with bug antennae. "My instructions were to send word ahead to the Fane, not the streets."

"We did as instructed, Commander," one of the bug headed riders said. "But news has a way of leaking through the hive."

"From the hive to The Causeway, leaving us with a crowd I'd rather be beyond," Mors said. "Move as quickly as possible. To the Fane, men."

Rich didn't get to see much of the city through the wall of giant horses. Beyond that was only the press of the crowd, a sea of faces that seemed to go on forever. Aians of the bug, cat, fish, squid, snake, and other persuasions Rich couldn't quite name crowded around, trying to get a peak. Above them, more aians flittered on moth wings or soared by on bird wings. Some of the flying aians held kids, who looked down and pointed.

Some of the faces started changing. The people looking at them had eyes set far apart, like deer. They scowled with razor-thin lips.

Rich wondered what mark they had. Then a visual of some game artwork popped into his mind. These new faces weren't aian. He was looking at nasrans.

"Nasrans live here too?" Rich asked Jason.

"Yeah," Jason said looking with glee at the sea of faces. "Nasrans claim their race started here. It was originally their city. That's why it's called Nasreddin."

"So why do the aians live here?" Rich asked. Not only live here, but from what he saw so far, it looked like they outnumbered the nasrans and ran the place.

"He asks why we live here," Mors said with a scoff. He eyed the nasran onlookers like they were sewer rats. "Nasreddin is our holy city. This is where the Twelve ascended to godhood and saved our people."

"Look," Jason said, his eyes dancing more than usual as

he pointed up. "The High Fane."

Towers, parapets, spiraling stairs, it was all carved into the mountain itself. Protruding and receding along the natural face of the rock, the High Fane rested on many tiers. Next to it, the headwaters of the river fell over the mountain ridge as a grand waterfall into one pool after another as it wove its course down to the city. The High Fane flowed around the pools, using them as the centerpiece for many of its tiers.

Their escort dismounted at the gates of the Fane. A slew of young aian men waiting beside the gates took the reins of the horses and led them away. Three of those men reached for the hava-chaises instead of horses.

Rich didn't want to relinquish his hava-chaise. Not having it kind of cemented the fact they weren't going anywhere for awhile. But he followed Jason's lead and stepped off the platform. The aians taking the hava-chaises made no attempt to use them; they simply carried them away and followed the horses.

The High Fane was incredible on the inside. Polished marble columns, granite walls and high ceilings were home to thriving vines of ivy. Water from the adjacent waterfall pool washed onto the stone floor in places, inviting soft green moss to spread along the rock. It felt as if the inside of the Fane was a living, breathing rock giant.

"No one goes green like the aians," Rich commented.

"I'm a bit fuzzy, but I think this was originally built by the nasran," Jason said, looking around in wonder.

Mors took them to a grand chamber, where twelve thrones had been carved into the face of the mountain. He dismissed his team and then addressed Jason.

"Please wait here while I inform the Elevated of your arrival."

"You got it," Jason replied.

After Mors disappeared behind one of the many doors in the chamber, Melvin leaned close to the others.

"Now's a great time to run for it," he whispered as if there were others within earshot.

"Nah," Jason said. "We're better off here. I wouldn't exactly be inconspicuous with a whole city hoping to get a peek at me. We've got no hava-chaises. They've got big horses. Plus some of them can fly. No worries, we got it."

They were about to find out if they had it. Mors trailed behind three aians garbed in red and white robes with fine golden bordering. One had a mark of feathers, another had bug antenna, and the third had a pronounced horizontal ridge protruding from his forehead.

"It is as you said, Mors," the one with feathers said, a broad smile on his face as he looked at Jason. He knelt. "One of prophecy, you are well received here in Nasreddin. I am Targhos, Elevated of Demir."

"I'm Cephrin," Jason said. "Um, you don't need to kneel or anything."

"Listen to the stranger, Targhos," the one with the ridged forehead said. "We do not know with any certainty he is the one. The prophecy mentions nothing of an arm of bone."

"Indur is right," said the antennae'd aian. "For all we know the stranger is a corruption of Onus, sent here to deceive the righteous houses. Until we know for sure, we must maintain vigil."

"That's okay," Jason said. "My companions and I were just passing through the High Veldt. The last thing I wanted was to declare myself the chosen one or anything. We can just take off, you know."

"No," the ridge-headed one said, "we don't know. That

is for us to decide. I am Indur, Elevated of Sen." Indur gestured to the antenna-headed aian. "He is Taym, Elevated of Yol. And Targhos has already received you."

"Your mannerism is foreign, Cephrin," Taym said, "not like any of the dialects under the roofs of the eleven houses. Interesting."

"We would like to speak to the three of you, separately and in turn," Indur said. "Mors, show the mage and warrior woman to the guest quarters while we interview Cephrin."

Just like that, with Mors' hands on their backs, Rich and Melvin were led away from Jason. Now they had to stick to their story and hope it washed with the High Fane.

They reached Melvin's room first. As Mors led Rich away to another room, Rich heard Melvin scream with frustration through the walls.

"Pink! I hate pink!"

Rich's room was nice, for a prison. The bed looked soft. A picture window and patio way had been carved out of the rock in the back wall. Outside the window, the sun had descended behind the mountains, painting the sky the rich palette of early sunset. A waterfall spilled down into an unseen pool. Stone steps set into lush grass led the way down, discreetly hidden between some bushes.

He sat on the bed. The robed aians, the Elevated, seemed likely to hammer away at Jason with a million questions. Getting through all three of them would take hours, maybe even days. He had time to kill.

Rich pulled out the two books in his library pocket. He liked reading the *Birleshik Arcana*. The history of magic and the Hierophane were fascinating now that he was embedded in this world as a mage. The fact that Kaftar Friese had a theory involving prepayment for spells left him hopeful that maybe casting Kaftar's spell to cage the creature wouldn't be all that bad.

He opened his spellbook to the page Rew had transcribed in it. The page was a replica of a page in Kaftar Friese's own spellbook. He was looking at the words of the first Hierophant. Still, he couldn't understand a word of it.

One word caught his eye. Not the spell he needed, but near the bottom of the page, the word mushkul was scrawled. He had seen that before. He opened the *Birleshik Arcana* and scanned until he found it: a quote from Kaftar in the old words followed by a translation in contemporary language. It looked like mushkul meant "hardship".

It was some kind of hardship spell. What kind of hardship? Not that it mattered since Rich wasn't about to cast any unnecessary spells. Still, he'd like to know what it was he was casting on the death creature, but a cursory look at the *Birleshik Arcana* told him there just wasn't enough old language in it to translate the spell.

The dying sunlight killed his research. Outside, lamps stylized like tulip bulbs came alight. Their light was similar to the glow of fireflies.

In the glow, he saw bodies burning.

He pushed the thought away. Paying the cost was hard. Reliving it would drive him crazy.

He looked at the nightstand beside the bed. An empty bowl sat upon it. An idea he couldn't resist came to mind.

Rich filled the bowl with water. Then he cast his spell.

"I distinctly remember telling you a bowl of water was unnecessary," Rew's voice said behind him.

Rich turned. "I know. I just didn't want to ruin the tradition," he said with a smile.

Rew cracked a smile at that. She was in the veranda, the

same one they had shared a breakfast in. The Hierophane gardens were gloomy, the paper lanterns not yet on.

"I would hardly venture to call one scry a tradition," she said.

"Traditions gotta start somewhere," Rich said. "Now, we're at two."

"So we are," she said. She looked beyond him. "I see you've earned yourself a beautiful room at the High Fane. What did you do now; negotiate peace between aian and nasrankind?"

Rich held up his hands. "This time I'm innocent. Jason made some new friends. At least with the aians. The nasrans here didn't seem too enthused with us."

"Nasrans don't seem too enthused with anyone of late," Rew said, her face clouding into a grimace. "They attacked the Hierophane."

Rich's heart jumped. "Are you okay?" he asked.

She nodded. "I'm fine. It's sweet you should ask. They destroyed a tower. Beyond that the only injury is to my pride and sense of calm."

Rich was silent. He wanted to say something clever or something that would make her laugh but couldn't grasp a single notion which would do that. The silence stretched.

"You know, in my world," he said at last, "a lot of organizations have comment boxes, where people can drop suggestions for improvements. Maybe something like that for the Hierophane'll help keep the violence down."

Her brow furrowed in a look of complete puzzlement.

"Forget it," Rich said. "I have a stupid sense of humor. I just wanted to take your mind off it is all. I should go."

"Wait, Rich," she said. "How long will you be in Nasreddin?"

"I'm not sure yet. We're leaving as soon as we can… death creature to trap and all. But I figure we'll be here for at least another day. Maybe two."

"Great," Rew said. "I'll come see you tomorrow."

"Huh?"

"The Hierophane has a delegation in Nasreddin," Rew said. "There's a standing portal to the city from here. Druze is busy hunting down the rogues that destroyed the tower and that leaves me to slowly go crazy. I need to do something besides wait for news. Would you like company?"

"Uh… yeah," Rich stammered a bit before regaining his composure. "Yes, Rew, I'd love to see you."

"Then it's settled," Rew said, smiling. "Tomorrow. Meet me at the Mage Delegation Tower. Would you like me to bring anything?"

Inexplicably, mushkul came to mind. "Yeah," Rich said. "Do you have a book of the old words with current translations?"

Rew frowned. "Not many of the old texts have survived to today. But I'll see what I can find."

"Thank you," Rich said. He stood still, waving goodbye as he willed the scry to break. It seemed to take forever. And he waved the whole time. Finally, Rew and the veranda disappeared.

"That was smooth," Rich said sarcastically to himself.

Night had fully taken over at the High Fane. A sea of stars dominated the heavens and the glow of the firefly lamps gave a mystical sparkle to the falling water. The air was full of cricket calls.

Someone had come into his room, leaving dinner. But Rich was too stoked to eat right now. He decided to go out into the garden.

He navigated the steps and pushed aside foliage until he emerged in a clearing. The waterfall collected into a pool before spilling off to collect again a tier below. Flowers bloomed around the pool. Miles down, the lights of the city of Nasreddin stood stark and beautiful against the gloom.

Rich wasn't alone in the garden clearing. A woman in a sundress sat beside the pool, washing her hands furiously in the water.

As Rich approached, the woman became familiar. It was Melvin. Why was Melvin wearing a sundress?

Rich saw Melvin wasn't furiously washing his hands. He was dousing his steel bikini bottoms in the water, smacking them over and over again against the rocks.

"Come out, goddammit, come out!" Melvin swore. Rich couldn't recall ever seeing Melvin so beside himself, so full of frustration.

Rich got closer, slowly, until he was right behind Melvin. After another round of dashing and scrubbing, Melvin exposed the steel bikini's leather interior. A red stain stood prominent against the brown leather.

"Melvin?" Rich asked.

Melvin ignored him. He scrubbed at the leather as if removing the stain would erase what had happened.

"Melvin?" Rich grabbed his shoulder.

Melvin looked up at Rich, his eyes brimming with tears.

"I didn't ask for this," he said, "I just… I just need to get home."

Rich held him. Melvin didn't fight the embrace. He sobbed into Rich's shoulder. Rich didn't know if the tears were caused by a guy dealing with changes he had never imagined or a woman too overcome with emotion to keep them bottled up. It didn't matter. Rich knew his friend needed him.

He would be there as a shoulder for Melvin to cry on, even if Melvin needed to cry all night.

Chapter 22

The Sprawl

Mike felt seasick by the time Ruki Provos finally stopped the caravan. They had traveled two full days on that damn tank-train, eating meals on the go, sleeping and driving in shifts. They had put bat-out-of-hell distance between them and Ardenspar. Now the night sky was overcast, making travel in the pitch black not worth the risk.

They made camp in the middle of a desert. It was a lot like the Dry Flats, only drier. And sandier. Ruki constantly batted at the sand on his bedroll like it offended him.

"I go from the *Exquisite Promise* to this," he said, scowling and smacking at more dirt. "I've got half a mind to leave you all in this desert, turn tail back to Suusteren and hide in my uncle's basement for a couple of years until this blows over."

Everyone else ignored him. Savashbahar mended rips in her robes. Runt stirred the pot of stew hanging over the campfire. Mike leaned over the pot, smelling and waiting to eat with all the patience he had left.

"Anyone hear me above the roar of desert silence?!" Ruki asked.

The fire answered, crackling and sizzling over dry sticks.

Mike wouldn't hold it against Ruki if he decided to up and run. Probably no one else did, either. But Ruki wouldn't. He was compelled to live up to his word and make his delivery. Actually surviving the delivery was something he needed a security detail for.

Nothing like being back in the temporary unpaid employ of the Provos Trading Company.

Mike spoke into the quiet. "No one actually said it, but what's so bad about this place we're going?"

Despite having two days time to discuss it, most mention of the place was met with grimaces, scowls, or shakes of the head, followed by silence. Ruki called it The Sprawl, Runt called it The Crossbane, Savashbahar whispered the name *yasak toprak*—forbidden land—under her breath like it was a curse word. They all reacted to the place like fighting it out against the entire Hierophane was the better option.

The same dry crackling fire that had answered Ruki's question now answered Mike's. The silence was not comforting.

"One of you spill it, already," Mike said. "I need the distraction. Ruki?" Mike asked the trader, whose back was turned away from the fire as he lay on his bedroll. "C'mon, it's story time. Might make you feel better."

Ruki turned to face Mike, looking cross. "You want to know? Fine. If I was you, I'd rejoice in my ignorance."

Ruki got up and joined them at the fire. The flickering light gave his features a sinister look as he spoke.

"We all call it something different, The Sprawl, The Crossbane; aians call it House of Onus. No one knows its real name anymore. All we know is it's there, an entire city warped and broken, in the center of the desert.

"They say it was a city of people who wielded magic technology that defies understanding today. Men used these tools as if they were gods without consequences. The stories I learned as a child say megryms began there, as did weagrs, the results of experiments by deranged mage scientists who wanted their offspring stronger or able to regenerate limbs like lizards.

"No one knows what happened to these people. They say they destroyed themselves. All that's left of them is The Sprawl, a testament to the arrogance of the ancients."

"I don't get it," Mike said, "if no one's left, who are we delivering these crates to?"

"Lost Ones," Runt said. He held up the stew spoon, letting Mike know dinner was served.

"*Gavur*," Savashbahar said the name like another curse word.

"Dwellers, Sprawlcrawlers," Ruki said, holding up a bowl for Runt to dump some stew in. "I've heard they prefer the name Tech Romancers. A whole ruined city wasn't enough to convince these fools some things are better left in the past. They're one part stupid, one part crazy and both of those parts are depraved. They live there, divided into a bunch of gangs, fighting over scraps of the ancient technology they forage for amidst The Sprawl."

Mike dug into the stew Runt had ladled into his bowl. Savashbahar stopped her mending to join them fireside. It was quiet for a moment, aside from the *nom-nom-nom* sound of everyone chewing. Mike spoke around a mouthful.

"I dunno. We meet our contact, drop off the stuff and ride out. It sounds simple enough."

"There's a reason no one trades with these madmen," Ruki said. "Traders rarely make it out of The Sprawl once they go in. One Sprawlcrawler gang is indistinguishable from another, and even if you trade with the right guys they'd just as soon kill you as pay you."

"Which ones are we trading with?" Mike asked.

"The Sons of Kaftar," Ruki answered. "According to Grandlevoss, they're one of the big three along with

Clockwound Warders and Exhaust."

"Word," Mike said with a nod.

Savashbahar laughed. "Why do you nod, little one?" she asked. "Knowing more about *yasak toprak* and the *gavur* that prowl it did not ease your mind. It is in your shimmer. Unease is all around you."

Mike shrugged. "It takes care of my immediate future. Until I figure out how to find my brother, that's about all I got."

Savashbahar set down her empty bowl. "You have a destination without a path. Like you, my destination is clear to me yet my path is obscure. We need to blood whisper."

She took out her knife. Without ceremony, she cut across her finger.

"Ho! Wait, what are you doing?" Mike asked.

"Sus," she shushed him. "Trust."

She grabbed Mike's hand and cut his finger. He took in a sharp breath as the sting hit him. Savashbahar smacked his hand as he went to suck on his cut finger.

"Don't be stupid," she said. "You need the blood to blood whisper."

Savashbahar held up the knife and looked around the campfire. "Anyone else seeks a path?"

"Keep your janky blood rituals away from me," Ruki said, getting up and retreating back to his bedroll. "I already know my path; it's away from all of you once I'm out of The Sprawl," he said, smacking away more sand before turning his back on the camp.

She turned to face Runt.

"No need," Runt said. "I am at peace with my path."

She looked at Mike. "Follow my lead."

Her finger traced a pattern in the desert sand, all jagged

lines and unclosed circles. Mike followed suit, feeling like a dumbass all the while. But he didn't have much in the way of options, so if perverse finger painting gave him a clue on how to track down Melvin, so be it. He painted.

"The ground is my witness, as it is sealed," she said. She held her finger high. Granules of red-stained sand stuck to it. He echoed her words and actions.

"To the sky, who sends winds of change."

She held her finger of the fire and squeezed a drop into the flames.

"Blood burns in fire. Yet it burns in my body. It burns in my heart…"

She dabbed a drop on her head.

"…to know the way."

Mike stood there for a minute in silence, waiting for something. Pulsing lights or phantom words or the campfire to jump up with little fiery pictures of Melvin somewhere. Something. None of that came.

"That it?" he asked.

"Now we sleep. The blood will whisper," she said, heading back to her bedroll.

No wonder Ruki and Runt wanted no parts of it. What a gyp. Mike sucked his bleeding finger and was rewarded with the grit of sand in his mouth.

Mike went to sleep. If the blood whispered, it talked about impossible things. Melvin was attacking him in the middle of the street, like he didn't recognize Mike anymore. Then Mel turned on his own friends. It was like he was crazy, like the air was too thin for him in the mountain town they were all at.

Before it got any crazier, a hand was shaking him awake. His eyes squinted open to dawn breaking over the desert.

"Come, Mike Ballztowallz," Runt said. "We do not want night to fall on us in The Crossbane."

They ate on the moving caravan, a breakfast of dried fruit and jerked meat. Greenish-yellow sand and rock the same sickly green color stretched as far as the eye could see. Unlike the Dry Flats, there were no shrubs or occasional wildlife. There was nothing.

"Who the hell thought to put a city in the middle of this?" Mike asked.

"Was not always desert," Runt said. "The city gave birth to Dead Sands."

The engine chugged through the Dead Sands. Occasionally, jagged emerald-green and black quartz crystals jutted out from the rocks. Nothing moved out there, as least as far as Mike could see with his daytime eyes.

It was close to noon when Mike saw awkward shapes emerging from the flat backdrop of the desert. And not just in front of him. He panned his head from East to West. The beginnings of The Sprawl were everywhere, like a city that didn't end.

It took another twenty minutes to make the outskirts. When they finally got to the city proper, Mike understood why nobody wanted to come here.

The Sprawl was a tour through the Apocalypse. An endless ocean of broken buildings stretched as far as the eye could see, nothing but broken marble, shattered glass and charred rubble. Twisted metal struts jutted up from the rubble like rotten teeth. The roads, as big as ten lane freeways, lay disjointed and disconnected, raised up in places and sinkholed in others like the broken bones of a tortured giant.

They were on one such road now. Despite its grand size, Ruki had to slow down and steer carefully to navigate between massive chunks of marble and stone debris.

Mike looked back. The Dead Sands had disappeared from view. Nothing but The Sprawl was all around them, as if the city had swallowed them up.

"How do you know where to deliver this stuff?" Mike asked.

"Grandlevoss was precise about the route through the desert," Ruki said, keeping his eyes on the road's many hazards. "He said it would lead to this street into The Sprawl. According to him, if I just stay on this road I'll get to a circle where my contact will be."

The place was library quiet. The rhythmic chug of the engine, barely noticeable in the Dead Sands, seemed deafening now. Mike could almost feel the small chunks of stone and marble the tank treads rolled over, like they were rocks in his shoes. He visualized those chunks by the sound they made as the caravan treads crushed them into dust.

Nothing stirred in the ruins. The lack of motion and noise set Mike on edge. No sound except their caravan was the equivalent of a brass parade in a deserted village. If someone wanted to find them, it wouldn't be hard. He already felt like there were a million eyes on him.

Mike scanned the empty wastes for any sign of movement. Nothing. The Sprawl rolled past them, empty, stuck in time at its last breath.

It felt like forever, with the city seeping past them, before they got to an intersection. It was a massive circle with offshoot avenues branching off in eight directions. A broken fountain stood in the center of the circle.

Ruki stopped the caravan. The silence rushed in and dominated the air. Everyone looked around. There was no one here.

"Did they all die?" Ruki whispered to no one in particular.

"I should kill you just for saying that," a voice said from out in The Sprawl.

Mike saw a blur of motion by the ruined fountain in front of the caravan. An aian with a ridged forehead stepped out of the blur, naked except for some black leather drawers.

Ruki smiled, all salesman. "Effective use of chameleon camouflage," he said. "The House of Sen always amazes me, my friend."

"We're friends now, us?" The aian said. "Because I thought you were just trader. Which are you… friend or trader?"

"Um… a friendly trader?" Ruki answered like it was a question.

"Ego!" the aian shouted at Ruki.

"Um… what?" Ruki asked.

"Ego!"

Ruki looked at his security detail like the answer on how to proceed was going to come from one of them.

"Judgment calls, tender, all is judgment calls," another voice said from the wasted city.

A human emerged, so well hidden in the rubble that no one had seen him. Wearing grayish-black leather, his eyes masked by blue-tinted goggles, the brown haired man strolled like he was in the park, twirling a black baton as he approached the aian at the fountain.

"Danda's judgment was to call for I, tenders," the man said as he patted the aian on the shoulder. The man smiled behind his goggles as he looked toward the caravan. "Ego is I."

"Right…" Ruki started.

"Shut up, tender," Ego said. "His judgment call for I was because your judgment call was to be both friend and trader to he."

Ego rested the baton on his shoulder and tilted his head like he was amused by Ruki.

"Cannot be both, you. Friends offer friendship. I for you, you for I. Traders offer trade. Money all you want. Supplies all I gets."

Ruki kept a smile but he looked nervous, the sweating-in-court kind of nervous. This wasn't a typical transaction in most people's customer service history. Ego seemed unbalanced to say the least. He kept going.

"What is a friendly trader? You trade friendship for I's money? You charge I for things friends give I for free?"

Ego's expression turned angry. "Friendly trader is like friendly leech. He a dead man to come to I's front door and lie to I," he said.

Just like that, the guy smiled again, like he had just heard a joke. "But forgiving is I, because you scared of I. You don't know what you say. So I ask again. Which you, tender?"

"A friend," Ruki said. "I'm a friend."

"Well, friend," Ego said, "meet I's other friends."

Suddenly, dozens of people emerged from behind rubble or from under it. Megryms and humans, nasrans and aians, all so well hidden that Mike could have stepped on them and not known it.

Ego pointed his baton at Ruki.

"Thing is, tender," Ego said, "Grandlevoss, him trader. Him already took I's money for what you bring to I now. How you and I friends after money changed hands?"

The gang of people approached from all sides of the caravan. They brandished clubs, swords and some had pistols.

The pistols sported cylindrical tops and crescent shaped barrels, but Mike had no illusions as to what they were.

"Them are friends, tender," Ego said, waving his baton at the advancing crowd. "When they bring to I, it's not for money." He rubbed his fingers together.

"List is short of friends who would take I's money," Ego said. He smiled a wicked grin. "And the list, it grows shorter all the time."

Chapter 23

Sons of Kaftar

Mike pointed to Ego as the crowd of goons advanced on the caravan. "The trader may be scared of you, but I ain't. I think you a hook-ass bitch, hiding behind your gang cause you ain't got it in you to come at me."

"I's offended by your mouth spillage, tender," Ego said, holding a hand over his heart. "You seek to challenge I, get I all sweaty and covered in your blood? What be the reason you want to make I work so hard? Eyes of yours don't see the fairness in the odds now, yes?"

Mike looked around at the horde. Had to be over two dozen leather and metal clad, angry individuals. "You damn right," he said.

Ego smiled. "I's always right. You the one wrong, tender. You brought one hand, three fingers," he said, holding up his fingers to illustrate. "You want to carry like I carry, you use both hands, all ten fingers."

Ego waved a dismissive hand at Mike. "Only way I carry like you carry is if you lop off seven of I's digits."

The crazy bastard wasn't so crazy after all. He wasn't going to go for the one-on-one. There was no guarantee Mike would've won that fight, but it was the only longshot he had to getting out of this mess. Now he was tapped.

Runt had his Z-blades disassembled into twin axes. Savashbahar had her dagger out. Mike hefted his club. The show of force made most of the gang smile as they inched closer. It damn sure didn't make any of them run.

"Fucking stellar," Ruki swore. "My life's going to end in The Sprawl, from a pipe smashing into my skull. All because of you stupid lot," he said, pointing at his security detail, "who have me out in the middle of total fucking ruin because you all decided it was a great idea to blow up the Hierophane!"

Just like that, the whole gang stopped in their tracks. They turned their heads to face Ego like it was choreographed.

Ego tilted his head again like he was curious. "What say you?"

Ruki looked around at the temporary pause to his demise with puzzlement. "Uh… I'm going to die in The Sprawl."

"You blew up the Hierophane?" Ego asked.

Ruki nodded slowly.

Ego turned to an ant-headed aian. "Them are the ones you talked about to I two days ago?" he asked.

"Can't say for sure," the aian shook his head. "Still just rumors in the hive. Could be."

"It was us," Ruki said, turning his salesman smile back on. "Grandlevoss needed someone to deliver to you guys and we needed to escape Ardenspar before we were caught. Otherwise, we wouldn't be here. We blew up the Hierophane."

Ego smiled. "Why didn't you just say to I you gave I a gift of friendship already?"

He shouted to the crowd. "These here friends of the Sons of Kaftar unlike any!"

The horde of murderous thugs cheered. They kept cheering, thrusting their weapons in the air like they had just won a battle. Ego walked through the throng to the head of the caravan.

"Time we gave you a friend's welcome, yes?"

The Sons of Kaftar treated friends much better than they did friendly traders. The most significant difference was them putting away their weapons. Mike also appreciated the flasks they brought out from their pockets. A bunch of the Kaftar kids jumped on board the caravan, where they toasted and passed their flasks and asked what it was like blowing up the Hierophane.

Ego was at the head of the caravan with Ruki, where they both smiled and laughed and drove the train together like they were old friends at reunion. Savashbahar was admiring the fabric of some of the gang ladies' attire, full of brass and chrome hardware stitched into gray-black leather. Runt and a big, ultra-buff aian catman were comparing weapons. All of a sudden, it was a party train.

"Not a bad lot, once you get to know them, right?" asked a human gang member next to Mike. His thin lips curved into a sardonic smile as he passed Mike his flask. "I'm Jal. Jal Messer."

Mike looked over at Ruki again. He and Ego were exchanging goggles.

"Guess not," Mike said, taking the flask. Unlike everyone else in his group, Mike wasn't quite as quick to forgive when people try to kill him. Where he was from, beef takes awhile to digest. It was probably for the best that this wasn't where he was from.

"I'm Mike," he said, taking a sip and welcoming the burn to his throat.

"Well, they say life is a dance, but we're all deaf to the music," Jal said, wiping sweat from his brow as he squinted at the sun. "I'm glad the dance took this turn. I've only been with the Sons for about two years now. Trader blood on my diskblades would burden my spirit."

"Why'd you join up with them?" Mike asked. "Hell, why does anybody join?"

"Oh, different reasons," Jal said. "A lot of us are natives like Ego. Sprawl born. Others seek to escape the trappings of their lives and come here to start anew amongst the ruins. Being a tech romancer promises advanced technology, adventure, a life without debts. Even the prospect of having a family is a powerful draw for the disenfranchised."

Jal took his flask back and grimaced as he downed a gulp. "I'm not any of those kind, Sprawl born or seeker. I was a trader, like your friend there," he said, pointing his flask at Ruki. "And like your friend, when I came here for business and they asked me what I was, I didn't pick trader."

Mike looked at Jal. "They made you join?"

He shook his head. "It was my choice. I just didn't know it at the time when they asked me. One of our rules is 'the only friend is a proven friend'. Joining was the only way to prove it."

Mike looked out over The Sprawl. The caravan crept through it, like it was a tour, like there was something to see. As the city rolled by it only offered more of itself, a seemingly endless vista of absolute destruction.

The question of how anyone could live here stuck in Mike's mind. He didn't ask it to Jal, self-confessed prisoner of choice.

"It's not a bad life," Jal said, seeming to know the question Mike hadn't voiced. "Apparently, I'm more of a warrior-poet than a tradesman. Besides," he said pointing in front of them. "You're about to see the perks."

The caravan had woven its way to what looked like a dead-end street. Ruki and Ego kept the caravan moving forward, toward a wall of debris as if they couldn't see the upcoming impact.

Just as suddenly as they had popped up to ambush them, more Sons of Kaftar appeared from the wall of debris. They cleared marble and large pieces of sheet metal from the road, revealing a downward ramp.

Any city this size would have an undercity. Mike knew that. Still, the sight of it was incredible.

The ceiling stood as high as a Gothic cathedral's. Where all the marble had crumbled on the surface, massive columns still stood down here. The marble had figures carved into them; on some, a single huge visage, while others held several figures depicted, frozen in the acts of war and love.

Megalithic crystals dangled in the air, suspended by nothing at all. Not only did they all shine with glimmering white light, each one looked like it was made of liquid. Smaller crystals constantly dripped from them, raining down into holes cut in the floor. The floor was illuminated by a river of glowing cobalt blue. The stuff flowed like water yet glowed like it was liquid neon. This same neon-blue water flowed down whole walls in places.

"That look says it all," Jal said as he nudged Mike. "Once you see this kind of wonder, it's hard not to take the Sons of Kaftar seriously when we say the future is in our past."

"Who? How?" Mike asked, looking at the giant crystals. Occasionally, a stream of small crystals would flow sideways from one giant crystal to another, lighting up the dark space around them as they passed.

"No one knows who," Jal answered. "The job of the tech romancer is to figure out how. We've learned a few things, like how to make diskbows and lightning gloves. Still, we've just scratched the surface of what's possible. The proof is all around us."

The caravan serenely motored through the huge rooms. It felt like a world away from the destruction of the surface. Mike looked at the giant gears and pistons embedded in the walls. Even though all of it was dead now, the machinery looked capable of moving whole skyscrapers. Mike felt like he was an ant taking a tour of the inside of an engine block.

"So, this is why you stayed with the Sons of Kaftar?" Mike asked, distracted by the flowing crystals and still machinery.

"Part of the reason," Jal said. "But I also believe in the cause. The mages have betrayed us all, starting five hundred years ago with the murder of Father Kaftar."

Mike already had his fair share of mage betrayal. Apparently, they had a tradition of dirty tricks that started well before they sent his little brother off on a suicide mission.

"What happened with Father Kaftar?" Mike asked.

"That was when the Hierophane first started out. The mage tower was good back then," Jal said.

"At any rate," Jal continued, "Father Kaftar and his apprentice Wozencraft went to a small mountain town called Olukent to destroy an evil monster. Father Kaftar fought and defeated the monster, but he was wounded as well. Instead of helping Father Kaftar, his apprentice, the dark Wozencraft, killed him while he was weakened so he could take control of the Hierophane.

"Wozencraft then tried to kill Father Kaftar's sons, the true heirs to the Hierophane. The surviving sons fled here looking for a technology to combat the power of the mage tower. That search continues today under Ego Friese, direct descendant of Father Kaftar.

"But while it continues, the Hierophane still maintains rigid control of all magical and techno-magical advancement.

They're forcing the whole of humankind to live under the heel of their factory mage boots," Jal said, shaking his head in disgust.

The caravan stopped. Dozens of folks were in the room, splashing in the neon blue water, smoking, playing with strange devices. But Mike was stuck on the room itself. It came with an epic view.

Instead of a wall, the room stopped at a sheer cliff. Beyond the cliff, the massive crystals shimmered like stars for what looked like miles, all of them raining crystals and shooting streams back and forth.

The room's remaining three walls flowed with the neon blue water, which ran into channels in the floor. The channels met at the center of the room in a pool, an infinity pool. The pool water ran off the cliff face, its neon water shining brightly as it fell into the unending darkness below.

"Welcome to the Heart of the Sons, home of the free," Jal said.

Ego stood at the head of the caravan, his arms out. "Today us and I celebrate, we feast to new friends!"

Cheers went up through the room. Everyone started piling out of the caravan, Mike's group and Sons of Kaftar alike, where everyone received a hero's welcome from the people waiting.

Mike felt a hand on his shoulder. He looked up to see Jal smiling back at him.

"Here we celebrate like this day is our last. It could be. Come, Mike."

Something nagged at Mike. It felt like a sense of danger, only it didn't come from the gang. Maybe it was something Jal said.

He saw Runt, Ruki and Savashbahar having fun with

everyone else. They knew how to let go of their trouble for a minute. He shrugged and followed suit.

◦§◦

Mike woke up with a fog in his head that only copious amounts of alcohol could conjure. He could have slept for another half a day if it wasn't for Runt, who had nudged him awake.

"What?"

"We leave soon, Mike Ballztowallz."

"Where we going?" Mike asked.

"Ruki and Ego discuss those matters now. First comes leaving The Sprawl," Runt said. "After that is another question. East or west our best options. South is mage lands, north, only the Eural Mountains, home to small mountain towns."

Small mountain town. It all came together. He remembered what Jal said and why it had bothered him. Maybe the post-binge cloud was good for something after all.

He saw a mountain town in his blood whisper. He saw signs, names in the street… the same name Jal had spoken: Olukent. That's where he'd find Melvin.

Mike jumped up in a rush. "We're going north to Olukent!" he shouted to Ruki, waking up a legion of sleeping Sons of Kaftar in the process.

Ruki and Ego turned and looked at Mike, Ego with that head tilt he did when he found something curious. "Why you head for the start of dark Wozencraft?" Ego asked.

"No, he's drunk. We're not going there," Ruki said. "A place nicknamed 'start of dark Wozencraft' is definitely not on my list of near future destinations."

"I gotta go," Mike said. "The Hierophane sent my brother out to do a job. He's going there. I need to stop him."

"That's our Mike," Ruki said, forcing a laugh. "Loves to joke. Excuse me a moment, Ego," he said, hurrying over to

Mike. "I need to discuss some things with my colleagues."

Ruki bent over and whispered. "What the hell, Mike? If we head north and the Hierophane picks up our trail, we're done for. Nothing gets over the Eural Mountains. We can't go backing ourselves against the wall like that."

"I gotta go," Mike said. "I'm finding my brother. You can come with or not, but I'm already out the door."

Savashbahar approached, pointing a finger at Mike. "You listened as the blood whispered," she said, smiling. "Mine whispered as well, and it showed me the Hierophane crumbled at your feet, all the Hollowers evaporating like dewdrops before the sun."

She looked at Ruki. "I go where he goes."

"So?" Ruki said with a shrug. Despite his nonchalance, he looked at Runt.

"No need to question," Runt said. "I see things through."

Ruki Provos bit his lip for a moment, then bared his teeth and growled with frustration. He turned to face Ego, "I need a route, friend. North to the dark Wozencraft start."

Ego smiled. He turned and shouted at his gang. "History is repeating! Our new friends are in the middle of this familiar stew! But this time I and us around to sweeten the pot, take the bitterness out. Sons of Kaftar see to that!"

☙❧

Less than an hour had passed since Ego had outfitted his new friends and seen them off when the tunnel scouts reported crazy news. The Clockwound Warders, them were coming in scores here, to the very Heart of the Sons.

Ego wouldn't have believed it but the scouts were always reliable. The Warders didn't have the numbers to risk a topside fight, let alone the force needed to press the Heart.

"Them must be a rage, up in arms about their fallen

leader's goggles," Ego said to Danda. "Wait for them to learn I traded those to I's new friend," he finished with a laugh.

Ego heard the sounds of skirmish in the east corridor. Revenge for their leader made sense, but not enough to try this suicidal attack. Ego had killed Pramus and deprived his body of the goggles six months ago. Why all the anger now?

The first wave of Clockwound Warders emerged through the corridor, them all wearing their signature eye goggles and chestpieces of turning gears. The Sons of Kaftar responded to their yells and raised clubs with well-aimed diskbows.

The sound of the high-tension springs in the diskbows releasing was music to Ego. Bladed disks shot out from the weapons and rained down on the Warders. Three steps into the room, and already that wave was cut into pieces.

Another wave was stepping into the breach. They were trying to gain ground while his men rewound their diskbow springs. Ego stepped forward with his lightning gloves. He separated his clasped hands and blue lightning arced in the gap.

Ego waved his hands and the lightning blasted out, sizzling through the Warders. They were just another wave of suicides to Ego.

More kept coming. While his men shot, Ego shouted at these warders and the ones behind them.

"You Warders have lost leave of your senses to come here to test I! Believe in I when I say the Sons of Kaftar will make you remember the fear you had for us after I killed Pramus!"

The Warders ran in, heedless of Ego's words. His men hadn't time to rewind their diskbows and it was too soon for his gloves to have built more lightning. Ego twirled his baton.

It would be mostly melee from here on out.

His baton took out one Warder with a sickening crack. Another Warder took the fallen's place. And another came at Ego from the side. He took them both down with quick, powerful strikes. Yet more came. They were attacking like they were mindless.

"It's not that they've forgotten their fear of you," a voice said from the corridor. Ego looked and saw something that made his blood boil with rage.

A purple robed mage stood in the corridor. Clockwound Warders streamed into the Heart of the Sons on either side of him, many of them already wounded, all of them with terror-stricken faces. The mage smiled as if he already owned the Heart.

"They still fear you," he said. "But that's my weapon. And they'll never be as afraid of you as they are of me."

Chapter 24

Diversions

The High Fane came for Melvin early in the morning. He was expecting it.

They had come for Rich last night in the garden, after Melvin had cried it out on his shoulder. Rich had refused to go until the guards had brought female attendants to see after Melvin.

Rich's demeanor was amazing. He wouldn't hear their protests or demands. He gave orders to those guards like they worked for him and looked at them like they knew better than defy him. The hesitant, scrawny kid Melvin had met half a year ago in the burbs had disappeared.

Now these same guards escorted Melvin down the hall for what amounted to an interrogation. Melvin walked confidently in his blue cloak and steel bikini. He was armed with an airtight story corroborating the others. And he was armed with a better mood now that the female attendants had provided the products that made monthly cycles manageable for a girl.

Thank you ladies, for showing me things most girls learn when they're twelve, Melvin thought. He recalled how Rich had talked with the attendants before he finally left, instructing them to take Melvin under their wings like they would a girl new to womanhood.

Thank you, Rich.

The guards brought Melvin to the same grand chamber that had the twelve thrones carved into the rock wall. Only this time, all the seats were full except the last one. The guards showed Melvin to a chair facing the thrones.

Melvin sat, expecting a litany of questions. What he got instead was a litany of introductions. Even Taym, Elevated of Sen; Indur, Elevated of Yol; and Targhos, Elevated of Demir introduced themselves like they hadn't already. The only ones who weren't Elevated were Nadi the cat guy, Ananna the spider lady, and Menanderus the squid dude, but they came with their own special titles and epithets that were even more drawn out and tiring to listen to.

The first to actually address Melvin was Dreva, Elevated of Eula. Eula was the house of moths by the look of Dreva's wings folded neatly behind her.

"State who you are," said Dreva.

"I am Zhufira," Melvin said. He didn't add anything to it. More conversation from him only meant more questions from them.

"How did you come to know Cephrin and the gray robe Razzleblad?" asked Geldin, Elevated of House Otam.

Melvin had a hard time placing Geldin, but from the ears it looked like the Otam house was horse. *Maybe it's ass*, Melvin thought. He suppressed a snicker and answered the question.

"I woke up with Cephrin and Razzleblad in Fort Law. I don't remember anything before that."

Durin, the one with the scales and forked tongue, leaned forward. There was no question about which animal characterized the House of Marad. He almost hissed his words even.

"Tell us what happened after you woke up."

Melvin kept it minimal. The fact that he knew they had already heard the story twice didn't put him in a storytelling mood. Besides, they were pretty much forcing him to tell it.

They couldn't have the full theatrical version.

More routine questions came from the fish man of House Baligoz and the question mark creature lady of House Zemishirus. What the hell was she? It'd be easier to tell if she had protruding ears like most of the Elevated, instead she had an elongated nose and some fierce hands, rough-looking and claw-fingered. Whatever animal she was, it was probably a burrower.

Melvin didn't have the same problem with Ananna the spider lady. Her hair flared out in stiff dreadlocks that framed her face with eight distinct legs. Plus she had mandibles.

"You have been through much," Ananna said. She had a regal composure as she regarded Melvin with her dancing eyes. "And you have come a long way. You must miss your homeland."

Melvin thought of manicured lawns, the one-hundred and fifty channels available through DirectTV, the convenience store up the street that was loaded with preprocessed delectables. He thought of dad watching the game with Mike. Melvin saw his brother looking tall and impressive in his Army dress uniform and remembered the look of annoyance on Mike's face when he agreed to play the game. Melvin sighed with regret.

"I definitely miss home."

"Who wouldn't, after such an incredible journey," Ananna said. "Tell me, what do you miss most about your homeland?"

Ananna was asking about where Zhufira was from, not the burbs. Melvin didn't know a thing about where she was from other than the climate must be hot enough to allow for her lack of wardrobe. It was a bait question… and Melvin had walked right into the trap.

"Just a feeling, you know," Melvin said. "A sense of comfort when I think of home. I can't remember anything specific though."

"Tragic, your memory loss," Ananna said. Her spider leg dreadlocks unfurled a bit. "And you think this black creature you uncovered at Fort Law is at the heart of your lost memories?"

"Pretty much," Melvin answered.

"A fearsome entity if ever described," Ananna said, her dreadlocks curling up close to her face. "Can you venture to guess why this black creature would manipulate your mind before you freed him and not after, when it could easily erase your recollection of its very presence?"

"Couldn't tell you," Melvin said shrugging. Now he was starting to feel like the prime suspect. "Maybe I went there to kill it in the first place and if I remembered that we probably wouldn't have freed it."

"Hmmm," was all Ananna said, leaning back into her throne.

Maybe it was spider lady's casual nonchalance about Melvin's capture. Maybe it was the seat he was in suddenly feeling hot. Either way, he wasn't a fan of their version of twenty questions.

"I appreciate you all being thorough," Melvin said. "But we've got some real evil out there. I know Jason doesn't have marks, but really, is it that big a deal?"

Ananna smiled. "Before Cephrin appeared, the last time an aian went unsheltered was thousands of years ago. In those dark days, no one had the salvation of the marks; our race was bereft of the eleven houses. If you had lived through the maddening times, you would know how important the marks are."

Melvin raised his eyebrow. "How would you know how bad it was? You weren't there either."

Ananna's spider leg dreads furled and unfurled. "Child, you have no idea who you address, do you?"

"Um…"

"Allow me to help," Ananna said. "I am Ananna, the Grower, Weaver of Fates, Protector of Destined Lovers. I am the Lady of the Third House, the house that bears my name."

She was the god of the house, or goddess rather. Melvin didn't stop to think these gods that Jason had talked about were still around, actual flesh and blood beings.

"Uh…" Melvin was at a loss for what to do or what to say or how to say it.

Ananna raised a hand to indicate two guys on her right, the squid and the cat. "Menanderus, Master of the Eighth House and Nadi, Master of Ninth House have seen the maddening times along with me and the other house masters. And if the others were in Nasreddin I'm sure they would attend you."

She leaned forward. "That is how important this is."

"I'm sorry, I didn't know," Melvin said.

"No need for apologies," Ananna replied. "It is hardly expected for you to know aian ways and heritage, especially considering your loss of memory."

Nadi, the cat god, stroked his chin as he spoke to Melvin.

"Tell us, why do you call Cephrin 'Jason'?"

ଓଃଡ

By the time they were done asking questions, Melvin felt drained like he had just taken an advanced placement test. How people could come up with so many questions for someone affecting memory loss was a true test of their creativity. He just wanted to get back to his ugly pink room and collapse on the bed.

Melvin opened the door to his room and saw a man he'd never seen before. Then he realized who he was looking at.

Rich had tamed his frizzled mop of gray hair. Now it was cut short, combed and neat, accentuating dark eyebrows which framed gentle eyes that turned down just a touch at the corners. His long, homeless man beard was gone, replaced by smooth skin that gave rise to a strong jaw and a grin that seemed to hint at something secret. He had traded in the baggy gray robe for a well fitting gray shirt, tucked in neatly at the belted waist of gray cotton pants. The new clothes hinted at a well toned body underneath.

Rich was handsome.

Melvin didn't mean that. Better… Rich looked better.

Rich put down the book he had been leafing through and smiled at Melvin.

"Finally over, right?" Rich asked.

"Wow," was all Melvin could say as he stared.

"I see you noticed," Rich said, rising from the bed. "This morning I decided I'd take advantage of the High Fane's male attendants."

"You look better," Melvin said. "I mean, you clean up well."

"I had to do something," Rich said. "I figured with Jason being the Chosen One of Prophecy, somebody had to fight the clichés we're riding. I'm just doing my part."

Melvin smiled. The silence stretched between them for long moments.

"So," Rich said, "did the High Fane tell you it was cool to check out the city?"

Melvin nodded. They also made it clear that Jason

couldn't venture out, but Melvin and the gray robe could come and go as they pleased.

Rich smiled again and his eyes sparkled with mischief.

"So what are we waiting for?"

True to their words, the guards didn't try to stop or delay the two of them. They functioned more as escorts, guiding the couple through the temple's many corridors and galleries to the entrance.

"How do you think it went?" Rich asked as they walked from the temple's entrance to the base of the hill.

"I dunno," Melvin said. "I figure they'll let us go. I mean, you can only say something incriminating if you're a criminal right?"

"Did you know Menanderus, Ananna and Nadi were three of their gods? We were getting interviewed by immortals—that's crazy!"

"Yeah," Melvin said dryly. He was nowhere near as enthused as Rich was with the session. "Like getting the third degree from Peter, Paul and Mary."

When they reached the base of the hill, it became obvious Nasreddin suffered from overpopulation. Crowds of aians and nasrans milled about densely packed streets, navigating around wagons and stalls and street vendors. It looked like pure pandemonium.

"Awesome," Rich said, smiling at all the activity. He didn't say another word. Instead, he grabbed Melvin's hand and led the way into the crowd.

Melvin allowed himself to be led. Rich went through the streets with enthusiasm. He pointed out the different architecture, homes that varied almost as much as the streets themselves. The houses mimicked nests and caves and burrows and dens, many looking like nature had placed them there without any intervention. They reached the river bridge, where Rich showed Melvin the underwater kelp houses.

Rich's happy vibe was starting to rub off on Melvin. Now he was also laughing at street performers who juggled or danced. He waved at the aian youths who flitted about overhead or chased each other with cat like agility. He marveled at the giant beehive buildings the nasrans milled about.

This was much better than crashing out on a pink bed. Melvin gripped Rich's hand a little tighter, silently thankful for the impromptu outing.

Finally, the couple reached a tower. Different than most of the buildings, it didn't subscribe to a natural aesthetic. The tower shot up into the sky, all stone and mortar. Rich led Melvin into the tower.

Inside, Melvin was surprised to find humans wearing brown robes. Most of them stayed hooded. They looked like monks. One of them, a middle-aged clean-shaven man with his hood down, looked at them with expectation. The interior was nothing ornate, just stone.

"Be right back," Rich said. It was only then that Rich let go of Melvin's hand. He went over and spoke to the middle-aged man, who must've been the head of the monastery. The brown robe showed Rich to a chair.

Rich created a bowl of water and set it down on the table next to the chair. Then he sat down and closed his eyes.

What was he doing, taking a nap? Melvin looked puzzled at the brown robe, who had already returned to some random task of sorting books. If it seemed out of place for people to stop by for naps, the brown robe didn't show it.

Rich's nap didn't last long. He was awake and on his feet in less than a minute.

"What was that all about?" Melvin asked.

"Just making a call," Rich said smiling.

"Well, let's get out of here," Melvin said. "We can check out the waterfalls." He grabbed Rich's hand and turned to go, all too ready to leave the monastery.

But Rich's body didn't follow despite Melvin's grip on his hand. Melvin heard the sucking sound of air getting pulled into a vacuum. He turned and saw the blue and white dazzle of a portal opening.

Melvin was about to protest going through the portal. The last portal didn't kill him like most times in game, but it didn't make him a fan of them either. He wasn't exactly fond of the memory of meeting two mages with murder in their eyes and fire in their hands.

But Rich didn't make a move toward the portal. Instead, a hooded brown robe emerged from it. The brown robe took down the hood, revealing the last person Melvin expected to see.

The Hierophant Majora looked at Rich with eyes that sparkled and a smile that radiated warmth like an oven.

"Look at you," she said. Her fingers found his whisker-free jaw and traced the jaw line up until those fingers ran through his hair. "You're positively handsome."

"I'm glad you like the change," Rich said as the Hierophant's fingers were discovering the shirt fabric and buttons around his chest.

"I do," she said. "I'm afraid I'm a bit underwhelming in comparison. Brown robes were the best choice in maintaining my anonymity."

"Brown robes or green nightgown, it's good to see you, Rew," Rich said. His eyes softened as he looked at her.

He was calling her Rew now?

"Come," she said, her fingers weaving their way down to interlock with his. Now Rich had both hands occupied as Melvin had kept hold of one hand while Majora held the other.

"There's so much to see and do in Nasreddin," Majora said. She looked at Melvin like she had just noticed he was there.

"Hello, dear," Majora said, her smile more customer service than it was for Rich. "I trust you can find your way back to the Temple of Houses, yes?"

She didn't wait for an answer. Instead she spoke to Rich.

"I can't wait to show you the Ascension Promenade," she said as she led Rich toward the tower exit.

Rich's hands pulled out of Melvin's grasp. He waved goodbye to Melvin, all smiles and happy eyed, before turning his back and heading out the door.

Chapter 25

The Hollow Truth

Mike looked out at the wasteland and grimaced. Now that they had seen how sci-fi The Sprawl's underbelly was, topside was even more depressing.

Despite the grim view, Mike felt good. He had a lead on finding Melvin, which was something he didn't have yesterday, voodoo mojo lead or not. Plus the Sons of Kaftar had taken good care of them.

The caravan got a serious upgrade. The Sons of Kaftar attached an iron triangle with wheels to the front, which allowed the engine to push aside small to medium chunks of debris without problem. They also loaded two barrels of glow water and an institutional-sized bag of rice on the caravan.

Mike and Ruki both got diskbows and lightning gloves. Ruki had his diskbow holstered at his waist as he steered through Sprawl debris, another tradesman turned warrior-poet in the making.

Mike didn't know why they called them diskbows. They were more like diskguns. You had to pull the tension spring back and forth until it clicked tight and it shot bladed disks instead of bullets, but it was still more gun than bow.

Runt had declined the lightning gloves. "Grip is bad," he said after putting on a pair and hefting his Z-blade staff. He didn't like fumbling with the diskbow tension spring either. But the buff cat aian had a weapon Runt did like, miniature dagger versions of his Z-blade. The aian had given Runt a spare set, which he was sharpening now.

Savashbahar didn't want any new weaponry. She swore by hexes and since they didn't have any, she preferred to remain hex dry. Instead, she received a couple of outfits courtesy of the Daughters of Kaftar. It was just in time, as her robe had been beat to shit after the escapades in Maltep and the Hierophane. Now she looked cool, with the leather pants and brassy hardware giving her a vibe of Victorian lady at the Thunderdome. She had body—who knew?

She looked at the Hexenarii tattoos on her exposed arms, shoulders and tummy. "It takes years to earn these," she said to no one in particular. "Understanding hex purpose, divining intent from its shape, mastering yourself. How strange the marks that men work so hard for and proudly display should be a badge of shame for me." She looked at Mike and smiled. "Showing them again, after so much time in the dark, it feels like flying."

Mike returned her smile. Things were looking up.

Well, not for Ruki Provos. He was driving angry. "I can't believe you have us heading to a place called Start of Dark Wozencraft," he said. "Fooling with you will likely be the death of me," he finished, turning to show Mike the sour look on his face.

That turn saved his life. A diskblade shot past, glancing across Ruki's neck.

Ruki yelled in pain and grabbed his neck. He instinctively ducked, which saved him from another diskblade aimed at his head. The whole crew took cover and looked out at the wasteland.

Whooping and yelling, their attackers broke cover. They rode towards the caravan in small, bug-like vehicles that scurried over the debris on five mechanical legs.

"Clockwound Warders," Runt said. He would know; he

had spent the night trading war stories with the Sons of Kaftar.

"Well, why are they attacking us?" Ruki shouted, looking at the blood on his collar. "Don't they know we blew up the Hierophane?"

"They don't care," Runt said, "Warders have no truck with the mages."

"Get us out of here, Ruki!" Mike hollered. He ventured a look out of cover and ducked again as three diskblades whizzed by. He popped back up to put his own diskblade into the chest of the closest Warder. That Warder collapsed across the controls of his mechanical bug, sending the vehicle's legs scurrying into the nearest pursuing bug and forcing both vehicles to crash into a marble pillar.

Little good that did. There were over a dozen more on his side alone. He looked at Runt.

"How many on your side?" he asked as he pumped diskbow tension spring taut.

Runt popped up and down. Two diskblades shot past.

"Nine," he said.

"There's a bunch in front of us, setting up barricades," Ruki said, barely peeking his head over the steering column. "Hang on for a hard left."

The tank treads squealed in protest as Ruki banked it hard. Mike crashed against the walls of the caravan. His brain raced to come up with something useful.

A hand grabbed the side of the caravan. A goggled face appeared, aiming his diskbow at Mike.

Savashbahar struck with blinding speed, shattering the Warder's goggles as she stabbed him in the eye with her dagger. She ducked a near-fatal diskblade as she made it back down.

Mike popped up and blasted another Warder who was

hanging onto the caravan. "Count your closest side!" Mike ordered.

Runt checked the side, and Savashbahar checked the back. Ruki popped up once, ducked quickly and then popped up again to put a diskblade through a Warder hanging onto the engine before he gave a count of what was up front.

The limited recon produced a count of three on the left, nine on the right and fifteen behind them. Several Warders from the sides had scurried their bug vehicles to the front, where they were trying to put a fair amount of distance between themselves and the caravan.

"They're setting up another barricade," Ruki said. "Looks like my only option is right."

They weren't just making these barricades because it was fun. The Warders were trying to corral them.

"No!" Mike yelled. "Ram the barricade!"

"Are you mad?" Ruki asked looking more shocked than when he got shot by a diskblade. "If smashing into it doesn't wholly destroy the engine, it will definitely slow us down enough for these Warders to catch up."

"Trust me, ram it!"

Ruki raised his head up, then down, then up, then down again. He pulled a lever, and the engine lurched as it gained speed. Ruki yelled over the whine of the engine.

"If we don't survive this, I'm going to kill you!"

They hit like a missile. The impact came with a deafening boom and an exploding white cloud of dust and rock fragments.

The caravan had pushed through the barricade, but now it was grinding to a halt. The white cloud of dust enveloped everything.

A crowd of Clockwound Warders slowly appeared in

the dust fog behind the caravan. They approached the stopped caravan with caution, probably trying to make sense of Ruki's suicidal ramming.

They were almost upon the caravan when Mike and Ruki popped up from the back. Mike smacked his hands together, activating the lightning gloves. Then he pulled his hands apart and a lethal dose of electricity erupted, blasting through the surprised Warders. Ruki followed up with a lightning bolt from his own gloves, bringing down the rest.

Ruki wiped dust and sweat from his brow and looked down at Mike. "Is every little purple fiber of you packed full of crazy?"

"I'm an unpaid employee," Mike said. "You get what you pay for."

"Bravo!" a voice yelled out from the dust cloud.

Everyone on the caravan watched as a shape started to emerge from the fog. The purple robed mage walked toward them, his hand claps jarring in the silence.

"One more turn and you all would have found yourselves at the wrong end of a spike pit," he said. "It would've been a quick death."

The purple robed mage flashed the perfect-toothed grin of a serial killer. "But where's the—"

Mike shot his diskbow. Fuck all that talking. If this bastard liked the sound of his own voice that much he could listen to it gurgling.

Whatever the mage was going to say was replaced by mumbo jumbo. He waved his hand and the disk veered off, deflected.

Ruki fired next.

The mage twirled and the diskblade curved around with the mage before finally coming back toward Ruki, who ducked as the blade shot past.

Now the purple robe wasn't all smiles.

Chains shot out from his sleeves. They wrapped around big chunks of debris. The mage hurled the boulders at the caravan.

The crew jumped off as the boulders crashed into the caravan, sending up a spray of neon blue water and rice.

"Insolent jackass!" the mage yelled. "You will learn to fear me!"

Mike sat crouched behind a crumbled marble wall with the rest of the crew.

"How the hell did this guy find us?" he asked.

In answer to his question a boulder crashed through the wall they crouched behind, showering them with bits of rubble.

"You can't hide forever," the mage said. "Hell, you can't hide at all."

They needed to put a little more distance between them and the mage. If he was going to throw stones, he was long on ammo and this wall was short on support. Mike motioned for the others to follow him. He ran in a crouch to another wall twenty yards away.

"Anybody got any ideas on how to bring this guy down?" Mike asked.

Another boulder crashed through this new wall, dangerously close to Ruki's head.

How'd this guy know where they were in this sea of ruins?

"I can smell your fear!" he yelled at them. "How do you think I tracked you to this wasteland? My dog left a nasty wound, didn't it love?"

If he was tracking them through fear then the guy

essentially had radar. Mike took his team further into the ruins. It wasn't going to help much, but it would buy them some time.

The mage laughed. "Look at you run, you little twerp! I can smell you. The scent of your fear reeks like alley piss. You're afraid you won't see your brother again… and you know something, you're right."

"Notice how that fear isn't of you," Mike called out. "It's cause I ain't scared of bitches in lavender dresses!"

The whole team had to dive out of the way as a boulder came down like it had been launched from a catapult.

"Way to improve our odds, Mike" Ruki said as they scrambled back under cover.

"Leave me," Savashbahar said. "He tracks us through me, from my fear exploited at the Hierophane.

She looked at them, her face grim. "You all must flee. Where ever I am, the Hollower will find me."

Mike didn't want to believe her, but there was no other way to explain how the mage got here. Whatever had gone down in the Hierophane had left Savashbahar with a scent of fear the mage could track til Doomsday. Mike was reasonably sure if everyone else got enough distance the purple robe wouldn't be able to sense them from their fears.

But leaving Savashbahar alone to fight this guy with only a dagger was condemning her to die.

Mike felt a hand yank him off his feet. Runt pulled him out of harm's way as a boulder crashed through the wall where his back had just been.

"Can't keep this up," the mage yelled out from the expanses. He was hidden, invisible in The Sprawl. "All this running is just making more rocks for me to fling at you. And I got a lot of rocks."

Mike had an idea. "Savvy, I need you to run some circles. Get the mage hot on your trail. Then meet us back at the caravan, hooah?"

Savashbahar nodded. "This I can do. How much time is a hooah?"

Mike smiled. He'd give her Army training later. "Twenty minutes. Stay a stone's throw away from this clown. Keep him talking."

Savashbahar darted, disappearing into The Sprawl. She turned long enough to see Mike, Ruki and Runt crouch run in the opposite direction.

The Hollower responded to their split party tactic with a hail of boulders for Savashbahar. She had to run and dodge as a rain of giant rocks threatened to crush her.

"You have chosen a beautiful place to die, Hollower!" Savashbahar yelled out. "The silence here will make your screams sound deafening."

"And who's going to make me scream?" the Hollower asked. "You, with your magic sticks? I already had you running scared at the Hierophane and Ardenspar."

He stopped talking long enough to launch some more massive boulders at her. Then his voice hit her ears again.

"Think your friends'll stop me? They can't get close without me picking up their scent. If they know what's good for them, they've already left you to die here."

Savashbahar darted from cover and the Hollower was there on her left. He raised his hands.

"*Tashbana chek!*" the Hollower cried.

A thousand small stones and rocks behind Savashbahar flew towards the mage. She had no time to escape. She covered her head and braced herself.

The rocks felt like punches. They hit her without mercy

as the mage called them toward him. Her body twisted and turned as the stones pushed and pummeled to get past her. She fell to the ground as the wave passed.

The Hollower didn't stop with calling the rocks toward him. He waved his hands and spoke and the small rocks melded together, forming a giant stone wall.

He pushed out and the wall careened towards Savashbahar.

She scrambled and dove for cover as the wall shot past to crash into the ruins behind her.

Bruised and battered, Savashbahar fought the instinct to lay there. She got to her feet and tried to put some more cover and distance between her and the Hollower.

"There's no chimney to scurry up this time," the Hollower called. "Nothing to come between our game of cat and mouse, my little hex rat."

"I still stand, the hex rat with a dagger in her teeth," Savashbahar called as she ran through a clearing to a broken wall. "How easy will it be for me to chew through you, a cat without claws, purring his empty threats and yowling fake fear."

That got his ire. He sent his chains smashing through the walls to get to her. She dodged his questing chains easily, her years as Hexenarii making her supremely agile. His anger made her smile with smug satisfaction.

Savashbahar finally made her way back to the caravan. The Hollower's rock assault had crushed the back wagon. Neon blue pools of water and mounds of rice littered the ground.

No one was there.

She turned and found herself facing the Hollower. He grinned at her, malice dancing in her eyes.

"Friends left you, eh?" the Hollower asked as he walked toward her. "I don't blame them. You're a death sentence."

She didn't blame them either. This was her fight. She brandished her dagger, fought down her manufactured fear of him. Not enough to completely dispel the terror, but enough for one final strike.

The Hollower's boots splashed in the water as he stood, reveling in his moment of victory.

"Time to scream, hex rat."

His chains shot out toward her.

She couldn't help her fear. She closed her eyes to it, the way of cowards.

Nothing came. She opened her eyes. The Hollower was shaking in place. Smoke came from him, the sound of his body frying.

He collapsed in the puddle of water. Savashbahar noticed a trail of neon blue going from the puddle. Her eyes followed the line to where it ended.

Several yards away, cleverly hidden in the rubble, were Ruki, Mike and Runt. Mike and Ruki were huddled over the water trail, smoke coming from their lightning gloves.

They hurried to her. The Hollower was coughing, trying to gather his wits. Mike kicked him in the stomach.

"Not so tough when you get set to extra crispy, are you?"

"Please," the Hollower coughed.

Mike gave him another kick in response.

"C'mon, man!" the Hollower cried. "This isn't how this is supposed to end," he said as he looked down the sights of Mike's diskbow.

"This is supposed to be fun," the Hollower continued. "A game, for Christ sake."

Mike raised an eyebrow. "Where are you from?" he asked.

"Chicago," the Hollower answered.

"The Windy City," Mike said.

"Yeah," he said. The Hollower's body wracked from a coughing fit. He spit blood and looked at Mike. "You?"

"I'm from Philly. Or at least was from Philly."

"The City of Brotherly Love," the Hollower responded.

The Hollower laughed and looked at Savashbahar. "You want to kill all the Hollowers, start with your little purple friend here."

The Hollower pointed at Mike, his wicked grin returning. "He's one of us."

Mike kicked him again and again.

"That's where you wrong, dude," Mike said. "There is no us. I ain't nothing like you."

The Hollower's laugh turned into a cough. He wiped the blood from his mouth. "Yeah, that's right, you're playing as the good guy. Well, here's where you let the defeated enemy go, good guy."

Mike shook his head. "I ain't the good guy. I'm the dude you tried to kill. There's real world consequences for that kind of shit, even in fantasy land."

He squeezed the trigger.

Chapter 26

In Mages Hands

Melvin made his way back to the Temple of Houses. He could always check out more of Nasreddin, but the city had lost its appeal. Now it was just a crowded, noisy, annoying place. He couldn't wait to leave.

The temple was considerably more tranquil. No heavy foot traffic or carts groaning or people yelling, just the sound of water cascading down rocks and birds chirping. He found his room, home of the ugly pink bed.

Melvin collapsed on the bed and found no comfort. He was restless, unable to nap.

There was always the High Fane. Melvin left his room and began to explore the new and undiscovered areas of the fortress temple. He found one room that resembled a church, with rows of wooden benches and an altar at the front.

This must be where they talk about how great it is to detain travelers.

He found another room that looked like an art gallery. Many of the pictures were of the gods in epic poses. Nadi the cat was bounding from one tree to another in the jungle. Menanderus the squid was underwater, battling a giant shark with a two pronged spear. Yol was below ground, holding a collapsing tunnel up with his ant strength.

Melvin paused at one picture. The aian in the picture had no discernible animal traits. Instead, the aian was being eaten away by maggots, his body falling apart to rot. The sun was eclipsed behind him, the eerie light playing against a crumbling temple in the backdrop.

"The Fall of Onus," a voice said behind Melvin. He turned to see Mors approaching. Mors stood beside him and looked at the picture as he talked.

"A powerful reminder of what it means to succumb to corruption," he said. His neck scales gleamed in the hazy light of the afternoon sun.

"What happened with this guy?" Melvin asked.

"Onus wasn't honest with himself or the others when he ascended," Mors said. "He didn't want to save aiankind — he wanted power. And someone who hungers for power will always stay hungry.

"Onus got the power he craved, but the corruption cost him. He is bodiless now, an evil force that feeds off his followers. The more followers he can add to his broken house, the more powerful he grows. That is why we are ever watchful of his influence."

Melvin looked at the picture of Onus. His face was tortured. Sickening dead flesh prevailed in the spaces where maggots were absent.

"Who'd want to follow him?" he asked.

"You'd be surprised," Mors replied. "Onus seduces with promises of power. He perverts the marks of the other houses, making them more potent but also more cruel."

Mors took his eyes off the painting to look at Melvin. "That's why Cephrin's arrival in Nasreddin is so important," he said. "The prophecy talks of one without a house, who will rise to reclaim the Twelfth House as his own and restore the broken pantheon."

Again with the prophecy. Melvin was tired of this layover in Nasreddin because of some pie-in-the-sky soothsaying.

"I wish they'd hurry up and make a decision already," Melvin said.

"They have made the decision," Mors said. "It is no accident I found you here. I came to escort you to Indur, who would like to tell you the decree himself."

They made their way to the audience chamber. Melvin's instincts told him not to expect confetti and a big brass parade for Jason's benefit.

When they arrived Indur looked like he was having a bad day. But he always looked mean because of that ridged reptilian forehead.

"We cannot substantiate whether or not Cephrin is truly the one of prophecy," Indur said. "So we will execute him tomorrow morning."

"What?!" Melvin cried. "How does that make any sense?"

"If we could verify his origins and appearance through the words of the prophecy, we would be able to welcome him and the new era he promises. But we cannot, because he claims lost memory, which means he could very likely be an agent of Onus. We cannot afford to take that chance."

"But what if he is the one of prophecy?" Melvin asked. "You just can't execute him!"

"You're right," Indur replied. "If he is the one of prophecy, we'll be unable to execute him. He will be heralded as the Chosen One. But if he does die, then he was clearly sent by the Corrupter to deceive us."

Melvin couldn't believe what he was hearing. If Jason died, which tends to happen at an execution, then he was evil. If he somehow miraculously survived being intentionally killed, then he was clearly prophetically chosen. "What kind of test is that?" he asked.

Indur looked implacable, as mean and cold as ever. "The only valid test we have."

※

Rew Majora sat on Rich's bed, enjoying the closeness sharing a book invited. Half the volume was on her leg, the other half on his. They read poetic passages aloud together, their fingers tracing the ancient language as they read.

"I would endure any hardship," Rich said, reading the modern language. *"Ben herang mushkul tahammul edibilirim,"* he said, switching to the old tongue.

He looked up at Rew, amazement in his eyes.

"This is crazy! Every passage, with the old words and translations. Where'd you find it?"

"It was no small task," she said. "If you notice, it's not a book of magic. I had to thoroughly search the dustiest library shelves to uncover it."

Rich looked back down to the book. He stumbled through the old language of the next line before saying the translation.

"These hardships would be my badge of love," he said. He looked at Rew. "What kind of book is it?"

"It's called *'The Song of Ardor Swain'*. It's one of our oldest written tales, about a youth whose betrothed is kidnapped by a water spirit. He travels the world's seas and rivers in pursuit of the water spirit to rescue his one true love."

Rew closed the book and handed it to him. "Take good care of this, Rich," she said. "There are a few copies in the old tongue and countless copies in modern language, but this was the only one I've found written during the Transition. It's extremely rare."

Rich took the book. "Thank you, Rew. Who doesn't enjoy a good romance novel?" he asked smiling wryly.

He set the book down and grabbed her hand. "And

thank you for showing me Nasreddin," he said, his eyes dancing as he looked at her. "I had a great time with you."

Rew returned his look and nodded. The thrill of this moment made her heart beat faster. Her blood raced with excitement.

Rich leaned forward, slowly closing the already short distance between them.

The door behind Rew burst open and shut with violent haste. It stole Rich's attention, making him jerk back and look up with alarm.

Rew turned to find the warrior girl, ashen faced and panic-stricken.

"They're gonna kill Jason," she said.

"What?!" both Rich and Rew said in unison, alarm in their voices.

The warrior girl went into detail about her conversation with the Elevated of Sen. She spoke only to Rich, as if Rew was invisible.

"Can't you do something?" Rich asked Rew. "Tell the High Fane he's on official mage business?"

"I hold no sway here," Rew said. "The Temple of Houses has always seen the Onesource differently from Seat Esotera. They see it as an entity, a god to worship. We see it as a force, like the wind, to be used for man's betterment. These differing views have caused a rift that makes dialogue between the two towers less than ideal. A human mage of any status hasn't a chance of telling the Council of Thrones what to do with an aian citizen."

"We gotta do something," the warrior girl said. "We can't just let them kill him."

Rew stood up. She drew the hood over her head and brought the folds of the robe up over her nose and mouth.

"I am here as a brown robe, a novice caster. I am no threat as it would appear. We have the element of surprise. Two highly skilled mages should be able to free Jason."

"I'm not exactly a kickball team reject," the warrior girl said, indignation on her face. She pulled out her sword. "I have this, you know."

"My dear, your skills are our last resort," Rew said. "Spilling blood in the Temple of Houses is one of their highest blasphemies. The Hierophane can apologize for a rogue gray robe and his novice accomplice, but bodies strewn through the High Fane would be nothing short of an act of war. Your edged weapon would only hurt our cause."

Rew looked at the girl. The sword trembled slightly in her hands as she returned it to its scabbard. She was still so far from her true potential.

"Besides," Rew said, "you are far from ready, girl. I see the fear of upcoming battle in your eyes."

The warrior girl glared at Rew. "I'm not," she said, gritting her teeth all the while, "a girl."

There was no time for this. "And I am not here to discuss your nature or preferences, dear. Now, hurry to your room and pack your things," Rew said.

She looked at Rich. "You too. As much as I delight in your new look, I think it's best if you don the robe again. It is a primary tool for a mage in the heat of combat."

Rich nodded. He had a focused determination in his eyes as he set his jaw. It was the look of a man ready for battle.

He unbuttoned his shirt and turned around to gather his robe. When he took the shirt off, he displayed the chiseled back muscles of a man half his age. A feminine gasp, barely audible, hit Rew's ears.

She turned to the warrior girl. She was still as a doll, her eyes locked on Rich's body.

"I told you to pack," Rew said.

The girl dry swallowed, nodded, and fled the room. Rew stayed and helped Rich gather his things. When his bag was packed, she looked over his robe, adjusting it in places.

"Remember, Rich, bend the robe. Alter it. It is an extension of you, a primary material for you to exercise your will over."

"I remember. A highly effective battlemage bends and alters."

Behind Rich, the glowlights had come on and the waterfall garden carried the gloom of night quickly approaching.

She touched his face. "Stay safe. Now let's save your friend."

Rew opened the door. Without warning, she bent her robes. The sleeves shot out, smashing the two guards in the back of the head. She used the sleeves to pull the unconscious guards into the room.

Rich led the way to Melvin's room. When they got there, Rich bent his robes, making the sleeves smack the guards in the face. The force smashed the backs of their heads into the wall. They crumpled to the floor.

"Be prepared," Rew said as Rich and the warrior girl stowed the unconscious bodies. "It will not be this easy where we're headed. No doubt they have Jason quartered in the Overwatch. We'd need the full force of the Hierophane to go against the guard directly. We must rely on subterfuge where we can."

Rich and the warrior girl were fairly adept at keeping noiseless footfalls, making it easier to navigate around the roving patrols. Moving through the temple bred a high caliber of danger. The chameleon followers of Sen could blend to look like part of a deserted hallway. One look from a follower of Yol and their unauthorized presence would be broadcasted through the hive mind.

They took every new corridor and hallway with care. Rew didn't know how long she had before either the unconscious guards came to or the roving patrols raised the alarm because the guards were missing from their posts. Either way, she knew time was growing ever shorter.

She peeked around the latest corner and her hopes for a smooth rescue dwindled. Five armsguards watched the ramp leading up to the Overwatch.

"House of Yol, three of them," Rew said. "We can't take the chance of them alerting the hive."

Rich looked for himself. "I think I have something that'll work. Get ready to go around opposite of my direction."

Before Rew could protest or ask what his plans were, Rich cast illusionary fire on himself. He looked like he was burning, but it was a harmless trick for novices.

He ran out from cover, screaming and flailing his arms.

"Help me! Auugh!! It burns!" he cried, running into the adjacent waterfall garden.

Four of the guards set off after him, the fifth stayed at the Overwatch ramp, but even he got near the end of the ramp so he could see some hint of the action.

Rew and the warrior girl moved with the opportunity. They snuck past the remaining guard, who was looking at the other four hard at work putting out the fire blazing in the garden.

The two of them were now safely in the Overwatch, but how was Rich going to make it to them?

Just as soon as Rew asked the question to herself did

Rich come running into view behind them.

"I knew it would work," he said with heavy breaths as he tried to recover from the run.

"How?" Rew asked.

"A guy on fire's bound to get people's attention," Rich said. "Once I had that, I killed the fire spell on me and lit up some of the shrubs. Aian eyes aren't too keen at night. I figured they'd think the fire blazing in the garden was me. You know, the old bait and switch."

"Clever," Rew said smiling.

They rounded the corner and an armsguard from House Nadi sprang into action. Rew sent her sleeves at him, but the guard easily dodged them with his cat-like agility. The guard ran up the wall and jumped over Rich's bent sleeves. He ran fast at them, sword raised and voice yelling alarm.

Rew began speaking a creation spell, a passageway through solid rock.

Rich was trying vainly to hit the nimble cat with his sleeves.

Rew focused on creating the passageway. She needed to build a tunnel from this room to the one below.

The armsguard lunged at Rew, his sword's edge wicked and close.

The building material for the tunnel was her robe.

The aian's sword met Rew's robe as the robe collapsed, taking Rew and the armsguard with it as it reshaped itself into the floor. Rew, wearing the robe, was safely anchored. The armsguard wasn't and found himself falling through. The temple's high ceilings did not lend themselves to the aian's plight as he landed with a crunch on the level below.

Killing her will to maintain the passageway, it closed, causing the floor to push Rew and her robe back up. Rich and the warrior girl looked at her with new eyes.

"Sweet!" Rich said.

"The alarm is raised," Rew said. "We must be quick."

The three of them ran through the Overwatch. The only factor to guide Rew to Jason was guard density. Between her and Rich, they were able to robe bend and alter through two packs of guards. Their large numbers in such a small space allowed the mages to grab the guards with their sleeves and use them as blunt clubs on the others.

They turned a corner to a ramp that ran upwards for several spans. A solitary iron door stood at the end of the ramp. Around that door stood five aians of the House of Demir, included the house's Elevated. They made no move toward them, but rather stood their ground, waiting.

Jason must be in there.

"Hold trespassers," a voice called behind them.

Rew turned and saw Ananna with a legion of guards. The last time she had seen the goddess was ten years ago at a nasran-aian peace agreement. Tonight the Queen of Spiders had a wrathful countenance.

"You humans think to overturn the will of Immortals? There will be no quarter for those who seek to profane this sacred hall with violence."

One moment Ananna was aian, the next she was a monstrously massive spider. She was fearsome, with a bloated green, purple, and black body and venom dripping from her mandibles. The spider leapt.

Rich spoke. The look on his face was of sheer terror yet the words came fast, smooth, eloquent. Rew could only pick up parts of the spell, it was so intricately layered.

A destruction spell for stone, a creation spell for wind, altering spells for rock, all tied together throughout with binding spells and bending spells that hinted at length and height, density and distance.

At the end of his incantation, Rich pushed out with his hands and the walls of the High Fane in front of him literally broke apart. Rew watched in mute disbelief as Rich pushed the part of the fortress containing Ananna and her guardsmen off the mountain. The huge block of temple fell, disappearing into the darkness below.

Rew stared at the chasm that now existed between them and the remaining Overwatch. It was as if Rich had been a giant with a hot knife. He had carved out a section of the Temple of Houses like a piece of cake.

"Blessed Onesource," she said.

Rich looked at her like he was an errant boy caught without an excuse.

"Get your heads back in the game," the warrior girl said. "We still got the flyboys at the door."

They closed the distance to the door, but none of the guards pulled their weapons. Instead, they bowed, led by the Elevated of Demir. Rew remembered him as Targhos.

"We prayed to the Onesource you would come," Targhos said. "We stand ready to fly you all and the Chosen One to safety."

"What of the decree of the Council of Thrones?" Rew asked.

"Their decree is that Cephrin be executed. If he is truly the one of prophecy, his premature death would be impossible," Targhos said. "But the House of Demir believes ordinary people are the agents of miraculous works. You are here, are you not? Ready to bring the Temple of Houses down around us to rescue Cephrin. Your very arrival here is the work of miracles; the House of Demir is at your disposal."

The warrior girl rushed past the aians and opened the door. Jason was there, in a room without roof or walls overlooking a severe drop to the ground below. A look of relief played across Jason's features.

"God, I'm glad you guys are here," he said. "We gotta bail, these jerks want to kill me."

Rew and Rich entered the room, followed by Targhos and his guard. Rew looked at Targhos.

"Please, fly us to the Mage Delegation Tower."

"At once, Hierophant," Targhos said with a slight bow.

Rew instinctively felt the folds of robe covering her nose and mouth.

"Your cover is intact," Targhos said. "But a novice robe doesn't give directives when a mage of gray is present. Worry not; your secret is safe with House Demir."

Rew nodded her thanks. She would have to trust Targhos, as she had little alternative.

Targhos raised his head to the night sky and he and the guards of House Demir unfurled their wings in unison. The feathery span of them all made the guardsmen seem bigger than the room.

"Epic," Jason said in awe.

It was a quick, uninterrupted flight to the tower. Targhos and the guards set them down at the entrance.

"Safe travels, Chosen One," Targhos said before he and his contingent flew away into the night.

Rew took down her hood and led the others into the tower. Inside, she created a bowl of water and held it out to Jason. Without any other prompting, Jason pulled off a bone finger and dropped it in.

"Northeast," he said before the finger settled to reveal the direction. He had called it true.

"The Hierophane has only one portal northeast of Nasreddin," Rew said, "the mountain pass town of Nev Shahir."

She looked at the Breunan, the tower keeper. "Bring him a brown robe," she said, pointing to Jason. The brown robe nodded and disappeared down a corridor.

"Nev Shahir sits at the only pass through the Eural Mountains," Rew said. "It is trade lands, full of many different races."

Breunan returned promptly, offering the brown robe in his hands to Jason.

"Put it on," Rew said. "Keep your head down and your arm covered. Word of what transpired here will follow you to Nev Shahir through the House of Yol."

Rew opened the portal to Nev Shahir. A fully robed Jason was the first to enter, followed by the warrior girl. Rich looked at Rew.

"You should come with us," Rich said. "It's not safe for you here."

"I have portal waiting to take me back to the Hierophane," Rew said. "Where I'll be standing ready to apologize to the High Fane for a rogue gray robe and his apprentice."

Rich hesitated as if he was searching for the right thing to say. He looked at the portal and back to Rew like he wasn't sure how long the magic would last.

"Screw it," he said.

He stepped forward. He grabbed her and gently, strongly, surely pulled her close.

His lips found hers.

Rew felt her body melt in his arms, his kiss weaving powerful magic in its own right. It turned a moment into something timeless.

Then Rich was saying goodbye and disappearing into the portal, taking with him something indefinable from Rew but leaving her with so much more.

Chapter 27

Murderous Trip

Rich looked at the nighttime Hierophane library, with its ornate wood furniture and silver trinkets gleaming softly in the lamplight, and breathed a quiet sigh of comfort. He looked at his space, beyond the dividing line of the scry, to the dark, rocky expanse that came with being in the foothills of the Eural Mountains. Once again, he wasn't putting up his fair share.

He looked at Rew. Lovely in her green nightgown, her smile told him she didn't mind at all. Dark curls framed her face. Sexy.

"You," Rich said, "this… it's the best part of being on the road."

Truth be told, the scry was the only good thing to being on the road. They had left Nev Shahir as quickly as they had arrived, using the cover of night to make a clean break with Jason huddled under his brown robe. Once clear of the city, they traveled along the foothills of the Eural Mountains, to some unknown destination Jason felt in his bones.

After only one day of walking over rock-strewn ground with wind gusts blasting dirt and small gravel in their faces, he already missed Rew and their time together in Nasreddin.

"You feel this is the best part of our separation?" Rew asked, her smile sly. "Because I was planning to make it much better."

Her hand reached out to him. Rich looked on in shock when her fingers kept going past the dividing line of the scry to touch his face. All this time, he had just assumed they couldn't go past the line. He had never bothered to test the boundary. He thought about this new discovery and the needing a bowl of water to scry thing and came to the conclusion that he needed to stop guessing at the rules.

He welcomed the surprise as eagerly as he welcomed Rew into his arms. Her kisses were hot, passionate. He met them with equal ardor.

She pulled away. Her look was one of absolute horror.

"What?" he asked in alarm. "What is it?"

Rich saw his reflection in the library's full mirror. He looked down at his hands, gnarled and covered with liver spots. Then he looked back up in the mirror and his trembling, wrinkled hands touched his face, a face now decrepit and withered with age. His eyes were sunken into bony cheeks. Thin strands of gray hair clung to his liver spotted skull.

Rew laughed at him. She was still young, still beautiful.

"How did you think this was going to end?" she asked. "Rew Majora is virtually immortal and you—you already have one foot in the grave."

Rich felt his teeth falling out, one by one. The nature of all this unnatural horror made it clear what this was. He pointed a bony finger at Rew, his voice husky with age.

"Richard Bates," he said.

Rew smiled. "Richard Bates, Rew Majora, I am both of these and neither. I'm the cost, Razzleblad, here to remind you that power comes at a price."

Rich's horror turned to anger. Using Rew to get under his skin felt like a low blow, nothing short of a mental kick in his balls.

"That the best you got?" Rich asked, his geezer voice cracking as he spoke. He shook his fist, "I'll get you, you young hooligan!"

"You think this is funny?" Rew asked, her face turning serious. "This isn't some random villager up in flames, mage. What you're looking at is your heart's reality."

Now Rew laughed, a sharp, derisive knife in Rich's ears.

"You stupid kid," she said. "You're not looking at some theoretical future of what happens if you go mad. You're looking at fact. You will see Rew Majora forever as this, while you become that ancient, decrepit bag of skin and bones you see in the mirror. This is your future together. And that is unchangeable, no matter what you do, no matter how sane you are."

Rew circled him, talking in a taunting whisper.

"How funny do you think it'll be for her? A woman locked in the prime of her life watching you waste away; cleaning the shit and piss you soil yourself in, wiping the dribbles of slobber from your wrinkled lips."

Rew got in his face, close enough to smell the sweetness in her breath as she whispered venom.

"She's lived for over three hundred years. What makes you think she has it in her to suffer through burying another lover? What makes you think she'll want to put her heart into you, Razzleblad? You're just a kid with most of his life already eaten away. Gone," Rew said, snapping her fingers, "just like that."

Rich roared, enraged. He pushed at Rew, wanting to push away the reality she presented.

Instead of pushing, his hands came up wielding fire. The fire spread to Rew's face. She screamed in pain.

They were no longer standing, but sitting next to each other as they had been when the scry first started. Only now the magic fire was burning Rew. She screamed at Rich and reached for him, but was unable to touch him through the dividing line of the scry.

"Why?" she screamed through the fire. "You're hallucinating! Stop the spell, please!"

He didn't know how to stop it. The cost had come in the middle of the scry and—

"No!" Rich cried, "God, no! I can't! I don't know how!" he yelled. But his words didn't help Rew, who had opened her mind to him and received uncontrolled mage fire as result.

Rich yelled again, this scream following him into the waking world. The sun was just beginning its climb above the foothills. Melvin and Jason stopped stowing their gear to look at him.

"Glad to see you're violently awake," Jason said.

Rich grabbed his chest, where his heart was thudding in panic. He didn't know for sure, he just didn't know.

Was what just happened all cost, or part cost? Did he leave a real scry with Rew burning?

He looked around for something, anything to think it through. The sun's light answered his question. It was night in the scry, even near the end. It had been all cost.

Only now did he let out his bated breath. Melvin and Jason had begun packing again. Melvin spared a moment to look at Rich.

"You OK?"

"Yeah. Yeah, I'm OK."

"Those must be some seriously twisted dreams."

Rich swallowed and nodded. He didn't bother to explain or elaborate. He got out of his bedroll and began to stow his gear.

This is how day two started in the foothills of the Eural Mountains.

Time passed slow and uneventful. The only sound

between conversation was the click of their boots against loose rocks and the occasional howl of wind gusts. Conversation could only last so long. The dead space of silence seemed like a heavy burden they all shouldered as they made their way down one hill and up another.

"Anybody else got that going to Mordor feeling?" Jason asked.

They all laughed. And the mood lightened. The next round of conversation lasted a while, relieving them of the burden of silence until dusk approached.

Rich cast a fire. They all settled down around it, watching the remaining day seep away as they ate pack rations. When Rich was done, he took out the *Song of Ardor Swain* and his spellbook.

He had always liked puzzles, ciphers, and cryptograms. Trying to translate Kaftar Friese's spell page was a welcome diversion. He kept his spellbook open to the transcribed page, and placed the *Song of Ardor Swain* between the spell book pages, looking for words that matched.

By the time his eyes lifted from the pages, he had made serious headway. He had found a few words for most of the spells, including one of the words for the spell he had to cast. The spell was called "Something Something Chain".

Rich looked past the campfire to Jason and Melvin, both sound asleep in the dark of night. He hadn't realized how much time had passed since dusk.

Apparently, Jason and Melvin had nominated Rich for first watch. Jason had left out his hourglass, one of his rewards from the Sentry Triptoe fiasco. All the sand had settled to the bottom for who knew how long.

He woke Jason for watch before settling into his bedroll. But Rich didn't want sleep. The thought was there, hovering.

He knew what he wanted, and ignoring the thought only made it buzz louder.

Rich gave into it. He created a bowl of water and set it down next to his bedroll. The he cast the spell for a scry.

He turned and saw Rew's bedroom. She was sitting on a bed of soft looking white blankets, wearing the green nightgown he had recently set her on fire in.

"Rich," she said, smiling. "I was hoping you would scry with me tonight."

Rich thought of their kiss in Nasreddin. "You were?"

"Of course," she said, brushing loose strands of hair from her cheek. "Portaling you all to the base of the Eural Mountains with no resupply or transportation was far from the perfect way to enable your quest. How do you all fare?"

"Not bad," Rich said, a little let down her hopes were business-oriented. "Jason feels we're really close to the monster, maybe a couple of days walk."

"Excellent," Rew said. Silence prevailed between them for a moment before Rew smiled and spoke.

"I know your customs are as foreign to me as my customs must be to you, but here you're supposed to say 'thank you' when a girl invites you to her bedroom at night."

Embarrassment hit Rich like a hammer. "I, I'm sorry, I didn't know it was your bedroom."

"I knew it. And I still invited you. There are only a couple of things a woman expects from a man she invites into her bedroom at night, and a 'thank you' is one of that couple."

"Thank you," Rich said smiling.

Rew wasn't smiling. Her face was ashen, aghast.

Rich looked down at his hands—wrinkled, spotted, old. His eyes came up to the mirror, where he was a raspy, rickety, ancient man.

Rich looked at Rew Majora, his new Richard Bates, as she laughed with glee.

"C'mon," Rich said with his age-rusted voice. "Isn't the same thing a bit tired?"

"There's a lesson to be had in the same thing," Rew said. "And after you've paid, I'm sure you'll come up with the theme. You are, after all, a smart boy turned clever old man."

"So, this is how I'm going to spend this cost? With your grandpa jokes?"

"Why, Razzleblad, I'm offended," Rew said smiling. "I'm being generous. I'm giving you another future look at a tender love moment."

Rich felt his right side go numb. He tried to yell out but the words all came out as mush. Then he collapsed on the floor. His brain burned with pain and was unable to speak, unable to do anything but convulse as the pain shook his body.

Rew kneeled over him, concern etched in her features. "Rich!" she shouted. "Rich!"

Richard Bates in his black suit stood over Rich as he convulsed and Rew as she knelt over him crying in panic.

"You're having a stroke, old man," Richard Bates told him. "This is how you die, Razzleblad. This will be Rew Majora's last memory of you—you decrepit, tired, spasming to death on the floor."

Rew was crying, asking Rich to say something, to come back to her. Rich fought against the paralysis, raged against the helplessness he suffered.

He was able to lash out and grab Rew. But his hands came up with fire. The fire spread to Rew's face, where she screamed in pain.

Now they sat on her bed, as they had been when the scry first started. And the scene played out as it did last time, with Rew burning and Rich unable to stop the destruction he had caused.

Rich woke up just like before, screaming and unable to determine if any of it had been real. This time it was still night out, no sunlight to answer the question.

Melvin came over, it being his watch.

"I'm sorry, about what you're going through," Melvin said.

Rich nodded. He looked down beside his bedroll. The bowl of water he had conjured was still there.

"I don't know," Rich said. His eyes searched the darkness frantically for a way to work through it. "I just don't know."

"Know what?" Melvin asked.

Rich didn't speak the problem. The bowl told him he had set up to scry. The cost didn't start at any place identifiable. When did the real Rew stop speaking and the cost Rew start? Did he ever get to speak to the real Rew at all? These questions bandied back and forth in his brain but the big question loomed, ever-present, unanswerable.

Did he burn her mind away?

"I don't know!" Rich yelled in anguish.

"Shaddup," Jason muttered half asleep as he turned away in his bedroll.

Feminine arms came from behind him to circle around his chest. A soft, beautiful voice next to his ear whispered.

"Calm. Remember, it's not real. Calm."

Rich leaned back into the embrace. He couldn't trust what he saw. The cost wanted his madness. So he put faith in the voice. It told him it wasn't real; he wanted desperately to believe in that. Rich closed his eyes and relaxed in the arms that held him.

Before Rich knew it, he was stirring awake to the others packing in the morning sun. Wordlessly, he got up and stowed his gear.

The mood was even more somber today than it was yesterday. Silence sat on all their shoulders, heavier than the packs on their backs. Jason tried to introduce conversation, but Rich and apparently Melvin didn't feel like talking.

Rich felt old. He looked over to Melvin. He noticed her looking at him, concern and something else on her face, and whenever he met her eyes, she'd look away.

She. Rich had grown so used to seeing Melvin as a beautiful woman he almost forgot there was a dude underneath. He couldn't recall Melvin's real face. He could only see Zhufira, smiling or being worrisome or looking beautifully fierce. She felt realer than the kid from the burbs he used to know.

The landscape failed to change. Only Jason could measure progress. "Almost there," he said as the day waned, the sun setting over the mountains.

He looked at Rich. "Campfire time," he said.

"No."

Jason smiled. "C'mon. You're playing, right?"

Rich dug in his pack for his ornate tinderbox, the only gift he had accepted from the people of Triptoe. He tossed it at Jason.

"You want a fire, get to work."

"Seriously? You want me to smack rocks together and blow at sparks all night when it takes you half a second to make it happen? C'mon dude, get it crackling before it gets dark."

"Don't you fucking get it?" Rich snapped. "I'm only casting one more spell," he said, holding up a finger. "One.

And this isn't it. You want a fire, make a fire."

Rich walked away from the camp and from Jason's mumbling remarks. He looked down at the red gemstone on the ring Druze had given him. If it was marginalizing the cost, Rich sure couldn't see it. He paid the same price for conjuring a bowl of water and a camp fire as he did for going super Razzleblad and cleaving apart a piece of the High Fane.

That was it.

This was the lesson Richard Bates wanted to teach him. Small magic, big magic, it didn't matter—his price would be the same.

This ran contrary to what Rew had told him and what he had read in the *Birleshik Arcana*. Cost grows as spell power grows. Mages simply can't cast above their present level until they've mastered the level they're on. And once you master a certain level, the cost for levels below becomes almost negligible.

But he had never mastered any level. He was a novice, inside a body that touted some of the highest levels of spellcraft a human could wield. Razzleblad's mind was tempered to the cost. Rich's mind was baby fresh and raw to it.

He looked out at the barren landscape, darkening quickly as the sun threw its purple-hued death throes. Rich turned around to the camp, where Jason's sour look was illuminated by a small, sad campfire.

Jason tossed Rich his tinderbox as he approached the campsite.

"I hope this means you won't scream us out of our sleep tonight and you'll start tomorrow off without your period," Jason said.

"You never know," Rich said. The period remark made him look at Melvin, who looked away, cheeks reddening.

Rich did the same thing he did last night, attempt to translate Kaftar's spell. He managed to translate three other spells on the page.

The first was called "Equal Hardship" and it was ludicrous. The spell turned someone to stone at the cost of turning yourself into stone as well. Why the hell would anyone do that?

The others two were better, still a bit crazy but not outright suicidal. "Cursed Footsteps" made the caster lame for two hours but paralyzed everyone in the immediate area for twice as long. The other was "Mind Erosion," where he could erase a selective memory from another mind at the expense of having a random memory of his own erased. That seemed kind of useful, but kind of dangerous too.

None of this helped him figure out his spell. He got another word out of the title, leaving him with the ominous sounding "Life Something Chain."

He looked up from the books, his eyes strained and his body fatigued. Everyone else was out again, with the hourglass out of sand. Rich settled into his bedroll after waking Jason.

Thoughts of Rew started to buzz in his head. Was she OK?

He stopped himself. Not knowing was murder. But finding out could kill her.

One more spell, he told himself.

Chapter 28

Olukent

Melvin should have been elated when Jason pointed with his bone fingers at the town in the distance. Getting here meant the end of a hard road and life in the wrong body. Instead of elation, there was only a choking sense of dread.

The town was nondescript, like a mountain version of Triptoe. But above the town sat a massive cave carved into the hillside. Perfectly round, the cave gaped open like the gigantic maw of a hungry beast.

That's where Jason's finger pointed. Melvin guessed it wouldn't be monsterly enough for the black creature to hang out at the local pub.

"Well, guess we should end some evil, right?" Melvin asked the guys.

"You ready to cleave some zombies?" Jason asked. "Town's probably crawling with them."

The town wasn't. Living people milled about the town. Not a lot of people, but everyone there was very much alive. The first man to see the three of them smiled warmly at them.

"Welcome to Olukent," he said, taking particular notice of Melvin. "I knew the master's message was going to spread, but, my, I never expected it to reach all the way down to the Transvaal."

"Funny how word spreads," Melvin said.

"Well, you all have gotten here just in time," the man said. "We've less than three days left until the Rising."

The man looked around with a question on his face, like

the newcomers were missing something. "Where are your bodies?"

"Um…" Melvin began.

"They're close," Jason filled in. "We weren't sure how this all worked, so we wanted to come and investigate first."

The man looked shocked. "You have heard Master Izal's message, yes?"

"Meh. A little," Jason said, shaking his hand so-so style. "You know how word gets when it spreads, the message gets twisted around."

The man looked in awe at the death hand Jason shook casually. He stared at Jason. "You've been touched—directly—by the Death Null?"

"Yeah," Jason said, looking like he was bored with the conversation. "Kinda why we're here."

The man brought his head down. "I am not worthy to speak to you," he said. "You are a portent of the Death Null's promise. Please, come, you must meet Master Izal."

He led the way to the inn, where a small crowd had gathered around one man who looked like a cross between mage and clown. He wore black robes covered with white polka dots. His face was white from caked powder, his lips red from what could only be lipstick. The guy was talking to the people in a calm, soothing voice, like he was teaching little kids Sunday school.

"Master," the man interrupted. "I've brought more to the fold. One, the aian, has been directly touched by the Death Null."

The man's powder face cracked as his ruby lips widened into a heartwarming smile. "Burru, you have done well." His attention returned to the crowd. "Excuse me, my children, I have much to discuss with our new friends."

The crowd left without a word. Master Izal looked at Jason like he was Jesus Christ.

Melvin shuddered. He hoped this wasn't another Chosen One episode. How many freaking messiahs did this world have?

"I am honored to be in the presence of one who the Death Null has directly touched," Izal said with a bow. "None of us have earned its grace yet, not even I."

"Yeah, that's why we're here," Jason said. "We wanted to experience more Death Null and we heard a little of your message, but we didn't get it all. So what's your message?"

Izal smiled. "Why, brother, you've arrived at the gathering place fortuitously. In less than three days time the Death Null will stop taking our offerings, and grace our lost loved ones with his gift."

"What offerings?" Jason asked. "What gift?"

Izal frowned. "It's tragic, how distorted the message becomes once it leaves the hearth," he said. He explained, maintaining his eerie bible-study sermon voice.

"I told all interested in gaining new life for their loved ones to bring their treasured remains along with a stranger's corpse. The Death Null resurrects them both at the mouth of the cave. We allow the stranger to roam into the cave as an offering and the loved one we escort to the town jail."

Jason scratched his head, confusion all over his face. "Why do you lock your loved ones up?" he asked.

Izal laughed, a good-natured, friendly sound that ran contrary to the freakish look he sported. "Our loved ones would wander into the cave with the offering corpses and would be forever lost to us. The resurrection is incomplete, you see. Our loved ones are just a roaming shadow of their former selves until the Death Null bestows its grace. But when its grace comes, in less than three days now, all of our loved ones will be restored, body and mind."

Despite Izal's attempt at explanation, Jason looked more confused than ever. Maybe he just couldn't believe what the hell Izal was saying.

"What'd everyone do in this town before the Death Null showed up?"

"Why, this old mining town has been abandoned for countless ages," Izal said. "Our family comes here once a year at the start of autumn, to practice our resurrection rituals. We have done so without fail for centuries. This year we have been blessed with our unwavering faith by the coming of the Death Null. And in three days its grace will fall upon us."

"One more question," Jason said. "Why do you think its grace is falling in three days?"

"Our loved ones tell us," Izal answered. "In fact, since resurrecting that's all our loved ones say. They speak in unison the days left to make offerings, counting down starting seven days ago when the first of them rose. Now they uniformly say three days."

Izal put his hand on Jason's shoulder. "You all have come just in time, brother." He looked past them like he had just missed something important.

"Where are your loved ones and your offerings?"

"They're on the way," Jason said. "Our resident mage will send word right away. You'll see, gonna bring an army of offerings for Death Null."

"Glorious," Izal said. "If you excuse me, I must see to my children."

Alone in the inn now, Jason turned to the others, his voice a harsh whisper.

"Dude, we're in the middle of a resurrection cult!"

"So?" Melvin asked. "I say we head into the cave and catch us a Death Null."

"We can't just march in there," Jason said. "You think these cultists are going to stand by while we stop their Death Null from dropping grace on them? We've gotta sneak in."

Jason was right. They needed to make the cave without being seen. Getting discovered meant having a murderous town at their backs and a legion of zombie offerings at their front.

They walked around the town, assessing their options. The cultists approached them and talked with serene optimism, like Ritalin kids waiting for Christmas. Melvin kept his smile pleasant and his eyes peeled.

By the time they had talked to everyone and mapped the town out, it was late afternoon. One of the cultists, Crispin or Crispy or whatever, came rushing out of the jail.

"Two days! Two days!" he yelled.

Great. Death Null wasn't on standard time. One thing all three of them universally agreed on, whatever it had in store in two days probably wasn't good.

Getting to Death Null didn't look good either. The only way to the cave was through a building at the base of the hill. That building was heavily guarded by at least eight nutjobs with swords. Izal called them the protectors of the flock. Melvin called them impossible to get past.

"Maybe the guards don't hang out in the building all night," Melvin suggested.

"I'll take a look late in the night," Jason said. "We'll see."

Jason got V.I.P. treatment around the town. Everyone loved him. Two of the cultists even gave up their room in the packed inn for Jason and his friends. That's where the three of them were now, in the small, dusty room sitting on either of the two beds discussing strategy.

Jason popping over to the guardhouse in the wee hours wouldn't cause suspicion. Mage-clown Izal said he was even free to go into the cave to audience with the Death Null. Too bad Izal said Melvin and Rich weren't worthy, otherwise there'd be no need for subterfuge.

"I'm an awesome gamer," Jason said. "But this is starting to look like a quest that needs a bigger group."

"Well, we can cut down the guards," Melvin said a little half-heartedly. He didn't relish the thought of killing guys just doing their job, but they were devoutly in the way and he wasn't about to scrub the mission. "After that, I can bolt and lock the guard house and defend it while you two track down and capture Death Null."

"Can't," Jason said shaking his head. "My arrows are useless against the zombies. And Rich would be even worse."

"How can I be worse than your useless arrows?" Rich asked indignantly.

"Even if you were the magefire slut I wish you'd be, these zombies are numb puppets. They're kept up by magic more than their meat. You go flaming zombies and all you'll do is create a bunch of walking bonfires begging for a hug."

Jason looked at Melvin. "We need someone who can hack these zombies down. Arms, legs, heads have to come clean off. Rich and I can grab swords off the guards and help, but the two of us alone won't get far if they're swarming."

Melvin got up from the bed and looked out the window. Early evening cast the town in dark spots filled in with the flickering light of several torches. People were still out and about greeting one another, talking and laughing peacefully. These folks were peaceful because all was right in their universe. Soon as that paradigm shifted they'd be grabbing their torches and pitchforks.

"All three of us going into the cave means a whole angry town at our backs," Melvin said. He turned to face the guys. "It's suicide."

"It's looking like our only option," Jason said. "But they're people, angry, nut-filled loon or otherwise, I can shoot them down and Rich can flame them up while you work out on the zombies in front of us."

"Don't you remember Fort Law?" Melvin asked. "Nothing stays dead around this thing. All you'll be doing is creating more zombies, and Rich would be making flaming zombies. In the end, we'll being stuck in the middle of a zombie sandwich as the fresh meat."

They were quiet for awhile. Melvin chewed his lip and went over all the factors again, like the perfect solution was there, waiting for him to discover it. Nothing came.

"I'll check in at the guard house at like two, three in the morning," Jason said. "We may be able to sneak past the guards. We don't have a lot of time to plan, but we have some. Let's make the most of it."

After all their talking, the only thing they could agree to do was wait until later. Rich took out his books and began reading like he had done every night since leaving Nasreddin. Jason took off downstairs.

"Crazy people like drinking too," he said with a shrug. "Just the fact that we're setting up to do this job means there's a place at the bar for me."

Melvin didn't have a thirst. Being cooped up in this little room didn't hold any appeal either. He settled for walking about the town, hoping to find a yet undiscovered option.

The cultists greeted and exchanged small talk with him as he explored the streets. They talked about their loved ones and all the things they were planning to do once the shuffling dead were restored to life. Melvin tried to imagine all these folks with rage on their faces, him cutting them down with his bastard sword.

It's twisted. But you just might have to kill every one of them, he thought.

Melvin found no secret ways to the cave. It'd have to be the guard house. No miraculous better option came to him in a moment of inspiration. Eventually, he found his way back to the inn room.

Jason was still gone. Rich, still reading, didn't even look up as Melvin entered the room. Melvin took the empty bed and turned towards the wall in an attempt to sleep.

A vigorous shake roused him. Melvin didn't know how he had found sleep, but he did until that happened. He turned, squinting in the light of the room. Jason stood over him. Rich was awake on his bed, looking up from his pages at Jason.

"Bad news," Jason said, looking tired. "They go down to six guards at night, two asleep in different corners. Even if Lady Luck was on our side and strip-teasing to distract the guards, odds are we can't stop all six from yelling out and waking the town."

Jason shooed at Melvin with his bone hand. "Move over. We'll plan in the morning. Sleep now."

Melvin had to dodge Jason's hefty aian frame as he dove onto the mattress. He stood, looking at Jason, whose body sprawled haphazardly across the mattress.

Rich closed his book.

"Over here," he said, putting the books into his robe. "I'm not as bulky as Jason anyway."

Rich turned to face the wall, leaving a decent amount of mattress space empty. It was better than the floor. Melvin sat on the bed and noticed something missing.

"No bowl of water tonight?" he asked.

Rich didn't turn from the wall. "No. No water," he said.

Melvin lay back to back with Rich. If nothing else, he was eager to get back to sleep.

He was semi-conscious when he first heard Jason's voice. Before that, he had only a sense of comfort. His hand had found a soft, ruffled pillow that felt good to rub back and forth. Then Jason had said something and it jarred the comfort.

"Awkward," was what he said.

Melvin's eyes opened and the situation became clear. Rich was asleep next to him, but sometime during the night his hand had found Melvin's hips. Melvin's hand had found Rich's hair, which he had been tousling as Rich breathed heavily into his neck.

They were spooning.

"This is his fault," Melvin said, rising to a sitting position as Rich kept slumbering.

Jason's eyes danced as he looked at Melvin. "You're becoming more Zhufira, I mean, more woman, every day."

Melvin laughed. "I was minding my business. He spooned me."

Jason shook his head. "I can see farther. Rich wheezes when he runs. We're all slaves of some kind to our bodies."

Melvin thought about Nasreddin. Rich in his new clothes popped into his mind. He choked out the visual. It was something he didn't want to think about.

"All the better we hurry up and get back, then, isn't it?" Melvin asked.

"You bet," Jason said behind a wan smile.

They woke Rich with little planned other than to watch the town. Perhaps an opportunity would present itself. If nothing changed, the standing plan was still to run into the guardhouse at two in the morning and start carnage.

Out in the streets, the morning autumn air was crisp. Melvin was glad the Hierophant had given him the cloak. This mountain town was no place for underdressed warrior girls.

An hour of watching the town yielded nothing but pleasant cultists going about the start of their day. Some hauled barrels, others moved wheelbarrows full of random materials and still others did nothing but roam about being friendly. Then Melvin saw dust rise in the distance, moving toward the town.

Melvin started to worry as the dust column grew closer. With their luck, it'd be an army of resurrection seekers, all with their two corpse minimum. They should have just gone in last night, unprepared as they were.

The thing stirring the dust got clearer at the edge of town. It was a rickety half-tank, half-train that barely moved faster than a power walk, it was so beaten up and broken looking. A guy in goggles drove it.

Melvin's breath caught in his throat. Next to the guy driving was a big man he instantly recognized. Runt Half-weagr. Right beside Runt was a little megrym, smiling a slick smile at Melvin like he had just bet the devil himself and won.

Chapter 29

Family

Mike was welcomed to Olukent by a parade of hugs. Not just his brother, but by Melvin's two friends too. Then Jason and Rich went to hug Runt up, leaving Melvin to spout a million things at Mike.

"How'd you find me?" Melvin asked. "Man, I'm so glad you're here. I was so worried after Fort Law. This is incredible. Now I don't have to search all over this world for you after we're done here and we can all go home and forget this ever happened. Aw man, it's so good to see you, you just don't know."

"It's good to see you too, bruh," Mike said, stepping back from his brother's embrace. "It's no accident I'm here. I owe it all to Savvy's mojo," he finished, pointing to Savashbahar.

Savashbahar harrumphed and retreated from the group, going instead to lean against the stopped caravan. She was still mad at Mike for being a Hollower, even accused him of lying in his shimmer. Even though he had apologized and explained it all and told her he hadn't known, she wasn't about to smile about it. He couldn't blame her; no matter how you sliced it, it had to feel like cavorting with the enemy.

Probably didn't set good with her coming to meet a whole group of Hollowers. It was going to get cold on the caravan.

Ruki Provos tapped Runt on his shoulder. "Who's the beautiful barbarian girl?" he asked.

"Mike Ballztowallz's brother," Runt said flatly.

Ruki raised an eyebrow, looking like there was a question on his face he couldn't begin to understand or ask.

"You and Runt and your other friends couldn't have come at a better time," Melvin said. "We need your help."

"Help?" Mike asked, his face turning sour at the mention of the word. "Man, I came to get your stupid ass before you kill yourself out here."

"I wish we could leave, Mike," Melvin said. "But we can't leave, and I mean really leave, until this is done."

Mike's response was interrupted by someone clearing his throat. Mike turned to see a clown dude in polka dot pajamas.

"You must be the ones Cephrin mentioned," the clown said, his voice soft like he was a part-time hypnotist. "Welcome to Olukent, where new lives begin."

"Yeah, yeah, not looking to buy a timeshare," Mike said, waving his hand dismissively before turning his attention back to his brother.

"You can't go until it's done?" Mike asked. "It's done now! How you gonna go back home if you're dead? Those fools at the Hierophane should've never put you up to this."

"We were the most capable people they had," Melvin said.

"That's what they told you? Jesus, Mel! This is Mission Goddamn Impossible. You don't see none of the mages up here helping you, do you? That's cause there ain't no coming back from this. They sent you here to die, man."

Melvin shook his head. "If we don't do what they ask, not only will something bad go down, but there'll be no going home for us."

The clown dude interrupted again with a throat-clearing, hand-raising gesture. "Excuse me," he said. "But where are your offerings and loved ones? Your caravan looks exceedingly empty from my vantage point."

Mike glared at him, a look reserved for dumbasses that had certifiably lost their mind. "Motherfucker, don't you see we talking? Kick rocks, clown."

This time, Mike kept his eyes locked on the clown's. In his mind, Mike was daring this fool to say one more word. First sign of a syllable and Mike was going to club him a goodnight lullaby.

Whoever dude was, he got the message. He backed away, giving Mike his space. Mike returned to the matter at hand, his idiot brother.

"What we're doing is getting the hell out of here," Mike said. "We ain't bargaining with the mages for whatever the secret is to going home. We taking it."

The matter was closed. He grabbed Melvin by the hand and turned to put his ass on the caravan.

Mike felt Melvin's hand twist out of his grasp. He turned to see his brother, towering Amazon that he was now, standing his ground.

"No," Melvin said. "We have to do this. I have to do this."

"You my little brother," Mike said. "All you have to do is what I tell you. Now let's go."

He grabbed Melvin's hand again. Again, Melvin twisted out and looked at Mike with defiance in his eyes.

"I may be younger, but I'm no longer little," Melvin said. "I had to grow up out here. And I won't be pushed and pulled around, Mike. Now, you can either help me or stand aside. But I'm going to finish this out."

"What?" Mike couldn't believe what he was hearing. "You telling me it took time as a woman for you to become more of a man?" Mike laughed. "Hell of a time for you to grow balls when you're rocking ovaries. Meanwhile, you too busy being a grown man slash big girl to see I am helping by saving your ass."

Mike grabbed Melvin's wrist and pulled. "Now get on the caravan."

Melvin whirled and in a flash Mike was flying through the air. He crashed into the side of a building and landed in a heap of trash.

In the trash heap, Mike heard one of Mel's friends.

"Oh shit, he just went into Zhufira mode!"

Oh hell naw. Now, Mike was hot.

Mike emerged from the trash to see Melvin in a fighting stance, his hands up, fingers locked and rigid like knives.

"I warned you, Mike."

"Warned me? Bitch, somebody should've warned you."

Mike charged in. Melvin's hands came fast at him. Mike ducked into a slide like he was making home plate, then sprang up with a gut punch.

Bowled over, Mel was just the right height for a punch to his face. Mike came down with it, and Melvin dropped into the dirt.

"You ain't too pretty to get beat the fuck up," Mike told him.

But Mel wasn't beat. He turned on his back, spun his legs. The kick knocked Mike off his feet, but before he hit the ground, Melvin was up and putting a well placed knee into his back. Mel finished by grabbing two handfuls of Mike's shirt and tossing him into the dirt.

Mike rolled in a ball, rocks tearing at his clothes and skin, before coming to a stop on his back. He heard Melvin's friends panicking.

"Dude, we gotta stop this, they're gonna kill each other," Rich said.

"Not only do you wanna come between family," Jason said, "but you want to step in between a Khermer warrioress and a megrym Knuckleduster. Are you crazy?"

Melvin ran up on Mike. He picked up the megrym and tossed him, this time aiming at some crates. Mike exploded into the empty crates, sending fractured wood everywhere.

Mike, on his back in the wood pile, felt Mel running up again. This time, Mike brought both legs up as Mel stood over him, kicking him hard between the legs.

If he had grown some balls in that body, they wouldn't be there after that.

Mel cringed in pain at the kick. Mike shot up, giving him another gut shot that bowled him over. Then he chopped Mel in the throat.

"You may be tall, but I'll break that ass down," Mike said as Mel choked for air.

Mike grabbed him by the hair and rammed his head into the nearest barrel. He brought an elbow down into his back and Mel hit the dirt.

This time, he best stay down.

"Step away, Mike," someone called out.

He turned to see Jason aiming an arrow at his face.

Mike's crew moved in a blur. Ruki brought up his diskbow, Runt pulled his Z-blade, even Savashbahar ran up from the caravan, her knife at the ready.

Rich turned on them, calling fire into his hands.

"Jason!" Mike whirled to see Melvin, his lip bloody, his face a torrent of rage. He had his sword out, pointing it at his friend.

"I swear on everything in me," Mel said. "If you don't

put that down I'll cut you into pieces so small, even the big chunks will still slip through the fingers of rats."

Jason lowered the bow. "Dude, I was just trying to help."

"Save it," Melvin said.

He put his sword away. Rich killed the fire in his hands and Mike's crew put their weapons down. Melvin looked at his brother.

"We don't have time for this," Melvin said. "Look, maybe you're right. Maybe the Hierophane sent us up here as patsies, but that doesn't change the fact that we can stop something bad from going down. We're the ones that set this thing loose. That makes whatever happens our fault."

He went over to his brother, got down on one knee and put a hand on Mike's shoulder.

"I'm asking for your help, Mike. Without you, it's a suicide mission, but it's still a mission I have to do. I can't walk away and leave this world with our mess to clean up. I just can't."

Mike looked at his brother. "You ready to throw your life away trying to fix something we shouldn't have even been around to mess up?"

Melvin nodded. There was resolve in his eyes. Mike wouldn't have believed it a week ago. His kid brother, a grown ass man slash woman.

Mike looked at his crew. Runt nodded, always down without having to say a word. Ruki Provos shrugged. A slim smile creased Savashbahar's lips.

"Aight," Mike said. "Let's kill us a big, mean, evil son of a bitch."

"I knew it!" a voice screamed behind Mike. He turned and saw the clown dude, pointing at him.

"No offerings, no loved ones," he said, "You are all interlopers, here to stop the Death Null's grace."

Clown dude turned to face the crowd that had gathered in the street, drawn there by the fight. "Children! They are frauds! Frauds! Frau—"

Ruki's diskbow muzzle, rammed into the clown's throat, killed his announcement. Ruki's other hand wrapped around the clown.

"I recognize a resurrection cult when I see one," Ruki said to the clown. "Tell me, do you want to take the chance of resurrecting without a head?"

"No one fears your trinket," clown said. "Nothing that small can take a head. He bluffs, children! He bluffs!"

In a second, Ruki pointed the diskbow at a bystander, squeezed the trigger. The disk shot out, taking some dude's arm off at the elbow and burying into the stomach of the guy behind him.

The diskbow was back on the throat of the clown. Ruki hadn't even waited to see the result of his shot.

"Ruki Provos doesn't bluff," he said. Ironically, he was bluffing now since he needed to crank the diskbow to get another shot out of it.

Mike and his crew, Mel and his friends, they all huddled close to Ruki while the crowd closed around them.

"Where we going with this, Mel?" Mike asked.

"Uphill," Melvin said, indicating the place with a nod. "There's a guard shack up there."

They worked their way up hill, the circle of angry townfolk slowly parting ahead and closing behind them. Any time the clown would try to yell out, Ruki cut off his air by jabbing the muzzle into his neck. If he couldn't yell orders, then the crowd stayed passive and disorganized. Mike almost felt proud of Ruki.

Once they arrived at the guard shack, the crowd in front of them melted away and eight armed guards stood ready. These guys weren't going to charge in, but neither did they move when Ruki threatened to off their leader. Mike got the impression their orders were no one got past them, even if it meant the leader's death.

The guards were close together, a tightly knit, organized group. Big mistake.

Mike stepped in front of Ruki. He smacked his hands together, activating the lightning gloves. The electric arc shot out and put the guards down as the lightning jumped through them. The crowd around them stepped back and exclaimed in fear.

"Holy shit," Jason said, "Where the hell can I score some of those?!"

"Inside, dumbass," Mike said.

Everyone piled inside while Ruki turned to face the crowd, bringing up the rear with the clown in tow. Before stepping in, Ruki pushed the clown into the crowd. Runt and Savashbahar closed and bolted the door behind him.

Outside the guard shack, the clown was yelling, his Mister Rogers voice well past gone. "Idiots! My life is not worth losing the Death Null's grace. Quickly, get the weapons, get the swords, the maces and axes. There is still time. Fly children!"

The door barely moved to the beating from outside, but the two windows weren't as stout. The left one broke first, accompanied by someone's head emerging through it.

Savashbahar was next to that window, her back against the wall. She thrust out with her dagger, catching the man in his throat with the quickness of a prison shanking. Nobody else's head came through.

Ruki Provos cranked his diskbow taut, rolled over to that same window and let a diskblade go into the crowd. He moved out of sight again and cranked his diskbow up.

"So, what do we do now?" Ruki asked.

"You're doing it," Melvin said. "Mike, I need you and your team to hold the cult back while we go into the cave and stop the Death Null. Think you can handle it?"

The right window shattered. Whoever's hand it was that broke the window lost it as Runt came down with his Z-weapon.

"Shit, you see my squad," Mike said. "We got this. What about you? Think you can handle the Thriller video waiting for you up there?"

"Hell yeah," Mel said. "I'm still mad about getting my face slammed into a barrel. I can't wait to take it out on those corpses."

"Go. Take a dump on Death Null then write 'Melvin Morrow wuz here' in it with your sword."

"See you when I get back."

With a nod, Melvin directed his friends to grab swords and the three of them were out the back door. Mike watched his brother disappear into the mouth of the cave.

I better see you when you get back, Mike thought.

An excited tapping on his shoulder brought him back to the guardhouse. Ruki Provos was pointing at a window.

"What kind of madness did you drag me into this time?!" he asked, his voice panicked.

Sticking their heads and arms in the window were two guys. One was a guard Mike had fried and the other was the dude Savashbahar had stabbed in the throat. Both of them were unblinking, glassy-eyed… very much dead.

Mike pulled his club.

"If you wanted better security, you would've paid for it, Ruki. Strap in for a siege."

Chapter 30

Death Null

Melvin was Zhufira. His blade *danced*.

He let out all his frustration. Anger at Mike, angst at Rich, and his body and the jumble of emotions, the conflicting confusions, wants and desires. There was no need to translate it here. His bastard sword understood all. It did the talking.

Just a few feet into the cave they met a pair of zombies. Melvin whirled between them and they were down in pieces before Rich and Jason could get in a sword swipe of their own.

Deeper in the tunnel, guided by Jason's bones and shown the way with Rich's fire-filled hand, they met another half dozen undead. Melvin wasn't sure if Jason and Rich were able to help this time. All he knew was he took off two heads in one stroke, cut off countless arms that reached with futile earnest to grasp him, and danced with his blade until he was in the center of a ring of severed parts.

It felt good, being Zhufira. Not just for a second, not just for short moments of uncontrolled anger, but as a standing vehicle for his aggression. She didn't keep anger and pain bottled up like Melvin. She was catharsis.

Well into the cavern now, the tunnels began to branch out in many different directions. Some ramped up, others down, and more went left and right. Melvin looked at Jason.

"We've got a problem," Jason said. "The feeling, the Death Null's presence, it's all around me."

"Maybe putting a bone in water will help," Melvin said. "There are too many passages to guess at this."

Keeping his magefire burning in one hand, Rich dropped the sword and conjured a water bowl that he held in his free hand. They all looked by flickering firelight at the suspended finger bone. It whirled in a circle ceaselessly, a magnet caught up in its own Bermuda Triangle.

Melvin felt the zombie before he heard the footstep shuffle up behind him. He whirled and his blade flowed like wind. Three passes, like an upward slanted Z, and the zombie was left with in as many parts: head, torso and a pair of disconnected legs. Jason ran over and cut arms so the torso section wouldn't crawl around.

Melvin looked at Jason.

"The 'always left' approach to maze traversing?"

Jason nodded.

They got started.

※

Mike sat in his chair, worried. Melvin and his friends had disappeared into the cave hours ago. His instincts told him to go in there after him. But combat survival training told him it was suicide to ignore your base when it's being overrun.

If nothing else, the cult built sound defenses. This guardhouse was definitely made to keep people from breaching. The door was iron, hinged on the inside. The windows were small, making it difficult for a person to crawl inside. Mike turned difficult to damn near impossible by tossing the beds and wedging the bed frames against the windows. Now nothing got through the windows except arms begging to get chopped off.

But no structure is impenetrable, and the will of the cult was making a way.

Close to an hour now, chipped rock fragments had been flying into the entryway. The cultists were taking axe picks or shovels or something and attacking the walls around the iron door frame. They worked both sides, now the trails were nearly quarter way up the door. Mike could see the fading light of day streaming through the carved lines.

Eventually, sometime well into the night, the door would fall inward. Then it'd be the four of them against total bedlam.

Waiting was hard. Well, not for Runt, he was power napping on a tossed mattress. Guess a lack of bed frame and an angry horde outside the walls didn't phase a half-weagr. He was a good dude to have with you in the foxhole.

Ruki came over to sit beside Mike. His initial panic from seeing the walking dead had subsided a couple of hours ago. At first, looking at a dismembered torso crawl around on its hands had turned him into a suburban housewife watching a mouse scamper across the linoleum. Luckily, Savashbahar was the man of their house, coming to the Ruki's screaming rescue and carving the torso up like a Thanksgiving turkey.

Even now, Ruki gave an occasional eye to the undead chunks.

"So," Ruki started, "uh, when you say that's your brother, um, do you mean some sort of warrior-brother-in-arms kind of brother?"

"I mean brother."

"I see," Ruki said, grimacing as he nodded. "Um, how long has your brother been your brother?"

"Why you wanna know?"

"Well, your brother is a woman. And exceedingly comely."

"Mel's been my brother long enough for me to club you brain dead over," he said. "That answer the question?"

Ruki nodded. "Yes, clears that matter up," he said. "At least until I find a quality helmet."

Mike looked at the spray of some more rock chips shooting from around the door. He looked back toward the massive hole of the cave.

What the hell, Melvin? Where you at?

⊙⊙

Melvin was tired. The "all lefts" approach was time-consuming. Chopping down zombies only added to the fatigue.

Fortunately, not too many remained. The big, roving zombie bands seemed to be all gone. Now they encountered a random one or two in the tunnels. It was a good thing too, as his romp through the tunnels as Zhufira had ended hours ago.

Rage, no matter how therapeutic, wasn't something indefinitely sustainable. Luckily, the three of them proved more than capable of rendering a zombie. Unlike the undead residents of Fort Law, these zombies were weaponless. Most of them seemed more eager to announce one day left rather than lunge out and attack.

"I wonder how Mike's doing?" Melvin asked. He led the way through this newest tunnel, guided by the light of a torch made from a stick, swaths of zombie shirt, and Rich's magefire.

"Hopefully, better than we are," Jason answered. "This maze sucks."

He was right about that. Twice now "all lefts" had returned them to where they started, where the tunnels branched and their direction finding failed. Jason had the good sense to use coagulated zombie blood to mark the spot with an "X" on the wall. They even had to stop for rest and food, eating jerked meat and sharing silence. At least it had been silent until the roaming zombie had come upon them to remind them there was one day left. It felt like they had been down here all their lives.

"Look at it this way," Rich said, fatigue wearing heavy on his face. "We've been down here so long that we're bound to find it soon."

A few footsteps later and the tunnel opened up. Melvin could no longer see the sides or ceiling. He was about to bear left until his torchlight illuminated the one wall until a light in the midst of the cavern made him stop.

Darkness pervaded everything, and the light seemed more of a silhouette. Just a thin line of white in the pitch black, showing the outline of a giant man-shaped creature. Two all white eyes of light looked out at him.

The Death Null.

They made their way to it without difficulty. There was no more zombie resistance. Melvin got close enough for the torchlight to illuminate its all black body. Still, the Death Null did nothing but look at them.

"Well…" Jason said, trailing off as if he was expecting the Death Null to roar or something. "… lack of endgame boss fight aside, guess it's time for you to do your thing, Rich."

Rich swallowed. "Ok, here goes."

"Wait," Melvin said. He looked at the others. "Does this feel right to you?"

"All the way," Jason said. "It's a death creature. It makes zombies."

"Yeah, but still," Melvin said. "Something's off. I mean, it's just sitting there. It's not trying to kill us, run, nothing."

"You killed all its zombies," Rich said. "Makes sense to me."

"Yeah," Jason added. "I think you're just girling out again. It's not a lost puppy, it's a zombie factory. Stop empathizing with it."

"Look at it, you idiots," Melvin said. "It can lash out at

us but it doesn't. It can punch out of here like it did at Fort Law but it stays put. Outside of controlling things that were dead anyway, what truly evil thing has it done?"

The Death Null's mouth opened, a white light cutting through a sea of black. "One… day…" was all it said.

"See?" Jason asked. "What about the countdown? It's probably got all its evil planned for tomorrow. We can't risk it."

"That doesn't make any sense," Melvin said. "I mean, at Fort Law it could have killed us but it just wanted us to free it. And once it got its freedom, it came here, where it wasn't bothering anybody. The death cultists were the ones that came to it, feeding it bodies. It wasn't like the Death Null was rampaging through cities, creating a corpse army."

Jason nodded. "Girly sensibilities or not, you've got a point there."

"All I'm saying is if it wanted wanton destruction or a zombie nation, it could've had that a long time ago," Melvin said.

A flash of red pierced the cavern. Melvin's eyes followed the light to the source. Rich's ring glowed with a stabbing brilliance. Then the ring shattered.

Suddenly, the air rushed together and the blue and white blinding light of a portal swirled into existence. Melvin had to shield his eyes from the light. Once it died, his eyes adjusted to see a man in black.

Druze.

"Rich, I can't believe I had to come here to urge this matter," Druze said. "Cast the spell. Cage this fiend."

"Dude, what gives?" Rich asked. "You told me that ring was supposed to mitigate cost. You had me wearing your portable portal?"

"It was a portal and scry," Druze said. "You think I'd trust a matter so important to a bunch of pendulum rejects?"

Druze walked over to Rich and put a hand on his shoulder. "I followed your progress every step of the way, Rich, waiting to jump in and take over in the event you failed. But you haven't failed. Don't fail now. Cast the spell."

Rich looked at Druze's hand, then stepped away, out of his reach. "I don't appreciate being lied to. And I'm with Melvin on this. She—I mean, he's—had a great nose for keeping us out of trouble so far. If you want to cast Life Something Chain, go for it. I'm not."

Druze's look of friendly earnest disappeared. Rage took over his features. He spoke and his robes lashed out.

※

Mike sat uneasily in an off-balanced chair that he had placed outside of the guardhouse. The legs were on uneven ground where the slope of the cave hill was just starting. He looked back into the building, at a doorway that was almost totally chipped away.

The cult's hours of labor at the door had given Mike and his team time to set up secondary defenses. Furniture framed the guardhouse exit and ran up the sides of the hill toward the cave mouth. Broken glass littered the ground around the furniture and extra swords and spears were entrenched in the ground at strategically deadly angles.

What he wanted was a bottleneck. With this setup, attackers had to take the hill one, two at a time tops. He hoped it was enough.

He made peace with Melvin's fate. If he wasn't dead in there, Mike couldn't do squat to help him now. He had his own survival to worry about. A broke-down pitched battle was moments away.

He turned in his chair. Savashbahar was a little further

uphill, sitting on the ground. Her head was down, apparently focused on sharpening her dagger. He went over to her.

"Hey," he said.

She said nothing. The high-pitched twang of her knife scraping against the sharpening stone set the mood in the atmosphere.

"Look, Savvy, I can't change how I got here and what that makes me. After we get out of this mess, if you want to blaze a trail as far away from me as you can, I'll understand. I just want you to know that you good people and I always got your back."

The knife stopped scraping against the stone. She looked up from her dagger, her face displaying utter disbelief.

"Stupid megrym," she said. "The dogs of war claw at the door, and you talk of sentiments? Does my feeling toward you matter more than final battle preparation?"

"Damn," Mike said, scratching his head, "I mean, when you put it that way…"

Savashbahar went back to sharpening her dagger. Mike turned to go, but she started speaking over the scrape of the knife.

"When I was a maiden, I made the choice to seek the way of Hexenarii. It was a choice forbidden to women by my clan. That choice made me outcast. But I was still the same woman, the same Savashbahar that was loved by all before my skin was marked. What kind of person would I be to spurn you for being something you had no choice in?"

She looked up from her task. A smile played on her lips.

"If I wanted nothing to do with you, I would not be here," she said. "Still, you need to learn where your words belong. If you speak of sentiment now, does it mean we've prepared as much as possible?"

Mike with a broad grin. He looked back at the iron door, which shuddered as the rock chips at the top of the frame flew. "Savvy, we're as ready as we'll ever be."

༺༻

"Cast the spell!" Druze yelled. His robes shot out again, knocking Rich down. The blackness of the robe made it impossible to see.

Rich saw that blackness wrap around Melvin and Jason and toss them into the walls.

"Why?" Rich asked. "Why do you want me to cast it when you can cast it yourself?"

Rich stood up and called illusion fire into existence around him. The light flickered through the cavern, illuminating the farthest reaches along with the enraged mage before him. He wasn't about to be sneak attacked again by hard to see robes.

"Life Ending Chain," Druze said. "The spell you worked so hard to translate is called Life Ending Chain. And I'm not casting it because I know how it works. After all, I was right here when Kaftar used it."

Rich couldn't believe what he was hearing. Life Ending Chain. He had no doubt it worked as advertised. And the name Druze dropped—

"Kaftar?" Rich asked. "He was the first Hierophant. That had to be—"

"Five hundred years ago," Druze filled in. "And back then, it took a lot to convince Kaftar to cast it. I had to make him believe this thing was the biggest threat imaginable. And then I had to convince him the death defying power of the monster would negate the spell cost."

"Only it didn't," Rich guessed.

Druze smirked. "It did, if you count his lifeless corpse rising up and saying 'free me' over and over until I incinerated him on the spot."

Druze called netherfire into existence. His hands glowed with the brilliant blue of it. Rich had seen the process for creating netherfire; he remembered marveling at the insane intricacy of it. Druze was showing off, giving Rich a display of the power he wielded.

"You must know, there's no escape for you here," Druze said. "But there's hope for your pitiful friends. All it takes from you is a single spell. Cast it."

"Hey, asshole!" a shout came from behind Druze.

Rich turned to see Melvin with his sword out, looking fierce. Zhufira fierce.

In another corner of the cave, Jason was nocking an arrowing.

"You messed with the wrong pendulum rejects," Melvin said. He charged at Druze, yelling the same battle cry he had ages ago during akhta.

"Ildasleen!"

☙❧

Mike and Ruki Provos had turned the first two waves of angry humans into the crispy undead thanks to the lightning gloves. Now it was Fort Law all over again. Mike and Runt stood side by side, facing the unending undead horde rushing through the bottleneck.

These things were hard to put down, so the best option was to send them over the side of the hill. It would take them forever to get back around, if they could even make the return trip.

Unlike Fort Law, the undead had half a town of breathing accomplices helping them out. While the undead rushed to get up the hill to get to the cave, the ones still alive hung in the back, trying to destroy the barricades and open the bottleneck.

Ruki tried to keep the cultists off the barricades with diskblades. His shots were good at disruption, but the cultists didn't stay away long. They saw how precarious it would be for the four defenders if the zombies were able to swarm. The cultists always came back, pushing and kicking and swinging at the barricades.

Runt swung his Z-blade, dropping another zombie down the side of the hill. Mike had his hands full with his own zombie. Another zombie rushed in and stabbed Runt in the side with a knife.

Runt roared with pain.

Savvy rushed in, her dagger lashing out in flashing blurs. The zombie's knife hand came away severed. She grabbed the thing by its hair and as she serial stabbed it she dragged it up the hill, where she proceeded to carve it out of the fight permanently.

Runt laughed. Loudly, thoroughly, madly. It was the first time Mike ever heard him laugh. The sound boomed out over the battlefield. He followed it up with a yell as he broke his Z-blade into twin axes.

"Now! Now, it's a fight!"

☙❧

Druze threw his netherfire volley at Melvin. Melvin, in mid-sprint, dashed left past one fireball. Then he made a whirling jump over the second fireball. He came down and kept charging at Druze like lethal fire jumping was a rehearsed part of a show.

Jason let an arrow fly. He nocked another one and let it go in a blur of speed.

Druze aimed his arms at Jason and Melvin. His sleeves came alive. One swirled into a black whirlpool, catching Jason's arrows. The other shot out at Melvin.

Melvin side-stepped the sleeve and closed the gap to the

mage. His sword stabbed out at Druze.

Druze slid back like the wind pushed him. The sleeve Melvin dodge earlier came back around. It hit Melvin in the back and pushed him into the mage.

The black robes swallowed both Druze and Melvin. They became a black sphere that swirled like a storm. Then the sphere exploded.

With a piercing scream, Melvin shot out of the explosion to land in a heap. Druze stood, unscathed and unmoved by the blast.

Almost like he was swatting a fly, Druze batted at another arrow with a sleeve. He turned to face Jason, who was in the midst of aiming another arrow.

Druze took two steps toward Jason. Casting a spell with each step, he knelt and picked up giant scoops of cavern floor. He threw the massive boulders with blinding speed at Jason.

Jason hit the floor. As the boulders passed, Druze spoke another spell and pressed down with his palms.

The boulders shattered, raining rock shrapnel on Jason.

Both Jason and Melvin were on the ground, groaning in pain. Rich had to do something. He had no clue what.

He cast the only thing he could think of at the moment and sent a pair of fireballs at Druze.

Druze said something quick and blew. The fireballs went out, like he was making a wish on a birthday cake.

"This is novice magic, boy!" Druze yelled. "I'm a five-hundred-year-old spell crafter. If you want to duel me, you're going to have to step into your gray robes. But you can't, can you?"

Druze tapped his temple. "I know. I've been watching, listening. The only way you can access Magelord magic is if you're in fear of your own life. But I'm not going to try driving an axe through your face. Or turn into a giant, venomous spider."

Druze smiled. "I'm going to torture your friends while you watch. Their only mercy will be your Life Ending Chain."

☙

Mike stood side by side with his crew. They all swung clubs and swords at the zombies. One of the barricades had failed, opening up the bottleneck. It took all of them to keep the tide at bay.

The cultists below were going to town at the remaining barricade. Even if Ruki Provos didn't have his hands full dealing with zombies, he was disk dry. It was only a matter of time before it came apart. Then the swarm would overrun them all.

Dawn was breaking over the horizon. Mike looked out at his high vantage point above the town, where the wan light revealed dark bodies moving rapidly through the foothills. A large force, an army, was heading towards the town.

"You guys seeing this?" Mike asked as he bashed another zombie off the hill.

"Maybe they're peacekeepers coming to put an end to this blasted resurrection cult," Ruki said.

The army was at the outskirts of town. Their individual shapes came into clear view.

"Not that lucky," Mike said. "They're nasran. They who I think they are, Savvy?"

"Yes," she said, swiping her dagger back and forth at a zombie. "Maltep has found us."

"Blessed Onesource!" Ruki cried. "How the hell did they find us?"

"My blood is their blood," Savashbahar said. "If they wish to listen, it will whisper to them."

Explosions started going off in the town. Yells, fire,

smoke, all the signs of fighting hit Mike. Maltep was coming for them hard.

"Children! Children!" the voice of the clown dude could be heard over the noise of battle. "Leave the offerings to their work, our backs are exposed! We must last, grace is almost at hand!"

The cultists working apart the barricade left it and disappeared into the guardhouse. There was still a legion of zombies to deal with and a larger opening to the bottleneck. But at least now they didn't have to worry about an all around swarming.

The Maltep nasrans had afforded them a temporary reprieve. A sick feeling washed over Mike, something that ran much deeper than the zombie gore he was covered in.

⊗

"Time grows short, boy," Druze said. "Cast the spell."

Druze had summoned magic chains that wrapped around the arms, legs, and necks of both Melvin and Jason. The chains kept them standing and rooted in place. Netherfire burned in front of Melvin, so close that the fire was slow roasting him. Druze was casually flicking razor sharp sleeves at Jason, cutting away the skin on his chest and flesh arm, one piece at a time.

"Ok," Rich said as he looked at his screaming friends, their faces looking sickly under the pale blue light of the netherfire torturing Melvin. "Just let them go."

The sleeves stopped flying. The netherfire winked out of existence, returning the cave to a dark calm. Jason and Melvin's chains remained fast.

"Just tell me why," Rich said. "Why is trapping the Death Null so important to you?"

"Haven't you figured it out yet, boy?" Druze asked. "How else is a human able to live for centuries without tapping into this thing's death negating abilities?"

"You… Rew!" He spat as the realization dawned on him. "You both feed off it?!"

"Exactly," Druze said. "This thing sits in some forgotten corner of the world, silently keeping death at bay for us. That is, until you freed it. Now it's time to set things right."

"You think this is right?" Jason shouted. "Die already, like everyone else!"

Druze's sleeves shot out. Jason yelped as the sleeves cut across his cheeks.

"Shut up, boy, robes are talking," Druze said. He looked back at Rich, disgust in his eyes. "But I can scarcely call you a robe. Before Rew was born, before she devised her witchlock, I sent real mages to their death renewing Kaftar's spell. Accomplished, powerful mages—some of them my own sons."

He walked over to the Death Null, looking it up and down before he turned to face Rich again.

"The last thing I'll let happen is watch their sacrifice go in vain, ruined by a child scared of magic."

Druze walked back over to Rich, pointing at his bound friends. "Now cast. Or the fire gets hotter and the blades get sharper. If it's any consolation, Rew was innocent in this."

"Innocent?" Rich asked. "She's feeding off an innocent creature and she's the faultless one?"

"Look at it!" Druze yelled, pointing to the Death Null. "Does it look innocent? Rew went with the same assumption you made when you saw it, the same assumption everyone makes. Can you blame her?"

Rich looked at the Death Null. It was tremendous, dark, terrifying. They had trekked all over the world just based on how it looked. He couldn't blame Rew for using it to extend her own life; he would've taken the same offer if he just had the visual to go by.

"We've wasted enough time here," Druze said. "Rew truly doesn't know the deadly consequence of the spell. That was before her time and her lock. In her eyes, you will have died a martyr, saving us all from evil. Now cast."

ଔଞ୍ଚ

Savashbahar was proud of her companions. There had been no escape from death visible anywhere, yet they all continued to fight on bravely. Together, they had seen victory over one battle.

Runt and Mike sent the last two zombies over the hillside. It was quiet on the hill now. Most of the undying ones were either cut into pieces or over the side of the hill, unable to return to the fight. But the quiet was deceptive. The town below burned.

A familiar voice shouted at them from beyond the guardhouse.

"Savashbahar is with you. Send her down to us."

"Go to hell!" Mike yelled.

"Wait!" Savashbahar yelled. "I am coming."

She looked at Mike. "This is not your fight. Not this. If it was, I imagine you would fight bravely. And I would be at your side, fighting with you."

Savashbahar put her hand over Mike's mouth before he could protest. She exchanged nods with Ruki Provos and Runt. None of their blood would be on her hands.

She put her knife away and walked with deliberate care down the hill, past busted barricades and broken bodies. She kept her chin high. There was no manufactured fear in her heart to dishonor her. She would die proud.

ଔଞ୍ଚ

Rich took out his spell book. He flipped pages slowly,

trying to think of a way to save himself and his friends.

"Don't think about casting something other than Kaftar's spell, boy," Druze said. "I recognize the difference between the old tongue and modern spellcraft. Remember, I used to be alive when people still spoke it."

Rich got to Kaftar's page. There was nothing else to do. Nowhere else to go. He swallowed, a dry, harsh feeling.

He was about to speak his own death.

Rich looked up at Druze and recited Kaftar's words, loud and clear so the mage could hear they were from the old tongue.

༺༻

The last time Savashbahar had seen Demirtash, he had been prepared to kill her. She had aided foreigners, stolen, even extinguished Maltep's sacred fire. Now Maltep's Chief Hexenarii stood in front of her, his face grim and taut.

Behind him, the faces of many warriors looked toward her.

"Kill me quickly, Demirtash, for it looks as if you've emptied half of Maltep to deliver your justice."

Demirtash took a step toward Savashbahar. He stood for a moment, looking at her in silence.

Then he reached out fast.

Savashbahar did not feel the bite of his dagger.

Demirtash's arms were around her. For the first time since she was a young girl, her older brother held her in his embrace.

"Sister, you were right," he said, "To fight, to help those foreigners, to strike at the mage factory. A hundred Hollowers came to us, led by the mages. If we had listened to your call to arms we could have struck first. Now we are all that remains of sacred Maltep."

Maltep was no more. It was news to make the ancestors

weep. She returned his embrace.

"I am sorry, Demirtash."

"We need to fight," Demirtash said. "We need Hexenarii. All our Hexenarii. You are outcast no more, dear sister, but the bravest among our chosen warriors."

The warriors shouted in unison, a cry a woman from Maltep had never heard.

"Hexenarii! Hexenarii! Hexenarii!"

☙❧

Rich finished casting the spell. He closed the book and dropped it.

Druze looked at him, anger etched across in his features.

"Where's the chain? You expect me to fall for your utterance of random words? I am out of patience! Now—"

A strangled sound came out of his throat. He reached for Rich. If he was trying to talk, nothing but choking came out.

"I wasn't trying to fool you with random words," Rich said. "This is one of Kaftar's spells, the one called 'Equal Hardship'. I couldn't beat you, Druze, so I had to join you."

Rich dropped to his knees, feeling heavy already from the weight of the spell. He looked over to his friends. The chains around Melvin and Jason dissolved, and they ran over to him.

"Dude, that was epic!" Jason said. "What'd you do?"

Rich pointed. Druze was frozen in his reach toward Rich, horror on his face. Gray stone grew, spreading upwards to his face, outwards to his hands and feet.

Rich looked down at his hands, white marble grew from his fingertips and spread up his hands.

"No!" Melvin cried. "God, Rich, you didn't have to do this!"

"C'mon," Rich said. "We've seen the movies. The bad guys aren't exactly known for their big hearts. He was going to kill the both of you after he got what he wanted. Hell, he even sent his sons to die. I don't think today was the day he learned charity."

"Shit!" Jason swore. "Dude, is there a way to negate this?"

The white marble was up to Rich's shoulders. His back felt solid, dense.

"If there is, I'm sure you'd be the one to find it," Rich said.

Rich felt the marble spreading up to his neck. He couldn't move, so he settled for a wink at Melvin.

"See ya around."

He saw no more.

Epilogue

Melvin sat in the cavern, his hands holding his knees. Mike was on one side of him, smoking a weird reddish brown cigar he got from the nasrans. Jason sat on the other side, looking at the last bit of grains fall in his hourglass.

Just a few feet away from the gray statue of Druze, the Death Null stood quietly. It acted peaceful, even if it didn't look it. If anything, it still looked ominous, powerfully evil, and dangerous.

Melvin hoped they had done the right thing.

Nothing happened after the last grains fell to the bottom of the hourglass. Either Jason's calculations were off or the Death Null's countdown was a lackluster affair.

Suddenly, a brilliant white light filled the roof of the cavern over the Death Null. Black streams descended from the light over the creature. The Death Null reached up towards the light. Then the light flashed, too bright for eyes.

When darkness returned to the cavern, the Death Null was gone.

"I've got a strong feeling all Death Null wanted was to go home," Melvin said.

"Of all the things to peg that creature," Jason said, "wayward traveler stuck in this world wasn't one of them."

"Does everything in the universe get stuck on this rock?" Mike asked, smoke following his words as spoke. "Bet if we look hard enough we'll find all the socks ever lost in the dryer."

Melvin's eyes went to the kneeling marble statue of Rich. His face was serene in the torchlight. He looked noble, like something Michelangelo would've carved.

"I was kind of hoping Izal's cult was onto something," Melvin said as he looked at the statue. "Rich could use some of that grace about now."

"Yeah," Jason said, "but grace would've brought back that evil immortal prick too," he finished nodding at Druze, forever frozen reaching out with horror on his face.

"I should've hit that fool harder," Mike said, puffing on his cigar.

Jason flexed the hand of his bone arm. "At least this still works," he said. "There's grace in that."

Melvin stood up. The others followed suit. Melvin gave his brother a helping hand; Mike looked beat to hell after the night he had.

"What do we do now?" Jason asked.

"What else would we do in a fantasy world of magic?" Melvin asked, letting a smile play across his lips.

"We get Rich back."

About the Author

James Beamon is a science fiction and fantasy author whose short stories have appeared in places such as Fantasy & Science Fiction Magazine, Apex, Lightspeed and Orson Scott Card's Intergalactic Medicine Show. He spent twelve years in the Air Force, deployed to Iraq and Afghanistan, and is in possession of the perfect buffalo wings recipe that he learned from carnies. He currently lives in Virginia with his wife, son and attack cat. He's serious about the attack cat... do not point at it. Pendulum Heroes is his debut novel.

Check out more of what James is up to at his site: http://fictigristle.wordpress.com

Coming Soon

Pendulum Shift (Pendulum Heroes Book 2)

But before that...

Did you enjoy the book? Let others who may be curious know what you liked and what you didn't. Your review is a powerful magic in its own right, better and more effective advertising than even big publishing houses can buy. Consider helping an indie writer out!

Made in the USA
San Bernardino, CA
07 June 2018